EZRA'S WALK

BY
BLAIR GREIMAN

ELECTOR PUBLICATIONS

ELECTOR PUBLICATIONS
818 MADISON STREET
VERMILLION, SD 57069

Printed in the United States of America
by

PRINTING SERVICES OF IOWA
BELMOND, IOWA 50421

FORWARD

The book you hold in your hands is unique in a number of ways. Not only does it introduce an exciting new author to the field of Christian fiction, it is written with the intensity and absorption of someone who has experienced much of the lives about which he writes. Of course, this is true of many interesting novels, but we are seldom in contact with literature that can speak so powerfully about crime and punishment, and Christianity and unbelief. This is because Mr. Blair Greiman is not only a serious Christian, he is also a convict, doing life without parole in a maximum security state prison.

Our Author has not only concocted a fascinating plot with interesting and surprising outcomes, he deals with some of the great issues of life and philosophy, not from an ivory tower but from the nitty-gritty of daily life inside and outside of prison. Mr. Greiman writes with a rare authenticity, and an intensity that may at times put off the more dilettante reader. Nevertheless he also writes with a soft and loving heart. *Ezra's Walk* is a story in which good triumphs over evil, the real kind of evil that lurks in human hearts, and comes to action in the works of the violent criminal.

Our author is only in his mid-thirties, and yet has spent over half of his life in jail, having been incarcerated at the age of sixteen. He has literally grown up among hardened criminals. And yet, strength has replaced hardness, and the criminality is gone.

We place this first novel of Mr. Blair Greiman before the public with great expectations that it will not only entertain and enlighten its readers, but that it will also challenge them to examine once again their own take on the universe and on the God who created it, as well as on the nature of the human beings who inhabit it.

Dr. Robert Grossmann, President
Elector Publications

PROLOGUE

"If only I could go back and start over again, knowing what I know now."

The quietly desperate wish of many hearts. Expressed or implied, the theme of many words. To prosper and not fail, to right a wrong, to erase a mistake, to retrieve a shameful secret from its public display— varied are the reasons, but the longing remains the same.

And what of those reasons? On their surface some seem benign enough. Good even. And then there are those for which we can construct no credible pretense of goodness whatever. For even as we would return to the past with our "knowledge" in hand, we dream that the others there remain ignorant, that by our advantage we might better manipulate, conquer and possess, arranging all substance and souls in our personal orbit.

Truth is, what we know now is pretty much what we knew then. Oh, not the details of the intervening history of course, the particular tack that lives and events would take. But the precepts— the principles by which it would all unfold— these we knew already. And that we now yearn to evade the result as it finds us, to renege and start over, has its root firmly lodged in all those times that we disregarded the things we already knew to be true, dreaming ourselves somehow exempt from the plainly evident rules by which all things, corporeal and otherwise, are so clearly and unalterably called to submission.

Would it really make a difference if the past could be lived over again with the advantage of knowing all that would happen and possessing every wisdom of humankind? Would any of it really make a difference if the life were still lived in the same slavery to unquenchable appetites, still bound to the concealment of a corrupt nature? Is it possible for a life dedicated to itself to arrive at a destination other than misery?

Yet and still, reality confronts even while things that are not real whisper sweet promises, lulling and luring into sleepy fantasy. "If only— oh, if only! by some strange, great miracle, I could go back and start over...knowing what I know now."

CHAPTER ONE

A lot of folks on a cross-country bus would rather be somewhere else. More than the general discontent rooted far down in the average heart, it's a specific desire to be traveling by some other means, though they find themselves here. The long-faced elderly on their way to and from relatives, not always welcome, their retirement too meager and their strength to depleted to hang onto the cherished independence of a car. The willfully dull-eyed young carried along by their sweet delusions from the known things of home toward things unknown and most often worse. The destitute chasing rumors of opportunity. The aimlessly drifting.

Among the high-backed vinyl seats of this particular westbound bus, near the rear and left of the aisle, Janet Slater sat next to the window, flanked by her six-year-old daughter, Kendra. They did not fit neatly into any of the typical bus passenger profiles, but, though she tried to maintain a mask of pleasantness for the child's sake, Janet Slater loathed this bus ride more than any of the other passengers. The pretty twenty-nine-year-old was college educated. She held a responsible office manager job at a respected architectural firm. And she considered this experience in mass transportation a most humiliating event, well beneath her proper station. But, she was a divorced single mother, and even with a decent job, it was a struggle to make things work. Her aging car had been in the shop again when she received the news of her Aunt Helen's death. Though she had never been particularly close to her aunt, her mother had been distraught and had pleaded that she and Kendra come to Illinois for the funeral. There had been little time to make other arrangements. She had few options but to buy bus tickets. She was not about to ask Kendra's father for help. Even if he would have, he'd have thought it entitled him to…something.

In any event, the ordeal was nearing an end. They had endured the trip east, the funeral, the looks and whispers of people, many of whom had attended her wedding and were only then learning of her divorce. In a few more hours they would be back in Haverston. God knows she never thought she'd be glad to get back to that uninspired little city on a nearly treeless prairie.

The bus trembled gently, idling at the Orde City bus station. A mild September rain fell in the early Friday afternoon while five people disembarked and two boarded. The first, a fastidious-looking elderly woman, carried a large canvas handbag. She eyed the other passengers suspiciously and chose the seat directly behind the driver for refuge, clutching the handbag tightly to her chest. The second boarder was a thick-figured, reticent-looking man of, perhaps, late thirties. The man's closely butched hair line receded on a bony, rugged skull. His dark eyes peered tentatively, almost apologetically, from drawn, scarred features. This all seemed as if it were foreign to him. He moved with exaggerated care as if afraid of violating some unknown custom. Carrying a large gray duffel bag and dressed in loosely fit jeans, worn leather work boots, and an odd thigh-length denim coat, he studied the seats and the passengers as he made his way down the aisle.

Approaching the rear, he stopped at the empty seat across from Janet and Kendra Slater. Extending his duffel over the seat, he looked aside at the mother and daughter as if to ask permission. Janet shrugged and turned her face away, indicating indifference. At close range, the man's eyes bore an ever-so-slight, but quite unmistakable smile and something more. A distant sadness subtly flashing from unspoken depth drew the notice of the child and her mother. As the man took his seat, Kendra watched him with unabashed curiosity while her mother sneaked furtive glances from behind her feigned indifference.

Rumbling to life, the bus began to roll out of the Orde City terminal. The man stirred, appearing anxious at the bus's movement. Catching the watchful eyes of Janet and Kendra, he smiled timorously and then turned his attention to the world gliding by his window. The youngster whirled her blond head around and gazed up inquisitively into her mother's face, silently gauging whether her mother was as intrigued by this stranger as she was. Eagerly, she turned back again, closely watching the man even as he watched the scenery outside his window slipping by with increasing velocity. Still covert in her interest, Janet paged through one of her magazines. Perhaps mother and child were both tempted, as people often are at first encounters, to make extravagantly

2

optimistic suppositions about the stranger. So often, reality later disappoints.

After staring out the window for a long time, the man finally drew a long breath through his nostrils and sighed it out slow and quiet, seeming to relax. Slumping a little from his disciplined bearing, he folded his hands in his lap and lowered his head, staring at the floor. Soon his eyes fell shut.

With an excited whisper, Kendra reported, "Mom, he's sleeping."

Janet glanced at the stranger and then down to her daughter. "Don't disturb him," she whispered back. "Why don't you finish the school work Mrs. Daller sent along."

"I did it, Mom. Don't you remember?"

"All of it?" Janet questioned, her eyes resting on the stranger.

"Yes," the girl insisted. "Don't you remember the 'Sam and His Cat' story? That was it!"

"Okay, all right. I just want to be sure. You've missed three days right at the beginning of first grade. I don't want you to fall behind."

Janet moved her attention to her daughter's face, smiling mildly before she resumed browsing her copy of "Independent Woman." Kendra, meanwhile, returned her full focus to the motionless subject of her curiosity. In time the inquisitive girl with the freckled face and softly rounded little nose edged out of her seat and into the aisle. Bracing her small hand on the edge of the stranger's seat, she leaned in close to study his face.

The man's eyes opened, expressionless at first, analyzing the large, bright blue eyes gazing up at him. The contrasting image of delicate blond head and the large, rugged-boned skull little more than a foot away was striking. The man's face warmed into a smile, halting at first, then finally certain and reassuring. The girl sounded an audible "hmmm" as she burst into a bright reciprocal smile.

"Kendy! I told you not to disturb him." Janet wearily plopped her magazine down.

Kendra recoiled across the aisle, her smile receding quickly. The stranger lifted his eyes to her mother. The woman's dark brown eyes glinted from fine, well-favored features. She was neither thin nor heavy, but full and pleasingly figured. Her skin showed itself a soft, subtly coppered tan where it emerged from the sleeves of a tightly knit white sweater and the cuffs of fashionably cut designer jeans down to her low-heeled, open-toed dress shoes.

"She is no disturbance," he said with measured tone.

"I'm sorry. She's not used to riding on a bus. We don't normally do this," Janet assured. "We don't belong with these...I work at an architectural firm in Haverston. I have a car. It's just that it went on the fritz and we had to go to my aunt's funeral in Illinois and there wasn't time to get it fixed and...There just wasn't time to make other arrangements and..." The more she tried to explain, the more rattled and warm-faced she grew. Both the stranger and her own daughter stared as she fumbled to regain her train of thought.

"I'm sorry," the man said, finally. "This is my first time on a bus, too. It is..." he paused thoughtfully, then smiled, "Not so bad." His easy, resonant voice and untroubled manner were engaging and soothing to both mother and child. Janet had scarcely realized how much tension had built up within her the past few days until a good measure of it dissolved into this stranger's gentle company. "I guess you're right," she agreed. "I suppose we can deal with it if you can. We're almost home now anyway."

"Haverston?" he repeated the place she had mentioned.

"Yes, that's where my ex dragged me after we got married, for his job." She rolled her eyes. "Now I'm stuck there raising a child on my own."

The stranger watched the little girl's eyes looking at him with apology. She was pained at being a source of restriction to her mother.

"Your husband left you?"

"Huh," she huffed. "He may as well have. He was never home anyway. Always out with his friends or working on his hot rod or something. He spent all our money on himself. Didn't have any time for me or even his own daughter. And when he was around he had to be the boss of everything. Mr. 'I know everything about everything.' He doesn't care about anyone but himself." She shook her head with disgust. "He showed his true colors when Kendy was

4

born."

The man watched the little one's eyes drop mutely to the floor. "You divorced him, then."

"Oh yeah," the woman confirmed with exaggerated indifference. Her moment of coolness fled in an instant, though, when she saw what the stranger's eyes were fixed upon. The lowly hung little blond head. "So— -" Janet began to rub her daughter's back soothingly, suddenly eager to change the subject, "Where are you headed?"

The man's eyes held their faint smile on Janet for a long moment. "I don't know. Wherever I find some use for myself, I guess."

Janet was puzzled. "Did you lose your job?"

A grim reticence passed over his face. He searched for words, then shrugged. "I had a position with the state for a number of years. But I've been let go and I'm obliged to move on."

Kendra eyed him with genuine concern. "Don't you have a family?"

"No, not the kind you mean, blue eyes," he smiled. "But I hope to make new friends wherever I go."

"That's an upbeat way to look at it," Janet said. "I don't think I could handle something like that as well. I wish I could be more easygoing like that, more positive."

"Mom, he could live at Mr. Porter's place!"

"Oh— -"Janet chuckled, rubbing her daughter's back again. "He doesn't want to get stuck in Haverston, sweetie." She was thoughtful for a time, though, then added, "Not that you couldn't, I suppose. There is an empty apartment in our house. It's a big old house converted into four apartments. The owner Mrs. Peterson lives in one downstairs and we live right above her."

Kendra nearly whispered, "Mr. Peterson died."

"Yes," Janet softly confirmed, "Just after Christmas. Mrs. Peterson hasn't been the same since." She shook her head with slow resignation. "And Calvin hasn't made things any easier for her. For any of us."

The stranger narrowed his scarred brow curiously.

"See, Calvin— Calvin Miller— is this big, scary guy that

moved into the other downstairs apartment back in June when he got out of jail," she explained. "Only Mrs. Peterson didn't know he'd been in jail. She didn't know anything about him when she rented the place to him. Now she can't get rid of him. He and his friends do dope and drink. They make incredible noise all night long. A bunch of people in the neighborhood have had stuff stolen. And he's always real intimidating to people. Everyone knows how violent he is and they're afraid of him. He was in jail for beating up a Haverston cop in a parking lot," she said with foreboding. "The Christians family, they live in the house next door, called the cops on him in July because of all the noise. The next night somebody shot a gun through their front door! It was on the news and everything. Everybody knows it was Calvin, but they can't prove it."

Janet sighed and rubbed Kendra's back some more. "Everyone's afraid to say anything now. I guess we're all just holding our breath and hoping he'll move out or get locked up again or something. Poor old Mr. Porter couldn't wait anymore though. He lived in the apartment right above Calvin's, across from us. He couldn't take the noise anymore and moved out. That's the apartment Kendy's talking about. Pretty appealing, huh?"

The stranger smiled politely.

"If it goes on much longer, I'm thinking I'll have to move us out, too," she added. "I can't even let Kendy play outside because of him and all his creepy friends downstairs."

"He called Mom bad words," Kendra said, her blue eyes reaching up into the stranger's face.

So it was that the bus continued westward and the stranger continued to quietly listen to his new acquaintances.

Wovoka County Sheriff Alvin Skoda sat at his Jasper Mills office desk stunned into silence. Scarcely did he hear the voice of Jim Ryan on the other end of the phone. In his forty-one years as a law officer, Skoda had come through many hard moments and appraised himself pretty steady under pressure. But the news that

6

the assistant security director of Kalbourne, the state's highest security prison, was giving him now left him cold. Ezra Jacob Watt had been released from custody that morning.

"Did you hear what I said Sheriff?... Sheriff Skoda?"

"What's that again?" Skoda's voice waxed parched and hoarse.

"I said please don't tell anyone where you got this information. Same as I told the reporters, don't use my name. We're not supposed to give out this sort of thing because he's served out his sentence. Right to privacy and all that. I could get in some hot water, you understand?" Ryan's voice was noticeably taut.

"Don't worry, Mr. Ryan. And I appreciate you sticking your neck out for us."

"Well, I don't normally do this sort of thing," Ryan assured, "But I've never forgotten the Watt case. I just had to warn someone. Especially you folks up in Wovoka County."

"But he was sentenced to fifty years," the old law man complained. "It's only been, what? Twenty? And you say he's served his full sentence and can't be held a day longer? That's the thing that really gets me. I know they get some time off for good behavior or something, but come on!"

"I know it. And I agree with you," Ryan said. "If he were sentenced today it would be different. But back in '78 the sentencing laws were more liberal. Not only did he get day-for-day good time to cut the sentence in half, but he also was credited another ten percent of his sentence for honor time. We have to go by whatever laws they're sentenced under."

"Good time. Honor time." The sheriff's voice edged incredulous. "That's hard to swallow. What goodness? What honor? He doesn't have any. He doesn't know the meaning."

"Yeah, I know it. I know." Then, after an awkward pause, Ryan added, "Look, Sheriff, there's something else and I hesitate to even mention it. But there are some people down here, even among the staff if you can believe it, that seem to think that Watt went through some sort of change while he was here. They think that he's a .... well, something of a Christian now."

"Oh wonderful," Skoda's voice was soaked with sarcasm. "So everything's all right now, huh? I'm sure the families will be happy

7

to hear it. Give me a break. What was he trying to do? Get even more time off?"

"Hey, I'm with you, Sheriff. Who knows what the guy was up to. God only knows his motives."

Ryan gave Skoda more of the details of Watt's release. The two men exchanged parting courtesies and then hung up.

The old white-haired sheriff's weathered face was ashen as he sat at his desk. A wave of two-decade old memories crashed down on him. In the late spring of 1978 he had been a senior deputy with the department when it had all begun.

A local farmer had found the body of what turned out to be nineteen-year-old Brian Helms in a soybean field. The former Jasper Mills High School athletic standout had been murdered, killed by a single twenty-two caliber gunshot to the head. Even more disturbing was the evidence that this strong young man had been bound and methodically beaten and tortured with mind-numbing savagery. Much of the cruelty had been visited upon him before he was shot. But the medical examiner had also concluded that someone had continued to mutilate his body even after he was dead.

A crime of such viciousness was virtually unheard of in this mostly rural part of the state. The twelve-man Wovoka County Sheriff's Department and the eight-man Jasper Mills Police Department had soon recognized their own inexperience in such a case and had called in state criminal investigators. The case had been puzzling. Clearly someone had harbored a personal hatred for Brian Helms, yet everyone they talked to insisted he was well-liked, that he had no enemies. He had just finished his freshman year down at State University. Good grades. No apparent problems. He had returned home for the summer to work odd jobs and spend time with friends. Indeed, it was with a group of these old high school buddies that he had gone to a keg party at the farmstead of a friend, not half a mile from the field where his body was found.

By all accounts, there had been scores of high school and college age young people from the surrounding communities and rural areas, coming and going from the party late into the night. In those days the drinking age was still eighteen and even underage

8

drinking was more tolerated. Lists were compiled and everyone who might possibly have been there was questioned thoroughly. As witnesses remembered it, Brian had left the large shed, where the focus of the revelry had been, sometime after ten and somewhat intoxicated, to get some air. A couple of people recalled seeing him walking among the chaotically parked cars, but no one had seen him leaving with anyone. His buddies all swore they left without him, assuming he'd found another ride, and several other party-goers confirmed their assertions.

Then one evening in late June, while the people of the Jasper Mills area were still trying to come to terms with the Helms murder and investigators were still coming up frustratingly empty, Gerald and Sandy Guiness called the Sheriff's Department in rising panic. Their seventeen-year-old daughter Amanda was missing. They had taken their eleven-year-old son Danny to his little league ball game earlier in the evening, leaving Amanda by herself on the family's farmstead. When they returned around nine p.m., she was missing. Deputies tried to reassure her parents that she had probably just gone off with friends, while her parents had insisted that she was a good, responsible girl and would not take off in such a manner. Her parents were right. The next morning's sunlight revealed Amanda's clothesless corpse on a muddy creek bank just a quarter-mile from her home. Though, plainly, she had been horrendously brutalized and, the medical examiner would conclude, most probably raped, an overnight thunderstorm and the rushing creek had conspired to frustrate investigators in their search for clues. One piece of evidence was unmistakable, however. The twenty-two caliber bullet recovered from the girl's brain had been fired from the same weapon that killed Brian Helms.

If they had not been before, people were truly outraged and terrified in the wake of Amanda's murder. Before, a good many had quietly held that Brian Helms had probably fallen in with the wrong sort down at the university and it had followed him home. People were reluctant to believe that such brutal depravity could lurk among them. But, as Amanda's broken vessel was lowered into the ground, everyone had come face to face with the sickening realization that there was a monstrosity growing right in their midst— no doubt greeting them politely and smiling in their faces.

More investigators poured into the county. Law officers from most of the surrounding communities and counties eagerly volunteered their off-duty time to help. Nearly every person in Wovoka County, at one point, had been questioned and many, re-questioned. Anyone deemed even mildly suspicious came under scrutiny. Anyone who had ever crossed the law in even a minor way. Any man who anyone found to be even negligibly antisocial or, in some way or another, odd, deviant, or new to the area, or whose neighbor just didn't like him— had always had a "funny feeling" about him. Still nothing. Nobody emerged as a strong suspect. And the succession of atrocities most certainly would have continued unchecked were it not for a most fortuitous turn of events on the night of August the seventh. Events that would later be ascribed by many to Divine intervention.

As a matter of long standing routine, the elderly Lilian Hoyt and her husband Horace were all but never up past ten at night. But for some reason that, to this day, she can't quite put her finger on, Lilian Hoyt felt out of sorts on that evening and had been unable to sleep. Going down to the kitchen of their farm home to warm some milk, she had just scarcely noticed, while glancing out the window over the sink, an ever-so-faint flicker of strange light beyond the rise of a hill in their hayfield. So faint was it that she had sought to dismiss it as nothing important. Yet, for some reason, the remote flicker bothered her until, at length, she woke Horace and asked him to go and see what it was. And, though reluctant to get up, Horace's wife persisted until he finally dressed and drove his pickup out to investigate.

After only a few moments the pickup had come racing wildly back over the hill and out of the hayfield, skidding to a stop on the gravel farmyard. Frantically, Horace had called out to Lilian from the yard, telling her to call for an ambulance and for the sheriff. The old man struggled to carry the nearly nude body of Lynnette Younger from the cab of his pickup into the house, laying her gently on the kitchen floor. He had found the twenty-year-old Jasper Mills woman lying in the freshly cut alfalfa in a disoriented stupor not fifty feet from her burning car. She was badly beaten

10

from head to toe. She was cut. She was singed. And she was bleeding profusely from a wound on the back of her head. Had she not been found until morning, she would no doubt have succumbed to the loss of blood and overnight chill. But she had been found and she was very much alive.

Indeed, while still on the Hoyt's kitchen floor, covered in quilts, she began to regain her senses and wasted little time telling what had happened to her.

Just days from starting her junior year of college, the young woman had been returning from a visit to a friend's rural home south of town when she had come upon a person dressed in dark clothing walking along the gravel road in the waning light of dusk. The events of earlier that summer had set everyone on edge, but as she drew near, she had recognized the young man as someone she had gone to high school with when she was a senior and he a freshman. On occasion she had spoken with him both in high school and in subsequent summers when she was home from college. About to begin his own senior year of high school, he had grown somewhat bigger, but remained very polite and well-mannered, if not a little shy, and so Lynn Younger had harbored no misgivings about stopping to offer seventeen-year-old Ezra Watt a ride.

Lynn had cheerfully greeted Ezra as he got into her car and had asked him what he was doing walking so far from his home at dark. "Hunting," had been his quiet reply. The young woman had not grasped Ezra's perverse joke until he slipped a pistol from his windbreaker and put the muzzle right to her head. In the stark, adrenaline-filled moments that followed, Lynn had filled with near paralyzing terror as Ezra forced her to turn off the road at a field access and drive far out into the Hoyt's deserted hayfield.

The things that Lynn suffered at the hands of Ezra Watt in that darkened field— the depraved sexual abuses, the brutal and sadistic inflictions of pain and humiliation for no more apparent reason than to glory in her agony— were sufficient to turn the stomach of every arriving lawman and ambulance attendant and to set every jaw with bitter resolve to see justice prevail without a moment's further delay.

When Watt had finally finished torturing Lynn, he had matter-

11

of-factly pushed her face down onto the front floorboard of her car and shot her in the back of the head. Then, after starting the seats of the car on fire, he had just walked away.

But what Watt had not realized as he slipped away was that the bullet he had fired at Lynn Younger's head had ricocheted— some would later say miraculously— off of her skull rather than piercing through. She was knocked senseless by the impact, but not killed. No doubt, Watt had looked back from his trusted cloak of darkness, believing the evidence of his treachery was being purged in the flames. In fact, the "evidence" regained enough consciousness and marshaled the tenacity to pull herself up and fall out of the open driver's door, crawling away from the flames and smoke before they could take her.

Even before they finished loading Lynn into the ambulance, the sudden explosion of traffic on law enforcement radios across that corner of the state began drawing a sea of clear-eyed officers to the Hoyt farmyard from every direction. And when the ambulance finally made its way out of the yard for the hospital, the undivided attention of a gathering army was turned upon one Ezra Jacob Watt.

Local accountant Noah Watt and his wife Ida had always been known as gracious, temperate people. They had born their only son relatively late in their lives and had raised him with strict, but gentle, nurture according to their firmly held religious views. As the nearly retirement age couple slept in the waning hours of August seventh, they had not heard their son slipping back into his bedroom through the window of their modest home on the edge of Jasper Mills. Nor, apparently, had they ever had any knowledge of any of Ezra's nocturnal wanderings, believing only that he was a quiet, private boy that preferred the solitude of his room.

But those kindly, trusting parents had their tranquil life and innocent presumptions forever wrenched from them just minutes before midnight. An incomprehensible wall of lawmen from every department and agency in that part of the state fell upon their little home without warning. While the couple was still blinking, trying to fathom what was happening, a swarm of officers had already stormed the house through splintered front and back doors, quickly filling every room. They dragged off a thoroughly surprised Ezra, handcuffed and pajama-clad, to the back of a squad car even as they escorted Noah and Ida, in their night clothes, out to the front porch to explain and to question. The eyes of the horrified couple had searched the faces of the lawmen trying to comprehend their words. Noah's frantic countenance had searched the windows of the squad cars, desperate for a fading glimpse of his son.

But in a few minutes more the case had seemingly been cinched tight even for Ezra's parents when officers found a cache under the floorboards of his bedroom closet. Among other things, they found a twenty-two caliber pistol and bullets that, it would later be determined, had been stolen from a Wovoka County farm home almost two years earlier and would subsequently be matched to all three attacks. They found other weapons and instruments of torment. They found books and handmade diagrams on torture and killing. They found pornography of the most vile sort, some of it disturbingly hand drawn. They found dark clothing with incriminating blood spatters. And, as if all of these things weren't distressing enough, they found stacks of meticulous, hand-drawn maps detailing the better part of Jasper Mills and the surrounding Wovoka countryside, bearing designations of scores of potential prey.

In subsequent days, though, the relief of having solved the crimes and stopped the carnage soon gave way to sinking horror as an unaccountable error came to light. Upon arriving in town, the expensive downstate trial attorney that Noah and Ida mortgaged their home to secure for Ezra, formally requested to examine all of the evidence against his charge.. .and the search warrant by which it had been gathered. In the zealous haste and confusion on the night of Lynn Younger's attack, it had not been entirely clear which agency was in charge of what. Was the sheriff's department leading the arrest and search or were the state's investigators? Was it still the Wovoka County Attorney's case or the state attorney's? Each had assumed another was appearing before a judge that evening to obtain the requisite search warrant for the Watt home. Each had assumed another carried that warrant with them. In fact, no one had obtained it.

Wovoka County Prosecutor Avery Loomis fought with rare

desperation to hold onto the evidence seized from the Watt home. But, in the end, as earnestly as Judge Ronald Skoda had sought to side with Loomis, the elder cousin of Alvin Skoda had never circumvented the written law, whatever his personal desires, and he would not do so then. The law he was sworn to adhere to was plain. The gun was excluded from evidence. The other weapons were out. The clothing was out. The books, the diagrams, the maps —all out. Nothing gathered from the Watt home could be used against Ezra. The embarrassed, frustrated Loomis was left with the testimony of Lynn Younger and the evidence gleaned from her person and charred crime scene. Sufficient to convict Watt of Younger's kidnapping, abuse, and attempted murder. There was nothing left, however, but pure conjecture to link him to the murders of Brian Helms and Amanda Guiness, the only crimes for which he could be sentenced to life without parole or death. Even the bullets taken from the victims were rendered useless because there was no longer any gun recognized by the court to connect them to.

Perhaps Loomis should have withheld the murder charges in the hope of finding more evidence at a later date. Perhaps Judge Skoda should have made him hold back the charges. But, Loomis pressed ahead with all of the charges. Probably, both men calculated that the sheer force of the community's outrage would result in a jury conviction no matter what had happened to the evidence. But Ezra's attorney was unpredictably shrewd. Though he was unable to prevent the seventeen-year-old from being tried as an adult, he recognized in Judge Skoda a man who would not yield to public sentiment or private turmoil, and, thus, opted to bypass a trial by unknown jurors in favor of having the old judge himself hear the case.

Throughout the autumn of 1978, Watt's trial played out. Some tried to fathom just what it could be that had motivated the boy to such heinousness. Many more didn't give a damn what his problem was. For his part, Avery Loomis asserted that Ezra Watt was an immutable sociopath. Whether born or fashioned, it mattered little. He was said to possess no conscience like a normal person. Where Lynn Younger was concerned, Loomis established his case firmly.

14

Though clearly afraid and still recuperating from her injuries, the young woman delivered unassailable testimony. But, where the murder victims were concerned, the prosecutor was left with little but naked speculation before Judge Skoda.

In his arguments, Loomis theorized that Ezra had wandered about in the night, watching people from the cover of darkness. Waiting. Fantasizing all manner of evil. From the darkness at the edge of the keg party he must have spotted a vulnerable Brian Helms, who had, on occasion, bullied the younger Watt in high school— and slipped from the shadows to take him away at gunpoint and exact a murderous revenge. Having crossed over the line between fantasizing and doing, the prosecutor speculated that Watt must have found the experience to his liking and, thereafter, began to look about for an opportunity to satiate his more prurient dreams. He must have found that opportunity in an isolated Amanda Guiness, just as he would later in a trusting Lynn Younger— neither of whom, so far as anyone knew, had ever slighted him in the least.

Ezra's attorney had simply stressed to Judge Skoda that there was not one shred of "admissible" evidence to tie his client to the Helms and Guiness murders and that even the prosecutor's rampant speculations were built upon an inadmissable foundation. Henceforth, he had ignored the murder charges completely, focusing the balance of his efforts on the Younger charges. But, finding no credible defense against the physical evidence, much less Lynn's unshakable testimony, Ezra's lawyer diverted to a most unusual stratagem. Much to the community's disbelief, he asserted that his client was mentally incompetent, that he had suffered grave abuse at the hands of his parents and, therefore, could not be held culpable for any crimes he might have perpetrated. The irony was, so far from being abusive, Noah and Ida Watt had been only too willing to climb up on the witness stand and offer themselves up, humble sacrifices for their son. While Ezra sat by idly, making no effort to bear any responsibility, and while the rest of the courtroom squirmed uncomfortably, Noah and Ida publicly shamed themselves, attempting to disgrace their own standing as good people in a desperate bid to bear their son's guilt for him.

But this was not a stain that Ezra's parents could wash from his hands. Judge Skoda vindicated Noah and Ida Watt, you could say, when he convicted their son for the attack on Lynn Younger. But, though he agonized over his decision for more than a week, the old judge had found no honest way to avoid finding Ezra "not guilty" of two murders which he and everyone else knew full well the boy had committed. Murders for which he could never be tried again.

The maximum sentences on all the Younger convictions added up to fifty years and Judge Skoda had wasted no time in sentencing Ezra to the maximum with an emphatic proviso to the state's corrections department that Watt never be so much as considered for any type of parole or early release. Still, many believed it was the weight of his responsibility in the Watt case that brought the old judge to a series of strokes, culminating in his death not two months beyond the trial.

And that was not the only fallout. The prosecutor Avery Loomis was so embittered and guilt stricken at the trial's outcome that he cursed everyone involved. Most especially Judge Skoda, whom he felt had betrayed him. Loomis vowed vehemently to anyone who came near, that if it meant spending every waking moment of his remaining life, he would never let Wovoka County's people down again and he would never— never— be thus vanquished in a courtroom again. In the subsequent years, he would prove as good as his word, forsaking all else in his life, including his wife and children, and striking genuine terror in the hearts of even the most minor of Wovoka County wrongdoers.

Feeling responsible for the search warrant debacle, the sheriff at that time resigned from the office and Alvin Skoda had then ascended to the post, remaining ever since.

The Guiness family was devastated beyond words. They say Amanda's little brother Daniel was never seen to smile again and Sheriff Skoda knew that it was so. The parents of Brian Helms came apart in divorce under the terrible strain, the pieces of their remaining family scattering away from Jasper Mills. The Younger family struggled every day to cope. Lynn began to slip ever farther into a dark, uncommunicative depression, sheltered in her parents' home, never returning to college.

Most people tried not to judge Noah and Ida Watt for the sins of their son, but the rapidly frailing couple never really recovered from their heartbreaking sorrow. Indeed, it seemed as though everyone had been horrendously affected by Ezra Watt's crimes, except Ezra Watt. While yet a deputy, Skoda had been one of the officers assigned to transport Ezra down to Kalbourne. Watt had sat in arrogant silence in the back of the squad car. The few words he had expended were filled with concern for himself— the unfairness of his sentence... hoped his attorney could get him out of it... could they stop for pizza on the way down.

Sheriff Skoda finally breached the surface of the engulfing memories and returned to the present with a shudder. Now Mr. Ryan had just given him the details of how this same amoral, predatory beast had, this very morning, been released from Kalbourne— fifty pounds larger, three times stronger, most of a library craftier, and countless prison battles more capable of brutality. They had escorted him out from behind the walls after twenty years, with all of his worldly belongings in a duffel bag and taken him to the local bank where, in cash, he had collected the $5,100 saved from his forty-cent an hour prison woodshop job. They had driven him to nearby Orde City and dropped him at the bus station. No warning to the public. No supervision. No forwarding address.

"A Christian," Skoda muttered. He had looked into those dark, arrogant eyes after the mask of innocent school boy had been removed. Ezra J. Watt gave no evidence of a conscience, not a hint of remorse. Such a rabid aberration of nature could no more turn to goodness than a snake to warm blood. Not in twenty years. Not in twenty lifetimes. It was not in his nature.

* * *

The afternoon rain had subsided and the stranger's dark eyes methodically surveyed the wet city street in front of the Haverston depot as the bus faded into the distance. Janet and Kendra watched him keenly while he scanned one direction, then the other.

"What do you think" Janet queried. "Not much to the place,

17

huh?"

"Looks all right to me." He looked up into the sky. "Bigger than my last place."

"Yeah, there's definitely plenty of wide open space. Unfortunately, part of it is about nine blocks to our apartment house. A long walk, I'm afraid."

The stranger slung the gray duffel over his shoulder, draped his coat over one of the Slater suitcases, and picked them both up. "Not so far," he assured, casting his stare on their attentive faces. "Lead on."

They began to walk and after some time, Janet eyed the man inquisitively. "You know, I just realized that we got so wrapped up in telling you all about us that we never even asked you your name."

There was a quiet space as they walked on in silence for another thirty paces or more. "You can call me E.J.," he finally answered.

CHAPTER 2

The gentle, heartsick sounds of weeping filled a quaint, pastel Jasper Mills living room. Forty-year-old Lynn Younger sat on the edge of the sofa waging a panic-laden, watery-eyed struggle to catch her breath and hang on to some semblance of composure. Gripping Lynn tightly around her shoulders, her elderly mother Alice heaved soft, grief-stricken sobs while, in the middle of the room, stood a defiantly postured Dale Younger. Tears of pain streamed from under the retired grocer's spectacles. A bitter mix of anger and fear quivered his jaw as he faced a somber Sheriff Skoda, the reluctant messenger standing in the passageway between their foyer and living room.

"Fifty years!" Lynn's father bellowed hoarsely. "They said fifty years! It's only been twenty! What the hell's going on, Alvin?!"

"I know it, Dale. I know it. I'm so sorry. The same thing went through my mind when I heard the news. But they did say when he was sentenced that some time would be taken off the stated term."

"Not thirty years!" Younger protested. "Nobody said they'd give him thirty years off!"

"According to the law he was sentenced under in 1978, he's served all of his time." Skoda looked away from the elder Younger's eyes.

"The law?! The law?!" Younger's voice choked with disdain. "Look what he's done to Lynn! Look what he's done to us! To everyone! Look what he's done! Where's the law?! Where's the justice in any of it?! Somebody should kill him! That'd be justice!"

The sheriff's eyes rose up quickly to meet Younger's. "Dale, don't even talk like that." Skoda searched earnestly for something encouraging to say. "He won't even come back this way. No reason to. Noah and Ida are gone, and he doesn't have any other family here about. No reason for him to come back this way. I'm sure he's already a long way from here by now."

The sheriff thought that he perceived some easing in Lynn's breathing at his words of assurance. Her father shuffled over to the far end of the room and plopped himself down dejectedly in an arm chair. "Why wouldn't he come back?" his voice rolled with sarcasm. "He can finish what he had all mapped out now. He can kill the whole town!"

The man saw the carelessness of his words as his daughter visibly tensed. Her deep brown eyes darted wildly from her father's face to the Sheriff's, trying to gauge in panicked silence if they really believed Ezra would come back.

"No, no, dear. He didn't mean that." Alice Younger squeezed with renewed vigor and brushed her daughter's shoulder-length brown hair from her cheek.

"Lynn, I really don't think so. I really don't believe he's coming back," Skoda quickly added. The old white-haired lawman now desperately hunted more than ever for words of comfort, something of hope that he could give to the devastated family. Anything. "Look," Skoda hesitated, gathering all the sincerity he could muster upon his face, "I was actually given a real encouraging report from the Kalbourne prison concerning Ezra. They seem to think that he really changed a lot while he was down there and it sounded like a legitimate evaluation to me." The sheriff raised his brown encouragingly. "They seem to think he's become a Christian now."

"Ohh! Ohh! Ohh!" Dale Younger sat forward in his chair, his hands raised above a vehemently shaking head. "How can you even say something like that to us, Alvin?! We don't want to hear that kind of rot! Who are you trying to sell that to?! People like that don't change...ever! No way!" The old man slumped back into his chair. "And who the hell cares if he did."

The entire living room was abruptly started by yelling out in the front yard. "Move away from the house!" a distressed voice boomed. "Get back!"

Lynn cringed and her parents craned to see out of the window behind the couch. Recognizing the voice, Sheriff Skoda's brow furrowed. He turned and crossed the foyer to the front door. Outside, a bewildered Jim and Betty Johnson stood frozen at the end of the walkway leading up to the Younger home. Midway up the walk, barring their way, was the deputy that had accompanied the sheriff as he delivered the news to the families. Jim and Betty were long-time neighbors of the Youngers. Their children had grown up together. And they were also friends and fellow Catholic parishioners of the sheriff. They looked past the deputy to Skoda with alarm. Betty clutched a freshly baked pie and Jim held her shoulder protectively.

"Dan, take it easy. It's all right," Skoda eased his deputy. "They're friends of the family. Let them by." Lifting his voice, he called down the walk, "Jim, Betty, please come on in. Dale and Alice will be glad to see you. They could use the company about now."

Warily, the Johnsons walked past the agitated, hulking deputy and up onto the porch. "We heard the news, Alvin. It's all over town," Jim explained. "We wanted to lend some support to Alice and Dale and to poor Lynn. We didn't mean to cause any trouble."

"No, no, you're not causing any trouble," Skoda reassured. "We're all just a little edgy with the news. You folks go on in. I'll be in in a minute." The sheriff let the door push shut behind him. He stood on the porch staring down at the deputy turning to face him from the walk. "Now Dan, I asked you before we left for your folks' place if you needed some time off to deal with this. You promised me you were okay, that you were going to be able to handle this business all right." The old sheriff's tone was gentle, but stern.

"Sorry, Sheriff," the deputy quickly adopted an easy affect that was suspect. "I just didn't know who they were, that's all."

"Well they're obviously not Ezra Watt," Skoda chided. "All right? Keep your head, Dan." The sheriff studied his deputy with concern. "You sure you don't want to come inside?"

The deputy shook his head.

"All right. Just take it easy out here, then."

Deputy Daniel Guiness watched Sheriff Skoda disappear back inside the Younger home. The kid brother of murder victim Amanda Guiness was fighting an extraordinary internal battle to maintain his composure and bide his time. From within the house he could hear yet another round of muffled sobs and anguished voices. He had to hold on and wait until the time was right. He had worked too hard and waited too long to come undone now.

21

From the summer night when his parents had brought him home from little league and discovered his sister missing, his life had been permanently altered to a most severe course. The strapping blond farm boy had been a happy-go-lucky first baseman and the premier hitter on his team of fellow fifth-graders when they drove up into the farmyard that night. The memory of the half-eaten strawberry malt his folks had bought him, falling from his hand to the dusty drive as panic swept over their family, was still so intensely vivid in his mind, even twenty years later, that he lived the sounds, smelled the scents, and felt the compressing dread in his chest. His big sister had been so good to him. He could still feel her hand mussing his hair, the warmth of her patient smile. When the sweeping agony of the next morning's discovery had reached his ears, he had wept long and bitter. And he had put down his ball glove with the rest of his childhood, never to be retrieved.

That fall, as the events of Ezra Watt's trial and sentencing unfolded, the unseen heart of an eleven-year-old quietly galvanized in the background. As he heard them say that Watt would get out of prison one day, every diverse aspect of his life became ordered and focused toward one end. Everything he had done since then— the school work, the boyhood boxing and karate lessons, the military training and service after high school, the law enforcement training and service after that, the madly intense, daily weight training sessions, the endless target practice, everything, all of it— had as its sole purpose just one moment. That singularly sweet moment when he would come face to face with Ezra Jacob Watt.

Inside, they were lamenting Watt's release. Outside, Deputy Guiness' temples throbbed rhythmically as the muscles of his gritted jaw flexed. The thirty-one year-old man's thickly muscled, two hundred forty pound, six foot-three frame stood with motionless discipline. Glassy eyes fixed on a point beyond the present, the sounds around him fell away to a distant, unperceived whisper and he was, once more, in a familiar, comforting place. Here, his mind began again to review the well-worn visualizations of their meeting, accounting for every conceivable contingency, countering and devastating every possible defense, cutting off every avenue of escape... The others grieved Watt's release, but he did not. This was the whole point of his life. It was Watt's turn to be hunted. Let them all mourn if they must. He would not. This day had been twenty years coming and he was ready.

CHAPTER 3

The waning Friday afternoon sun had nearly dried the sidewalk running parallel to Seventh Avenue. Janet, Kendra and the man who called himself E.J. walked along the west side of a large, two-level brick house. To the south of the house, in the back yard, they had passed a sizeable shed of matching brick. An old garage, perhaps, with large, white wooden double doors at its west end facing the avenue. Rounding the corner onto Oak Street, a large, covered porch that took up the whole north end of the house was revealed. The porch's roof was supported by massive, square brick pillars along its front and sides. The exterior of the house betrayed signs of neglect. Some of the brick mortar joints were beginning to crack. Old, loose paint flaked from the wooden window and door frames. Grass and weeds grew undeterred around the house and porch and at the edges of the yard. Branches, discarded wrappers, cans, and bottles, some broken, littered the unkempt grounds of the spacious corner lot.

"This is where we live!" Kendra announced. The man trailed the girl and her mother up the porch steps and through the front door into a small foyer area. To the left was a set of bare wooden stairs to a landing and, presumably, doubling back and up to the second floor. To the right, a lightly hued oak door with heavy raised panels.

"Mrs. Peterson, the landlady, lives there," Janet pointed. "We hardly see her at all since Mr. Peterson died. She's kind of let the place go." Janet lowered her voice, nodding indirectly down the hallway. "They don't help things."

The dimly lit hallway led straight through the center of the house to a door opening onto the back yard. Midway down the hall, on the left, was the partially opened door of the other downstairs apartment. From within came the monotoned, staccato strains of trash metal music. Loitering out in the hallway was a ragged, skinny couple of twenty or so. The young man's and young woman's vacuous, darting eyes and unnaturally gaunt faces suggested the excessive use of stimulant. Their contemptuous glare fell on Janet and Kendra with well-practiced ease. When the mother and daughter had meekly averted their eyes and turned aside to ascend the stairs, the couple gained a better view of the man that followed, carrying their suitcases. When his unflinching eyes met them, the young people's haughty expressions abruptly sobered and it was their eyes that found the floor. Only when the man had turned to follow up the stairs did the gaunt couple hazard another glance, cautiously studying the bulky, six foot form slipping from the foyer.

Atop the stairs was another foyer area and directly across from the steps was another oak door.

Kendra pointed to the door eagerly. "E.J., we live here!" Pointing to another door across the foyer, just around from the steps, she added, "That's where Mr. Porter lived! You can live there!"

"Hope you like noise better than he did," Janet reiterated. "Calvin and his friends, like those two, don't even get warmed up until after midnight. You'll be right over top of them. Mr. Porter tried asking him to keep it down. So did Mrs. Peterson and a couple of the neighbors. Even me. He doesn't care. Thinks it's funny." Her voice lowered. "Since the shooting no one says anything at all." She paused, eyeing the untalkative man. "Just want to be sure you know what you're getting into."

Her blue eyes heavy with concern, Kendra reminded, "He called Mom bad words."

Staring down into the little earnest face, Ezra Watt answered simply, "Ya."

Janet unlocked her apartment door. "It's about supper time. Will you join us, E.J.?" She flashed an intriguing glance at him as she and Kendra went inside.

Ezra set their suitcases down just inside the doorway and straightened. "I need to see the landlady."

"Are you going to come back and eat supper with us, E.J.?" Kendra echoed her mother with a hopeful face.

Ezra stared at the child's face. "Sure."

Kendra suddenly bolted from the entry and scurried away into the apartment. "I'm going to get my pictures ready to show you when you come back!"

25

Ezra looked back into Janet's face with unexpected hardness. It caught her off guard and made her uneasy. "She means drawings," the woman explained. "She draws pictures...with crayons."

Ezra said nothing, only nodding slightly. She was a little unsettled by his manner. Something in his expression. Maybe he was just studying her. She just wasn't sure. He was hard to read and she was hesitant to ask. Whatever it was, Janet was relieved when, at length, he turned and left.

* * *

The early evening news blared from the large television in Edna Peterson's dimly lit living room. The grief-weary widow sat slumped in an overstuffed arm chair, staring at the screen with blank resignation. Having reached the retirement age that she and her husband Ben had so long worked and planned for, life seemed to have little point without him. This apartment house that they had labored half their lives to buy and renovate for a secure "golden years" income had been taken over by hooligans. The deed listing her as owner may as well have listed her as prisoner. The violent bully across the hall had clearly taken ownership of the place and no one seemed particularly interested in stopping him. Even her son-in-law, for all his incessant bluster, had shrunk away, saying there was little he could do and that she should consider selling the place and moving to a "home." He did say that he would be glad to handle the finances for her so she wouldn't have to "worry" about anything. She stayed. If only to thwart his transparent greed for her and Ben's lifetime of work, she stayed. And maybe out of some lingering sense of loyalty to Ben, she stayed.

Her last refuge had become sitting before her TV from morning until late in the night, with the volume uncomfortably loud in order to block out as much of the clamor from across the hall as possible.

Now there was a knock at her door, filling her with dread. It was too late in the day for an after-school visit from her grandson Michael. In the back of her mind, with numb trepidation, she often wondered when Miller and his friends would finally burst in and take over this last little corner of her world. Still, as she approached the door, she did note that the knocking seemed uncharacteristically gentle for one of them.

Easing her door open, Edna peered out at a lean, stocky man dressed in jeans and a neatly tucked blue pocket tee-shirt. A dark denim coat was draped over a gray duffel in his left hand. Looking up to the man's eyes, Edna supposed she would find menace, but detected none.

"Mrs. Peterson?" The man's voice suggested a certain strength to her.

"Yes," she answered.

"My name is E.J. I am a recent acquaintance of your upstairs tenants Janet and Kendra Slater. They tell me that you have a place for rent. I was hoping you might consider renting it to me for a while."

"Oh." Edna's face brightened and she opened the door wider. "Please come in and have a seat." She extended a hospitable hand in the direction of the dining room table before disappearing into the next room. "Let me turn off the television."

Shortly, the sound of the television ceased, unmasking the muffled, jagged noise from across the hall.

"I'm afraid I'm not dressed for company," she said, referring to her worn, ankle length housecoat and slippers. Her mostly gray hair bore only remnants of a once stylish permanent. The deep character lines of her face spoke of a woman who had smiled happily through her life, though she now appeared haggard and careworn. "Would you like something to drink?" she offered.

"No." Ezra set his bag and coat on the floor at the corner of the table. He pulled out the chair at the end of the table and offered it to the widow.

"Oh—" Edna's character lines promptly warmed to a smile. "Thank you."

Ezra settled in the chair around the corner.

"Well, okay," Edna sighed. "I could sure use the rent. I'm down to one paying customer." She affected a light-hearted chuckle, trying to put on a cheerful face for her polite guest. "But it's only fair to tell you that the reason the place is vacant is because the previous tenant couldn't take all the noise from my downstairs tenant, Mr. Miller." She tried to conceal her bitterness, nodding toward the jagged noise. "I've had some problems with him and his friends. Young people these days, you know. They make an ungodly racket at all hours of the day and night. I think they've been breaking things, too. I've heard horrendous banging and crashing. He's very violent. The whole neighborhood's afraid of him. My neighbor's home was shot into after they called the authorities about him." She lowered her voice, leaning forward. "He was in jail, you know. I should have known better than to rent to someone who's been locked up. He—" the widow began to stammer with rising emotion. "He hasn't even paid any rent since he moved in. And he— he's chasing away my good tenants."

Ezra listened in silence. His eyes followed her face as she spoke. The woman paused awkwardly, fighting a gathering flood of emotion. Patiently, he waited as she attempted to regain her composure. She had only just met Ezra, but she felt as though she sensed something unusual about him. There was more to him than the rare politeness, she thought. Something...dauntless.

Lonely and withdrawn all these months, for some reason, the widow took the occasion of Ezra's presence to feel eased, perhaps a little safe, even. Scarcely before she realized what was happening, a deep well of anguish gushed up from a heavy heart. Embarrassed though she was, Edna Peterson cried. Just sat there looking across the table with pained eyes and cried. Ezra watched. He listened. He was quiet.

"I'm so sorry," she finally sobbed. "I don't know what's the matter with me. I guess I'm afraid the Slaters will go, too, and I'll have nothing left. Who could blame them? He doesn't care about anyone," she pointed a trembling finger at the noise. "Doesn't have any idea about what people spent their whole lives building. He's just an animal. No good in him at all."

For a good, long time the two sat without speaking while the old woman's sobbing gradually subsided. Finally, Ezra placed a large, reassuring hand atop the woman's. "God is good," he said simply. "He will take care of you."

The words seemed naive to Edna, yet he spoke them with such

surety. And she noted that the hand covering hers was, most certainly, not the hand of a sheltered man. It was callused and rock hard. The tops of the fingers and enlarged bony knuckles were wickedly scarred.

"What do you charge for rent?" he asked.

She retrieved her hand and wiped her eyes. "Four hundred per month."

Ezra reached down to the coat folded over his duffel. "May I give you three months?"

"Oh, certainly." The widow's watery eyes brightened. Ezra straightened with a wrinkled bank envelope in hand and retrieved twelve one hundred dollar bills, placing them on the table.

"Thank you so much," she sniffed and smiled, a measure of relief apparent on her face.

"I saw a shed in the back." Ezra returned the envelope and straightened again. "You use it?"

"Well, no, not really," she answered. "It has a lot of my Ben's old tools and such. He passed away last Christmas. My grandson Michael likes to play out there sometimes. I think he misses his grandfather."

Ezra's eyes appraised the woman as he seemed to calculate. "If I take care of this place for you, could I use the shed to do some woodworking?"

"Oh— well, my goodness yes!" Edna's enthusiasm was hushed. That sounds like just what I could use. This place is a mess. More than I can handle. Ben was a good handyman— until he got sick. But I'm just lost." She paused in consideration. "I should reduce your rent."

"No." Ezra rose from his chair and collected his things. "The use of the shed is enough." On his way to the door he stopped and tipped his head toward the noise. "How much does he owe you?"

"Oh, I— I don't want any trouble." A sudden twinge of apprehension took hold of the landlady.

"Me either." Ezra's smiling eyes evinced reassurance. "All the same, if you don't mind, I'd be curious to know."

"Well, June, July, and August," she answered. Quickly she turned for the kitchen. "I'll get your key. We can get your phone turned on tomorrow."

She returned with his key. "The kitchen is furnished, but there's not much other furniture to speak of," she explained.

"It'll be fine," Ezra smiled. "Beats my last place."

Edna's curiosity was piqued. "Where did you live last?"

"Back east," he answered in a kind enough tone, though with a certain terseness that suggested his history would not be the topic of further discussion.

"I see," she said, studying him closely. "Now you said your name was E.J.?"

He nodded.

"Is that short for something?"

"Yes, it is," Ezra nodded politely and pulled the door shut behind him.

CHAPTER 4

The early autumn sun was mostly set. A weary Alan Hunt slipped on his suit jacket and placed papers in his briefcase, preparing to flee his office. The deputy warden of Kalbourne Prison had sent his frayed secretary home hours ago, remaining behind in the now empty administrative offices to field a continuing stream of phone calls from the media, from concerned and frightened citizens, and, as a matter of course, from an unyielding line of perpetually campaigning politicians, all noted experts on the criminal justice system. Now the phone had finally ceased its complaining ring and Hunt was more than ready to get home and salvage what remained of this Friday evening with his family.

But as he turned off the office lights, the phone sprang to life again. Weary, he stood in the darkened doorway, listening to the ringing. A dull, throbbing headache pounded at his skull. He told himself to let it ring and leave. He was under no obligation to stay and answer the phone after hours. Letting go a sigh, he flipped the lights back on and picked up the phone. "Kalbourne State Prison," he greeted.

"Warden?" a man on the other end eagerly asked.

"No, Deputy Warden Hunt speaking."

"Ah, good. I'm a deputy too. Glad I caught you. Name's Dan Guiness. I'm a deputy sheriff up here with the Wovoka County Department and I've been assigned to determine the current location of Ezra Jacob Watt." Guiness had adopted a friendly, engaging tone.

"I don't mean to be flip, Deputy, but your guess is as good as mine." Hunt's voice bore cracks of fatigue. "Do you suspect him of committing a crime today?"

"No," Guiness' voice tensed a little, "but he did do his previous crimes here and a lot of people are concerned that he might try to come back. If we just knew where he was, I could— I mean, we could make sure that... I mean, we could just give everyone some peace of mind and ease their fears if they knew he was a long way from here. I'm sure you understand."

"I do understand the concerns, Deputy," Hunt agreed. "I've

been flooded with calls all day from a lot of very worried people. Many have given me a lot of helpful suggestions on how to better run our prison. But as I've been telling them, we don't make the policies down here. We just carry them out. And one of those policies is that when a man has served out his sentence we let him go and he doesn't have to tell us where he's going. Inmate Watt did not see fit to tell us where he was going, if he even knew himself. I wish to assure you, however, that had we ever become aware of any evidence that Watt intended further harm to your community, we would have passed that along to your department or whoever needed to know. We never found any indication of this. In any event, his sentence was completed today and we were required to discharge him. We successfully contained him within our walls for absolutely as long as the law permitted us to do so. Something we rarely do these days, I might add."

"Well as far as future crimes go, you don't expect he'd just tell you what he was planning!" Guiness waxed incredulous.

"Not directly, Deputy. But it has been our experience, in long years at this job, that it's very difficult for an inmate to spend a substantial portion of his life with us and not have his true motivations show through, sooner or later. In truth, Deputy, most of the prisoners who spend a lot of time with us tend to grow pretty tired. Tired of the violence. Tired of the chaos. It's generally a young man's game, you know. Not the ones you hear about in the media, but they are the vast majority. There are the notable exceptions that end up coloring the world's view of all the rest, but the fact is, if the older ones make it back out of here alive, they're not likely to cause anyone serious trouble."

"Not always though," Guiness pressed. "Like you said, there are exceptions."

"There are," Hunt affirmed. "But in this case, Deputy, Watt's record reflects an increasingly subdued inmate beginning eight or nine years ago, even though there was little incentive for him to behave. You understand, he knew that he wasn't getting out early regardless of how he behaved, that he was going to do all the time allotted by the system."

"Okay, all right," Guiness persisted, trying another avenue. "If you don't have a location on him, could I at least get a copy of those prison records you're referring to? You know, just to review."

"Deputy Guiness," Hunt's voice grew weary. "As I intimated earlier, unless you're conducting a current criminal investigation, we're not able to give you Watt's records without his permission. I gather from the day's events that someone down here has already leaked information, but you'll not be getting anything under the table from me, Mr. Guiness."

Dan Guiness came close to pleading. "Look, Mr. Hunt, I'm not sure you realize just what kind of animal we're talking about here. He acted normal back then too. That's what he did to you people. He fooled you. He's not like your other inmates. He isn't going to change. He's a monster! If I— I mean, if we could just find out something— any known relatives, friends, associates... anything!"

"Deputy, I'm sorry," Hunt grew terse and a little suspicious. "Perhaps you should transfer me to your sheriff and I can explain things to him for you."

"The sheriff isn't in the office right now," Guiness said, the easygoing facade he had started with now completely abandoned.

"Well, you can have him call me Monday, okay?"

Guiness' voice turned cold. "Yeah, I'll sure do that."

"Goodbye Deputy Guiness," Hunt said with finality. Waiting for a response, he received none and so, hung up, finally and quickly making his escape from Kalbourne.

* * *

Dan Guiness sat still at his kitchen table for several minutes, listening to the dial tone at his ear and staring blankly at the wall. In the next room, his wife Susan, six months pregnant with their third child, sat reading to their first two— Jeremy, six, and Amanda, four.

Susan and the children all flinched in sudden, stark fright as the telephone crashed into the kitchen wall. The children fixed wide, fear-filled eyes on their mother's face as their father growled eerily and shouted obscenities amid more thunderous crashing and cracking.

"Jeremy— Mandy, go to your rooms right now," Susan ordered in an urgent, hushed voice, her protective hands gently compelling the children toward the far hallway of their Jasper Mills home. Unnerved by what she saw upon returning to the kitchen, she began to cry. "Dan, what have you done? What's happening to you?"

Menacingly, Dan stood over the splintered remains of their antique kitchen table— the one Susan's parents had given them for their wedding. The shattered telephone lay on the floor in a small pile of rubble beneath an ugly, gaping hole in the wall. "That sanctimonious piece of crap wouldn't give me anything! Not one damn thing! He acts like that monster is just magically okay now! What a stupid! blind! jerk!"

"Dan, please. Just please, please calm down. Please." Susan's voice wavered with fear. "You're scaring the kids. You're scaring me."

"I told you, Sue! Didn't I! I told you when we met in San Diego! You remember? You're the one who wanted to get married! You're the one that wanted to come back here with me after the Corps! You wanted to have kids and act like everything was normal! I told you I had business with this animal! I told you!" With his whole hand, Dan wiped away the spittle from the corner of his mouth and the tears from his eyes.

"I know you did, Dan." Tears streamed down Susan's paled face. "I thought it'd be a long, long time. I thought you'd forget— that you'd let it go."

"I'll never forget!" he hissed. "I'll never let it go."

"What if you get hurt?" She wiped tears from her face with a trembling hand. "What if you get in trouble? How am I supposed to take care of Mandy and Jeremy and have another baby by myself?"

"I told you, Sue. You're the one that wanted all this." His hand made a wide sweep indicating their entire life. "Anyway, there's no way that punk is going to hurt me. I'm ready. And I won't get in trouble. No one will even know who did what, unless..." His eyes grew frigid looking down into his wife's face, "Someone tells them otherwise."

34

"I won't." She verged on tears again.

Dan retrieved his automatic pistol from the kitchen counter. "You got your gun with you?"

"No," Susan answered. "You know I don't like it, Dan."

"Where is it?" he demanded.

"I locked it in the desk." She began to sniffle back fresh tears. "Away from the kids."

"Oh, it's going to do you a lot of good there, Sue," his voice filled with disdain. "Keep it with you like I taught you. He could be anywhere."

Retrieving his shotgun from the entry closet, Dan headed out the back door.

"Dan, where are you going? Your shift is over." Susan pleaded weakly. "Please don't go back out."

"I have to patrol," he shouted from the drive. "He could be here already. There's been enough time. Don't worry," he assured. "It's under control."

Dan drove away into the night and Susan stood gazing at her trashed kitchen, wiping her face with the back of her wrist, and wondering just what it was that her husband had "under control."

* * *

Some folks eat their meals a little slower, some a little faster. Then there was this E.J. fellow. One moment his head had been lowered in some manner of private prayer. Janet and Kendra had scarcely looked down at their own plates, taking a measured bite or two of their Salisbury steak and potatoes, exchanging a few pleasant words. When they looked up again, he was wiping his plate clean with the last of his bread. It wasn't that he was ill-mannered. They hadn't even heard him eating. He simply seemed accustomed to eating very quickly and with a single-mindedness that evidently excluded superfluous pauses or conversation.

"Would you like some more?" Janet reached for the bowl of potatoes.

"No." Ezra put up a hand, then hastened to add, "It was very good. But if I eat too much I'll ruin my girlish figure."

35

Janet chuckled and Kendra supported her forehead with the heel of her little hand, giggling at the unexpected silliness delivered with such a straight face by the stranger.

Ezra regarded the giggling child and then dryly accused, "You don't think I'm pretty, do you?"

"Noooo eehee hee," she laughed even harder.

"Come on, Kendy. Eat your supper," Janet finally prodded after a time and the girl resumed her meal, though still breaking a periodic smile and an audible "hmmm" as she ate.

"Will you look for work in Haverston?" Janet asked.

"I told Mrs. Peterson I'd look after this place and she's going to let me work some wood in her shed out back."

"Oh, that will be good for Mrs. Peterson," Janet exclaimed. "Sounds like just what she needs. That's really nice. You know how to do woodworking, huh?"

"A little." He sat quiet for a time, looking about the kitchen, studying its details. "If I need more, I'll find something else. Don't guess it takes a lot for an old single guy to live on, though."

"I suppose not," Janet smiled. Turning serious, though, she complained, "There aren't many good jobs around here."

Ezra feigned concern. "Only bad ones?"

"No, you know what I mean," she smiled and tried to clarify. "Good careers with job security, you know?"

"Job security?" He pondered the words. "No, I don't expect someone to guarantee me a job. They can't know the future any more than I can. How can they protect me from it?" He pondered a moment. "I figure most anywhere you go there are people that need stuff done and are willing to pay for it. Guess the only thing I'd be looking for is honest money for honest work...when I've finished the work. Not looking for more."

"Maybe," Janet said. "As long as it's dignified work, though."

Ezra's face filled with humor. "Only undignified working people I've ever seen were the ones turning up their noses and bellyaching."

"You got a point," Janet agreed.

When Kendra had finished eating, Ezra rose and began taking dishes to the sink. Janet scrambled to her feet, collecting her plate and silverware. "That's okay. I'll do that, E.J."

"I don't mind," Ezra assured, picking up the potato bowl from the table.

"Well, I do." Janet moved close to him, taking the bowl from his hand with gentle firmness as she looked into his face. "Really, E.J. Please let me do it. You're a guest. Why don't you go into the living room. I think Kendy has some pictures to show you."

"Yeah!" The child's eyes grew bright. "Come on, E.J., I'll show you!" The girl tugged at a pair of his fingers, leading him from the kitchen and into a brightly colored living room. She pointed to the far end of a faded yellow couch. "You sit here. I'll get my pictures." Inhaling with anticipation, she bounded from the room.

Ezra sat quietly in his assigned seat. In a short time, Kendra returned with a carefully ordered stack of crayon drawings on thick, cream-colored paper. She stood in front of him as if to audition for a part, clutching her drawings close, so not to reveal them out of turn. She withdrew the first drawing and presented it. "Okay, look at this one first." With much anxiousness, the girl watched Ezra's face as he took the paper in hand and examined her work.

What he saw was a work he reckoned quite good for a child of six. Much time and effort had plainly been expended to depict trees, grass, and animals of recognizable form and color. And dominating the center of the page were three people. Though a little stickish and not entirely proportionate, they were clearly a man, a woman, and a girl.

Ezra's face warmed with recognition. "A family."

"Yeah," Kendra exhaled through a relieved smile. "They're at the park."

"Very good," he praised. "You like the park, yes?"

"Yeah. My dad— my dad used to take us to the park in his hot rod! But..."her enthusiasm faded, "That was when I was five."

"I see." Ezra stared intently into her face.

"Yeah." She came closer and pointed a finger at the man in her picture depicted with yellow hair and two blue dots for eyes. "But somebody else could be the dad."

Ezra's eyes lost some of their happy glimmer. He beheld the

anxious face and absorbed her words. Finally, he pointed a rugged finger to the same figure. "This isn't somebody else. This is your father, yes?"

The girl's eyes dropped and she nodded quietly.

The man's eyes fell as well, yielding to a surge of heaviness. He drew a long breath and eased it out again, returning his eyes to the endearing blue-eyed, freckled face with the gently rounded nose. "Come on, kid. Show me another picture."

When Janet had finished the dishes, she stood in the archway, drying her hands on an embroidered dish towel and watching the interaction between her daughter and their new acquaintance. He seemed, to Janet, unduly cautious with Kendra. Not unkindness or dislike. But, as on the bus earlier in the day, he seemed to harbor a certain strangeness, an unfamiliarity, to the setting. Kendra kept edging closer as she showed him her pictures. Soon, she had turned about and was standing right next to him in a manner that her mother recognized as the girl's unspoken way of asking to be picked up and held. But E.J. did not oblige. More than once, Janet saw him lift a hand as if he would wrap it reassuringly around Kendra. But each time, he would hesitate and stop short, then return the hand to his side.

The dish towel still in her hand, Janet watched from the archway with interest for a long time. Eventually, she began to see the telltale signs of sleepiness descending on Kendra and she spoke up. "It's about time for your bed young lady. You've been up since early this morning and it was a long bus ride."

Kendra protested. "I can stay up a little longer, Mom."

"No, you can't," she answered firmly. Tossing the towel back inside the kitchen, she came across the living room. "Come on. Pick up your pictures." While the girl complied, restacking her work, Janet studied Ezra. Then, flashing inviting eyes at him, she added, "Maybe E.J. would like to help tuck you in."

Ezra passed his eyes from the expectant young face to her sweetly smiling mother and swallowed uncomfortably. "No," he answered simply.

"Really, it's okay," Janet tried to reassure. "Kendy would like it if you did."

"No."

Surprised and a little embarrassed by his rejection, Janet's sweet smile faltered. "Okay. Well, I'll just be a few minutes putting her to bed."

Clutching her drawings close, Kendra turned away with a certain sleepy somberness. Before the child was gone from the room, Ezra called after her, "Hey, blue eyes."

"Yeah?" She turned back.

"Thanks for showing me your work. You're a good artist."

The child brightened and Ezra bid her a "good night."

Janet followed Kendra from the living room and Ezra got up from the couch. The woman turned back, speaking in a hushed voice. "Don't go yet, okay? I'll just be a few minutes. Okay?"

He turned a blank expression toward her. She didn't know how to read him. She liked him, the quiet sturdiness, the cautious, gentle manner, but she had the feeling there was something more she wasn't seeing.

After a moment, he gave a simple nod and retook his seat. Janet disappeared down the hallway. Ezra smiled to himself, hearing the girl whisper to her mother, "Mom, what's an art—artist?" In a few minutes, he heard mother leading daughter in bedtime prayer. But Janet's voice seemed calculated to project from the back room and Kendra stumbled and stammered with the words, waiting for, and then mimicking her mother's lead. It didn't strike Ezra as a normally practiced routine, so much as a scene orchestrated by the mother to endear them to a man they had observed praying over his supper.

Indeed, in the child's room, Kendra looked up from her pillow with a measure of confusion as they finished. Janet gazed back at her daughter, then smiled sweetly and gently touched the girl's nose with her finger. "Sleep tight, bunny."

From the living room, Ezra could heard the girl's bedroom door pull shut. There was some gentle clinking and rummaging in another of the back rooms, then softly approaching footsteps. The barefoot woman returned to the living room, still dressed in her fashionable denim, but sporting an old, comfortable looking, turquoise jersey in place of the white sweater. And when she passed near, a subtle, arousing scent that Ezra had not noticed before wafted over his face.

"Would you like something to drink?" she asked.

"No."

"You sure?" she pressed. "I have some wine or a cold beer."

"I'm sure."

"Okay," she relented, coming back to the couch. She sat down near Ezra. Much nearer than he would have anticipated, her knee coming to rest on the edge of his hip, her supple foot curling beneath her other leg as she turned herself toward him. "Can I ask you a question?"

The warmth of her soft breath touched the side of Ezra's face. His pulse quickened. He nodded, staring across the living room, not daring to turn his face toward hers.

"You said you're single, right?"

"Yes."

"You seem like a real nice guy. Kind and quiet. But you seem— I don't know— sort of sad or something. Did somebody hurt you? You know, break your heart or something?"

Considering her question, Ezra turned himself somewhat toward Janet, though still not venturing a look into her face. He gazed blankly at the turquoise jersey draped loosely from the softly rounded apex of her breast. "No," he finally answered. "In fact, my whole life, people have always been very good to me. Better than I've had coming."

"You shouldn't be so hard on yourself." She leaned in still closer, her warm, minted breath mingling with the perfume and filling Ezra's head. "I think you deserve to be treated very good," she said very softly.

When, finally, he raised his face to hers, she fastened deep, liquid brown eyes onto him with unnerving intensity. Ezra was suddenly warm. Close up, her complexion was smooth as silk, her lips, delicate and... he was very warm. His breath came shallow. Her eyes held him immobile. He was uncomfortably warm. At last, Ezra drew in a long breath through widened nostrils and, letting the air fall away, pulled free of her magnetic stare. "You can't know what I deserve," he said, turning back toward the living room.

Without looking at her, he redirected the conversation. "Where's your husband?"

"What do you mean? I told you, I'm divorced."

"The little one's father, I mean. Is he still around?"

She leaned back on the couch and sighed. "He lives here in Haverston. Has the same job at the utility company that brought us out here to begin with. But what's that got to do with anything?"

Ezra drew his shoulders up in a slow shrug. "The girl seems to see something between you guys that gives her reason to hope."

"E.J., she's just a kid. She doesn't know what's going on."

"I don't know," Ezra said. "Youngsters see more than you think. Is she wrong to hold on to hope for her family?"

"No,"Janet conceded. "I mean, yes," she changed her mind. "No— I don't know," she resigned. "But she hasn't even seen Robert, her father, more than a couple of times since we split. And then it was only because he came over here trying to give me money when he knows he's supposed to send it through the agency."

"Maybe he wanted you to know he was trying to give something of himself for a change," Ezra suggested.

"What do you mean?" she frowned.

"Well, I don't know," Ezra tried to explain. "It just seems like when a person does work, they're laying down a piece of their life. So whatever money they have to show for it is like little pieces of their life. And whatever a person spends his money on, is what he's given his life for." Ezra considered his words. "Unless it's inherited or stolen. Guess that would be spending someone else's life. Anyway, maybe he's trying to give you guys something of himself for a change. Maybe he's sorry."

"Not likely," Janet contended. "You don't know him like I do."

Ezra turned his face toward her again, considering her for a long moment. "Where I came from there were many men who would treat their wives or girlfriends very badly. Put them through hell. And when the women would finally leave, I guess some of them didn't really care and some were angry or hurt, but they weren't really going to change the way they were."

41

Janet nodded agreement.

"But some of them," Ezra continued, "Some of them were sorry. Affected by the loss in ways that the people who knew them would never have expected. You might say changed, even. I remember one fellow, probably about the worst of them all. He used to treat his wife like a slave. He tried to control her to the point of absurdity. But when she left, he was broken. Never the same again. His whole personality and everything about him changed. I think he was sorry. I don't guess he wanted much more, in the end, than for her to know that."

"Did she take him back?" Janet asked.

Ezra studied her hopeful face for a moment. "No, she didn't. Did you want her to?"

"I don't know. If he was really changed... I don't know."

Ezra smiled faintly. "Doesn't it seem as though we have hope in us to see other people forgive and be reconciled, to have a happy ending, but forget to hope the same for ourselves, sometimes."

"I know what you're saying," Janet agreed. "But it just doesn't always work out, you know? Sometimes people fall out of love. They have to do what they have to do to take care of themselves."

"Is love so fleeting?" Ezra questioned. "Is it something we just fall into and out of like an accident we can't control? Because I'd like to think it's more than that. Something we have in us to give or not. How else can we promise it for a lifetime regardless of how we will feel at any point along the way? We've got to have faith that if we keep giving the love and devotion that we've promised, the good feelings we long for like happiness and contentment in doing the right thing will grow out of it." Ezra peered hard into Janet's face. "Either we control our feelings and they serve us, or our feelings control us and we are slaves, yanked about by erratic masters. We do one or the other. We can't do both."

There was an awkward pause and then Ezra's eyes began to smile again. "Think it's about my bedtime, too," he said, getting up from the couch.

Janet followed him to the door. "I know what you're saying, E.J. I just think it takes both people, you know?"

"I reckon you're right about that," he concurred. "I have this

42

notion in my head," he said, opening the door. "Families, marriages and such are like living beings with a heart of their own. Each one greater than the sum of its parts. It's a hell of a thing to see one die. Hell of a thing. And you know what they like to call folks who cause death..."

Ezra shrugged and smiled, leaving Janet alone in her entry, uncertain of him— and most everything else.

* * *

In the darkened living room of his new apartment, Ezra lay on the carpeted floor in a pair of worn sweat pants. His rolled up coat resting under his head, he stared up at the ceiling. Owing more to a general, day-end release of tension than any specific emotion, tears slid from the corners of his eyes.

What a day it had been, beginning with his eviction from home. And Kalbourne really was home to him. Comfort had long ago replaced the claustrophobia. His cell had felt familiar... good. When they locked it each evening he would relax. The same mass of concrete and steel that had protected the outside world from him, had also insulated him, snug and safe, from the often incomprehensible outside world. But this morning had found him uprooted from the security of his home, the long-ingrained routines, the surety of his woodshop job and the status accrued in the course of living twenty years within those foreboding walls. This morning he had stood anonymous at the Orde City depot, and dread had begun to creep in on the realization that nothing was any longer familiar. No routine. No job. No status.

Only in the last few years, since Holbert's death and his time of reckoning, had he harbored anything like genuine faith. Faith that was supposed to calmly accept everything, pleasant and painful, as Divine dispensation meant for his good. But perhaps it had been easy to trust in Providence from a rent free cell with three meals a day whether he worked or not. He knew he wasn't supposed to, but he had found himself fretting as he boarded the bus this morning. As the bus had begun to move down the highway at speeds most unsettling to a man so long confined to his feet, the pointlessness of anxiety had informed his thought and he withdrew to the cool, comforting cocoon of quiet prayer. Not so much for food or shelter did he petition, as a direction to go and a purpose to serve. It was from this cool place that he had been drawn to see the little blue-eyed face looking up at him. Such a sight was never seen in Kalbourne. Alien. But, hearing the mother speak of their troubles and seeing the heaviness that rode the little one's heart, he had quietly wondered did Providence thus answer his request of purpose so immediately? He did not know, certainly, but he had decided to follow them and see where it might lead. It seemed as good a direction as another.

It had become routine to review the day in this manner, to carry on a mental dialogue, prayer, if you will, before sleep. And, with his other routines gone, it became even more important to him now. In youth he had fantasized wildly and plotted darkly before drifting into fitful bouts of guilt-ridden sleep. The first decade of Kalbourne had seen this raw prurience supplanted by eastern ideas of oblivion, examining every recess of his mind and zealously chasing after the shadowy promises of self-developed knowledge and power. But, aside from summoning destructive bursts of adrenaline and numbing the conscience to the aftermath, these had provided no abiding peace. Satisfying sleep continued to elude. When it seemed everything under the sun had been explored, he had found himself forced to acknowledge, if only to himself, that the long search within had discovered nothing but hopeless corruption, weakness, and darkly shaded ignorance. Left to itself, his foundering mind had always tended toward labyrinthine, self-serving delusions of hypnotic complexity, while consistently and obstinately rejecting the plain, child-like, ego-canceling Truth. Words from his upbringing kept pushing their way to the surface of his awareness, insisting that he finally reject his own and look without. "Be still and know that I am God," the Psalm said. In the very heart of the conscience, beyond all the pretense, hadn't he always known that the One responsible for reality was the only One who could ever reveal it? Was not the One who conceived life, Himself alive, first and foremost— sustaining, continuing, and watching? If a person could be liberated from designs on the future

44

and somehow relieved of what had gone before, if he were truly content with whatever came, entrusting all to the One who made it and continues it, would that person not be rewarded with the sleep of an unlabored conscience, deep and satisfying? Surely, an hour's worth would be sweeter than a lifetime of the schemer's fits and the pretender's dance.

At the moment, there were a few muffled sounds from the surrounding Haverston nighttime. Some nearer, some far. But, compared to his previous environs, it was incredibly quiet. Not since his youth in the nocturnal Wovoka countryside had Ezra experienced anything like real quiet. Kalbourne was filled with noise that never slept. The clanking of steel and whirring of exhaust fans. The heavy footfalls of ever-patrolling boots, jingling keys, and blaring walkie-talkies. A ceaseless din of talking, hollering, laughing, crying, coughing, snoring, excreting, flushing... Hundreds of open-ended, five by nine cells stacked into a huge block, all spilling noise out onto the ranges, reverberating off the massive cellhouse walls and blending into one homogenous, progressively sublimated drone. With the sounder sleep of recent years, he'd grown fond of waking up in the very early morning and using the comparative quiet to read or to think until they opened the doors at six and it was time to work. Only now was he becoming aware of just how much noise there had been, even in an early morning Kalbourne, as its sudden absence left his ears literally ringing. Ezra breathed deep and rode the glorious ringing off to sleep.

It must have been sometime after one in the morning when Ezra was lifted out of his sleep by noise from below. Banging doors, yelling, unnaturally raucous laughter, and that abrupt, brittle wash of metallic monotone. Gathering his bearings, he stared at the darkened ceiling and listened for a time. He must've slept about four hours, he figured. It was enough. He felt good. But there would be no placid reflective time amid such racket. He rose and dressed. He washed his face and readied for the day.

45

Leaving his apartment, Ezra quietly descended the stairs. He walked partway down the lower hall and stopped before the Miller apartment door, listening to the strident, grating mindlessness on the other side. For all its noise, Kalbourne had its way— often brutal— of dealing with those who exceeded the accepted norm. For years, Ezra had himself maintained a kind of noise curfew from evening until morning over "his" corner of the cellblock. Some of the older inmates had even flocked to cells at this corner of the block, affording him a certain, largely unspoken, respect and consideration all around the institution in gratitude for this zone of relative peace. His head bowed, Ezra now listened to the banality on the other side of the door a little longer. Between the jerky breaks in the music, he could even hear voices vulgarly boast of waking all the "so-and-so" neighbors. He looked at the oak door, solid and sturdy. It may as well have been paper to a man so long accustomed to massive steel barriers. His acute eyes piercing the dark, Ezra turned from the door and walked the remainder of the hallway. Slipping out the back door, he descended the steps of a small concrete porch and stood in the grass of the rear yard.

All the activities of Kalbourne were conducted in daylight. Inmates were always locked within the cellhouses before dark for security's sake. Ezra had not been outside in the dark for more than twenty years. It did not take long for him to realize, whatever else of him might have changed, the boyhood exhilaration of being alone in the dark had not left him. He breathed in the crisp September night air while the pupils of his eyes slowly remembered how to stretch wide and allow in the nocturnal landscape. He buttoned up the dark denim coat and wandered off into the dark.

CHAPTER 5

The Saturday morning sun shimmered just behind the horizon. Lynn Younger tended to horses on either side of the long, wide aisle of the east barn, faithfully bearing water, hay, and grain, currying coats and easing anxieties as a mother her children. But, since hearing the news of Ezra Watt's release the previous afternoon, she had been unsuccessful in controlling her own anxieties. She tried— desperately, she tried— to own a satisfying breath, but could not. Her heart raced and would not cease its relentless pounding, pounding, nor would the painful knot in her stomach relax its grip for even one blessed moment. Lynn distributed grain and hay with jittering hands. The fresh alfalfa's aroma, to this day, sparked unsettling flashes of the Hoyt's hayfield. On constant verge of tears, she struggled, expending great effort just to maintain a flittering composure. Though they tried to feign calmness in her presence, her parents were faring little better. She'd been unable to accomplish more than a few tense moments of semi-sleep. So she'd opted to come out to her work at Grey's Stables even earlier than was her custom. Grey's had long been her refuge.

A few miles north of Jasper mills on old Route Forty-three, Grey's Stables was a popular horse boarding and riding establishment, catering to equine owners and recreational riders from Wovoka County and surrounding parts. Desperate to comfort their ailing daughter, Dale and Alice Younger had brought Lynn out here one Sunday afternoon more than eighteen years ago. She had remained in a severe, intractable depression long after the corporeal wounds of her attack had healed. Remembering how she had loved the horses and ponies at the county fair as a girl, her parents had earnestly hoped, even prayed, that being around the animals might kindle memories of happier times. Lynn had been unwilling to go riding that first Sunday, but as she petted and nuzzled the gentle creatures, her parents had believed they saw the first signs since the attack of something other than abject misery in their daughter.

The owner Bill Grey had soon noticed the drawn-looking couple bringing their grown, uncommunicative daughter to his stables several times a week. When he had learned that this was none other than the Younger family, and recalled the horrendous events that had befallen them a couple of years previous, he made a decision to offer Lynn a job helping to care for the horses in his stables, an act that had been met with tearful gratitude from her parents and silent acceptance from Lynn.

It was an act that Grey had never regretted. "Best horse person and best employee I'll ever have," he would often tell people in private. Ever since the first day Lynn had been unshakably devoted. She showed up early, left late, accepted her paychecks only as an afterthought, and regarded even the suggestion of a day off as an insult. As long as she was left to herself with the horses in the east barn, as long as no one tried to engage her in conversation or get too close, she seemed generally content. Whenever the stables would acquire a new horse that was particularly frightened or skittish, oft times due to the abuses of a previous owner, the animal would be sent to the east barn and placed in Lynn's care. She seemed to have a special affinity for such creatures and invariably they would sense the trustworthy nature of their new caretaker. Soon, they would calm and all but melt into her tender, wordless attention.

Lynn was, at once, embittered by the injustice of Ezra's release and terrified to the brink of paralysis. But she was determined not to abandon her charges to another's care. For so long, fear had permeated every aspect of her life, holding her captive as much as Ezra had. It sprang from somewhere deep and indefinable, causing both heart and mind to race away uncontrollably. It made her sick, this fear. It was a beast with a mind of its own, unwilling to heed her conscious yearning to calm down and let it go. Grey's had long been her one great refuge. Over the years, the fear had, by gradual degrees, relaxed its grip. Perhaps even lulling her into believing it had gone. But now— now it was back with a vengeance, seizing hold of her as tight as ever it had and Grey's tranquil barns and pastures weren't keeping it at bay.

Though she very much wanted to, Lynn would never forget the strangely detached Ezra Watt that had savaged her in 1978. Like some kind of machine that didn't even hear her, he had posed, abused, and tortured her in precisely ordered procession as if following some malignant, well-rehearsed itinerary— as if she had not even been present, but merely an object in his macabre production with no wishes or existence to even consider. In subsequent years, if she would glimpse footage of snakes or sharks with their disconnected stare, it would fill her with the nearly irrational dread of recognition. Others now tried to reassure her, but others had not seen Ezra completely devoid of his carefully fashioned facade. She had seen him without the mask, the true, unconcealed essence of Ezra Watt. The fact that Ezra knew she was a living witness of his true nature was no small source of terror now. Everyone kept saying he wouldn't come back to Jasper Mills, but they didn't seem especially convincing to her. Some even tried to soothe her by suggesting that he might really have changed in prison. But in the Hoyt's hayfield she had not seen anything alive to change. Nothing but emptiness. Probably, he had simply fashioned a more sophisticated veil with which to shroud his evil heart.

Lynn had cared for old Bender since he was brought here as a neglected, frightened colt more than fifteen years ago. In time, he had grown into a huge bay quarter horse gelding more than sixteen hands tall and he and his quiet keeper had grown into a most trusted friendship. When she neared his stall, bearing the grain bucket, Bender plainly sensed the distress in his friend. All but ignoring his morning rations, he reached his great, brown-black head over the stall gate, gently nuzzling flaring nostrils to the side of Lynn's face, earnestly searching the nature of her pain. The feed pail slid down the side of Lynn's leg to the concrete aisle. She grasped hold of the animal's massive, docile head with wilting arms. Bender stood uncomplainingly still while his keeper clutched his head and wept aloud.

* * *

On the curb of Seventh Avenue, just off the southwest corner of the apartment house, next to the tenants' parking area, Ezra set yet another plastic bag full of refuse. He'd noted several dented

49

metal trash cans there, all but one missing their lids, and decided this must be the trash pickup spot. He remembered reading about how people separated different kinds of garbage now in order to recycle it. So as he cleaned up the yard and shed in the hours before dawn, he'd been careful to separate the refuse into categories of plastic, glass, metal, paper, and one final pile best depicted as miscellaneous, partially rotted branches, boards and stuff.

With the growing light of dawn, he was able to closely examine the wooden frames of the back door and windows. They needed scraping and repainting, but the wood was sound. Likewise, the heavy lumber picnic table in the grass between the house and the shed needed refurbishing.

Ezra re-entered the shed through a small door on its north side. He had opened up the double doors at the west end and uncovered all the small, four-pane windows, allowing light to stream in from all directions. He could see his cleaning efforts better now than under the three bare light bulbs at night. He'd swept and cleaned the concrete floor. He'd cleaned and organized the workbenches and cabinets. And he'd examined and inventoried all the tools, parts, materials, and miscellaneous items. There was an old, but solid, Rockwell table saw in the center of the floor. A band saw to one side, and a sturdy old drill press on the other. There was a lawn mower and a pair of ladders. There were miscellaneous wrenches, hammers, and other hand tools of the sort. But Ezra also noted the conspicuous absence of several tools, mostly smaller power tools, for which silhouettes were painted on a shadow board above the east workbench. Someone had apparently helped themselves to the widow's property.

Emerging from the opened double doors, he went around to the south side of the shed and began pulling weeds and picking up assorted junk and refuse that had been discarded in this dim, narrow space between the backside of the shed and the neighboring property's wooden privacy fence. Working his way back into the dense undergrowth, Ezra came upon a sight that was at once unexpected and disturbingly familiar to a distant childhood memory. Carefully hidden beneath a pile of debris were the remains of a dead cat. Nearby, within a small plastic bag, were several wadded pieces of tape with the animal's hair still clinging to them, suggesting the means by which it had been restrained and perhaps killed. Kneeling down on the balls of his feet to study the sight, what the new caretaker saw prompted him to lower his head with grimness. Covering the creature from head to tail were severe, small diameter burns seared through both fur and flesh, a most cruel and protracted torture. Upon kneeling for some time in careful thought, Ezra picked up the cat and put it far down in his garbage bag. He covered it with more trash and set the bag on the curb with the others.

* * *

Edna Peterson woke from a dissatisfying sleep about seven-thirty. She was tired and disappointed. Though he had not expressly promised, she had gathered the implication from her new caretaker E.J. that he might, somehow or another, manage to quell some of the noise from the Miller apartment. But, like so many nights these past months, she'd been startled awake after midnight by the inane bedlam and unable to find sleep again until it subsided sometime after four. She tried to shake her disappointment. After all, what was it she expected this new man to do that no one else was willing or able to do? Given their past dealings with Calvin, Edna wondered if even the Haverston police were reluctant to confront him, perhaps hoping he might just eventually move on and become someone else's problem.

Rummaging about her bedroom at the back of the house, Edna glanced out her window and then stopped to look more carefully. She walked over to the window in disbelief and gazed out. As if by magic, her yard had changed appearance overnight. The litter was gone. The tangled weeds, the growth around her shed and at the borders of the yard, all gone. While she stared, disbelieving, her eye caught movement within the shed. Soon her new caretaker emerged, a scraper and sandpaper in his hands, and he began to work on her picnic table.

Watching the stranger work, the landlady was intrigued. To have accomplished so much, he must have begun working in the middle of the night. While she lay in a sleepless fume, while the hooligans partied mindlessly, he must have been quietly laboring in the dark. She thought he seemed very conscientious, meticulous even, as he worked on the table. He was not rushed nor apparently concerned about anything around him. He moved about with the relaxed, measured gait of a man who had no other engagements pressing and no intention of ceasing his labor anytime soon.

CHAPTER 6

Midmorning, Saturday, a bright sun streamed into a book-laden study. The receiver of a rotary phone to his ear, Reverend Otto Hartmann sat straightly at his sturdy old desk. "It is good that you did not come back here, Ezra. There is much upset." The wiry little old widower of eighty-seven years spoke in a stern, high-pitched voice that still bore the traces of German accent passed from his immigrant parents. "It is good that you have found a place so soon and proper work to do. Remember, Ezra. Do not forget. You have not merited this liberty nor life itself. But our Father has given you both in abundance and the heart with which to face them. Do not squander what has been given you. Flee temptation at every turn, my son. Do not allow yourself time for sloth. Do not live for your own, Ezra."

The old man listened intently while Ezra responded on the other end. "Good, good," Reverend Hartmann said stoutly. Then Ezra bid him goodbye and he responded in kind. "Ya, very good then, Ezra. Jesus will watch your soul then, yes? Go with God, my son. Go with God."

Replacing the receiver in its cradle on the desk, the austere old preacher waxed deep in thought, surrounded by a lifetime of books that mostly covered the four walls of his parsonage study. He had served several churches around the country before arriving at the small, rural Wovoka Christian Church some thirty years ago. When his Rachel had passed on and been buried here in the cemetery behind the church ten years ago, he'd decided to finish out his service here, as long as the parishoners would have him and until the Lord sent for him and they could lay his bones next to hers. Though approaching ninety, the lean, spry man had never permitted his mind idleness in all those years and was still clear and bright. He attended the needs of his two hundred parishoners, mostly farm families with a few from Jasper Mills. He baptized the newly arrived, educated both young and old, married the passionate, visited the sick and buried the dead. And he still delivered powerful, Bible-anchored sermons every Sunday morning. He taught the Word of God not with words only, but by his own unwavering example of discipline and faithfulness. A faithfulness that would not exclude even Ezra Watt.

Noah and Ida Watt had been devout parishoners of Wovoka Christian, attending every service and Bible study and always bringing their son Ezra. As Ezra grew, Reverend Hartmann had diligently instructed him in the Bible, in catechism, in church history, and in theology. Ezra's had been a religious and moral education rarely seen by children of this day and age. And he'd been a bright student, memorizing and reciting large tracts of Bible and catechism easily and expounding doctrine perceptively.

Nevertheless, with great sorrow, Reverend Hartmann had witnessed Ezra exposed as a perverse criminal— a traitor to his victims, his family, his community, the church before whom he had feigned a right heart, and a traitor to the God in whom he had professed faith. The preacher watched as Ezra's gentle parents suffered overwhelming heartbreak and guilt for their son while Ezra had seemed quite oblivious to anyone's pain, save his own. He had ministered to the elder Watts as they receded into the gentle relief of the grave.

And Reverend Hartmann had done something else for the past twenty years as well. Quietly, faithfully, in his carefully preserved, thirty-year-old Dodge, he had made the long drive south to Kalbourne every three months. He had done what no one else would do, what, in the end, even Noah and Ida were unable to continue. He had visited Ezra.

With vivid clarity, the old preacher could still recall his first trip to Kalbourne and his encounter there with Ezra in the prison's visiting room. "Ezra," the uncompromising cleric had looked squarely into the boy's face. "This Bible tells me that we have all transgressed our Father's good strictures and that we rightly deserve death. And if this is so for even the most diligent, how much the more for you?! Not only in our Maker's pure stare, but even in our own clumsy eyes you merit incomparably worse than you've received. But our God has seen fit to spare you. He has showered you with such mercy that it defies understanding and our notions of justice. I have not come here to show you sympathy, Ezra. I have not come here to say comfortable things to you. I have come to deny you the luxury of drifting further in numbness and fantasy, to take from you the pleasure of your secret schemes, and to deny you self-pity. It is my intention, if God is so willing, to relentlessly irritate your conscience, to place it before you again and again, that you may stumble over it and fall on your arrogant face!"

Ezra had presented himself contritely at that first visit. He had agreed with everything the preacher said and had even admitted his guilt... now that he could not be tried. In fact, Ezra said all the right things just as he always had in Bible and catechism classes. But his eyes would not meet the preacher's and his words were empty. By then, Reverend Hartmann had been wary for Ezra's wiles and had easily discerned the conspicuous mask of falseness. But the preacher had also noted something else that first visit. Despite his feigned happiness to receive the visit, Ezra had been most uncomfortable at the preacher's presence. "Good," the old man had thought. He knew that God would select and regenerate whomever He wished. It was the Lord's business. Regardless of his feelings, the Reverend was to do his duty and, by virtue of his church and his parents, Ezra was plainly his duty. So he would challenge Ezra with the Word and he would pray earnestly for him as many others in the home church would quietly do also. If Ezra continued obstinate and false he would only multiply the destruction that was being withheld from him. The end would be, as always, God's domain alone.

"God gave you great blessings and every advantage from birth, Ezra. You eagerly destroyed it all. You thought you could do better yourself, abandoning the very One who holds your existence. You spit on your Creator and His creatures. And yet, by Grace beyond definition, you continue to sit here with breath in you, with blessing and advantage anew. Someday, it seems He may even permit you to walk out of here. You deserve it not. Will you continue to ignore your Maker and His works? To lie to me and everyone else? Will you continue this futile struggle to serve yourself? Will you spit on all of us some more? What lies at your end, Ezra? What will it be? Our Father alone knows and you would do well to fear Him. He lives beyond the boundaries of time and even now awaits you at your end."

CHAPTER 7

The Haverston noon whistle slowly wound down in the distance. Ezra stood on a stepladder, prepping a window frame on the east side of the apartment house for repainting, scraping away old paint chips and dirt and sanding the wood smooth. Though his phone conversation with Reverend Hartmann was more than an hour old, his mind was still occupied by the preacher. How he had once dreaded that little old man and his visits to Kalbourne!

Growing up in Wovoka Christian Church, he'd privately considered his parents, the church, and Reverend Hartmann ignorant, weak people, their religion illogical and foolish. Was he to believe that of all the religions in the world he just happened to be born into the one true one? After all, they sent him to a public school in Jasper Mills all week long that showed him how the world was in reality driven by unconscious forces, that we were all simply chance biochemical occurrences. There was, then, no more compelling point to life than the instinctive avoidance of pain and the pursuit of whatever desires inhabited one's mind. All else was cumbersome superstition and weakness.

From an early age, Ezra had noted in others an eagerness to ignore their own publicly avowed morality in the pursuit of various urges when they believed no one of consequence was watching. So the idea was to conceal one's more presumptuous and destructive desires behind a montage of artificial words and motives when people were watching. The school, the television, the books— they all tended to agree that people's urges, even the prurient and destructive, were merely the product of genetic fortune or the environment, both beyond one's control, and if he had found within himself certain disturbing urges, already well-developed as he emerged from the murky haze of infancy, it only confirmed what they said. There was no reason to suffuse such things with guilt. He could not help the way he was born. It was beyond his control. Guilt must be the most useless and sinister of human inventions.

The animals all about devoured, copulated, and killed as their natural born cravings dictated and their strength and cunning permitted. They did not apologize. Any fool could see that the people who met with the most success on this planet— the ones who best avoided pointlessly uncomfortable burdens, the ones who secured to themselves the most power and luxury— cast aside all but self-serving concern for others, wove the most ingenious devices to gain their desires, and left behind any pangs of culpability. Who could say that anything had a moral aspect to it anyway? We just were what we were, born of unconscious lineage, so much cosmic, biochemical soup, individualized for an accidental moment.

All the same, to avoid unnecessary hassle in his youth, he had memorized the words, espoused the creeds, and fashioned a highly useful shroud of virtue.

Still, as he had entered Kalbourne those many shadows ago, along with the obligatory fears of prison, there were other things that incessantly nagged at his mind. For instance, he'd been quite certain that he was smarter than the people around him. He was sure of it. Surely this hadn't been a delusion. Yet these ignorant, superstitious people had caught him and were no longer willing to accept his masks of deception. But this collapse of his carefully woven devices, this exposure as a pretender, had only come by the incalculable chance occasion of Lynn Younger's survival. And chance must surely be all that it was. It could not have been anything other...

And there were the unfulfilled promises. From earliest remembered childhood, the unrelenting fantasies had promised untold pleasures, the gratification of the secret urges that spawned them. But when he had finally attempted to transform his dreams into reality, the images were not sensuous as promised, but ugly, the feelings not euphoric, but sickening. The lusts were less satisfied, more consuming, than the start. And those pangs of useless guilt were far more formidable in person than had been imagined from afar. Beneath a well-practiced veneer of calm, his mind raced blindly, his heart pounded and would not be reasoned with. The stomach would not unknot. Yet and still the appetites roiled and the fantasies vowed anew, pleasure most glorious and blissful relief from all guilt and despair lay just beyond the next crest of raging self-indulgence.

The overwhelming power of the prurient and the violent to seize hold of the heart, to prod and to sear— arising from somewhere deep down in that unconscious mire of infancy. He could not attribute it to another. He often did not want to be this way, wanted to be "normal," but, just as often, was enthusiastically beguiled. It would not release him. It simultaneously tortured and entranced, divided the mind against itself and gave it reason for living. He did not want to be this way and at the very same time was unable, indeed unwilling, to turn away.

This guilt, what was its point? Why should it pursue him so into Kalbourne? No one there bothered him about his crimes. They were content to allow him his schemes even as they pursued their own. It must have something to do with that meddling old preacher, he had decided. Every visit rendered his private thoughts jumbled, his heart disquieted, for days, then weeks. Why should that old man's presence disturb him so? What was he trying to accomplish anyway? Didn't the preacher know that he couldn't change even if he wanted to? He had tried as a boy many times. He couldn't. Why didn't the Reverend just forget about him? He wasn't hurting anyone anymore. The guilt, the preacher, everyone— why didn't they all just leave him be in the comfortable, dark caverns of his heart? The mind raced on, unable to settle on anything. The heart would not cease its irrational pounding. That damned seizing in his gut would not let go.

But in time. In time he had learned, degree by degree, to numb the turmoil. In the long search for oblivion he had managed to deaden the roiling, seizing symptoms and even to forget about all the beguiling childhood fantasies, creating the strong delusion of peace in his mind. He had, at one point, put the prurient monster into such a deep sleep that he thought it dead and gone. Old man Holbert had helped teach him these things mostly by example. The eye of the hurricane— it can lull the unaware.

Ezra's mind came back from the past to the window frame in front of him. The German-accented words in his head insisted, "Pay attention, Ezra! Work hard! Do not be slothful!" Repositioning the ladder, he resumed his scraping and sanding on another frame. The window on which he worked was partially open and, through the

58

screen, from within the apartment, a booming, angry voice suddenly yelled out, "You better knock off that damn noise, you son of a—! I'll bust your head! You woke me up, you f— jerk!"

Ezra stopped scraping and set down his tools. Quietly he spoke to the angry voice in the apartment. "I am sorry to bother you. I know the feeling. Only last night people of similar character woke me up, too."He paused with measured thought. "I'll find something else to do."

* * *

"Yeah, whatever," Calvin Miller muttered. "Stupid piece of crap." The dead tired young man rolled over amid the mess of sheets, clothes, and garbage on his bed. Exhausted and ailing from the dull, persistent throbbing in his head, Miller was in no mood to put up with some stupid hick interrupting his sleep and disrespecting his quiet. He wasn't the kind to put up with people's stupidity for long. And he wasn't about to let anyone disrespect him. At six feet two and better than two hundred pounds, leaned and drawn tight by amphetamine, few people tried. Often wired on meth, with long, unruly blond hair and a wild-eyed, volatile demeanor, he was avoided by most everyone except those few who shared crystal with him. Though not yet twenty-one years old, Calvin already had a fearsome reputation in Haverston and the surrounding communities. He'd been in jail more than once, mostly for assaulting people, including the infamous incident with the Haverston cop who'd tried to hassle him for drinking in a parking lot— a feat in which Calvin derived much pride. Perhaps, the boasting and whispered rumors had grown larger than the facts of the incident. Suffice to say, with the aid of a second officer, Calvin had been subdued and no one had required intensive care.

No sooner had he drifted back into a fitful twilight than he was startled back to consciousness by a lawn mower sputtering to life out in the yard. Calvin yelled out unintelligibly, jerking and flailing up out of his bed. He staggered about, struggling to manage his jeans on and muttering a steady stream of expletives. He stormed out of his apartment and down the back hall. Slamming the back door open with great violence, he flew down the porch steps and out into the back yard, proceeding in a great, menacing stride. He rounded the corner of the house and gathered his first glimpse of the man responsible for his torment, maneuvering the small Lawnboy at the edge of the property and more substantial than he had anticipated. The angry young man's threatening gait faltered subtly as he approached.

He screamed over the mower's engine, "What the f— your problem, man!? I told you I'm sleeping! Ain't you got no respect?"

Holding Calvin in his periphery, Ezra stopped and killed the mower. The engine rattled to a stop and he straightened to face the taller young man.

Calvin hissed through gritted teeth, "I ain't going to put up with your disrespect no more, man! That's on my honor, bud! You got that?!" His fists were tightly clenched and his whole body seethed and tensed with adrenaline. He displayed his fiercest mask of bug-eyed savagery, a tactic that invariably produced cowering retreat in people. Yet far from shaken, this man looked directly into his eyes without waver, with what appeared, strangely enough, like a smile.

"You all right, partner?" Ezra asked.

"There ain't nothing wrong with me, bud!" Calvin's eyes flickered and began to dart about. Burgeoning cracks in his mask betrayed glimmers of doubt. "You're the one with the problem!"

"I'm sorry to upset you," Ezra soothed. "But it is customary to do work during the daytime."

Calvin could discover no suggestion of fear in Ezra. Rattled, he shook his head with vigorous obstinance and redoubled his determination to give this interloper a clearer understanding of just who it was he was crossing. "Look, bud, I done too much time in the joint to put up with disrespect from anyone, man. That's on my honor, bud. I've hurt some dudes real bad before, man, including a cop. It don't matter to me, man. I don't give a f— who it is. You got that?"

Ezra was quiet for a time, studying Calvin's face with unnerving ease. "Well," he finally said, "I suppose since you're a paying tenant I could arrange my work to suit you better."

Calvin's tautness relaxed some. The man seemed to be backing down. "Yeah, that's what you better do all right."

"You are a paying tenant?" Ezra emphasized the word "paying" in his question.

Calvin's eyes widened and he tensed anew.

"I only ask," Ezra assured, "because there seems to be some confusion about overdue rent. But, like you just said, you're a man of honor. So I know it's got to be a misunderstanding. A man of honor would never deprive a grieving widow of her living."

Calvin's shame swiftly put on the veil of anger and he menaced from gritted teeth once more. "You better get your nose out of my business. You got it?!" He held his finger up near Ezra's face and glared at him long and threatening, but received no response beyond the smiling dark eyes. He turned to leave.

"There is one other thing," Ezra gently prodded with an air of mirth.

"What!" Calvin yelled, spinning back around.

"Well, there's some talk going around that you and your friends make too much noise and keep your neighbors up at night. Even some slander that you're slinging poison out of Mrs. Peterson's house. Hate to hear that sort of thing being said about a man of honor."

"What, you some kind of cop or something?" Calvin glowered.

"No, just the new caretaker," Ezra shrugged. "Don't want to see your reputation sullied, that's all."

"There ain't nothing going on in my apartment!" Calvin's finger was at Ezra's face again. "Far as you're concerned, there ain't nothing going on. Didn't I just tell you to keep your nose out of my business?! I'm not telling you again! I'm done talking! You got it?"

"Got it," Ezra answered, dipping his head in polite acknowledgment. "Nothing going on. Done talking."

Calvin turned, fists still clenched, and stalked back to the house, telling himself he was satisfied that he'd made his point. But there was something strangely disquieting about the new caretaker.

CHAPTER 8

Edna Peterson's television shrilly bellowed another early evening sitcom. Slumped in her chair, the woman neither laughed at the banter nor reacted to the buffoonery. Through spaces in the artificial laughs, she heard the knocking at her door. Pulling herself up out of her chair, she shuffled to the door and opened it on a pleasant-faced Ezra. He looked freshly scrubbed. His butched hair still glistening, he wore a clean pair of jeans and his seemingly trademark blue pocket tee-shirt, neatly tucked.

"Evening, Mrs. Peterson," he greeted. "Want to let you know what's done thus far and get your okay on some things."

"Oh goodness," Edna emerged from her lethargy in his presence. "Please, please come in. Come in the living room and make yourself comfortable." She hurried to turn off the television. "Can I get you something to drink, some tea?"

"No thank you."

"How about something to eat? Have you eaten?"

Ezra smiled and assured, "I'm fine, thanks."

"Okay," she relented and soon sat down, sinking back into her chair while Ezra took a seat on the corner of a matching sofa adjacent to her. "Well, my—" she exclaimed. "You've done so much already, I can hardly believe my eyes. My yard looks brand new." She leaned toward him, lowering her voice. "I see you mowed the lawn later. I heard the mower earlier and then I heard him storming around, making a frightful racket." She spoke hesitantly, nodding toward the Miller apartment and searching her caretaker's eyes anxiously.

A subtle wryness colored Ezra's face. "Said the noise was disturbing him. Felt it was disrespectful. So I waited until he left to finish."

"Oh pooh." The woman threw a disgusted hand toward the Miller apartment. "He's a fine one to complain about noise and respect. Phew! But, of course, better to avoid trouble," she quickly added.

A glimmer of mischief flashed through her caretaker's eyes for just a moment. "Of course," he agreed, then quicky turned his

62

attention to other matters. "Let me tell you what's been done so far. The yard is cleaned up, as you know. The shed is cleaned. I made an inventory of the things you have there." He withdrew a neatly folded paper from his shirt pocket and handed it to her.

"I don't even know what Ben had out there," she apologized.

"It looks like there might be some missing tools, the smaller, power ones," Ezra explained.

"I just don't know what Ben had out there." She shook her head slowly.

"That's all right," Ezra soothed. "I can put locks on the doors if you like. Might keep things from walking off so easy."

"I guess that'd be good," Edna agreed. "How much do you need for that?"

"Not enough to worry about." He moved on, steadily. "I found some other things— small sweatshirt, toy gun, so forth."

"That's probably my grandson Michael's. He likes to play out there sometimes."

"That's right, you told me that," Ezra nodded, pausing in rather grim-looking thought before catching the widow's eyes and quickly smiling. "I also checked the plumbing in the basement and cleaned your boiler. You'll need to fill the fuel oil tanks before winter."

"Ben always did those things," she fretted. "I don't even know where to start."

"It'll be okay," Ezra eased. "We'll get it figured out."

"Well, yes," her rich character lines warmed. "I suppose we will."

"Also, I'm prepping the window and door frames for painting," he pressed on. "You want them white again or something else?"

"I just don't know. What do you think?"

"How about a nice forest green," Ezra suggested. "Might go good with the brick."

"Yes, I think you're right," the landlady agreed. "That sounds just fine."

"Forest green it is," her caretaker smiled. "I'll paint the shed trim and the picnic table to match."

Ezra continued on, telling Edna of several more things that he had done or checked and obtaining her approval for many repairs and improvements, none of which, it seemed, would cost her anything. Finally, her words laden with emotion, she gushed, "Thank you so much for everything you're doing, Mr. E.J. I just don't know what to say. Everything just fell apart after Ben...You're a real godsend. I haven't been able to bring myself to do much of anything but watch that." She pointed at the television.

"Ya, they say that thing grabs ahold of people." Ezra studied the set with interest. "Sort of a window, isn't it? Looks out on one sort of world. There's another window that looks out on a different world." He dipped his head toward her living room window. "There's no doubt that world's hard to wrestle with. We got to go out and meet it and we can't change the channel when it doesn't give us what we want. But it's sure enough real." He gazed at the TV again. "That one brings a world right to you. Even tells you what to think about it. Doesn't seem to have much realness to it, though."

Edna chuckled her assent, "Oh, you're sure right about that. You're sure right. I just can't seem to face things out there anymore, though. With Ben gone and my daughter and her family... well, they don't need me. There just isn't much that an old woman like me is good for. I'm pretty useless," she chuckled again from eyes that lacked any corresponding humor.

Ezra took in his landlady's face a long time. "Mrs. Peterson, that just isn't so. I don't guess our Maker continues anything without a purpose. Especially people. You got a good heart and hands with a lifetime of living in them. There's plenty that need what you have to give, that need a caretaker just like you do."

Edna chuckled again, this time with a certain warmth. "Well, I— I suppose. I guess there's plenty of people who do need that."

Her caretaker nodded and smiled, watching her face. "Well," he abruptly stood. "Time to get back at it."

"Oh, it's late in the evening for work, E.J. You should rest."

"I will rest," he assured. The glimmer of mischief peeked out of his eyes again. "It's a nice evening, though. And there's one or two things to be done before bed."

CHAPTER 9

It was getting on past eleven this Saturday night and the jagged music was reverberating throughout the apartment house. Edna Peterson lay awake in her bed, verging on frustrated tears. She thought about the words her new caretaker had said to her, but she didn't know how she could even begin to face the kind of callous world that seemed to so disregard her in her own home. She began to get out of bed, to go and blare the late night TV, as was her habit when the Miller apartment began shaking. But this time she hesitated. And then she did something she hadn't done in a long time. Resignedly, wholeheartedly, she prayed.

Above her, Janet Slater sat on her bed, trying to focus on a magazine amidst the racket when Kendra entered the room, dragging her pillow.

"I can't sleep again, Mom."

"I know, sweetie. Come and do like usual." Janet patted a spot on the bed next to her.

Kendra crawled onto the bed and curled up next to her mother, placing her pillow under the side of her head and one of her mom's pillows over the other side to muffle the din. Rubbing her daughter's back, Janet continued her efforts to read.

Out front, Ezra lingered, mostly invisible, amid the shadows at the east end of the porch. Quietly, he worked on a window frame, rubbing it with a small, folded piece of sandpaper. The gaunt couple that had been standing in the hallway the day before pulled up out in the street in a dented, rusty old Chevy. They sauntered up the walk and ascended the porch steps, wearing their dull-eyed masks of indifference. They did not notice the caretaker in the shadows until he spoke.

"There's nothing going on in there, man," he said without so much as looking up from his sanding.

Stopping short of the door and spinning about, the startled couple momentarily lost their veil of coolness. They stared uncertainly at the silhouette stooped in the darkened corner and the young man nervously asked, "What did you say?"

Ezra straightened and turned toward them, the glint of his eyes piercing the shadows. "There are some unfortunate rumors that Mrs. Peterson's house, Mr. Miller's apartment, more exactly— is a place of loud parties and poison," he explained. "But Mr. Miller, a man of honor, has personally assured me that there is nothing going on in his apartment. Just wanted you to know that, in case you thought otherwise."

Though unsettled by Ezra, the gaunt couple feigned incredulity. Shaking their heads, they sounded manufactured laughs of disdain and continued into the house. Ezra stooped and resuming his sanding. In just a few moments, he heard the door to the Miller apartment crashing open and the sound of screaming rage thundering down the hallway. Deliberately and without excitement, Ezra straightened once more and turned. Still gripping the small, dusty fold of sandpaper between the thumb and fingers of his left hand, he took a couple of measured steps forward and planted his feet squarely just as Calvin Miller burst out onto the porch in rabid, bug-eyed rage.

"I told you to stay the f— out of my business!" he screamed. "I told you I was done talking!" Gritting his teeth with wide-eyed ferocity, he hop-stepped and accelerated swiftly toward Ezra, his left fist raised before his face, his right cocked far behind in preparation for a colossal blow. "I told you!" he snarled gutturally in the adrenaline warped moment before impact.

Much can happen in such time stretched moments, appearing but an instant to the bystander's eye. With disconcerting calmness, Ezra tilted his head just slightly, allowing Calvin's left to graze by his ear. At the same time, with deceptively fluid speed, he raised his own left in a short back-fisting motion, his granite knuckles cracking against the young man's forearm and sending the wildly looping right fist flailing uselessly to the side. And, though his blows had just so quickly been brought to nothing, the momentum of Calvin's charge continued him right into the firmly planted caretaker. Ever-so-subtly, Ezra snapped his chin downward, his forehead forward to meet the bridge of the taller young man's nose with a dull, hollow crack that turned Calvin's knees to rubber. The verdict of this meeting was Calvin stumbling awkwardly backward several feet and crashing, unceremoniously, onto his rearside while

Ezra remained planted where he had begun.

Calvin raised his hands to his face, touching the blood trickling from his nostrils and from an opening at the bridge of his nose with trembling fingers. A great knot in the muscle of his forearm shot pain through him when he tried to re-clench his right hand. Over the ringing in his ears, he heard his friends stepping out onto the porch behind him, the sound of the gaunt young woman's gasp of surprise. And, looking up, he saw the caretaker watching him with those damned, smiling eyes. The embarrassment in front of his friends, the apparent lightness with which the caretaker took him— it was more than Calvin could bear. Freshly enraged, he climbed back onto his feet and began bouncing on his toes in gravely fierce fighting stance.

Evidently unimpressed, Ezra still stood with his hands at his sides, gripping the sandpaper and making no effort to brace himself for impending attack. "Well, come on then," he said matter-of-factly.

Calvin moved in cautiously this time. Setting his left foot in close, he faked a jab at Ezra's face even as he kicked his right foot forward with all of his might toward the intersection of the caretaker's legs. Ezra lifted his right foot and twisted, allowing the young man's shin to smack against the bend of his knee with dull resonance, then replaced his foot on the porch while Calvin cried out in pain and reached for his injured leg, crumpling at the caretaker's feet.

"Circle's turning pretty tight for you tonight, partner." Ezra examined the sandpaper in his hand, then dropped his eyes to Calvin's face. "You're reaping pain just as fast as you try to sow it."

Standing over the gasping, writhing Miller, his feet still established where they began the fray, Ezra gazed at the shaken gaunt couple. With a regard-filled nod and no-nonsense tenor he bid them simply, "Good night." And needing no further convincing, the gaunt ones hastily abandoned the porch and their friend, Calvin, rattling away in the beat up old Chevy.

Ezra finally yielded his spot, setting the piece of sandpaper on the nearest window ledge. Peering up from a miserably blood-stained, tear-streaked face, Calvin whined, "My leg's broke, man!"

"Na, would've felt it crack," Ezra calmed. "Probably just dented your periosteum."

"What— what?" Calvin stammered.

"The fibrous membrane around the bone," the caretaker explained. "Lots of nerve endings. Painful, ain't it?"

"F—!" Calvin complained. "It hurts like hell!"

Ezra smirked. "I don't guess it hurts that bad." Suddenly feeling very much alone and helpless with the caretaker looming over him, Calvin was swept by fear and braced himself, not knowing what the man intended. Reaching down with one hand, the caretaker gripped Calvin by the arm and, with frightening ease, hoisted him straight up onto his one good foot. "Come on, big guy, I'll help you to your apartment." The caretaker half lifting him off the ground by his arm, Calvin hobbled into the house and down the hallway toward the blaring music. "You shouldn't speak so crudely," Ezra added. "It doesn't suit a man of honor."

When Calvin had been brought through the open door of his apartment and deposited on the stained and torn couch to the left, Ezra made his way through the deafening brittle noise to the stereo on the far side of the room. He examined the myriad buttons, knobs, and fluctuating lights, then pulled the plug from the outlet on the wall with a satisfied sigh.

Edna Peterson, still praying in her room, the Slater's upstairs nearing sleep— they had all flinched dreadfully, as much feeling the crashing doors and monstrous raging as hearing it. Now, just a few moments later, the music abruptly ceased, mid-song, and silence prevailed. They remained braced, awaiting the next explosion of rage. But it did not come and it did not come and by degrees they relaxed, soaking in the quiet… and quietly wondering what had just transpired, hoping with all earnestness that the peace would hold. "Thank You," Edna whispered, drifting blissfully off.

In Calvin's apartment, the young man sat on the couch with his injured leg propped up on the small scratched coffee table, ever-so-gingerly rolling up his pant leg. Across the room, Ezra fumbled with the silenced stereo until he managed to extract the small metallic disc. "So this is a CD," he said in quiet amazement. "Isn't that something?"

Hearing the caretaker's words, Calvin looked up sharply at his back, but held quiet.

Turning about, Ezra read the words printed on the disc. The name of the group was "Wicked Legion." The title of the disc was "Dealing Death." Among the songs were titles like "Killer Stomp," "Dead Man's Thrash" and "Suicide Ride." His eyes lifted from the words on the disc to Calvin's face and Calvin's eyes dropped away to the floor. "Must be an acquired taste," Ezra offered, setting the CD on a shelf next to the stereo. He took note of the large, blue-black knot already well-formed on the center of Calvin's shin. "I'll get some ice," he said, heading toward the kitchen.

He returned with a can of beer. "You don't have ice," he said. "Put this on it."

Calvin winced and flinched as Ezra pressed the cold can to the knot. The young man grasped the can weakly with his sore right grip and held it in place. Prickling panic began to creep up his spine as he noticed the caretaker looking at the small plastic bag of lumpy powder on the lamp table at the end of the couch.

"Those skinny folks must have left that," Ezra offered. "If I was you, I wouldn't sprinkle that stuff on my corn flakes. I think it's making them sick. All bones and sunken eyes. Maybe they meant you harm." Calvin stared up blankly from the couch, not a clue how to respond and beginning to wonder about the caretaker's sanity. The blood had mostly dried and caked on his face and Ezra offered to find a towel to clean him up, disappearing down the apartment's back hall for the bathroom.

Now when Ezra returned to the living room with a wetted towel, he was faced by a badly shaking Calvin gingerly balancing himself on his one good leg... and pointing a semiautomatic pistol. Miller's eyes flickered and darted with trepidation even as his voice attempted to feign confidence. "Yeah! Yeah, bud! Now what do you want to do, huh?!" His words cracked dryly. "You don't know who you're messing with! I'll kill you! I'll kill you, dead!"

"So what." Ezra stared hard into the young man's face.

Calvin was bewildered.

"Everyone's a killer." Ezra tilted his head with a strange air of merry menace. "Who hasn't thought about killing and every other kind of evil. It's all the same. There's nothing new about it. Pulling the trigger won't make you someone different. It'll just confirm what we already knew. Your finger won't be guilty, will it? But the heart that thought on killing and gave the finger its command will be. Even if the finger never pulls the trigger, the heart that dreamed on murder is already a killer to the One who sees all things."

With an increasingly unsteady grip, Calvin continued to point the gun at the caretaker's face even as that face smiled at him. "Much as I'd like to be in heaven tonight, I got a feeling our Maker's not going to let me out of here so easy. Besides, it'd be a shame for you to display your heart to the world so openly. You could do better."

Calvin was thoroughly confused and frustrated. Confused— this man spoke as one who had concern for him. Frustrated— he'd never encountered anyone so, through and through, unshakable. It was terrifying. How could it be that the one holding the gun was in fear and the one facing the gun, odd as it sounded, was rather enjoying himself. Yet, even as Calvin was overtaken by the creeping realization that his gun held no influence with this strange man, he persisted in pointing it at him.

"Anyway," Ezra smiled, "You got enough prisons to deal with already. You don't need to put your bones in one, too. You brag about jail, but it really is society's garbage pile, isn't it? All the openly displayed vileness of people's hearts exposed, raw and stinking. I expect all that misplaced pride would get overwhelmed by the stench pretty quick in a serious prison."

Ezra fell quiet for a time. He looked about the room at the piles of trash and clothes. "This place is a bit of a garbage pile itself, isn't it?" He stooped down and picked up a cardboard box near his feet. "Could do with some cleaning," he said, picking up trash and depositing it in the box.

Ezra neared Calvin, continuing to pick up trash. Calvin followed him with the gun's muzzle, fresh tears sneaking down his face. Straightening right in front of the gun, the caretaker looked squarely into the anguished, wide-eyed face and simply took the weapon from his hand. "Sit down," he said, turning his back on the deflated young man.

Staring, glassy-eyed, Calvin complained weakly, "That's mine, man."

"That right?" Ezra continued cleaning. "If you actually paid for it, it was with Mrs. Peterson's rent money. Which makes it more hers than yours. Somehow I doubt you even paid for it, though. It's not like you're a man carrying your own load. You're a baby living off other people's sweat. People who have to work that much harder just to carry you through the world." Ezra removed the clip and cleared the chamber. "Where'd you get it?"

Calvin looked at the floor without answer.

Ezra set the gun and clip on the lamp table next to the bag of dope. "If you ever get done playing with other people's things, you'll want to give them back and start carrying yourself. It's what a man of honor would do. I bet if you had to provide for yourself, you wouldn't throw your sweat away on poison and death noise." He nodded toward the CD.

"Man, you don't know," Calvin protested. "I got to get along any way I can, man. There ain't no good jobs around. I ain't gonna flip burgers or haul garbage for no minimum wage, man."

The caretaker studied the sulking young man. "You graduate high school?"

Calvin shook his head.

"You mean you weren't strong enough to do the work the other kids did, but now you want one of their jobs. You want to be, what? Their doctor? Engineer? Boss?"

"No," Calvin feebly replied.

"Calvin," Ezra's eyes fixed hard on Calvin. "You've been living on people's good grace for too long. Sneaking, lying, stealing, poisoning their kids, intimidating and hurting...flipping their burgers or picking up their trash for any money at all, is better than we have coming."

Calvin blinked. He thought he heard the caretaker include himself among the undeserving.

"Even so, we're going to give you a good job."

"What?" Now back on the couch, Calvin looked up in surprise. "You're giving me a job? What do you mean? Doing what?"

71

"Helping me do some honest labor," Ezra answered.

Calvin was skeptical. "You mean you're not kicking me out?"

"Nope. Going to put you to work. You can start earning your keep."

"I— I don't know," Calvin grew flighty. "What do you want me to do?"

"We're going to add value to raw material through good old fashioned labor. Only way I reckon we can make some real wealth." Humor filled the caretaker's eyes.

But Calvin understood that he was serious about working and his anxiousness multiplied. "I don't know if I can, man. I mean, I got a lot of other stuff I got to do."

"You got nothing to do all day long," Ezra countered. "You've been making a lot of noise about being a man, Calvin. Time's come to get on with it. You're not going to coward out from a little work are you? You going to lose heart and run away on me?"

"No." Calvin blinked blankly. "I ain't gonna run."

"All right, then!" Ezra beamed. "Monday morning we start. I'll come get you. You can be vice president of production," he chuckled. " A position befitting a man of honor."

Ezra caught sight of the clock on the wall. It was midnight. "Sunday," he said. "Time for rest." He opened the door to leave. "Oh, and Calvin," he paused staring back soberly at the young man. "If I have to come back down here because you're bothering the neighbors again..." He left without finishing his sentence.

Calvin remained on the couch, battered and disheveled. His face was still caked with dried blood streaked by tear trails. His head hurt. His leg throbbed. His arm hurt and he could only close his hand about half way. The apartment was eerily quiet. He could hear the buzz of the electric clock on the wall, his own uneven respirations. Calvin looked back up at the apartment door and swallowed hard.

* * *

Way out on the east edge of Haverston, where route twenty-six leaves town, you'll find Jillian's Bar and Grill. Bounded on two sides by a large gravel parking lot, Jillian's is a flat-roofed, concrete block building painted an insipid hue of yellow. As the name implies, there was always a generous flow of beer, liquor, and heaping plates of grilled food at Jillian's. Interest often centered around the huge projection TV with all the sports channels via satellite dish. For the most part, thirty and forty-something men comprised the regular late night crowd with a few women and a few older drunks filling in the mix.

About midnight, there were still better than two dozen boisterous souls mingling inside. Most were gathered along the bar, drinking, eating grilled brats and burgers, and watching an early-season college football game broadcast live from Hawaii.

Set apart from the revelry, on the far side of the room, Bobby Slater sat at a table with a young, pretty brunette woman. The woman was clearly bored with his conversation and looking for an out. Oblivious to her disinterest, Bobby talked with enthusiasm of his job at Mid-Prairie Electric. The thirty-two-year-old Slater's bright blue eyes shown from a sparsely freckled face with a gently rounded nose. He brushed the longish blond hair from his face as he talked. "See that's the thing about being the production crew chief. If I'm not right on top of the generator output curves all the time, over forty thousand people will either get surged or browned out."

"Wow," the young woman politely feigned being impressed.

"Yeah. Where did you say you worked again? Haverston Elementary?" he confirmed. "See, now you can tell your students you know the guy that makes the electricity."

"Yeah," she smiled. "That's really something."

"Yeah. So you said you're not married, right?"

"Yeah. Well, I'm really just here to drive my friend Kathy and her boyfriend Eldon home." She pointed toward a couple among the crowd at the bar. "I'm not really into the bar scene."

"Yeah. Guess it's not the best place to meet people. I'm not married either. Still looking for the right girl, I guess." Bobby fidgeted with the handle of his mug. "Just spend most of my time working and customizing my house. Did I tell you about my house?"

She shook her head.

"I built a real nice split-level out in the Woolridge Acres addition on the northeast side," he brushed the hair from his face and pointed north. "Did most of the work myself. Saved a lot of money that way and built it just the way I wanted it. Used three-quarter inch sheathing all the way around. A lot sturdier than most houses."

"That's really good," the woman nodded.

"Yeah, got it decked out real nice inside, too," he persisted. "Got a big screen TV with surround sound. Got digital satellite, digital stereo, the works."

"Wow." Her mask of interest only nominally covered her fleeting patience now. She got up from her seat, excusing herself. "Time for us to be going. Nice talking to you."

"You have to go already?"

"I'm afraid so. Have to drive everyone home yet."

"Hey, speaking of driving, did you see my car out in the lot?" Bobby's face lit up again. "The metallic green Charger with all the chrome?"

"I don't think so."

"It's a sixty-nine," he said with pride. "A real collector's piece. Built it up myself. It's got a four-forty block, dual carbs, racing cam, the works. It'll do one-seventy easy. Maybe you'd like to go for a ride sometime," he offered, flicking the hair from his face.

The woman stood by the table, not wanting to turn her back while he was still speaking. But when he paused, she did not squander the opportunity. "Well, if I ever need to go a hundred and seventy, I'll know who to find. I really have to go now. Bye."

"Yeah, all right. Bye," Bobby answered, scrambling up from his chair. "Nice meeting—"

The woman had already turned and fled for the bar. She whispered to her friend who glanced furtively in Bobby's direction, then whispered to her boyfriend. In a few moments, the trio had made their farewells to the others and were exiting the front door.

Bobby merged with the people at the bar. His buddies from work, Ronnie and Jake, both smirked at him.

"Damn, Bobby, we just got you free of one wench," Jake

laughed. "What are you trying to do? Get yourself all tangled up again? Bad enough having one dipping into your pocket already and a kid besides."

"Watch what you say, Jake," Bobby warned.

"Aw, man, take it easy, Bobby. I didn't mean nothing," Jake eased. "Mellow out, man. I won't bring up your ex or the kid no more, all right?"

"Besides," Bobby shifted focus. "I was just talking to that gal. She seemed nice."

Ronnie chimed in, "That ain't what Eldon said. He said she's real stuck up. Thinks she's too good to drink or have a good time with us working people. Says she even tried to get Kathy to dump him."

"Yeah, come on, Bobby," old Augie Weirls added his drunken voice to the mix. The sixty-something man was well-looped as usual. "Have another drink, Bobby. Don't pay them women no mind. I ain't never worried nothing about them and I done just fine," he slurred. "They ain't worth all the work. Hell, you don't have to work near as hard without them."

"Augie, you ain't never had a steady job in your life," Jake laughed and everyone else joined in.

"Yeah, but Bobby likes to work," Ronnie said, only half laughing. "Always busting butt at the plant, making the rest of us look bad." The humor faded from his face. "It's like I keep telling you, Bobby. Don't nobody give a damn if you work hard or not. They ain't gonna pay you more. I mean, who the hell's watching? They ain't. They don't give a damn about us working people. Why should we give a damn?"

"That's it, Bobby," Jake agreed. "You got to learn to relax, man. Take it easy on the work and the stuck up women, man."

Ronnie lowered his voice. "Man, I keep telling you, Bobby, if you want to get laid, just take Lizzy home." He nodded in the direction of the animated forty-year-old blond woman, drinking and loudly carrying on with several men at the other end of the bar. "She likes you fine and you don't have to do nothing but buy her a few drinks and maybe give her a little spending money. Ain't nothing to it."

"Hell yeah," Jake agreed. "She'll do anything you want. She's rolled most the guys in here... except Augie." They all laughed boisterously.

"I don't know," Bobby hesitated. "She's pretty and all, but she's got a husband."

"How many times we got to tell you, Bobby? Her old man's been in a wheelchair since he broke his back over on the Coop construction site. Don't do nothing but stare at the TV all day. You ain't got to worry about him. She just stays married to him so she can spend the disability checks. Life's too short to worry about it, man. Go for it, Bobby. Yeah, go for it, man."

Bobby looked over at Lizzy, watching her for a time. "Yeah, maybe. I'll think about it." He turned to leave. "Think I'll head home."

"Aw man," Jake complained. "What's your hurry, Bobby? It's still early, bro. Let us buy you another round. Ain't like we got anything to get up for tomorrow. What else you got to do, man?"

"All right," Bobby relented. "What the hell."

"All right, Bobby," Augie slurred. "Way to be, boy. Have another drink."

They all laughed uproariously at the old drunk.

"Hey, Bobby," Ronnie's beer-soaked smile grew broad and impish. "I ever tell you about the time me and Jake took a couple of Genoa cheerleaders out after we beat their football team thirty to nothing?" He paused. "We were both linebackers, you know."

"I know," Bobby smiled. "You guys tell me all the time."

"Yeah, yeah, we were good," Ronnie slurred. "Almost made it to state."

"Yeah, I know," Bobby said. "You know, you guys have told me about the cheerleaders a few dozen times."

"Yeah, yeah," Ronnie gushed on obliviously. "See they were all goody-goody and stuck up, see. But Jake had a case of cheap strawberry wine in the trunk like usual, see, and we got them to drinking, see ee hee hee. Man, we had them drinking that stuff like Kool-Aid. And, and, then, see, we took them out to the old quarry north of town, see..."

CHAPTER 10

Sunday morning dawned clear and bright, a radiant sun swiftly warming the crisp air. Kendra ran about happily in the freshly mowed yard while her mother and Edna Peterson stood on the front porch conversing in hushed tones concerning the previous evening's commotion. Noting drops of dried blood on the porch, they speculated as to what had happened. And while they were yet amid conjectures, Ezra appeared on the front porch, dressed in a simple black suit and loafers, with plain white shirt and narrow black tie, and carrying a small, well-worn brown Bible.

"Oh my." Edna Peterson exclaimed. "Don't you look handsome, Mr. E.J.?"

"You're kind to say so," he answered. "I walked uptown to Hamble's Clothing store yesterday when I had a few minutes. Seems to fit pretty well." He noticed the nervous glances toward the blood. "I'm sorry about that, Mrs. Peterson. I should have cleaned that up last night. I'll do it soon as I return if that's okay."

"Oh, that's all right, E.J. I can get it myself. But we were just wondering what in the world happened." The landlady looked at him with hesitant curiosity. "Is everyone alright?"

"Everyone's fine," he assured.

"We heard the noise," Janet pressed. "Was there a fight?"

"Na, just a little horseplay."

The women accepted his answer, though their faces said they were less than appeased.

"E.J., where are you going?" Kendra inquired, trotting up to the porch steps.

"Going to church, blue eyes."

"Hmmm," the girl delighted in her nickname. "We go there too. At Christmas time before I open my presents."

"Ah— yeah," Janet added. "We really should get there more often. Just get busy with other stuff, I guess."

Ezra smiled and nodded respectfully to the women before starting down the porch steps.

"What church are you going to?" Edna asked.

Ezra pulled a piece of neatly torn newspaper from his Bible.

"The local paper listed all the churches in Haverston with their schedules for the week. Thought I might try this Grace Reformed church over on Twelfth Avenue. The caption says they preach the 'plain Word of God'."

"Well, you know there's the New Vision Cathedral uptown," Edna offered. "They have a splendid, huge cathedral with beautiful stained glass all the way around. All the clergy and choir wear the most stunning robes and the music is just wonderful. Beautiful furniture, artwork, carvings, and statues— it's all quite breathtaking," she assured. "And some of the most prominent people in Haverston go there. Even some of the other churches have joined with them."

"Sounds like quite a show," Ezra agreed. "All the same, I like my preaching plain and simple."

He bid the women and child a good morning and set out westward, conferring well-mannered acknowledgments to people that he saw in yards and drives along the way.

* * *

There's a modest, one-level brick building at the corner of Twelfth and Maple in west Haverston. It used to be a community center, but interest waned. Now it was the home of Grace Reformed Church. Born out of division among the members of the much larger First Christian Church, Grace Reformed was only two-and-a-half years old. At the time, the vast majority of First Christian had voted to become part of the New Vision Cathedral uptown. It meant more money and benefits for the clergy. It meant vast and beautiful facilities, their former property being given over to New Vision for use in progressive forms of community outreach. It meant many grand and enlightened productions. Perhaps it even meant elevated status within the community for the parishoners. There had been the small matter of renouncing certain simplistic interpretations of the Bible that the highly informed New Vision clergy had advised "too constrictive and intolerant for modern peoples," but this was happily conceded by most. A few, though— about a dozen families and a handful of individuals— could not abide these erosions and so, dismissed as stubborn and ignorant, they were left behind without a building or a pastor.

It was then that an organization of churches scattered across North America known as the United Reformed Churches— URC for brevity— received an impassioned plea for help from these beleaguered remnants of the former First Christian. The URC ministers soon dispatched a young minister fresh from their Canadian seminary to Haverston. With his wife Rose, Reverend Brett Travis traveled to Haverston with instructions to establish a mission church for the URC upon the foundation of these stubborn Bible believers. With financial assistance from the URC churches, they scraped together enough for a down payment on the vacant community center and Haverston Grace Reformed was born.

Working odd jobs to support themselves so as not to be a drain on this small congregation's resources, Reverend Travis and Rose had devoted themselves to this mission for two and a half years. Yet they were often tempted toward frustration, having added just four new families to the official rolls in that time. Whenever they prepared another report to the URC, they worried that the hard-earned money sent them by the other churches would seem unjustified. But, unlike many churches of this age, they were unwilling, indeed unable in good conscience, to compromise their strict Biblical message, to accede to society's ephemeral notions in an effort to attract more people. They had not been sent to Haverston to tickle ears with fuzzy, feel-good mush. Some Sundays unfamiliar faces would appear in the pews. But, despite an always warm reception by the parishoners, they rarely returned more than a time or two. The life of devotion and service Reverend Travis called his listeners to, by his word and by his example, seemed entirely too severe to most.

On this Sunday morning, having concluded the Sunday school classes, the Reverend sat on a simple bench next to the pulpit, praying quietly in advance of the main worship service. To the side, Rose fingered an intricate classical prelude on the keys of a second-hand organ. From his heart, the Reverend asked that his Creator would use him to faithfully communicate his Word, and that this mission work might meet with success. As he finished and opened his eyes, he caught sight of the austere-looking figure entering the rear of the sanctuary. The stranger nodded, slow and respectful, to the very elderly widow Mae McVillian, sitting in the rear pew. He took a seat a few feet from the staunchly Christian woman, ninety years in age. The preacher watched as the widow and the stranger wordlessly studied one another from stone faces. Then, while he yet watched, the two warmed into bright, mutual smiles. The Reverend knew not if they were previous acquaintances, or if they had simply recognized something familiar in one another.

When Rose had finished the prelude, Reverend Travis stood and began the service. Familiar old hymns were sung together. Scripture and catechism were read in unison. Prayers were offered as from one body. All of these had their place. They prepared the assembled for the center of this, and every service— the sermon. The Word of God plainly asserted. Though he was still a couple years shy of thirty, no one questioned Reverend Travis' authority. Because genuine leadership owes not nearly so much to age as to demonstrated integrity, when the tall young preacher with the intense countenance and Canadian accent spoke, people yielded their ears.

"Brothers and sisters," he began. "This morning I want to speak of a dichotomy of views among people of this world, a schism that has existed since the first people. In this world, at the foundation of all thought, there are two opposing beliefs. Two views of the essential nature of human beings at unresolvable odds with one another. The view held by most amid their philosophies, theories, and religions, sees man as morally good of his own accord, an evolving creature or a reincarnating spirit developing into something ever better, stronger, wiser by some manner of inherent, self-possessed power. In one form or another, there is this notion of achieving righteousness and gaining entry into the very presence of our Creator by one's own wit and strength. In sharp contrast to this view, stands our Bible, asserting that since the first people rose up against their Maker, they have passed on to all subsequent people a natural born condition of willful unrighteousness, miserably corrupt, self-deluded, and deteriorating as individuals and as a species. Now the view that people are good of their own nature must believe that if a person does bad things, even outrageous atrocities, that they were shaped by forces beyond their control or, at the very worst, that they are an unnatural exception to the norm of human virtue. But the Bible says that when people do or say detestable things, they merely show outwardly what occurs naturally in every human heart. Sin and evil. This morning, I want to call three witnesses forth for you to hear. Creation, that is, what we can perceive and understand of the natural world. Conscience, that is, the primal knowledge imprinted on our very essence by our Maker. And the third witness is the Bible, that is, the book which claims to be the very Word of our Creator, uniquely preserved through history and establishing its authority with each of us by seeing through us and cutting our conscience in ways no human words ever could. Do you think these witnesses will disagree? Will you be surprised if all three testify in harmony?

"We all learned of the atrocities done by the Nazis earlier in this century. When we examine these things closely, we find not evil leaders and their henchmen only, but millions of ordinary people who, by their actions and inactions, were willing and eager participants. The ones celebrated for harboring and protecting the persecuted were the exceptions of human behavior, not the norm. And we well know that it was not just this one generation of people in this one country that happened to be so corrupt. We know that Joseph Stalin did not murder twenty million with his own hands, but with millions of self-willed hands. Likewise, Mao in China or Pol Pot in Cambodia, or Amin in Uganda or a thousand other places in this century alone, not to mention every time and place in history. Thievery, slavery, and murder in the guise of communism, nationalism, socialism, capitalism...religion. Or no guise at all. It's all the same. The fact is, not just Hitler and Stalin, but any human being remaining in his natural born state and finding himself in a circumstance of unrestrained power without apparent consequence, will quite eagerly steal, savage, and slaughter in a vain bid to reorder this world with himself at the center— a god. How did evil seduce the first people? 'You shall be like gods...'

"From Bosnia we are shown pictures of seemingly benign souls standing next to neighbors and friends with warm smiles on their faces and good will in their hands. We are told that, in some instances, only days later these self-same smiling souls, the threat of consequence seemingly removed, savaged and murdered these very same neighbors and friends. The true nature behind the smile is thus revealed. Again, we know that this nature is not exclusive to Bosnia. Brothers and sisters, do not allow this testimony from the world all around you to fall upon deaf ears and blind eyes. The fact is, your own neighbors and you yourself, anyone that is not providentially restrained by the threat of punishment or regenerated by our Maker, will zealously do the same things, given the opportunity. The evidence observed in the behavior of human beings throughout history does not tell you that human nature is good, but that the moral law that threatens immediate consequence is good. Wherever and whenever the moral law has succumbed to the natural urges, human souls have consistently proven themselves utterly vicious. Thus, we recognize truth in the testimony of the Bible when it says, 'There are none who are righteous,' that 'all have turned aside,' that their mouths are full of cursing and bitterness, and their 'feet are swift to shed blood,' 'destruction and misery are in their ways' and 'the way of peace they have not know.' They have 'no fear of God.'

"We are all infected. Psalm 51 testifies that we are diseased from conception. This is a real infection, both physical and spiritual. It compromises the most basic molecules of genetic information passed from the first people to all subsequent generations, corrupting both the body and the breath of life that inhabits these molecules. Contrary to evolutionary religion, time is only accumulating harmful mutations in our genes. It's not making them better. This infection manifests as a basic mistrust and defiance of the Creator that has brought about this existence and continues it all through each space of time. Sin contaminates our every perception, thought, word, and deed. Think of it. Each of our trillions of cells is formed and woven together with a complexity that abandons our comprehension at the starting line. They are held constantly in existence, divided, and regenerated apart from our consent, by a Will and a Power not our own, by uncountable decisions not of ourselves. And, though we daily witness this Power continue to uphold and actuate all things, animate and otherwise, maintaining each orbit from the intergalactic to the subatomic, we still find ourselves unwilling to trust Him for our own continued existence and ultimate well-being. Rather than existing in reverence of such a Creator, we despise his rightful authority and plainly evident order. Rather than gratitude for this fathomless gift of being, we charge Him and His creation with our self-imposed miseries. He has spoken, according to the Bible, literally "thought," all things into being by the unboundaried power of His mind while we, given a thousand lifetimes of unrelenting mental strain, will never squeeze out the faintest subparticle of tangible substance. Yet we would claim ownership of ourselves and this creation, blindly taking credit for things we had nothing to do with, arrogantly boasting over things we don't even begin to understand.

"The Bible says that we have no excuse for this behavior, notwithstanding our infection, that we've always perceived our Maker and His plainly evident ways. Romans 1 says that God has shown these things to us, that 'since the creation of the world, His invisible attributes have been clearly seen, being understood by the things that are made, even His eternal power... so that (we) are without excuse.' Psalm 139 says that 'my soul knows very well' that all is God's work and that it is 'marvelous'. Our souls know very well that if we exist, alive and aware, the one who made us existed first, alive and aware. How vain and deluded to appropriate such credit to ourselves or to any part of the created world. Romans 1 calls it 'exchanging the truth of God for the lie' and 'worshiping and serving the creature rather than the Creator.' This willful self-delusion is so utterly absurd in the face of the plain evidence all about us, that Adam and Eve were without excuse... and so are we.

"On all sides, then, the created world testifies of its Creator's goodness and faithfulness and, at the same time, of our unjustified mistrust and corruption. And now our own consciences give testimony.

"The conscience is an awesome thing. We often use the word carelessly, even suggesting that some people have no conscience. But the Bible says that we all have right and wrong written on our hearts, that our conscience is a witness either for or against us, our thoughts either accuse or excuse us. The problem is not that any of us lack a conscience, but that because it so often accuses us we learn to deafen ourselves to its indictments. As we emerge from childhood, in one manner or another, we begin practicing the subtle art of being "cool." This involves building a facade, an image, a falseness around oneself. We begin affecting an attitude of unconcern for the corruptness lurking in our hearts as well as a pronounced disregard for the interests and feelings of others. 'So what,' we say. 'I'm cool, man, doesn't bother me.' 'I don't give a— .' Some folks become so adept at anesthetizing themselves to the cut of their conscience that they are indeed easily mistaken for having none at all.

"But even as we justify, excuse, and trivialize our misdoings, we testify against ourselves, admitting what our mouths deny. When we cynically question and accuse the motives of others, be they our leaders or our neighbors, we further witness against ourselves. For we would not so readily see selfishness and falseness concealed in other hearts were we not so intimately acquainted with it in our own hearts. People do harbor secret desires and motives deep within. So guarded are these secrets that the soul seizes with abject terror at the thought of being exposed openly to others, brought to the light, as the Bible puts it. If you have ever been seized by this fear of discovery— and you all have— then you have already been convicted of evil by your very own conscience. It is that simple. Passages like Hebrews 10:22 and I John 3:21 assure us that we cannot be gripped by such fear if our conscience is clean, that we will have confidence before God and before men, even in the face of public ridicule, if we are right-hearted. The Bible says that Adam and Eve had such right-hearted confidence before God until they determined to spit on his authority and be their own gods. Immediately, they were seized by fear and they ran away and tried to hide. Their guilty consciences destroyed their confidence before God and they knew they were exposed, naked and vulnerable, before him and each other. They wanted to cover up, to hide. So do we.

"The Bible says 'it is a fearful thing to fall into the hands of the living God' and that no one can see the face of God and live. I once read an article in a journal about researchers who directed incredibly intense laser light through crystals. If there was the slightest flaw within a crystal, the light would be obstructed, building up heat within the crystal and vaporizing it instantly. But the pure, uncontaminated crystals were not harmed, the intense light passing through them cleanly and coolly without producing any damage. Our Creator is an unfathomably pure and intense spiritual light that our flawed souls cannot bear to face directly for even a moment. We need to be covered. We need to be purified. The notion of a gentle, New Age kind of light that can abide our defilement without discrimination may be a soothing anesthesia to our accusing consciences, but it is a delusion no matter how desperately we dream otherwise.

"And then we try to rationalize that we're not guilty of evil if we don't act it out. 'I haven't killed anyone,' we say or 'I don't cheat on my spouse,' or 'I haven't robbed a bank.' Still our conscience undeniably lacks confidence before God. We still try to hide. This is because our conscience well knows that sin does not originate in the body that acts it out, but in the heart that gives the body its direction— in the soul. From start to finish, our Bible says that it's the heart of a person that bears guilt. Proverbs 4:23 says to 'keep your heart with all diligence, for out of it springs the issues of life.' In the seventh chapter of Mark, Jesus tell us that 'from within, out of the heart of men, proceed evil thoughts, adulteries, fornications, murders, thefts, covetousness, wickedness, deceit, lewdness, an evil eye, blasphemy, pride, and foolishness,' that 'all these things come from within and defile a man.' It's one thing to be tempted. We read that Jesus was tempted in every way a person can be and did not sin. But when we take hold of that temptation, that passing notion, that fleeting urge, when we begin to mull it over, imagine ourselves doing it, dream on it and luxuriate in it, we've made that thing our own and we're not being tempted anymore. We are sinning. Jesus tells us that whoever looks at another to lust for them has already committed adultery in their heart. In Matthew 6, he warns that what we do in our secret place matters even more than what we do in the sight of people. And I

John 3:15 says simply that if we hate, we are murderers. It matters, what is in our heart.

"You may question how hatred can be murder. But, in all of its many faces, what does hatred seek to do, but divide and separate? And what else is death, but separation? Separation of life from body, soul from Creator, of families and friends— all of it is death. And that which seeks such estrangements and divisions is murderous. Jesus warns that men should not seek to separate what God has joined together. Has He not joined together body and soul, creature and Creator, spouses, families and friends— all things good, just, and plainly ordered? What is evil, but that which seeks from its heart to foul, corrupt, pervert, and destroy these unions? Backbiting, malicious words, deceit, unfaithfulness of heart, fraud, rage— these are but a few of hatred's faces and they all sadistically desire to separate another from family and friend, from the truth, from happiness, from property, from their very life. It's all hatred, brothers and sisters. And it is murderous.

"How many hearts are secretly giddy with excitement at the misfortune, trauma, and suffering of others, all the while feigning most sincere sympathy? Judge from the memory of your own heart and see if you like the answer. How many have gleefully awaited trouble to befall another without trying to avert it or even give warning? How many thieves have accepted wages with hands that rested idle when no one was watching? How many mouths have delivered words intended to divide another from faith, family, or friend? All in some asinine bid to make ourselves the center and purpose of being, exchanging what we truly are to try to be something we can never be.

"James, the brother of Jesus, writes that the law engraved on our hearts by our Maker is not many, but one. If we disregard it at any point, we are guilty of it all, no better than another who crossed at a different place. By our relative human standards, there are most certainly good people and bad people. But in our Creator's stare, fixed and pure, with the notable exception of Jesus, there is only deliberate ugliness and failure.

"The Bible says that the law of God has a special purpose in teaching us a hard lesson about our true nature. Romans 3:19 and

20 says plainly that the reason the law has been given to people is so that all the world might be shown guilty before God, that no one will be judged righteous by the law. The purpose of the law is to give us knowledge of sin, to plainly show it to us, lurking in every corner of our heart and unable to scurry away from the light of the law that illuminates every recess and crevice. Satan suggested to the first people that if they just broke faith with God and looked behind His law, they would suddenly know both good and evil. And, indeed, when they betrayed God they immediately knew good and evil. God's goodness, from which they were now estranged, and their own evil.

"Augustine writes of stealing fruit as a boy. Though he had plenty at his own home, he was convinced that the coveted bounty was sweeter to the taste. A beach-side hotel owner tells of having only minor problems with people fishing from the balcony until he posted a sign forbidding it. These anecdotes illustrate how a law, most any law, reveals a natural born mistrust in the human heart. It's a discontent that always believes the Sustainer is hoarding good things on the other side of righteous boundaries, an obstinance that refuses to accept that the Creator's order and law is for one's own well-being. This heart pigheadedly insists that if only it crosses beyond this stifling morality, it will discover all the wondrous pleasures that our Father cruelly withholds.

"Our three witnesses— creation, conscience, and Scripture— having revealed sin in humanity, go on to testify of its due consequence. In Genesis God cursed the ground, that is, the physical creation, when it became infected by sin through its very apex, human beings. We seem to have a hard time understanding how something spiritual like sin can have such an effect on the physical universe. But you need look no further than your own person to see how something spiritual, your mind and heart, has profound effect on something physical, your body. Is it really more difficult to discern that the universe as a body is affected by the Spirit that created it and sustains it? If that Spirit, repulsed by the malignance in its creation, turns away, will the creation not die? Can that which is sustained continue apart from its Sustainer? Romans 8 tells us that the whole creation groans under the weight of corruption. Not able to abide corruption, God is separating from His creation and, as He does, it dies. 'The wages of sin is death.' As the vital glow slips from a dying man's eyes, so the universe is losing its vitality, its energy. Plain observation of this entropic phenomena has yielded the second law of thermodynamics in physics which testifies that any system or entity in our world will run down, wear out, and disintegrate without a continual renewal of energy or organizing principle from outside of itself. In other words, there is nothing in our universe that is self-sustaining. Everything, from galaxies to individual particles, requires a constant sustaining force from outside of itself. As we observe stars destructing from across space, orbits gradually slowing, a planet losing stability, and our own gene pool accumulating more detrimental mutations with each generation, we see the progression of sin's wages for ourselves even as the writer of Psalm 102 observed that the heavens and earth grow old like a garment. Even the Greeks, upon whom we base much of our modern math and science, discerned the law of 'morpholysis,' meaning to 'lose structure.'

"Our witnesses continue on, speaking of justice. Physics observes that every action has an equal opposing action— balance. People of every culture have discerned that there is a balancing force at work in our world, that what goes around tends to come around. And our Bible confirms that people reap what they have sown— balance and justice. This knowledge of proportionate justice is also written on our hearts by our Maker. A sense of justice is woven into our conscience so that we will never be able to sincerely speak words like 'I didn't know' or 'I don't deserve.' The Bible says that every mouth falls silent in Jesus' presence, unable to refute his righteous judgment. For example, we all instinctively recognize that it is relatively more heinous when offenses are committed against children than adults and even worse when done to infants. We all have this inborn sense that the more innocent and pure the one victimized, the more wicked is the crime and the more severe the punishment must be to restore balance. Jesus concurs, saying that if anyone offends a little one, it would be better for him to be thrown into the sea with a millstone hung about his neck than to face what he deserves. We are told that even criminals in prisons hold their own in lowest regard, often brutally, who have victimized the young. The more pure and innocent the offended, the more evil is the crime, and the greater the punishment must be to satisfy justice, to restore balance. What have we just done in acknowledging this awareness of proportionate justice alive in our conscience, but condemn ourselves utterly? For we know full well, in the secret places of our hearts, in each of our consciences, exposed nakedly before its Creator, that we have repeatedly and knowingly betrayed, ignored, and purposely offended our Maker and Sustainer, whose purity is beyond measurement, whose innocence exceeds boundaries and that, therefore, we quite justly deserve punishment beyond measurement, retribution exceeding boundaries. Our own well-developed sense of balance tells us so. No wonder our confidence before God is so completely destroyed by sin.

"By His very nature, God cannot simply ignore or suspend His perfect justice. If it would be repugnant for a community to fail to punish a heinous criminal, how much more so to ignore justice where violation of the unfathomable Creator is concerned? The Bible says God is faithful, not just some of the time, but always. This faithfulness extends to all things, from upholding the physical laws that order our universe to guaranteeing moral justice. Do you worry that someone may get away with something? Do not worry. God is faithful and His justice will not be mocked. Every inequity will be balanced. Every penalty will be paid— either by the offender or by the Acceptable Substitute— but it will be paid in full. If justice is not always as swift as you would prefer, do not fret. Rather, take heed of what great mercy our God affords each of us in such apparent delays of justice, grace periods, if you will. Because for those who obstinately refuse to take heed of the grace given them, the bitterness of their end is only compounded. Justice will prevail in all things. On this you can rely.

"Jesus teaches us in blunt terms about the just end of sin, hell, that is. In the eighth chapter of Matthew he describes the separation of creature from Creator as a weeping and gnashing of teeth in outer darkness. And isn't it thoroughly just in so much as this is precisely what the unrepentant desires and strives after? To be free of god, separate and autonomous. To be one's own god. Such have convinced themselves that this kind of separation would be a good thing while their Sustainer knows sorrowfully otherwise. In this outer darkness, a disembodied soul has its much sought after separation from God and from all that belongs to God, namely, all of creation, including that soul's body. Such a one is now quite free to be its own god, free to create as much substance of its own as it has power within itself to create...precisely nil. In the waning verses of Mark 9, Jesus deems it important enough to echo Isaiah three times in a row concerning hell— 'where their worm does not die and the fire is not quenched.' Understand, brothers and sisters, that the worm is the conscience, wriggling and eating from within, no longer dulled by the anesthesia of this grace period, accusing without end and that the unquenchable fire is none other than one's own deepest, burning passions and lusts raging out of control in permanent separation from all things, beyond hope of satiation. No remedy or rest. No mouth to give voice. No one's ear to hear. Nor any further grace to mitigate the intensity of burning.

"So let's review the testimony of our witnesses. All of the observable world tells us of sin and its just, balancing penalty. Our own conscience concurs, lacking confidence before our Maker. And, through His Word, enlivened by His Spirit, God tells us these things directly. To deny sin and its just penalty in human nature, we must pronounce the Creator, His creation, and our own consciences all liars. As John writes, 'If we say that we have no sin, we deceive ourselves, and the truth is not in us... If we say that we have not sinned, we make God a liar and his Word is not in us.' If we accept none of these witnesses, what is left to trust in, but the shadows of covetousness, the empty whispers of lust-driven self-delusion?

"The evidence finds us in an utterly miserable place from which we are proven powerless to escape and yet the Word of God is a Word of hope. Our Father continues this dying creation in a period of grace and exposes our sin to our faces, not to pointlessly taunt, but to destroy our vanity and point out our need of rescue. In His unfathomable wisdom and mercy, God has wrought a way to satisfy

His justice in the wake of our sins and still salvage His defiled creatures, restoring us to right-hearted confidence before him. As Jesus says, 'With man this is impossible, but with God all things are possible.'

"Jesus Christ is the solution that God has wrought for this dilemma. The Bible testifies to this, and our Creator's living spirit confirms this reality in the mind, heart, and conscience of every believer. He is none other than the Salvation, the covering of the exposed conscience promised to the first people and subsequently believed on by all the people comprising God's holy church from the ancient patriarchs to the nation of Israel to an uncounted sea of souls suffused through all nations and cultures these past two millennia— not coincidentally, the same two millennia during which the overwhelming majority of this earth's population has occurred. Jesus is the junction of humanity and God, of finite creation and infinite Creator. Human, because only humanity can rightly satisfy the penalty owed by humanity. We experience our existence as individuals but, as descendants of the first human, we are all members of that same breath of life imparted to Adam by his Creator in Genesis 2:7 and passed down to us, many branches of a single root. A brother of this same breath and having overpowered the corruption that infects all the other branches, Jesus is the Acceptable Substitute to absorb the penalty of human sins and restore souls to God, grafting them into himself, a new and uncorrupted root. And He is truly God as well. Only the supernatural, that is, the nature transcending power of the Creator is strong enough to break the natural-born grip of sin on this human breath and only the One beyond measure can pay the price beyond measure that we owe, restoring balance and guaranteeing justice.

"If we made something that malfunctioned or became defiled we would probably throw it away. But, rather than throw us away, our Creator, exercising a forbearance and faithfulness we neither comprehend nor merit, has wrought this mysterious, fearsome union in front of the entire world on behalf of those souls on whom He will have favor. Philippians 2 describes how God, in the person of Jesus, willingly subjected Himself to the humiliation, misery, and death of His own creation. A great mystery.

91

"If we are to have a part in this mystery, overcoming sin's death-grip and having our just punishment absorbed, we must be genuinely united to Christ, to the undefiled Root. The Bible makes it clear that our Father joins people to their Salvation through the bond of faith. Galatians 3 says that we become children of God through faith in Christ Jesus. The writer of Hebrews devotes the entire eleventh chapter to explaining how paramount faith is for people of God. Many trivialize and scoff at this notion of being united to something real and solid by something as seemingly ethereal as faith. But what is it that unites us to material possessions, to family and friends, or to anything of which we feel certain and sure. A keen old preacher once pointed out to me that the only thing that ties me to anything in this existence is faith. I am Rose's husband and the old green Dodge out front belongs to us only because I and my neighbors believe that these things are true. There is no umbilical cord that attaches these things to me. Only the invisible, yet quite real, bond of faith. There may be some pieces of paper or bits of computer data at the courthouse signifying some of these beliefs— marriage, children, home, car— but the unions themselves are not discernable to any of the senses. We live every aspect of our lives by these connections of faith and if someone breaks these ties, we are offended.

"Brothers and sisters, we should have no difficulty understanding how it is that we are connected either to the ghostly promises of sin or to our Creator through Christ, by nothing more and nothing less than faith, by what we believe in our heart of hearts. What we truly believe will show itself in our thoughts, feelings, words, and deeds. And, in this case, what God has joined together will never again be put asunder. As Paul reassures his fellow believers in Romans, nothing can 'separate us from the love of God which is in Christ Jesus our Lord.'

"We began this morning by pointing out two opposing views of the nature of mankind. Having listened to all of the witnesses that speak to us on this matter, we have established the truth of our natural born condition and we have briefly touched on how our Maker has worked a remedy. Next Sunday, if God is willing, we will want to look at how our Father breathes new life into people, how he plants, nurtures, and grows this connection to Christ, reviving hearts that were dead in sin."

* * *

Zwingli Park graced an entire residential block in west central Haverston. And on any Sunday morning when the weather was nice, there were people scattered throughout the park's sprawling, tree-lined lawns, playgrounds and benches. Children played on swings and slides and merry-go-rounds. Teens and adults recreated and lounged about. In an open, sunny area at the south edge of the park, several teenage and preteen girls were sprawled about on blankets, sunning themselves, as was their custom when weather permitted. And, as was his own custom, a well-tanned and manicured man in his fifties sat on a nearby bench, arrayed in designer leisure clothes and expensive jewelry, carefully eyeing the girls over the top edge of the Sunday newspaper he pretended to read. The exhilarating thoughts these children inspired... He was not one of those perverts you read about that can't control themselves. He was a smart man. A man of culture and certainly not foolish enough to risk the consequences of his... No, what he did, he did within, nicely concealed from prying eyes. Was it anyone's business what occurred in the private recesses of his heart? Hell, he'd been this way since... well, since he could remember.

On one of his frequent glances around, the sort that one must constantly take to assure that no one is watching, this well-heeled man took passing note of a man in a dark suit a block away, walking along the sidewalk. He brought his craving eyes to rest on the oblivious daughters of Haverston once more and slipped back into a luxurious fantasy with practiced ease. But an odd gust of breeze soon drew him out of the dream as it whisked the front section of his paper from the bench. He turned to see where his paper had blown and saw the man in the dark suit picking it up from the sidewalk. When the stranger neared the bench, returning his paper, he noted the Bible in the man's other hand.

"Thanks a lot, there, fella," the rich man said.

93

"The news must not be heavy enough to stay put this week," Ezra joked and handed the section over the back of the bench. As he did, the front page story caught his eye. "Suspected Serial Killer Released and at Large," read the bold headline above an old picture captioned, "Ezra Jacob Watt at his 1978 trial."

The rich man took notice of Ezra staring at the headline. "A real outrage, isn't it?" He shook his styled gray head. "No way scum like that should go free. Should have killed him. That's what he had coming to him."

"Yes," Ezra concurred. "A man has the wages of his evil coming to him."

"Damn right," the man on the bench said. "And you know he's going to kill again. He can't help himself. Animal like that crossed my path, I'd likely put him out of his misery."

"Well," Ezra smiled, "We could always hope that he's changed. Maybe he won't take all that grace for granted."

The man looked at Ezra incredulously. "What are you talking about, fella? You know better than that. Don't be so damn naive. People don't change. Especially ones like that." He nodded toward the Bible in Ezra's hand. "You been listening to too much of that mumbo-jumbo."

Ezra shrugged. "Guess if I didn't listen to this mumbo-jumbo, I'd have to go back to what I was before I listened to it." He paused and considered. "No, I think I'll stay where I'm at."

"Suit yourself," the rich man flipped a dismissive hand. "My ex used to always try to get me inside a church. All they do is try to make you feel bad so you'll give them money. Hell, she's still giving them mine." He narrowed his eyes into a world-wise mask, staring off into the distance. "I've been in business thirty-five years. Been all around the country and overseas, too. I know more about people than any sniveling preacher. People just are what they are. They don't change."

"If they're left to themselves," Ezra agreed. "But if the One who made a person was of a mind to turn him inside out... well, I don't guess anyone's going to stop Him."

"Ahh ha," the man forced out a derisive chuckle. "I hate to burst your bubble, fella, but there ain't no one out there that made us. No one's watching. We came out of the slime. Science has proved all of that. Life's a bitch and then you die. There ain't nothing more to it. Don't get me wrong," he offered, at length. "I like religious folks good as any. Even got some working for me. I just don't come to the park on Sunday to get preached to. Hell, I'm a conservative at heart myself. Believe in low taxes and the death penalty for scum like that." He pointed to the newspaper.

Ezra nodded. "Me too. You involved in the conservative causes?"

"No," the man answered. "Got a business to run. Don't have time for all that. Besides, most of the folks involved in that stuff, politicians and such, are liars and hypocrites. Anyway, I don't have to do something to be a conservative."

"Yeah, I think you're right," Ezra stared past the man. "I reckon a man is what he is in his heart whether he acts on it or not."

"That's what I'm saying," the well-heeled one assented as he turned his face back toward the park to see what Ezra was staring at. When he saw that it was the young girls sunning themselves, he turned back quickly, supposing he would catch the church-going stranger in hypocrisy. Instead, he was met by chilling eyes, fixed hard on him, not a hint of hypocrisy in them. Some sort of primal fear of discovery suddenly sprang up and clutched the rich man's chest, as if a beast. And, though he thought it most unreasonable that this should be so, it nevertheless was. The stranger with the Bible couldn't possibly know... no one knew! His face grew hot. His heart pounded away from him irrationally. He swallowed hard and chuckled weakly, feigning ignorance. "Wha— what?"

Ezra's eyes softened after a time and he patted the back of the bench as he turned to go. "Sweet dreams, big guy."

CHAPTER 11

A car deprived of its muffler drew Ezra from his sleep as it passed by the apartment house and faded down the street. He reached for an old bandless quartz watch from among the things in his open duffel next to him on the floor. Just past one in the morning, Monday. He stretched and relaxed for a time, listening. The apartment was very quiet.

This was his favorite time of the day in Kalbourne. He would read or think in his darkened cell until the doors opened at six. Now he didn't have to wait for doors to open. It took getting used to. He could do as he pleased. No barrier hindered him. It was a largely forgotten concept, like a lot of things out here seemed to be. He could lie here all day and not do a thing if he felt like it... "Work hard, Ezra!" The insistent, German-accented voice barged into his head. "Do not be slothful! Flee from idleness, Ezra!"

Straightaway, Ezra got off the floor. He opened the apartment's windows, searching out cooler air. With its heated rooms, this house felt much too warm to him. He was adapted to colder environs. The dim Kalbourne cellhouses, with their massive interiors and dearth of sunlight, were much cooler in all but the very hottest weather. In the autumn, they didn't send steam through the pipes from the powerhouse until November or so and then only enough to keep the water from freezing. Many a morning he'd watched his breath escaping into the crisp air of his cell and imagined himself a kind of monk on a mountain. Reality would soon reclaim him, though, as waking souls began their daily banter from somewhere down the block. "Hey dog, you got some squares for a homey, man? I get you back next week, man. My woman gets paid then and she gonna send me some green, man. Can you help out a homey, man?" No, it definitely wasn't a mountain monastery.

Ezra thought the house quite soft as well. All wood and carpet and plaster board. Everything out here in the world seemed so frail. Cellhouse walls were four feet thick. A tornado would amount to a spring cleaning for such structures. All the furniture there was set in concrete or welded to the walls. The only thing breakable in Kalbourne were the men. The people and things out here seemed so very fragile. Much of these past few days, Ezra had felt as though he were some awkward beast in the midst of ever-so-delicate surroundings.

Washing his face, Ezra slipped into his comforting blues and left the apartment. He eased through the downstairs hallway and stopped at Calvin's door. Silence. His heart warmed and his eyes smiled in the dark. He continued out the back door and into the welcoming night.

* * *

Drenched in feverish sweat, Lynn Younger was thrown dizzily from her sleep by another nebulous nightmare, more thick, acrid darkness and panic than any discernable images. The clock on her nightstand had progressed just ten minutes from the last one. Abandoning any notion of further sleep, she sat up. It was too much to battle. Easier just to stay awake, though that wasn't really any bargain either.

The anxiety, the awful dread, had her clenched in a demon-grip she could not break. She kept trying to reason with the fear, to relax and gain a satisfying breath. But, day and night now, her heart pounded and her breath came in shallow draws over a constant, verge-of-tears knot in her throat. It was increasingly difficult for her to focus her racing, jumbled thoughts on anything for more than a scant few moments.

How could it be? How could he be out here walking around? It was so damned unfair. Where was the justice? He'd ruined her life! She had been doing so well at the university. In a couple more years she would've had her degree. Maybe even a master's degree beyond that. She was going to have a career helping people and making a difference. And a family with a good husband and happy children... Instead, she sat here in her parent's home, forty and still afraid to go anywhere except straight out to Grey's Stables and right back again.

Several men, over the years, had tried, ever-so-gently, to ask her out. She had refused all overtures, always careful to avoid even the briefest eye contact. Her family, a few old girlfriends— they all told her how deserving she was, that she should "find someone." They didn't understand. They didn't understand that she didn't even want to be touched by anyone. They didn't understand that she could see the leering in their eyes, no matter how nice they pretended to be. Even if she had trouble seeing it sometimes, she knew it must be there, lurking behind a friendly smile and gentle words. He had taught her that...

There was still Jess Anders. She had gone out with him a couple times in high school. To this day, he still came to see her every six months or so and would always ask if she wanted to go do something together. Everyone told her what a good man Jess was, how he'd worked since high school to build up a successful construction business, how kind and charitable he was to everyone in the community. He did seem nice. She was never able to sense anything sinister in his intentions. He was tall, blond, and handsome besides. A lot of other women around Jasper Mills surely coveted such an invitation from Jess. But he didn't appear interested. It seemed he was content to bide his time, building houses and waiting for her. Whatever Jess thought he saw in her, though, he was mistaken. He just didn't understand. No one did. It didn't matter how hard a person worked or how good he appeared to be or how patiently he waited. You could never see what was really inside them, what their true nature was. In the Hoyt's hayfield, all those years ago, Ezra had taught her that... She was not taking any more chances on people. She would keep to her safe routine. Home to Grey's, Grey's to home. Alone. Jess could keep building his houses. Alone.

It wasn't yet three in the morning, but she decided to leave for Grey's. There was no rest for her here. If she was to be weary with fear, she may as well be so amongst her big, gentle friends in the stables. If she stayed here until sunrise, she'd only have to see the look in her parent's eyes. Everyone was starting to look at her the same way they had back then, as if she were the most pitiful thing they'd ever seen. At least her charges at Grey's needed her. And she was sure of their hearts... Damn Ezra Watt! Damn him to hell! Why was he still alive?

A sturdy knocking at his door gradually invaded Calvin Miller's consciousness and pried him from a thick, headachy sleep. His clock radio read 4:46 a.m. Must've been a dream. Another volley of knocks struck his door. "Oh, man! What?" he muttered, dragging himself up out of bed and limping badly from the bedroom to the front door in his undershorts. "What?" He growled, opening the door, still half asleep. But he proved alert enough to lose his menace as soon as he recognized the caretaker's form.

Ezra stood holding a brown paper bag, his eyes filled with humor. Calvin loomed groggily in the doorway, his hair matted and tangled. The bridge of his nose was scabbed over and both of his eyes bore dark raccoon-like rings around them.

"Enough sleep. Time to work," Ezra said.

Calvin blinked over and over, like a deer caught in headlights.

Ezra brushed past him and entered the apartment. "I saw inside your fridge," he said over his shoulder as he set the paper bag on the kitchen table. "Brought you something edible for breakfast. They got a store uptown that's open all night long! Fresh fruit and everything."

"You mean the convenience store?" Calvin scowled.

"A convenience store." Ezra looked into Calvin's face. "Boy, it sure is."

"Oh, man. Where did you come from? You ain't never heard of a...." Calvin shook off some of the grogginess and whined. "Come on. It's too early."

Ezra was unmoved. "You're wasting time. Get dressed."

"What are we going to do at this time of the morning?" Calvin protested.

"We're going to make wealth," the caretaker answered, a hint of pride glinting from his eye.

"What do you mean?"

"I mean add value to something through honest labor. How do you think wealth is made?" Ezra studied the young man's glowering face. "You want to tangle?"

"Wha— what?" Calvin stammered.

"Do you want to fight?" the caretaker clarified.

Calvin looked about the room anxiously. "No!"

"You told me you wouldn't lose heart and run out on me," Ezra said. "I'm taking your word. So get dressed and get out here for your breakfast. We have work to do."

"Oh, man," Calvin muttered beneath his breath, limping to the bedroom. "I don't believe this sh— ."

"I told you about talking like that," the caretaker called after him. "It doesn't become you."

In a couple of minutes, Calvin returned to the kitchen in jeans and tennis shoes, pulling an old concert tee-shirt over his disheveled head. There was a place set for him at the table; a bowl of cereal, a sliced banana, an orange, peeled and sectioned, a glass of milk, a glass of grapefruit juice.

While Calvin sat down and ate, the caretaker stood by and studied the tangled mess dangling over the young man's shoulders to the middle of his back. "We'll be running some power tools today," he finally said. "You might want to bring a hair tie or something. You get that stuff caught in a table saw, it'll rip your whole head off."

Calvin stopped chewing, his eyes abruptly wide. Ezra pointed at the table. "Hurry up."

CHAPTER 12

From behind the desk of his cluttered, downtown Northfield office, private investigator Gilbert Harms listened carefully to the earnest Wovoka County deputy seated across from him. Harms had worked as a private investigator since he took early retirement at age fifty-five from his long time job as a Northfield police detective.

Unable to gain the information he craved through official resources, Dan Guiness had traveled to this larger town of forty thousand, fifty miles to the west of Jasper Mills in dogged search of someone who could help him find Ezra Watt.

" — So you can see why our department needs this done discreetly through a private party," Guiness explained. "Officially, we're not supposed to be looking for him. But we would feel a lot better about it if we just had an idea of where he is so we could, you know, just reassure some of the more frightened citizens in the community."

"So you folks don't want to make contact with Watt, then?" Harms clarified. "You just want to know where he's at, hopefully, a long way from Wovoka County."

"Right, exactly," Dan smiled benignly.

"Sure," the lanky investigator nodded, "I can understand that. I sure can. Don't know if you remember much about that case. I'm guessing you'd have been pretty young back then. I sure remember that summer. I worked over at the Northfield PD then. Bunch of us went over to Wovoka County that summer, trying to help out any way we could, mostly combing the ground for clues. A real bad time."

Dan Guiness started from a momentary glaze and nodded. "Yeah, that's what I hear."

"Okay." Harms focused in on the task at hand. "If we have Watt's Social Security number and date of birth, that'll help us zero in on him quick if he's not trying to hide. If he's not using his name or number, though, it'll be a good deal more challenging."

Dan put a tattered manila file on Harms' desk. "That stuff should all be in these old arrest records from '78."

"Now if this doesn't yield anything, I can go down and try to fish something out of Kalbourne," Harms explained.

Dan shook his head, subduing his contempt. "They aren't very helpful down there."

Harms smiled. "Given a little time, I might be able to snag onto something. If not," he paused, "Guess I'd have to try to pick up his trail along the bus route he took. Either way, could get time consuming and expensive if he doesn't want to be found."

"Well, the department has authorized me to pay your retainer, fees, expenses— whatever it takes," Dan assured, pulling a stack of folded over bills from his uniform pocket. "Will a thousand get you started?"

Harms eyed the cash with some hesitance.

"Discretionary funds," Guiness eased with a smile. "More discreet than a department check, you understand."

"Yeah, I guess so," Harms agreed. "But it might not take a thousand if I find him right away."

"If you find him right away, it'll be well worth it," Dan assured. "And if you don't, I... we can get you more. Like I said, whatever it takes."

"Okay." Gilbert Harms stood up from his chair and offered his hand. "I'll get on it, Deputy—" He hesitated, studying Dan's face. "What did you say your name was, again— Guiness?"

"Yes." Dan tensed, releasing his grip from the investigator's hand. "Why?"

"That name just sounds familiar." The old man's brow furrowed. "Can't quite place it, though."

"Pretty common name east of here," Dan offered. "Probably just read it in a newspaper or something."

"Maybe so. Maybe so." The old detective smiled kindly. "Well, you have yourself a good day, young fella."

* * *

Ezra quietly watched the scenery pass by the passenger window of Calvin's brown Ford pickup as they traveled along Oak Street, returning to the apartment house. Calvin was at the wheel, his hair now pulled back tightly into a pony tail. Not yet nine in the morning and the back of Calvin's truck was filled to the brim. There was three hundred board feet of what Calvin had heard them refer to as "four quarter" cherry wood. There was fifty board feet of "eight quarter" cherry wood. There was three quarter inch and one quarter inch cherry plywood, various knobs and pulls, drawer slides and miscellaneous hardware. And piled atop these things were many tools and machines as well. There was a planer, a jointer, a router, a drill, and more. There were piles of clamps, jugs of glue and finish, sheaves of sandpaper, sacks of screws, and a dizzying array of bits and attachments. All of these things were foreign to Calvin, but apparently quite familiar to the caretaker. He seemed to know exactly what he wanted. As they had cleaned and organized in the shed early this morning, he had watched the caretaker make careful notes and lists. Now, in the past two hours around town, Calvin had watched this E.J. purchase more than twenty-eight hundred dollars worth of materials, tools, and supplies, from a hardwood supplier, a tool retailer, and a hardware store, carefully inspecting each item and paying for all of it with cash that he kept withdrawing from inside his coat. The sight of that much cash stimulated Calvin's coveting nature. But the thought of crossing the caretaker again as quickly stifled his greed.

Nearing the apartment house, Calvin pressed, "What are we going to make with all this stuff?"

"You'll see as we go," was Ezra's answer.

Calvin considered some more, maneuvering the truck around the corner onto Seventh Avenue. "Yeah, but what was all that stuff about making real wealth? Money's money, man. Don't matter how you get it."

"I disagree," Ezra said. "If money was just paper or even gold, it wouldn't be worth a thing. Money has value because of what it stands for— work and the useful things that come from work like food and shelter and clothes. The way I see it, when people pay money for something, they're trading someone's hard work— their own or somebody else's— for what they want. Money's just easier to trade. You can't eat gold and a pile of cash won't protect you from a blizzard. They're just ways to represent the work it takes to grow the food or build the house... real wealth. Things of real value that keep us alive and comfortable only come from work, from someone laying down a piece of their life to take something out of the ground and sweat over it until it's something useful. Seems to me, the more people work to make the basic, useful things of life, the more real wealth they have to trade for things like medicine, government, and Disneyland. And the less people want to work, the more time they spend trying to figure an angle around plain, honest work, the less wealth there is for anything... no matter how much fancy paper they print." Ezra brought his face around to Calvin's as the pickup came to a stop outside the shed. "You and I are going to lay down a piece of our lives on that wood and make something real." He turned away and stared out the windshield. "Men like us need to carry our load, need to help others carry theirs. Otherwise, we're just sucking up air and fouling it while we wait to die."

The men got out and unloaded the pickup. They carried in the wood, stacking it neatly in a corner of the shed. Calvin was tired by the time they had finished and his bruised leg and sore arm ached. Sitting down on the pile of cherry, he exhaled dramatically. "Whew! What time is it?"

Ezra carried the planer and its stand to the far end of the shed and busied himself mounting the former atop the latter. "About ten, I guess. Unpack that jointer and set it up there." He pointed to a spot on the floor slightly offset from the planer's outfeed.

"Man, I don't know how to do that," Calvin resisted.

Ezra glanced up from his work with no-nonsense eyes. "You're not that helpless. Read the manual. Figure it out."

Glowering, Calvin got up from the wood pile and began to wrestle the crated machine across the shop floor, muttering as he went.

* * *

The Haverston noon whistle could be heard as Ezra and Calvin finished the last of the machine setup and calibration. The siren still slowly winding down in the distance, Calvin looked expectantly at

104

the caretaker.

Ezra brought a jug of water over from one of the workbenches and handed it to Calvin. He studied the younger man intently as he drank. "Hungry?"

Calvin brightened. "Hell, yeah!"

The caretaker nodded sober agreement and took back the jug. "Good feeling." He turned and headed for the wood pile. "Time to work wood."

Calvin's eagerness withered, his shoulders slumped in disbelief.

Ezra carried two eight foot boards past the young man on the way to the planer. "First thing to do is make the wood straight and true. Anything of quality must have a straight and true beginning. Piece of furniture, a house..." He considered for a moment, then smiled. "A man."

Calvin stood in sulking silence. Ezra tossed him a tape measure. "Come over here and tell me how thick our stock is so we know where to set the planer for the first pass."

Calvin fumbled with the measure on the edge of one of the boards for several moments before deciding, "About an inch."

"About an inch won't do it," Ezra chided. "Exactly how thick?"

Calvin stretched the tape across the edge again. "One little mark less than an inch."

"The little marks are sixteenths," Ezra offered. "So one mark under an inch would be what?"

Calvin shrugged blankly.

"You didn't figure you needed this sort of thing in school, huh?" Ezra watched the young man's face. "How many sixteenths of an inch in an inch?"

"Six— sixteen?" came a distinctly irresolute reply after several moments of careful deliberation.

"So one less is...?"

"Fifteen sixteenths?"

"Hey man, you got promise." Ezra's face filled with mirth as he set the planer and began to mimic, "I ain't gonna flip burgers for no minimum wage, man. Hee he he..." The caretaker laughed robustly as he turned on the planer and grabbed a board.

105

* * *

By four in the afternoon, Calvin and Ezra stood on opposite sides of a waste-high workbench that they had carried through the side door of the shop out into the yard, searching out the pleasant September sun. On the bench rested the fruit of four ceaseless hours of labor. In various lengths, widths, and thicknesses, there was stack after stack of precisely machined cherry wood. After planing the depths, jointing the edges, rip sawing the widths, and cross cutting the lengths, they had continued on, dadoing precise grooves into some pieces, cutting complex panel slots into others with a molding head, mortising square and rectangular holes with an attachment on the drill press, and cutting tenons at the ends of other pieces. All the pieces were marked lightly in pencil with a system of letters and numbers and organized in ordered stacks, a great wooden jigsaw puzzle arising from the caretaker's head with meticulous precision. What it was, how it all fit together, was still a mystery to Calvin, yet the caretaker had made him not merely help, but begin to learn each process, forcing him to pay exacting attention to every detail. By now, not only did Calvin's body ache from exertion and hunger, but his head throbbed and swam with all of the information on which he'd been compelled to focus all afternoon.

Now, outside at the workbench, Calvin believed that at least his next task of sanding boards would not require so much concentration. Across the bench, Ezra was applying glue along what he termed "F" joints in the edges of some of the shorter three-quarter and one and a half inch stock, then clamping them together to form panels. Calvin made as though he would begin sanding, then set his board back down, his brow crinkling with concern. "Man, I'm really hungry. When are we going to stop and eat?"

Ezra continued working without so much as a glance across the workbench. "I thought we might just keep going until our Maker brings us something to eat."

Calvin protested with all the gravity he could muster, "I'm serious, man. I'm hungry as hell."

Ezra finally looked up. "You don't think God will take care of us if we work hard and don't worry about it?"

Calvin shook his head. "No, man. That's stupid. I— I mean, no disrespect or nothing, E.J., but that don't make sense. We got to take care of ourselves. There ain't nobody out there to take care of us."

Ezra set some clamps up on the workbench. "You ask?"

Calvin frowned. "Ask what?"

"For food," the caretaker clarified. "You ask your Maker for some food?"

"Come on, man," the younger man whined.

Ezra worked some clamps around another panel. "I will ask for both of us," he finally said. "Mean time, we'll keep working."

Calvin stood staring across the workbench from glazed, disbelieving eyes. "Oh, man! I don't believe this—" Catching a warning eye from the caretaker, he did not finish his words. Grudgingly, he snatched up a board and began sanding, trying to console himself in the notion that he could relax and not have to concentrate so hard on the task at hand. No sooner had he begun sanding, though, and the caretaker was eyeing him.

"What!?" Calvin glowered.

"Look at your work," Ezra pointed. "You're just scratching the wood and making it rougher when you sand across the grain. Sand the length of the wood with the grain, not against it." He observed as Calvin began again with the grain and mused as he returned to his gluing and clamping. "Kind of like our Maker. Go with Him, things get smoother. Go against Him, everything gets rough and scratchy. Ha ha ha ha," Ezra laughed, quite pleased with his analogy.

"Oh, man," Calvin said beneath his breath.

They continued to work in the backyard through the late afternoon and, little by little, they were aware of more and more faces watching them. From a second-level window at the back of their apartment, Janet and Kendra watched intently. Below them, a light-complected, hollow-eyed boy stood next to Edna Peterson, both of them gazing out into the back yard. From the adjacent house to the east, the spectacled faces of a middle-aged couple and two teen-aged kids peered from a living room window. To the west, across Seventh Avenue, people returning from work and from school stood in several yards, quietly watching.

"Guess this doesn't square with your reputation," Ezra said.

Calvin shook his head in concurrence, unwilling to look up from his work at all the watching eyes.

"Who's the kid with Mrs. Peterson?" Ezra inquired.

"Think it's her grandson," Calvin shrugged. "Hangs around back here by himself a lot."

The caretaker absorbed the information. "We probably invaded his space."

Calvin nodded agreement, though not really listening. A distinct feeling of awkwardness was growing in him as the surrounding eyes continued to watch. He knew all the people were stunned to see him obediently working under the direction of this new stranger. He kept wondering why he was doing it himself. When this E.J. had woke him up so early this morning, and at least a half dozen times since, he had wanted very much to tell him to "go to hell" and storm off. Yet... he had not. Perhaps it was fear, but it seemed more than that. He was skeptical that the caretaker would really harm him if he walked away. But each time he contemplated abandoning his work and the caretaker, or going back and lazily laying about his apartment in his usual manner, a surprisingly strong grip of shame would lay hold of him, fixing him firmly in place. He did not know how he would face the caretaker again and look him in the eye if he deserted. It had not mattered to him for a long time what anyone thought of him, but, for a reason he could not quite put his finger on, it mattered what this E.J. thought of him. Though he'd attacked the caretaker and even threatened to kill him, the man didn't seem to hold it against him. And though E.J. had clearly demonstrated that he did not have to treat Calvin with respect, he nevertheless did. Indeed, the caretaker kept treating him like an honorable man. More than that, actually expected him to be one.

So they worked on and gradually, talking amongst themselves in guarded tones, the faces began to turn and disappear from the windows and the yards, settling into their respective evenings. Here and there, the faint sound of the telephone ringing in Edna

Peterson's apartment could be heart out in the yard.

About six-thirty, Janet came out the back door of the apartment house, carrying a cardboard box and trailed by Kendra, carrying a smaller one. "Hope it's okay,"Janet flashed a hesitant smile. "Thought you guys might like something to eat."

"All right!" Ezra smiled. "Calvin hasn't allowed me to stop for food all day long."

Janet's eyes darted nervously to Calvin, who was shaking his head in persecuted silence.

"E.J., I helped make supper," Kendra declared, proudly bearing her box to the workbench.

"That's cool, blue eyes."

"Hmm," she responded with her customary brightness.

Following Ezra's lead, Calvin helped clear a space at the end of the workbench and clapped the dust from his hands. The men flanked either side of the bench and watched as Janet unpacked the boxes. Plates and utensils, a stack of sandwiches, a bowl of pasta salad, another of sliced melon, a pitcher of iced tea...

Calvin's eye caught the humor-filled glance of the caretaker and he remembered their earlier conversation. "Don't mean anything," he said. "Just a coincidence."

"No such thing," Ezra quietly responded even as he smiled at Janet and Kendra.

Janet's brow lowered. "What are you guys talking about?"

"Just a slight difference of theology," Ezra said.

The woman seemed puzzled, but then brightened and, seeking the caretaker's approval, asked if he would say grace.

Ezra agreed and, as Janet lowered her head, Calvin retracted his hands from gathering food. Kendra looked on curiously while the caretaker offered a simple prayer. "Dear Father, our Creator, Sustainer, and Redeemer. May you make us aware of You in ways that we cannot ignore. And may we be truly grateful that You have remembered us even when we have failed to remember You. We pray by Jesus' name— Amen."

When he had finished, Calvin and Janet raised their eyes, relieved at his brevity, yet not unmindful of his words. Unable to hold back a moment longer, Calvin began wolfing down a sandwich.

Kendra continued to eye Ezra as he dished up a plate. "Did God hear you?"

"Yes He did, blue eyes. He hears everything that we say out loud... and everything that we say inside where no one else can hear."

The notion astonished the little one, her eyes growing wide.

Then Janet asked, "Do you really believe that God always remembers everyone?"

"I believe he constantly remembers everything that exists."

"What do you mean? How?" Janet pressed.

He set down his plate. "Near as I can tell, the Bible says that God both created and upholds all things by His 'Wisdom' or 'Understanding' or 'Word' — all of which can be translated from their Hebrew and Greek to mean 'thought.' So, literally then, He has thought everything into existence and, by His continued thought, holds all things in existence. All that is real, all that is true. If God stopped remembering something for even a moment, whether a little particle or a whole galaxy, it wouldn't exist anymore. How could it be any other way? How could anything exist except that the One who brought it into being continues to allow it and maintain it?" Ezra picked up his plate again. "When the Bible says God is faithful, that's an awesome statement. It means that reality and truth are solid and trustworthy only because their Creator is."

Janet reflected seriously on his words. "So we can't be independent and do anything on our own? We need God for everything?"

"I believe that's true," Ezra confirmed.

Listening as he ate, Calvin eventually spoke up amid mouthfuls. "Yeah, but it don't have to be Christianity, man. I studied a lot of other religions. I got into Buddhism when I was in the joint. That makes a lot more sense, man. You can find a lot of deep truths inside yourself when you meditate."

"Did you?" Ezra asked.

"What?" Calvin responded.

"Did you find a lot of deep truths inside yourself?"

"Oh yeah," Calvin assured. "I got really deep into it, man."

"What'd you discover?" the caretaker pressed.

"Well, you know... it's not that simple. It's more like really profound feelings, you know? Like, that everything's connected."

"I know," Ezra watched the young man's face. "A lot of people, especially rebellious young men, are attracted to ideas that make them feel strong, that make them feel like they have the power somewhere down inside to overcome their own corruption and even overpower death by thoughts or words or actions that seem noble or profound to them... You sure you understand what Prince Siddhartha was saying, though?"

"What— who?" Calvin's face fell blank.

"Prince Siddhartha," the caretaker repeated. "Your teacher, the founder of Buddhism, the Gautama Buddha. I thought you were deep into it."

"I— ah, it's been a while," Calvin shrugged, taken aback.

"Remember how the Prince was so disturbed by death and decay that he left behind his throne, his riches, his family and, finally coming to a tree, sat beneath it and vowed not to move again until he understood the truth of existence? After a long time he had his satori, his moment of enlightenment. And just what great truth was revealed to him?"

"What?" Calvin pressed, suspiciously like one hearing for only the first time.

Ezra smiled from tired eyes. "That all existence is suffering. Suffering brought about by human passions, lusts, and corruptions. And the pure Zen preachers that followed in China and in Japan, the ones who rejected the man-made traditions and pointless ceremonies of their times, the ones who longed for simple truth, they all came to similar conclusions. The great Zen preacher Bankei concluded simply that people are sinful and corrupt and life is miserable because of it. So these men hungry for truth— looking within, looking without— came to more or less the same conclusion that the first writers of the Bible had revealed a thousand years before. The Bible even says that the very first people were aware of this sin and misery at its beginning. But the ancestors of the prince and the Zen preachers had not thought it useful to retain the knowledge of salvation from this corrupt condition, knowledge imparted to their first ancestors thousands of years earlier. They were left without any remedy except to dream of becoming 'uncreated' as Gautama put it, or 'unborn' as Bankei longed for. They wanted to extinguish themselves and taught others likewise, to cease to exist as individuals. They hoped, dreamed, and strove to become one with everything so they might escape the misery and penalty their consciences told them was inevitable. Like a business man who goes corporate to avoid personal liability." Ezra smiled. "But even though they dream of undoing a creation they had nothing to do with, a least the Zen purists recognize the horrendous penalty associated with sin. They see the coming justice for wrong intentions, wrong words, and wrong actions. The Buddhist scriptures speculate that it must take an uncountable number of lifetimes over unmeasurable eons of time for a soul to be purified from its corruption. But a few centuries before the Buddha, Isaiah had already written that unless the Creator intervened through His Messiah, the soul could not overcome its corruption in any amount of time... 'Their worm does not die and the fire is not quenched.'

"Many other religions and philosophies try to ignore the conscience altogether, and dream that if they just work at being sincere or say some magic words or perform the right rituals that their Maker can somehow just ignore their corruptions and leave things unbalanced. But a Creator of perfect justice cannot turn away from justice. So, Calvin, you said there are lots of ways to God, that it doesn't have to be Christianity. But the way I see it, reality doesn't come from our imaginations. It comes from its Creator. And there's only one Creator and, so, only one reality and truth... whether we ever get it or not. It can be no other way, Calvin. One Creator, one truth, and only one Way to Him. Not the many ways we try to dream up, but the Way He has provided in plain sight of the whole world. Jesus."

Ezra finished his plate and politely thanked Janet and Kendra for the meal, then disappeared into the shed. Now well past seven as mother and daughter returned to the apartment house, Calvin stood by the workbench, freshly gorged, tired in the extreme, and wanting very badly to desert the yard for his bed. Ezra re-emerged from the shed, now slinging a ladder over one shoulder, a can of paint and a brush in the opposite hand.

"What are you doing now?" Calvin's eyes glazed with dread.

"Need to do some work for Mrs. Peterson before the day runs out."

Calvin shook his head. "Man, you're hardcore."

Ezra stopped and considered his new charge. "Can you get the work bench and the wood back in the shed by yourself?"

"Yeah, I guess so."

"Why don't you knock off for the day after you get everything inside."

Calvin brightened. "No problem!"

The caretaker continued on, calling back over his shoulder as he disappeared around the corner of the house. "See you in the morning."

"Oh, man," Calvin complained out of earshot. When he had finished dragging the bench and carrying all the wood and tools back inside, he trudged heavily to his apartment. Scarcely able to stay awake though a shower, he fell face-down on his disheveled bed and descended into depths of sleep so profound that the old Zen preachers would've been impressed. He was completely oblivious to the knocking at his door around nine. His buddies concluded that he wasn't at home and continued on their way under the watchful eye of the unnoticed silhouette atop the ladder at a darkened corner of the house.

CHAPTER 13

JoAnne Bundy stood by her kitchen table, trying to engage her husband Karl in conversation as he gulped and stabbed at his breakfast. "You know how hard of a time she's been having ever since Dad died," JoAnne said. "She's having trouble collecting enough rent. Couldn't we just help her out until things get better?"

"Damn it!" Karl garbled through eggs, his bearded jowls jiggling. "I don't drag myself down to that warehouse everyday, to a job I hate, so we can throw away money on your mother!"

"It's my money too," JoAnne argued. "I work."

"Right," Karl said through mouthfuls of toast. "You're gonna pay the bills on your six-twenty an hour receptionist job."

"I take care of the boys and the house," she protested. "You don't lift a finger to help. You're either watching TV or out bowling and drinking with your friends. I'm here doing everything myself. I don't ever get any time for me!"

"If you had to go to that miserable hellhole every day, you'd have to blow off some steam too!" the balding, pudgy man complained. "You don't have any idea what I go through there. I got to unwind. You're not going to make me feel guilty about getting a little bit of enjoyment out of life. I ain't going to blow what little I got on your mom!"

"She's my mother, Karl. My mother! At least say something to the guy that owes her rent. Get him to pay or leave or something!"

"Why should I stick my neck out?" he slobbered through his cereal. "I got enough problems. I'm not the one who rented to that animal. I married you, not your mother If she wants me to take care of her, she can sign over her stuff to us and go to a home. Let the government pay for it. We'll give her an allowance and keep the rest. Supposed to be our inheritance anyway."

"I can't believe you say things like that, Karl!" JoAnne shook her head. "I don't want to take my mom's house and money away!"

"Don't bother me about it then." He slurped the last of his juice.

Slumped in a living room chair, the pale-complected Michael Bundy listened to his parents arguing in the kitchen. From vacant

114

eyes, the twelve-year-old stared at his eight-year-old brother Jonathan. His little brother was sprawled on the floor, thoroughly absorbed in drawing a picture of cowboys riding horses with his colored pencils. In time their parents' voices subsided and Michael got up from the chair and strolled toward the kitchen, stepping squarely on the center of Jonathan's drawing and twisting his tennis shoe clad foot. Having shredded his brother's careful work, he continued on his way without any acknowledgment.

Jonathan's eyes welled with familiar hurt and rage. His big brother's abuse was visited upon him daily, yet he never managed to get used to it. Just when he thought he was prepared for it, Mike would suddenly be nice to him long enough to get him to drop his guard, then hurt him once again. Now, as so many futile times before, Jonathan sprang from the floor and charged his brother in a blinded rage, screaming unintelligibly and furiously swinging his small, clenched hands.

Turning about in the archway between kitchen and living room, Michael placed an outstretched hand on the head of his charging little brother, holding him beyond the range of the awkward, angry flailing. Then he released the stiff arm and stepped aside, his enraged little brother stumbling and falling face first into the kitchen floor.

"What's going on now!" Karl Bundy yelled. "Jonathan, stop that! Stop it right now!" he ordered as the younger boy sprang at his brother again, only to be met by another maddening stiff arm and deposited backwards onto his posterior.

"I don't know what's the matter with him, Dad." Michael appeared genuinely concerned and perplexed by his brother's behavior. "He's always attacking me or blaming me for something!"

"He ripped my picture!" Jonathan blurted through angry tears.

"Oh, I did not," Michael refuted. "He ripped it himself because he didn't want me to look at it. I didn't even touch it."

"No, I didn't!" Jonathan sobbed. "He did it! He—"

"Cut it out, Jonathan!" Karl interrupted. "I don't have time for your nonsense. Go in the other room."

"But Dad! He ste—"

"I don't care! I don't want to hear it! Go on!"

Sobbing and utterly defeated, Jonathan shrank from the kitchen, once more vanquished while his older brother, as always, somehow seemed to appear innocent.

"Go get ready for school, Jonathan," his mother called after him.

In the kitchen, Michael donned a mask of gravity. "I honestly don't know why he acts like that. I didn't do a thing to him."

"Well, he probably just wants more attention from his big brother," JoAnne ventured analysis. "He's at an awkward age. He just looks up to you and wants to be like you, Michael. Maybe you should pay more attention to him."

Michael nodded with sincere affect. "Maybe I should, Mom. Maybe that's it. Oh, by the way," he added, beginning to shuffle toward the back door. "You don't have to worry about Grandma anymore, Mom. There's a new guy that moved in upstairs and he's taking care of things for her now."

"What do you mean?" JoAnne asked. "What guy?"

"I don't know," Michael shrugged. "Looks like some kind of soldier guy or something. Grandma says his name is E.J. Said he was real nice. He even made that Calvin guy be quiet and help him work out back. I saw it yesterday."

"That's just great," Karl wiped his mouth with the back of his hand. "Strangers don't just show up and help old widows out of kindness. Probably wants her money. Probably fixing to rob her blind."

"Well, we wouldn't want anyone to take Mom's money," JoAnne retorted coldly. "Maybe you should go check things out."

Karl stared back at his wife and son in momentary silence, then concluded, "If she wants to rent to strangers and criminals she can deal with it herself. I got enough headaches."

* * *

With its many small windows clean and the doors opened wide, Tuesday morning's sunlight bathed the inside of the shed. The caretaker's knock had pried Calvin from his sleep before five again.

116

He had soon been fed and compelled to the shed once more. Already, they had cleaned and polished the machine beds and blades, the caretaker insisting that Calvin learn how to properly maintain each piece of equipment in painstaking detail. They had then continued gluing and sanding where they left off the previous evening. Now after eight, Ezra decided that they could machine the panels without waking the neighbors.

They were just about to start up the planer when a mild, hesitant voice from the far end of the shed drew their attention. "Excuse me. Mr. — Mr. E.J." A lean, middle-aged woman with glasses stood just outside of the opened double doors, clutching a wicker basket. "I don't mean to— to disturb you."

"Not at all," Ezra answered as he walked toward the woman, focusing his eyes until he recognized her as one of the spectacled faces he'd seen in the window of the adjacent house the previous afternoon. "How can I help you?"

"Well— ahm, my name is Clara Christians," she introduced. "We— my husband Lloyd and our children— live next door." She nodded eastward.

"Yes," Ezra nodded, recognizing the name of the family whose house had been shot at.

"Well, we noticed you working over here and—" her voice fell to a whisper, looking past Ezra to Calvin at the back of the shed. "We just think it's so nice, what you're doing for Edna." Reaching into her basket, she pulled out a large foil tin. "I was baking bread and thought you might like some," she explained, extending the dense, fragrant loaf.

Ezra took the loaf with both hands and brought it near his face. He drew in the warm, rich aroma and his eyes filled with delight.

"It's banana bread," Clara declared.

"It sure is," he responded with conviction.

Clara brightened at his response and hastened to add that it had "walnuts and chocolate chips in it," and hoped that was "okay."

"Yes it is!" He assured.

Eased, the woman chuckled, "Good."

The caretaker looked straightly in the neighbor woman's eyes. "Thank you, Mrs. Christians."

117

"Oh, you're very welcome," she beamed. But her face fell grave once more as she drew a second loaf from her basket. With guarded voice she explained, "I made one for - him." She ventured a look past Ezra to Calvin, quickly returning her eyes to the caretaker's face.

Understanding more or less what was occurring, Calvin stood in awkward silence at the back of the shed while Ezra quietly assured, "I'll see that he gets it."

When, much relieved and smiling, the woman had departed, Ezra turned and eyed Calvin with humor. He carried the loaves to the large workbench on the south wall and placed them in a drawer protected from the sawdust. Returning to the planer, he watched the wordless expression on Calvin's face and smiled.

"Don't worry, partner. Probably just a coincidence."

CHAPTER 14

A tattered card table with folding legs occupied the place in the Guiness kitchen where the walnut table had been. Young Amanda awkwardly spooned macaroni and cheese to her mouth, her large brown eyes following her mother about the kitchen. Her uniformed father sat across the table, home on his lunch break. The noticeably pregnant Susan was wearied from a morning of chores and grocery shopping after getting Jeremy to school. She fidgeted with some pans and dishes at the sink, hesitant to speak.

"I had a couple of contractions this morning," she finally said. "They really scared me for a while, but I haven't felt anymore. Just the usual kicking. So I guess everything's okay."

Dan stared at his soup and didn't say a word.

Susan sighed and turned toward him squarely. "Dan, I went to the bank this morning to put some money in our savings. The statement says a thousand dollars was taken out on Saturday. What's that for?"

"Never mind what it's for." He didn't even look up from the table.

She tried to choose her words judiciously. "I thought we were going to save everything we could, with the baby coming."

"I needed it," he snapped.

"Can— can I ask what for?" she probed warily.

The room was silent. Dan picked at the food on his plate with his fork. "I needed it and that's the end of it."

"Does it have something to do with him, with Watt?"

Dan poked at his food some more in silence.

"Dan," her voice began to waver, "Please. Please don't... Please think about what you're..."

Without speaking another word or even looking at his wife or daughter, Dan plopped the fork down in the middle of his uneaten dinner and headed for the back door.

"Dan, Dan, Dan, please don't leave," Susan pleaded. "Don't go away mad. Please. I'm sorry. I won't say anything more."

Without any break in stride, Dan continued out of the house. He got in his patrol car and drove away.

119

Amanda's muted, large-eyed concern followed her softly weeping mother.

* * *

The workbench was in the backyard again and Calvin and Ezra concentrated on fashioning a pile of precisely dovetailed half-inch stock into drawers. Now passing six in the evening, the men had worked straight through the day again without a break longer than the moments taken to swallow a little water here, a few bites of banana bread there. Inside the shed, resting on an open area of floor near the double doors, was the assembled body of a full-sized cherry rolltop desk. It presented handsome, symmetrical raised panels all the way around its back and sides. The top of the upper section was still missing and the carcass had no drawers, organizer, or tambour yet.

Working in the yard, their attention was soon drawn to the far side. With her large wicker basket in a firm two-handed grip, Clara Christians approached, her children and husband in tow.

"Hello again," she hailed. "We brought you some supper, if it's okay."

"Sounds good," Ezra answered. He passed a happy glance over Calvin and started to clear a space at the end of the workbench.

Calvin felt the caretaker's eyes as he helped clear items away. It was becoming increasingly difficult for him to discount these things as mere happenstance. And something more. Though he was again tired, sore, and, banana bread notwithstanding, quite hungry, he nonetheless noted an unfamiliar urge to continue working, to finish the drawers they were making. He was surprised, maybe even a little unsettled, to feel such an inclination. He kept these things to himself.

Clara huffed with exertion, hefting her basket up onto the workbench. "Mr. E.J., I wanted you to meet our family. This is our son Daniel and our daughter Lydia. And this character is my husband Lloyd," she proudly pronounced.

The caretaker greeted the rest of the Christians family. Meanwhile, Calvin's eyes grew wide, watching the energetic neighbor lady unpack a seemingly bottomless basket. She set out large bowls of pea salad, strawberries and melon balls, augratin potatoes, and another heaped with the most wonderfully smelling barbecued beef cubes. Among the plates, glasses, and utensils were covered pitchers of juice and milk and, of course, plenty of banana bread.

But Clara Christians hadn't completely finished unpacking her basket when Janet and Kendra pushed out the back door of the apartment house, each carrying a box. "I didn't realize you already had supper," Janet hesitated.

Ezra motioned them over and began stacking the drawers farther down the bench to make more room.

Janet set out hamburgers with cheese and all the fixings, pasta salad, and ear corn. Kendra proudly bore her box of utensils and freshly baked brownies. "I helped make brownies," she exclaimed.

Ezra helped her box onto the workbench and momentarily placed a gnarled hand atop her head. "If you helped make them, we know they're sweet, blue eyes."

The Slater boxes were not completely unpacked when Edna Peterson emerged from the back door, carrying a covered dish and trailed by her grandson Michael, bearing a pan and more utensils. "Oh my," she chuckled. "I didn't know there were so many people out here. I saw Janet feeding your last night and thought I might offer tonight. I see you already have—"

"Looks like a picnic," Ezra said. "Wouldn't be complete without you." He now began setting drawers down on the grass to make enough room.

"This is my grandson, Michael," she introduced the vacant-eyed boy who placed her pan cake on the bench.

"Hi," Michael greeted everyone, suddenly smiling with easy charm.

The others were quick to greet the boy, but Ezra remained quiet, his eyes waxing hard behind a pleasant smile as he studied the boy. Disconcerted, Michael's charming affect wavered and he eased himself to the far side of the gathering.

Soon, the group of people were engaged in happy conversation. But Calvin stood apart from them, absorbed in thought at the far corner of the workbench. He stared in disbelief at all the food crowded onto the bench. There was scarcely room for it all. And there was this sudden gathering of people, all happily chatting around the caretaker. Calvin had treated every one of them badly in the past and, if not for this E.J., still would be. They had avoided him, hiding in their homes. The caretaker hadn't been here a week and they were all coming out from behind closed doors and flocking to him, not wanting him to leave. And they didn't want him to leave, Calvin knew, because he made them feel safe, not from some vague threat, but from Calvin. Looking up from the abundance, his eyes were caught by the caretaker's, staring at him from within the busily chatting group of neighbors. His eyes were not unkind, but solemn, as if knowing what Calvin was thinking.

"Will you say grace again, E.J." Janet's question came from within the group.

Ezra looked about at all the expectant eyes. "Sure," he agreed. He motioned Calvin over to the group and laid a firm, paternalistic hand to the back of their nemesis' neck.

"Dear Lord, our Maker, Keeper, and Redeemer," he began, prompting everyone to lower their crowns. "You've said that there is none good but One. So while we share good food and good will, may we see Your hand in all of it. May You grow genuine gratitude in our hearts. We claim the right to ask these things of You by Jesus' name. Amen."

Several soft "amens" followed the caretaker's and the happy bustle of conversation and food being dished up soon ensued.

Clara gave the entire gathering occasion for pause, when she turned her attention to Calvin with a surprisingly maternal tone. "Calvin, you sit over here and I'll fix you a plate." She pointed to the empty picnic table near the workbench.

Calvin felt them watching, awaiting his reaction. "Yes ma'am," was his faint replay. He looked away and took a seat at the table.

While the others returned to their food and conversation, Clara dutifully brought Calvin a plate heaped with too much of everything. "I'll get you some milk and some napkins," she said, energetically returning to the workbench.

"Thank you," Calvin heard himself respond in near whisper.

His heart weighed full. A surge of hotness burned beneath his eyes. He didn't know why he should suddenly feel so on the verge of crying. But as he tried awkwardly to chew a small mouthful, he just knew that he felt desperately like breaking down. He fought hard, though, to resist this flood of feeling. He surely did not want to make a fool of himself. He thought Mrs. Christians might have caught his watery-eyed glance when she returned with milk and napkins. But if she did, she was kind not to say anything in front of the others. She gave his shoulder a passing, matronly squeeze and left him alone at the table.

As the conversation continued on, Ezra noted that the hollow-eyed boy had slipped away. A few minutes later he saw the boy coming around from behind the shed. When Michael's eyes met Ezra's, he quickly looked away. Bidding his grandmother a hasty "goodnight," he soon vanished.

In time, the gathering began to wind down and everyone started to pack up dishes and copious leftovers. Janet eyed the caretaker inquisitively, still thinking of the previous evening's discussion. "You know when you were talking about different religions last night and you said something about the first people?"

"Yes," Ezra answered.

"Do you really believe there was a real Adam and Eve?"

"I do," Ezra confirmed.

Janet was skeptical. "What about all the evolution they showed us in school?"

"I don't believe it," Ezra shrugged.

"Lloyd reads about that subject a lot," Clara spoke up. "Don't you?"

"Mmmm," the pleasant spectacled neighbor man agreed. "Evolution theory troubled me for a good part of my life, until I finally started to read seriously on the subject and give it some honest thought. You know, there's even a lot of folks within the scientific community that have a hard time keeping their faith in evolution. A Sir Fred Hoyle points out that the odds of even one information polymer, such as a simple DNA molecule, arising by chance from a random soup are roughly the same as filling our entire solar system, shoulder to shoulder, with blind men randomly shuffling Rubiks cubes and all, by pure chance, solving the puzzle at precisely the same moment in time. But it seems a lot of folks still find this explanation of our beginning easier to accept than that of living things coming from a living Creator. I suppose a dead creator, no matter how improbable, can't hold us accountable. So that's what people like to imagine."

Mr. Christians pointed north and east. "That Dahmer fellow over in Wisconsin— the one who killed all the people— he gave an interesting interview on the television when he was still alive. He said that he'd always thought about killing and such from the time he was a youngster. But it wasn't until he came to believe in evolution as a young man, that he decided it'd be okay to go ahead and carry out his thoughts. Since he believed we all just came from slime and returned to it again, he didn't figure there were any lasting consequences to one's actions and he could do as he pleased. It seems to me that a lot of folks probably try to use evolution in a similar way to give themselves license to do whatever's been in their mind from an early age. Anyway, it was interesting to see Dahmer having second thoughts about his faith in a dead creator after his evil had caught up with him.

"A lot of scientists in the field of genetics have been abandoning evolution as they learn more about the true nature of genes. You know, an organism's genes are like computer programs, each with a certain amount of information on it, a fixed number of rungs on a spiraled DNA ladder. As you would expect, a simpler organism has shorter, simpler DNA with less information while a more complex animal has longer, more complex, DNA molecules with more information. Evolutionists have always preached that when animals change some of their characteristics over time, like Darwin's birds adapting to different environments, that they are becoming more complex organisms, that the bits of information in their genetic programming, the rungs on their DNA ladders, are increasing in number and complexity. But what scientists actually observe is that when a gene mutates, one or more bits of its programming change their orientation, but the total amount of information, the number of rungs in the ladder, remains the same. It does not increase or decrease. So there is no way for a simpler organism to become more complex over time, but only to adapt to changing environments. No matter how many times a bacteria mutates to resist antibiotics, the number of links in its DNA chain remains the same even as they switch back and forth, adapting to changing conditions. It will always remain a bacteria, no more and no less complex than when it started. For thousands of years people have selectively bred animals for different purposes and conditions, but they all remain the same species that they started as. And Darwin's finches remain finches. Given a gazillion years, this is not going to change. Personally, I don't believe it's a coincidence that the Bible says all living things were created distinct kinds, or species, if you will."

"What about all the fossils?" Janet queried. "Don't they prove evolution?"

"I used to wonder the same thing,"Mr. Christians agreed. "But the more I've read about it and the more I've thought about it critically, the more the fossil evidence has led me to a very different conclusion. You know, all of the fossils that have been found are of distinctly different species without any of the thousands of intermediate forms that would be necessary if one species was to evolve into another.

"And when we just look at the plain evidence around us, we see that when animals and plants die, they don't naturally become fossils. They become dust. They are eaten by others, they decompose and so forth. Even if buried deep in the ground, aerobic and anaerobic microbes reduce these bodies to dirt. On the ocean floors, bottom feeders process all of the ocean creatures as they die and fall to the bottom. They don't become fossils either. Yet zillions of fossils are found the world over. And virtually all of them are found in a layer of sedimentary rock. That's the kind of rock formed out of sediments under the great pressures of very deep water. And this had to happen quickly enough that the normal process of decay could not take place. This is not explained by the long eons of time that evolution describes. It is, however, consistent with the world wide flood that the Bible describes.

"The Bible describes a world before the flood that did not have oceans, but small seas, lakes, and streams circulating water from 'fountains of the deep,' as they were called— great underground reservoirs of water. And it describes a great barrier of water vapor above the atmosphere, 'waters above the heavens,' they were called. It says that when the flood happened, those underground reservoirs flooded out onto the earth, perhaps driven by geothermal energy, and that the waters above the heavens, the great vapor barrier, fell down to the earth. With the cavernous reservoirs at least partially emptied and the nearly unimaginable amount of water weight then on top of them, they must have collapsed, forming the floors of our present day oceans. The Bible says that all the water receded from the higher land into these new ocean basins over the next year, carving much of the landscape we see today.

"But before the water receded into the ocean, all the sediments from the earth's surface that were roiled up in the flood, settled back out in layers just as sediment in a jar of water does, with the heavier particles settling first and the finest, lightest particles last, forming layers of sedimentary rock under the weight of the water, just as we find them today. Settling out of water at the same time as the sediments were all of the organisms and animals, with the smaller, relatively denser organisms and shelled creatures settling out first in the lower layers of sediment and the more buoyant, larger animals, such as reptiles and mammals, settling out in successive layers.

"An evolutionist can interpret these layers of sediment with different types of fossilized creatures as eons of time and evolution of species, but it is, by no means, the most plausible explanation of the evidences.

"In the end it comes down to faith. Even the most rational scientist can't escape faith. We all establish our view of the world on underlying first principles that cannot be proven and must be held by faith. Evolutionary religion holds as a first principle that everything becomes more highly organized and complex over time even though the world around us, from decaying matter to a dissipating cosmos, gives evidence of a disorganizing principle at work. Evolution holds by faith that organized, conscious, living things have come from a disorganized, unconscious, dead source... that all has come from nothing. Others believe the Bible when it says that organized, conscious, living things have come from an organized, conscious, living Creator. Which belief seems absurd to you?" Mr. Christians asked Janet.

Janet hesitated. "When you put it that way, I'm not so sure."

Gradually, the people receded from the yard, bidding the caretaker— and Calvin— a good evening.

Once again, Ezra had Calvin put their woodworking away in the shed for the evening, even as he retrieved the ladder and tools from the shed and set about working on Mrs. Peterson's property.

CHAPTER 15

Wednesday unfolded much as the previous day. Ezra drew Calvin from his bed well before dawn for another day of steadfast labor. By four in the afternoon, the desk had all of its drawers installed. Above rested a labyrinthine organizer and to one side, the partially constructed tambour. At the workbench on the south wall, Calvin stood, eating a hunk of banana bread, and carefully watching Ezra draw on a plain white piece of paper as he explained exacting details of the desk's tambour. For the past three days, Ezra had taken pause at every new process to sketch what they were doing on paper, adding precise dimensions and explanations, and storing all of the papers in an old blue folder left behind by Ben Peterson. What amounted to a nearly complete set of technical drawings for a rolltop desk now occupied the folder, every dimension, angle, and arc flowing fluidly from the caretaker's head to the paper before Calvin's eyes.

When Ezra had finished his explanation, the men turned to continue their work and noticed the watchful presence of Mrs. Peterson's grandson, holding a schoolbook and standing well outside the shed doors.

"Hi, Michael," Ezra greeted.

The boy abruptly assumed an easy smile. "Hi."

"Come on in," the caretaker invited. "I think I found a couple of your things when I was cleaning."

Calvin watched Ezra walk back to the far drawer while the Bundy boy tentatively entered the shed at the double doors. Returning, Ezra held out a toy cap gun and a roll of caps.

"These yours?"

"Yeah," Michael affirmed demurely. "Thanks."

"Sure," Ezra replied, apparently unmoved by the boy's charm. His other hand moved subtly into view at the side of his leg, holding a roll of tape and a box of matches.

The boy's easy smile flickered. "That— that's not mine."

"Didn't say that it was." The caretaker watched the boy from a stone face. "Since you mention it, though, it does occur to me that you could have used these to play with the cat."

As if suddenly seized, Michael's smile vanished into a reddening face and shallowed breath.

Seeing the boy's reaction, Calvin's eyes whirled swiftly to the caretaker. "Whoa! What'd the kid do?"

"I didn't— I don't— wha— what cat?" Michael stammered. "What are you talking about?"

"Found a dead cat hidden out in the weeds behind the shed here," Ezra explained to Calvin as if the boy weren't even there. "Taped up and tortured with burns. Suffocated."

"Whoa!" Calvin looked incredulously at Michael.

"I didn't do it!" Michael insisted. "It must've been somebody else!" He eyed Calvin. "It could've been him."

"Why you little—"

Ezra interrupted Calvin's words with a cautionary glance. He considered the boy's accusation, then shook his head. "I doubt it. Calvin's old enough that if he acted out those kinds of things, it'd be people who suffer. No, I reckon doing such things to animals comes from a younger mind... still rehearsing for people."

"It wasn't me!" Michael squeaked on the verge of tears.

The caretaker studied the panicked young face. "Maybe I'm mistaken," he finally shrugged. He picked up a piece of the tambour and joined Calvin in sanding. "Too bad, though." He continued to stare at his work. "It'd be good for a fellow like that to be exposed to the light of day before he does something worse and destroys his whole life."

The sounds of sanding prevailed for a time while Michael stood inside the doors, calming and regaining some of his facade, not sure whether to leave or to stay and continue protesting his innocence. Then, still focused on his work, Ezra added, "I knew a boy once. A boy who had those same kind of urges and went down the same sort of road. He was real clever at hiding his darkness, though, and no one found him out until it was too damn late."

Ezra worked on and Calvin, looking at the caretaker and the boy and sensing this was a time to hold his tongue, worked on without comment. For his part, Michael now stood waiting for the caretaker to continue and, when he didn't, a rising curiosity laid hold of the boy. "What happened to him, to the boy you knew?"

"Michael," Ezra chose another tambour piece to sand, "The boy I knew came out of infancy and into his first memories knowing already that he was messed up. His thoughts, his desires— they weren't right. They were all bad. Real bad. But you know how it is, even though he knew his urges were wrong, he wouldn't turn away from them. He enjoyed them, you see, these fantasies of his. Like nothing else."

Michael was now listening intensely and Calvin was more going through the motions than accomplishing real sanding as he awaited Ezra's words.

"Some believe that everyone is born with bad desires," Ezra continued. "I guess most are able to keep these things pretty much to themselves or else make excuses or try to make whatever it is socially acceptable. They say something like, 'Since I was born with this urge or that urge, pursuing it should be accepted as a valid lifestyle.' But you see, Michael, this particular boy knew already at a surprisingly early age that he would never be able to contain his urges as mere fantasies and that the things he was driven toward would never be mistaken as socially acceptable. He was aroused by the notion of hurting others, you see. He dreamt almost continually of stalking, of capturing, of dominating and inflicting pain, motivated by a sense of revenge for some perceived wrong, by an innate love of violence, and most of all by a drive to possess and control all the people and things around him that he saw as desirable and beautiful. But, whatever his reasons, whatever his fantasy, it all came down to his wish to be the center of everything around him, to violate and to destroy those around him in some endless effort to be the center and purpose... a god. Sounds terribly absurd out here in the open. But evil always looks pretty asinine out in the light. That's why it spends so much time hiding.

"You understand, Michael, there was a part of this boy that not only knew his thoughts were wrong, but was scared of them, even sickened by them sometimes. Part of him didn't want to be the way he was, wanted to be normal like others seemed to be. But he just could not make the thoughts stop. Growing up, people saw him as normal and bright. A nice boy. But, day and night, he struggled inside with these thoughts, always careful to hide this constant tension behind some cleverly formed disguise of normalcy. If a childhood friend caught a glimpse through a momentary crack in his mask here or there, they never really understood what they were looking at. He didn't know why he was this way. He just was. He would try to convince himself that it was just a passing phase, that he'd grow out of it and be normal. Deep down, though, I think he knew that it wasn't going to go away. Then he'd tell himself it was all just harmless daydreaming. Wasn't hurting anyone. Wasn't guilty of anything. He was free to think whatever he wanted in the privacy of his own mind, he told himself. Still, if he was so innocent, he wondered why he was always so careful to hide himself from everyone. I mean parents, friends— everyone. Why was he so damned terrified of being found out?

"And even while he was still thinking all of these things at a young age, he was already beginning to practice his urges on animals. He'd choose the wild, hard-to-catch ones, the ones that would provide the most thrilling challenge. He devised ingenious ways to lure them, to make them feel at ease and then make his capture. He would restrain them and keep them from making too much noise. He'd inflict pain on them in any way he could imagine and watch the writhing and struggling with great fascination. Much like the one who hurt this cat must have. Over and over and over he'd strangle or suffocate these animals just to the edge of death only to revive them and do it again. Only when the thrill of his little rehearsals passed over its apex did he either kill the animals or just as often, since they couldn't tell on him, simply let them go. After all, such animals, now highly motivated by fear, would make an even more challenging hunt the next time."

As Calvin listened to Ezra and watched Michael, he grew increasingly unsettled. The kid didn't seem terribly surprised by what he was hearing, as if the man's words bore familiarity with him. And this E.J.— well, it just seemed to Calvin that he knew an awful lot about the inner thoughts of this "boy he once knew." But Calvin held quiet and continued to listen.

"You know, Michael, this boy never did get caught in his childhood. His secrets stayed hidden. So he grew a little older, a little bigger, and the animal play just didn't cut it anymore. As he'd

131

always known he would from the age of three or four, he began to hunt people. At first he just watched from a distance, hidden by shadows and anonymity, carefully observing... planning. Several times, despite that part of him that struggled against it, he chose a target and followed his plan to the brink of attack, turning back only at the very last moment— his adrenaline quietly dissipating, his intended prey often smiling politely back at him, never realizing what so nearly happened. And then one day, when he wasn't so much older than you are right now, Michael, when most still took him as a nice kid, he came up to that brink once more. But this time he did not turn back. He jumped off the edge of his fantasy world and landed squarely in reality, capturing and taking someone away, hurting this person very, very badly. And since a person can tell a fellow's secrets, he killed his victim. He murdered."

Michael and Calvin both swallowed hard. With unflinching eyes, Ezra stared into the boy's face. "You want to know something, Michael?"

"What?" The boy's weakened voice was scarcely audible.

"All the promises of those fantasies turned out to be lies," Ezra answered. "The dreams had promised awesome pleasure and power if he would only hurt people. But when finally he did their bidding, he didn't find any pleasure. Only ugliness and dread. Instead of the long dreamed of feelings of control and power, he found himself losing control. But even so, the urges came back, stronger than ever and promising that the next time would be different. The fulfillment of all his dreams was just beyond the next conquest. So he attacked more people. He caused unrepairable damage to entire families and communities and still no satisfaction came. All the while, an awful fear was wrapping its fingers around him. A sickening dread that the powerful dreams and urges that had controlled his whole childhood, his whole life, were just empty lies... and that his evil deeds were now hunting him and would not be escaped." Ezra sighed and chose another piece of tambour to sand.

"Did he get caught?" Michael asked.

Ezra looked at the boy, examining his face. "Of course he did, Mike. Hidden things are always revealed sooner or later. Darkness is always overpowered by light. It never wins. Lies and evil secrets are like empty, vacuumed spaces surrounded by truth, like air, on all sides. The truth watches and waits and surrounds, never going away for even a moment. It presses inward relentlessly. And whether it seeps in gradually or breaks in suddenly, the lie is always destroyed. The carefully hidden secret is always discovered and overwhelmed by the simple truth. The boy was found out and caught like one of his own prey, though treated much better, I must say. He was exposed to everyone for what he was. Can you imagine, Michael? All those inner secrets he was so terrified of being discovered were laid bare before everyone, his charming disguises and clever words rendered useless." The caretaker fell silent once more, working his wood.

But Michael would have none of it now and he pressed the caretaker closely for more information. "What did they do to him? Did they punish him?"

"What do you think?" the caretaker responded.

Michael stared at Ezra as if he felt sick. "But that's the way he was born," Michael argued. "He doesn't— he didn't know why he's like that. He can't help it. It's like you said, he wants to stop, but he can't. How can they blame him?" He spoke most earnestly, Michael did, his eyes filled with great concern.

Ezra wiped a suddenly weary hand slowly over his face. "Well, it sounds very good, doesn't it? Almost sympathetic, really." His hand dropped back to his work. "But then, the boy wasn't split into two people, was he? He was just one. It's not as if half of him wanted to think and do evil while the other half didn't. It's more like his whole will went eagerly down that monstrous path while the winces of fear and conscience tried in vain to counsel some kind of restraint or compromise. But the will, eager to get on with its evil, argued that it couldn't help it, that it was just born this way and the conscience should stop nagging and let things be as they were. It was only after the climax of the thought or the deed, after the damage was already done, that his heart would sink low for a time before growing hard once more. And even in those fleeting moments of remorse his dark heart strongly resisted any rash notions like exposing itself in the light of confession, preferring to hang on quietly while the sorrow passed and the hardness returned." Ezra looked straightly at Michael once more. "The boy didn't really want to stop, even if he told himself he did. He knew he should. Had those fleeting moments when he thought he just might. But if he had really wanted to stop with all his will, he would have. The very thing he needed to resist evil— his will— was the very thing so infected and taken with evil from the beginning. He wanted to, willed to, think and do those dark things And in those rare moments when he didn't, he had no strength of will to break free. So he was guilty, Michael. And they rightly blamed him and punished him."

Michael gazed back at the caretaker with the sickened concern coloring his pallor. Surprisingly nigh to tears, he asked, "So the boy couldn't ever change?"

It seemed to Calvin that the caretaker now began to soften toward Michael. Perhaps even, to be quietly moved.

"He had no strength to change himself, Michael," Ezra answered. "Not even the desire. Like most folks, he was driven by the shape of the particular thoughts born into his head. And as you know, the shape of his natural born drives wasn't the sort that could be overlooked or excused away. Most believe that people are what they are and they don't change." Ezra paused, carefully considering his next words, "But there are some who believe that the One who made us is alive and that He can change anyone, if He's of a mind to, that He can free a person's very will from even the strongest grip of evil and cause even those things which were once craved the most passionately to become ugly, shameful, and despised. He can even cleanse the evils already done by the hearts and the hands of these fortunate souls through His Redeemer."

"You mean Jesus?" Michael asked.

"You've heard of Him, ay?"

"Yeah, sure," the boy affirmed.

"I guess most of the people who've ever lived have heard of Him, either before He came or after." Ezra lowered his voice and leaned in close. "You know, Mike, there are those who believe that if God decides to change a person and save them from their darkness, that person can't even stop Him from doing it, that the Maker of all things has power over all things, even a will that loves evil. I guess that's the only way it's going to happen. People sure don't seem to be able to change their hearts on their own, do they?"

Michael shook his head somberly.

"The way I see it, Mike, if God has seen fit to arrange things so the person who destroyed that cat has a chance to hear about the boy who used to do similar things... well, just maybe God intends to send a message to that person. Maybe He's even fixing to wake that person up from his dreams and drag him into the light, to rescue him from his own evil-loving will before he goes further and does more harm. Wouldn't that be something, Michael?"

The boy nodded.

"And if this person were to discover a genuine desire growing down inside of himself that wished very much for these things to happen to him, for all that old struggle and darkness to be taken out of him, and replaced with something honest and good, if, from the most secret place in his heart, he were to confess these things to his Maker and ask to be changed— well, I do not believe that our God will turn His back on such a request. When it's all said and done, I believe it will be shown that even that first sprouting desire for change found growing inside was put there by our good Maker, planted and protected every step of the way. That's the way I see it, Michael. If you should happen to come across the person who tortured the cat, would you tell him about the boy I once knew? He might need to hear it."

Michael gazed at the caretaker's face with wide, sorrowful eyes and nodded slowly.

"Well then, you probably should be on your way now," Ezra suggested.

The boy nodded again and turned to leave, but then turned back once more. "The boy you knew?" Michael asked gravely. "Did God change him?"

Ezra escorted the boy through the doors. "Some say yes. Some say no. But only he and God know for sure."

Calvin stood, dumbfounded, watching the boy leave. Ezra returned to work without further comment. At length, Calvin picked up a piece of the tambour and continued sanding, even as he shook his head in quiet disbelief. "Damn, man." Could it actually be that

E.J. was really able to know that the boy had done these things? And why did E.J. know so much about this stuff anyway? Calvin was sure of one thing, "Don't ask."

CHAPTER 16

Exhausted and sulking, Janet lay on her couch Wednesday evening. Her day had been long and frustrating. Having taken Monday and Tuesday off from work to deal with her car and to have some time for herself after her aunt's funeral and the bus trip, she had gone to the office early this morning at Bolan and Meyer Architectural. Besides Monday and Tuesday, she had been gone most of the previous week as well without notice. So she had worked hectically all day at her office manager post, frazzled and frayed, trying to catch up, only to have several of the architects and their staff hassle her about dwindling supplies. To top it off, her boss, Mr. Meyer— the Meyer in Bolan and Meyer— had called her into his office in front of everyone to "talk." He chided her for falling behind and for missing so many days. He made an act of seeming concerned for her.

She had tried to explain to him all the pressures she had in her life. She pointed out that he didn't know what it was like to raise a child alone. Still he had warned her to get caught up with her work and not to let things fall so far behind again, that they had important projects and deadlines and couldn't afford to be out of supplies.

So she had been forced to find somebody to watch Kendra on a moment's notice so she could work late. Her latest sitter refused to keep the child after five-thirty and several others said they couldn't on such short notice. She wasn't about to ask Robert. She'd have quit her job first. In desperation, she had asked Mrs. Peterson, who had agreed to watch Kendra with surprising eagerness. Now home at last, Janet didn't even want to think about tomorrow. Still trying to catch up, she would have to work late again. She wanted to sleep for a month.

"Mom." Kendra's voice startled Janet just as she was drifting off. The girl stood at the couch holding a stack of children's books. "Mom, I still have to read my books to you so you can sign my reading sheet for Mrs. Daller."

"Oh, Kendy. I'm so tired. Let's do it tomorrow night."

"But, Mom," Kendy argued, "You said that last night. You

137

said we'd do it tonight. I have to give my sheet to Mrs. Daller on Friday, Mom."

Janet reached wearily from the couch. "Here, just give me your sheet and I'll sign it for you."

"No!" Kendra protested, stepping out of reach. "I have to read them to you! I'm not supposed to cheat!"

"Kendy!" Janet's voice rose in exasperation. "Just— just. We'll do it tomorrow. I promise, okay?"

Perturbed, Kendra took her books to her school bag near the front door. "I wish Dad was here," she muttered. "He would let me read to him."

Janet sat up on the couch, rubbing her eyes. "How many times do I have to tell you, Kendy? Your dad isn't coming back. He doesn't want to read books with you. He doesn't even want to pay your child support."

Janet watched the girl's face sink. "It's not your fault, sweetheart. I told you before, your dad and I just don't get along anymore. We don't love each other anymore. Sometimes people just stop loving each other."

The girl eyed her mother with heavy concern. "What if you stop loving me, Mom? Where will I go if you divorce me like Dad did?"

"No, sweetheart. Come on, it's not like that. Your dad didn't divorce you. Just me and him got divorced from each other. It doesn't involve you. I mean... I'm not going to stop loving you, ever. Love is just different between grownups, see? It's not the same thing."

The girl's wide blue eyes searched her mother's face. "Why?"

Janet stared into her daughter's trusting face. "It's just different, Kendy. It's grownup stuff." She looked away. "You wouldn't understand. Life if just more complicated when you grow up."

"But, Mom," Kendra's voice lowered with gravity, "I say my prayers every night," she tried to reassure her mother, revealing this guarded secret. "Really, Mom. It's like E.J. said, Mom, that God hears inside me. And when we were at Grandma Perry's house last week, she said that if I ask for good things, Jesus will answer my prayers. She really said that, Mom. She did. And I asked Jesus to make you and Dad so you're not mad anymore and then you won't be divorced anymore and—"

"Kendy."

"And— and that's a good thing to ask for, isn't it?"

"Kendra."

"And, uhm— uhm." The teary-eyed girl interrupted, stammered and stalled, not wanting to hear her mother's words. "Uhm— uhm, isn't that a good thing to ask for, Mom?"

"Kendy, I'm sorry," Janet broke in softly. "But this is real life, not one of your grandma's fairy tales. I don't want to be with your dad anymore. He doesn't treat me the way I deserve to be treated and he's not going to change— even if you pray. Men like him don't change. They can't. I'm so sorry to disappoint you, sweetie, but he's not coming back. He doesn't want us and I don't want him. You have to learn to accept that."

A tear sliding mutely down her freckled cheek, Kendra turned away and quietly retreated to her room.

Janet put her weary face in her hands and sighed, "Great. That's just what I needed. Thanks a lot, God. The perfect end to my day."

* * *

Kendra sat on the bed in her darkened room, the covers draped over her head to form a tent-like space of privacy. "You're not a fairy tale," she whispered with steadfast determination. "You're real. I know You are. I saw E.J. talk to You. You can make my mom and dad love each other. I know You can!..."

* * *

Around the side of Jillian's Bar and Grill, the sound of two pairs of shoes scraping along the gravel, echoed across the darkened parking lot. Dulled by his regimen of beer and greasy food, Bobby Slate shuffled along toward his green Charger at the far end of the lot, followed by Lizzy, close at his side and sillied by the drinks he'd bought for her.

"So what'd you have in mind, Bobby, asking me to go for a spin?" she giddily asked as Slater unlocked the driver's door.

"I don't know. Thought maybe we could go back to my place. I can show you my new house or something."

"Oh yeah?" Lizzy gnawed at her gum. "Whatchya gonna show me, Bobby?" she brushed by him provocatively, getting into the car.

Bobby slid down into the driver's seat behind her and closed the door.

"It took you long enough to take me home," Lizzy cooed through her intoxicated smile. "I was beginning to think you didn't like me or something."

"I like you fine, Lizzy," Bobby assured. He put the key in the ignition and turned it. Nothing happened. Frowning, he tried again. Still nothing. Not a sound.

"What's the matter?" Lizzy began to giggle. "Can't get it started up?"

"Must be an electrical problem," he said, all but ignoring the woman. "I'll take a look under the hood."

"Take a look under my hood, Bobby," the well-endowed woman mimicked his serious tone, briefly flashing her shirt up, then laughing uproariously.

Bobby acknowledged Lizzy with a half-smile as he got out of the car. He circled around the open driver's door to the front of the car and raised the sparkling, metallic green hood.

From within the car, Lizzy continued to tease with drunken boisterousness. "Come on, Bobby! Start me up!" But Lizzy's eye caught movement in the shadows at the edge of the lot and as she watched a stout figure emerge from the darkness and stroll toward the front of the Charger, her face began to sober. An unsettling prickle scurried up her spine as the stranger's hard eyes passed over her before he disappeared behind the raised hood.

"Problem?" the man asked Bobby.

"Huh?!" Bobby jerked up with a start. "Oh— I'm not sure. Won't start."

"Hard to believe," the man said. "Looks like a well cared for machine."

Bobby smiled proudly. "Like it? Built it myself from the frame up."

"Must've taken a lot of time."

"It sure did," Bobby agreed, jiggling the battery cables. "I'm going to give it another try."

When he got back in the car, Bobby tried the ignition again, but still nothing. "Damn," he complained. "I don't understand it."

"Who's that guy?" Lizzy whispered.

"I don't know. Just trying to help, I guess."

"Well, he gives me the creeps," she declared. "I'm going back inside. Come get me when you're ready to go." She slid out the driver's door behind Bobby and strode briskly across the lot, glancing back nervously at the stranger several times before rounding the corner of the building.

"Wife?" the stranger asked when Bobby returned to the front of the car.

"No," Bobby laughed. "Just a good time, if you know what I mean." He looked into the man's face expecting a reciprocal smile, but discerned no change of expression. Bobby turned and began fumbling with the engine's wiring, this time in a more systematic fashion, and he ventured to change the subject. "Yeah, this car's my baby. Probably got more than three thousand hours into her."

"That's a good piece of your life," the man quietly observed. "A lot of men don't put that much into their families."

Bobby looked back sharply, then nervously chuckled, "Yeah, I suppose. Car's a lot less aggravation, though. And it won't get tired of you and throw you away."

"They're similar, in a way, a car and a family," the man said. "If you don't take care of them, they'll fall apart."

"I suppose you're right about that," Bobby agreed.

"I don't guess there's too much in the world that won't fall to pieces without a caretaker." There was an earnest edge to the stranger's voice. "A home, a family, a community— they all need good caretakers. I once read that the word 'husband' even means 'caretaker.'"

141

"Huh," Bobby huffed from under the hood as he fidgeted with the distributor wires. "A man can't take care of his family if the woman won't respect him, you know? He doesn't have any control."

The man considered Bobby's words. "I think if a man turns away from his own desires and serves the needs of his family without worrying anymore about himself, his wife and children will be more of a mind to respect and follow him. The man who dreams of being a king in his home with his family as servants, the sort that demands and threatens, will probably lose the very respect and authority he makes such noise about. No, I don't think that true authority comes from the selfish use of strength. I think it grows out of devotion and self-sacrifice. Out of love."

"So you're saying a man has to be a servant to get respect and be the head of his house?" Bobby was skeptical.

"A caretaker," the man nodded. "A husband."

Bobby shook his head, returning to the engine. "That doesn't make sense. Besides, even if a man and his ex don't get along any more, that don't mean he doesn't love his kid. He'd still give his life for his kid."

"Give his life," he man repeated Bobby's words aloud. "You mean jump in front of truck or take a bullet or something similarly epic that isn't likely to ever happen?"

"Well— yeah," Bobby was hesitant.

"As opposed to the mundane and mostly unnoticed ways to give one's life. Not just dying for someone, but living for them." There was definitely a heartfelt edge to the stranger's words. "If a man says he'll give his life for someone, then he should stop waiting for some fantasy scenario and get on with doing what he says he'll do. If he spends the few hours he's got left on earth devoted to a child, a wife, or anyone else who needs him, that's when he's giving his life. Not when he hoards those hours, indulging desires he can never satisfy anyway, while he boasts of going out in some moment of glory."

Bobby gazed back critically from under the hood. "If a man works all day, he shouldn't have to feel guilty about having something for himself and getting a little enjoyment out of life."

"If a man feels guilty, why shouldn't he?" the stranger countered. "If he has done as his heart knows he ought, I don't reckon anyone can make him feel guilty. If he hasn't, I don't guess anyone can keep him from it. How does a man get any enjoyment out of life, if he knows he hasn't done as he ought, if he's left duties undone, words unkept? A lot of folks spend up all the time they'll ever have, chasing after enjoyment and never catching up to it. I once read that we only find true enjoyment in being caretakers anyway, that no matter how much selfishness promises happiness, it never does deliver. People are designed by their Maker to be servants and we can't ever find real contentment until we forget about trying to satisfy ourselves. I even read that whoever tries to hoard his life ends up losing it and that whoever gives his life away in service to his Maker finds it returned to him. Something happens inside a person, sometimes, and they can't even stop it. Everything that had always seemed so important and promised so much pleasure, all of a sudden, loses its luster and becomes ugly, even while the obligations that had seemed so heavy and confining suddenly become the very thing desired."

"You read all that, huh?" Bobby said. "Where'd you read stuff like that?"

"The Bible."

"Oh." There was an awkward silence. Bobby jiggled some wires. "No offense, Mister, but I don't really know you. You're not going to try and 'save' me or something?"

"No, that sort of thing's between a man and his Maker, I reckon."

"Yeah," Bobby mumbled.

The stranger was quiet for a time, watching Bobby work. "Wouldn't it be something to see, though? A man's heart turned inside out. His whole view of the world dumped upside down. It'd be a miracle."

"I guess it would be," Bobby shrugged. "Guess it would."

"Why don't you give the car another try," the stranger suggested.

"Haven't found anything wrong with it, yet."

"Maybe it was just a loose connection," the man encouraged.

"Give it a try."

"All right," Bobby relented. He walked around and plopped in the driver's seat. When he turned the key, the engine growled to life instantly.

"Hey!" Bobby exclaimed. "You were right," he shouted over the engine as he got back out to close the hood. "Must have been a loose…"

The stranger was gone. Bobby looked in every direction, but the man had vanished. Finally shrugging, Bobby closed the hood and turned toward Jillian's where Lizzy was waiting. He took a step or two in that direction, then another. He hesitated as if suddenly unsure what he wanted. His freckled face scrunched with a wave of apathy and he turned back toward his car. In another minute, the sparkling green Charger had slipped from the parking lot and Bobby went home alone.

* * *

Books were strewn all over the Bundy's family room floor near the bookcase. From the relative safety of the next room, young Jonathan curiously watched his clearly agitated older brother Michael frantically rifling though the books looking for… Jonathan knew not what. Evidently not finding what he was looking for, Michael tossed some of the books back on the shelves with haphazard results and moved on quickly to the nearby end table. Rummaging through its contents he soon complained under his breath, "Aw, dang it!" He looked about, seeming to gauge where he might search next. As he scanned, he caught the eyes of his little brother watching him.

Bracing, Jonathan blinked at his big brother's stare. Michael paused a long moment considering his young brother's face. He saw the familiar apprehension— the dread. This should have brought him glee. He much delighted in provoking fear. But fingers of shame seemed to lay hold of him now. Fear, even. For a fleeting moment, he thought he caught a glimpse of himself through his brother's eyes. The words of his grandmother's caretaker swarmed in his head— the boy who enjoyed hurting others…. He shook his head, trying to clear it. Even if his heart repulsed him, how could it be changed? How long would this wish for a change even last before the familiar tide of darkness rose up again?

Jonathan tensed as Michael approached, his eyes filling with the memories of abuse, even while his jaw set with an ever-defiant resolve to stand his ground and gain his brother's respect. But Michael walked right past Jonathan, not venturing the slightest insult. And, it seemed to Jonathan, that there was an odd sort of sorrow in his brother's face.

Jonathan flinched. A trick it must be! But no blow came from behind and, as he turned around, he saw Michael already heading up the stairs. With much curiosity, yet ever-so-cautiously, Jonathan eased up the steps. He heard more rummaging noises from down the hall. Very carefully, he ventured a look around the corner from the stairs and glimpsed the back of Michael sticking out the door of the closet at the far end of the hallway.

"Ah ha!" Michael finally exclaimed from the closet. Backing out, he neglected to even close the closet door as he hurriedly turned and headed down the hallway with the stiff, black vinyl bound book in hand. He rushed past his little brother, still crouched at the top of the steps, and disappeared into his room at the other end of the hallway, accompanied by his new found Bible, the door slamming shut behind him.

CHAPTER 17

Fine dust swirled and mingled with the afternoon sunlight streaming into the shed. Calvin and Ezra were absorbed in carefully sanding all the parts of the desk before finishing and final assembly. With ever finer grits of sandpaper and several time-honored techniques, like raising out the rough fibers with a damp rag, Ezra taught Calvin how to render wood exceedingly smooth. With a steady, wordless pace, the men worked on.

The faint, rhythmic sanding sounds drifted out into the back yard. At the picnic table, Kendra sat snugly next to Mrs. Peterson, the elder woman's arm draped comfortingly around the girl. Exercising much concentration, the girl read aloud from one of her books.

"…and Booboo the kitten was not sad any mo— more. She li— lived hap— happy and saf— safe with her family ever aft— after." Kendra gazed up eagerly into the landlady's eyes.

Edna's face beamed brightly from beneath her reading spectacles. "That's right dear. That's very good," she chuckled warmly, squeezing the little one's shoulder. "You read very well."

"Hmm, yeah." A relieved smile on her face, the girl basked in the woman's attention, but her brow waxed concerned again and apology filled her voice. "I still have to read three more."

Mrs. Peterson just chuckled all the more warmly. "Well good, sweetheart. That will be fun."

"Hmm, yeah."

* * *

The sprawling Carr Industries warehouse enclosed nearly an acre on the western edge of Haverston, serving the sundry and varied manufacturing interests of Carr Industries. At the back of the facility, in the manager's office, Karl Bundy sat at a leisurely incline in the chair behind his desk. His old pal and coworker Al Lemley leaned back in his chair as well, his feet resting atop the desk. Lemley flipped another page of his magazine— a "skin rag" as he called them— and held up the picture of another contorted,

146

clothesless young woman for Karl to see. "Get a look at that, huh?"

"Mmhmm," Karl smiled approvingly. "I'd like to have some of that."

"Looks better than the old lady, heh?" Al chuckled.

"Hell," Karl complained. "The old lady don't want to do anything anymore, except nag me about her mother."

"I hear you, buddy. Been there. Best thing I ever did was unload that bag of mine and her whining, better-than-thou parents. Don't know why you keep putting up with it, Karl."

"Well, the boys are still kind of young, you know. And she'd probably take everything I got."

"Heck, there are ways to hide your stuff," Lemley assured with a wink. "Besides, poor but free is better. You know what I mean? As far as kids go— Kevin and Julie were younger than yours when I cut loose from Carmen and they've done fine. It ain't a big deal to them. Most their friends' parents are split, too. Heck, Julie's going to graduate from State college this year summa... cumma something or other. She's doing just fine. Kind of snobby like her mother, though."

"How about Kevin?" Karl asked. "Ain't heard how he's doing in a while."

"Aw, he's getting along all right. Shacked up with another cute little thing over in Omaha now. The last one's harassing him about child support and stuff, but the contractor he works for pays him in cash so she can't get at it, heh heh."

While the two men chuckled together, Dale Johnson, one of the newer employees at the warehouse, walked in the office with his time card. "Mr. Bundy, my wife's sick today, so I stopped home to check on her after my last delivery. It's about a half-hour. I wrote it on my card for your signature, so I don't get paid."

Bundy and Lemley looked at one another, humor gleaming from their eyes.

"Who the hell cares if you went home for a little while?" Karl said.

"I don't want to cheat anybody," Johnson contended.

"Listen boy," Karl chuckled. "Lewis Carr's got three factories and half the real estate in the county. He's a stinking billionaire. He isn't going to miss a half-hour of your miserable pay. Lighten up."

The two elder men smiled knowingly. But Johnson remained steadfast. "If it's all the same to you, I'd like you to sign off on my card. Don't want what isn't mine."

Al and Karl's smiles dimmed. "Fine with me," Karl shrugged, accepting the card and initialing it. "It's your paycheck."

When Johnson had left the office, the two men shook their head with disdain, their faces lapsing into masks of weary, world-wise experience. "The guy's way too honest for his own good. Must think he'll get a damn reward or something."

"You know, you have to watch a guy like that," Lemley lowered his voice. "First chance he gets he'll try to make you look bad in front of the boss. I seen his kind before. Always busting butt even when everyone else is laying back."

"Yeah, I know what you mean."

"Ayhey!" Al exclaimed, flipping to a new page in the magazine. He held up the picture of the naked girl in the convoluted pose. "Huh? How about that?!"

"Oh, baby!" Karl groaned. "I'd like to do her!"

The men laughed together.

The telephone on Bundy's desk rang a half dozen times while the men continued to look at the magazine. Karl finally sighed with obvious irritation and gruffly picked up the phone, bringing the receiver to his fat, bearded jowls, "Yeah, what."

"Oh, hello Mr. Carr. How can I help you, sir?" Karl rolled his eyes contemptuously as he listened to his employer on the phone. "Ah, one moment, sir. I'll check the manifest." He fingered through the manifest of shipping orders on his desk. "Ah, yes sir. Here it is— twelve-thirty-four. Yes, it was delivered here last week and was supposed to go out to the plant like you say. One of my people must've dropped the ball. We've been real swamped lately, heh heh." Karl listened again while Carr spoke. "Yes sir. I'll see if I can't free somebody up to get that over to the plant right away. I'll take care of it for you personally, sir. ASAP. Yes, sir. Goodbye."

Bundy drew back the corner of his mouth derisively as he hung up the phone. "The jerk won't give us anything but cost of living

148

raises and wants us to jump and sweat over every little order."

"I hear you, buddy," Al agreed. "Need something delivered?"

"Oh, supposedly the production line at the implement plant is held up, waiting for that shipment of wheel bearings we got in last week. Order twelve-thirty-four."

"I guess I could load them up and take them over." Lemley got up from his chair.

"Yeah, all right," Karl agreed. "You take them over. But get Johnson to load them up for you. He wants to kiss butt so bad, he can lug those heavy dogs."

The two men laughed as ones full of wisdom.

"I tell you, Al, I sure wish I'd hit that lottery so I could get out of his hellhole. This place is killing me."

"You and me both," Lemley concurred, shuffling slowly from his office. "You and me both."

Bundy's face quietly glazed over as he returned his eyes to the girl in the magazine atop his desk. But after a few moments, he was aware of someone at the door watching him. Looking up with a start he recognized his son Michael staring at him. Awkwardly, he slid the shipping manifest over the magazine.

"Michael, what are you doing here? Don't you have school or something?"

"It's after four, Dad. School's out."

"Oh— well, what's up?" Karl asked. "You get in trouble at school again?"

"No, Dad. I just came out to talk to you about— about a problem I have."

"Problem? What problem?" Karl's brow furrowed. "Come in here. What's going on?"

Michael paused an awkwardly long time, stepping into the office. "Do you ever have bad thoughts and— and urges, Dad? Really bad ones?"

"Wha— what the hell are you talking about? What thoughts? What urges?"

"I mean to do really bad things to people," Michael elaborated. "To use them for... to do terrible things to people just because it seems like it would feel good."

149

"For goodness sakes! Of course not! Never!"

"Never?" Michael pressed.

"No," his father insisted, sliding the shipping manifest, with the magazine beneath, into his desk drawer. "What is this all about, Mike? Why are you asking such crazy questions?"

"Dad," Michael hesitated gravely as if about to lunge off a great cliff, tears welling in his hollow eyes. "I gotta tell you something. Something I can't keep to myself anymore."

Karl Bundy's face began to lose its pretense. His eyes filled with worry. "Close the door, Michael."

* * *

Bobby Slater sat at the bar in Jillian's, his regular evening beer and brat remaining untouched in front of him. He kept trying to eat, but just couldn't seem to do it. It wasn't that he wasn't hungry. He'd worked all day and his stomach was growling for its routine to be satisfied. And he wasn't sick either. Yet he just couldn't muster the will to eat or drink for some reason. Several times he tried to take his glass in hand, but his hand remained on the rail. He didn't know what was happening to him. Everything seemed... strange.

At a table full of men behind him, Lizzy was telling her vulgar jokes and laughing with unusual uproar. She wouldn't look at him, much less talk to him, yet it seemed she was determined that he notice her as she laughed, then whispered to others about him. Apparently, she wasn't happy about being left behind the previous night. As he considered it, though, her chill wasn't really what was bothering him. It wasn't as though he'd hoped to have a meaningful relationship with Lizzy. She was clearly bent on being a public commodity.

No, it wasn't Lizzy that had hold of him and he didn't guess it was his buddies either. They sat on either side of him, Ronnie and Jake, carrying on at the top of their smoke-filled lungs as was the custom. Bobby's ears were numb from the noise. From time to time, an elbow would poke his ribs and someone would yell some alcohol-soaked, spittle-splattered words in his face, then laugh raucously. He wasn't even comprehending them anymore. Just senseless garble. It didn't really matter. Same old noise. He just smiled and nodded blind agreement.

Bobby lifted his eyes to the huge television screen behind the tender. Another game from somewhere. The players taunted one another, puffing and prancing about, flashing eyes of violence. To the delight of the raging, bulge-eyed crowd, each strove not for the victory of his team so much as self-attention bought with the utter destruction and humiliation of an opponent. Bobby turned his face away.

The impassioned strains of a song from the juke box on the far wall made their way through the unintelligible noise to his ears. With ever-rising waves of gut-wrenching emotion, the singer declared the purity and timelessness of his love for another. A love that would never forsake. Bobby called to mind the piece he'd just read about that same singer in one of those celebrity magazines— how he was getting married for the fourth time and, after extensive therapy, had finally come to realize how his parents and previous spouses and lovers had all victimized him and damaged his "self-concept" through their insensitive and oppressive shortcomings. Bobby tuned him out.

Staring blankly through his beer, he listened to the voices that filled Jillian's, swirling and reverberating about his head. The voices complained bitterly about everything. The voices lied. They were filled with envy and venom. They boasted. They threatened. Each droned on, enamored with itself, never really hearing another. And the laughter. For all his time and participation here, Bobby had never before just stopped and really listened to the laughter. Dry cackling, furious and forced, devoid of any genuineness or heart, desperately striving to drown out the same uselessness that he, too, felt.

Uselessness! That was it. That's what was eating at him. Pointless and useless. All of these things that surrounded him. All of these things that he continuously strove for, that seemed so damned important. All this shameless greedy groping to appease hungers that were never going to be appeased. He started from his trance and looked closely at the things and the people around him.

151

This was what he wanted? This? What had that man in the parking lot said to him about a man trying to satisfy himself, about the real point of life being usefulness? Who was that guy? Bobby had inwardly scoffed at what that stranger said, and yet, didn't he suddenly feel the near-panicked impulse to flee from all of this and from the pointless appetites that had lured him here?

He looked around the room again. He listened carefully once more. Then, though his words were drowned in the sea of revelry and heard by no one, he spoke them aloud, nonetheless. "What the hell am I doing here?!"

Bobby Slater stepped down from his perch at the bar and, turning his back on everything there, headed for the door with a sure stride.

"Hey, Bobby! Where you going, man? — Bobby! Where the hell you going?"

He didn't look back. There was not even the suggestion of a waver in that sure stride as he exited the door.

"Aw, man, he's been acting weird lately. Who knows what's got into him?..."

CHAPTER 18

Friday had begun very early, as usual, for Calvin and Ezra. The first hour of this morning had been devoted to cleaning the shed from top to bottom, even vacuuming the rafters and mopping the floor. Ezra explained that the shop would have to be very clean when they put finish on their work or dust particles would mar the end result. The shop needed a regular cleaning anyway and finishing day provided the opportune time.

When the cleaning was finished, they applied a clear sealer to all the parts of the desk, then sanded the surface of the sealer with a very fine paper and wiped all the parts clean again with tack cloths. Thereafter, coat after meticulous coat of clear finish was applied to the unstained cherry wood.

By midmorning the finish had dried and the two men sat on the shed floor attaching the top to the pedestals and installing the drawers. Suddenly, the sound of an approaching angry voice came from out in the backyard. "Where the hell is he?! Is he in there?!"

"Karl, wait a minute," Edna Peterson's voice strained from a point more distant. "I'm sure there must be some misunderstanding. Karl. Be caref—"

"Which one of you is the piece of sh— called E.J.?!" Bundy's voice boomed in the double doored entrance. When the eyes of the heaving, red-faced man were able to focus on the two forms rising from the floor, he knew already that he'd greatly overstepped his capabilities, but his anger kept him from retreat.

Flashing jealous for the caretaker's honor, Calvin lunged forward, halted only by Ezra's hastily extended arm. "Who are you calling sh—?" Calvin snarled.

Lurching backward, Bundy swallowed hard, his lungs searching for an elusive breath. But Ezra held back the wild-eyed young man while out in the sunlight, Edna Peterson watched with trepidation.

"Stop it," Ezra commanded Calvin, his voice calmly insistent.

"But you heard what he said!"

"It doesn't matter. Get back."

Calvin relented and backed several feet into the shed, his menacing stare riveted on Bundy.

153

"I'm E.J.," Ezra said to Karl Bundy.

Bundy mustered renewed courage from Ezra's restraint and, jutting his jaw, pointed a quivering finger and bellowed, "I want to know what you did to my boy Michael! If I have to get the cops down here to find out, I will!"

"What's the problem with Michael?"

"You tell me!" Bundy heaved. "He was just fine, never had a problem until he talked to you! Now all the sudden, he thinks there's something wrong with him! Thinks he's got evil inside him, that he's going to do all kinds of terrible things unless he gets 'changed.' All because he killed some damn cat!"

Calvin broke his stare from Bundy and looked at Ezra. "Man, you were right. The kid did do it."

"Mr. Bundy," Ezra addressed the man with unruffled clarity, "I did suggest to Michael that he might be the one who tortured and killed the cat I found out back but he denied it and I didn't press him further. I merely told him about a boy I once knew who did such things, the sort of thinking that caused it, and where it all led him. Now as I see it, if Michael recognized something of himself in my words, your contention really isn't with my words so much as your boy's conscience."

Bundy's breathing was labored. His dry, wavering voice crackled. "All I know is my boy never had any problems. He was just fine until he met you. Now he wants to spill his guts about all kinds of twisted nonsense. Stuff that should be kept to himself! Stuff I damn sure don't need to be hearing about! Now... Now his mother's got it in her head that she's got to take him to a shrink! I have enough troubles! I don't need this sh—."

Ezra looked the man straightly in the eyes. "I'm sorry for any increase to your load, Mister. But like I said, I only told Michael about somebody I once knew. I can't search a heart or rattle a conscience. Somebody else does that."

"Yeah, whatever." Bundy barked. "You just stay away from my boy! I don't want you talking to him anymore!"

"Okay," Ezra replied.

"I mean it!" Bundy postured. "I'm serious!"

"I believe you."

"You better," Karl Bundy warned as he backed from the shed. "I'll have the cops down here so fast it'll make your head spin!" He turned and stalked away, muttering derisively at his mother-in-law as he passed her. "Michael won't be coming over here again. Not as long as you have creeps like that living here."

Edna watched her son-in-law storm away. When he was out of sight, she turned back and hesitantly approached the shed doorway. Her troubled eyes lifted to Ezra's face. "You found a dead cat?"

"Yes."

"I had a beautiful orange tabby with a white nose and four white paws. I haven't seen her for several weeks. Was— was that the one you...?"

"Yes."

"Oh... my." The troubled woman turned and went away.

As Ezra turned back into the shed, Calvin's eyes followed him. "How come you let that guy talk to you like that? You could have trashed him easy, man."

The caretaker retrieved a couple of small boxes and a handful of soft rags from a drawer. "I don't want to trash anyone, partner."

"You did me," Calvin contended.

"My friend," Ezra returned to the desk with a happy twinkle in his eye, "I believe you mostly did that to yourself."

Rubbing the bridge of his nose, Calvin finally smirked sheepishly, "I guess so."

One of the small boxes that Ezra placed on the desktop read "pumice," the other "buffing compound." Calvin watched the caretaker's face quizzically. He saw that glint of mischief in the caretaker's eyes again as he was handed one of the soft rags.

"You familiar with the term 'elbow grease,' Calvin?"

* * *

In her favorite sweatshirt and tattered jeans, her feet liberated from the confines of shoes, Janet lay on the couch staring blankly at the television. She was finally caught up at the office and had been able to get home at a decent hour. She didn't have to think about Bolan and Meyers again until Monday. On the floor nearby,

Kendra labored with crayons and paper, forming another image of the world for which she still harbored hope. The television show was contrived and predictable. Janet's eyes wandered on the ceiling and she sighed resignedly. "Whoopie," she thought to herself. "Another exciting Friday night." Soon, a gentle knock at the door interrupted her boredom and brought Kendra to her feet.

"I can get it, Mom," the girl assured, heading for the door.

"All right," Janet agreed, though she still got up and followed. Before she had rounded the corner to the entry, she heard the door open and Kendra's shrill excitement. "Daddy!"

"Hey there, Kendy," came her father's soothing voice. "How's my girl?"

"Good!" she assured with much enthusiasm.

When she did round the corner, Janet saw Bobby kneeling in the doorway hugging their daughter. He stood again and placed a gentle hand atop the whirling head. Father and daughter both gazed back at Janet with identical pairs of bright blue eyes. "Hi Jan," he greeted.

"Robert."

Bobby had nearly forgotten the uniquely formal manner in which Janet always spoke his name. It had always seemed to grate at him when they were married. Funny, he couldn't remember why now. It kind of made him feel warm, even if she wasn't happy to see him.

"What are you smirking about?" she snapped.

"Aw, nothing," he smiled. "Would it be okay if I visit Kendy for a little while?"

"Yeah!" Kendy agreed.

Janet answered with deliberate ice in her voice, "If you really cared about her, you'd pay her support," she braced for his familiar anger.

The entryway fell silent. Bobby absorbed her words. "You're right," he finally said and retrieved a check from his jacket pocket, extending it to her.

"You know you're supposed to make your payments through the agency, Robert. You can't just give it to me. They have to record it. It's not my responsibility to tell them."

"I know, Jan. I know," Bobby eased. "I made up all the payments with the agency. You should get a check from them next week."

Janet looked down at the four figures in her hand with suspicion. "What's this for, then?"

"Just call it a late penalty or something," he shrugged. "I'm just... Jan, I'm sorry I played games about it."

She examined the check again and then thrust it back at him. "I'm doing fine by myself, Robert. I don't need your help."

"You're doing real good," he agreed, their eyes connecting. "I know you don't need the money. But I really don't need it either. I'd just blow it on nothing. You know me. We can put it toward Kendy's college or something." He rubbed the girl's back. "It's all right, Jan. There aren't any strings."

Kendra carefully watched her mother and father staring at one another. Janet was put off balance by her ex-husband's demeanor. He seemed different than she knew him to be. So still. He was always restless. She knew he had to be up to something. She knew him too well. Always trying to control. Always wanting to manipulate things to be his own way. And always, always, getting angry when he didn't get his way. So she fashioned another volley calculated to set him off and expose his game. "This doesn't mean anything," she chided, stuffing the check in her jeans. "You can't just come over here. We have a life of our own now, and it doesn't include you." She braced herself once more for an angry tirade.

But it didn't come and, a little sad, Bobby quietly agreed. "I know. Maybe Kendy and I could visit out on the steps for a little bit. Or I— I could come back when it's better for you."

Janet was confounded by his calm and influenced by her daughter's pleading stare. "No," she finally relented, her tone softening. "You can come in for a little while."

"Yes!" Kendy pumped a little fist into the air and, taking one of her breaths of anticipation, bolted from the doorway. "I'm going to get my pictures for you, Daddy!"

Janet and Bobby were left studying one another in the entry. "You better not hurt her feelings," Janet warned.

"I know."

"Well, come in, then." She stepped back from the entry and Bobby obliged, closing the door behind. He went into the living room and she headed for the kitchen. "I think I have some beer in the back of the fridge."

"No thanks, Jan."

Janet's head popped back out from the kitchen. "You don't want a beer?" she clarified with disbelief.

"Na."

"Huh," she mumbled, turning back into the kitchen. "What's got into you?"

"What?" Bobby asked.

"Nothing."

For a long time, Janet aimlessly shuffled and clattered dishes about the sink— dishes she'd already washed— while she listened to their daughter's joyful banter with her father in the next room. In time, she abandoned her pretense and peeked into the living room. Sitting on her dad's lap, Kendra was cozied into his arm while her little fingers tenaciously gripped his. His head bowed down to meet hers, they chatted happily over her drawings like two old pals.

"These sure are good, buddy," Bobby complimented. "You're a real good drawer."

"Yeah," the girl basked in her father's attention. "E.J. said I'm an artist."

"E.J." Bobby repeated.

"Yeah. He lives over there," she pointed. "He was on the bus. He made Calvin stop bothering everybody. He ate supper with us. I showed him my pictures, too."

"I see." Bobby's voice grew soft.

Janet took the opportunity to emerge from the kitchen. "He's the new caretaker for Mrs. Peterson. He's a really good man." She emphasized the word good. "He's taking care of everything around here." She measured Bobby's quiet stare. "Been real good to me and Kendy, too. He and Kendy get along really well together."

Bobby slowly nodded acknowledgment of his ex-wife's words. He lowered his head back to Kendra's even as the girl tightened her grip on his fingers.

158

The words still resonated flatly in her own ears and Janet regretted them already. "He— he's just a friend." She clarified.

Now Bobby and Kendra both raised their faces and watched her from quiet blue stares. It seemed to Janet that she was always finding herself at the awkward end of such curious stares. "I mean, you know, just an acquaintance. We're not seeing each other or anything like that."

Bobby nodded again and he and Kendra returned to one another's attention. Janet stood awkwardly silent in the living room for only another moment before pangs of self-consciousness sent her retreating back into the kitchen. And after a few more minutes with Kendra, Bobby came to the kitchen doorway.

"I'm going to take off, Jan. Thanks for letting me see Kendy. I know I should have asked before I came over. I told Kendy I would ask you if I could come by tomorrow and spend longer."

As he spoke, Janet stood up quickly from her seat at the table and turned her back to him. He could see that she was wiping her eyes with the heels of her hands the way she always did when she cried. "Won't that interfere with your weekend?" she sniffed. "I know how you need to be with your friends."

"To tell you the truth, they don't seem like all that much fun lately." He paused and the kitchen was very quiet, but for the buzz of a clock and the sounds of Janet's quiet sniffles. "Jan, you all right? I didn't mean to upset you. I'm sorry."

She turned around, trying to hold her reddened eyes widely open. "No, you didn't... I'm fine." Tears began to well again in her eyes. "What's going on, Robert? Why are you being so nice?" she pleaded. "Did something bad happen?"

"Nothing happened, Jan. Nothing bad. Everything's fine. I just... I just sort of caught a look at myself. Didn't like what I saw. Feel like I want to do better... where I can."

Her eyes closely followed his face watching for the old masks of insincerity.

"Anyway," he finally added, "thanks for letting me see Kendy."

"Okay," she sighed unevenly.

"Can I come by tomorrow?"

159

"I guess so." She wiped an eye with the heel of her hand again.

"Thanks." He paused again, watching her. For a moment he leaned in subtly, as if he wanted to come to her and... In the end, he made an awkward waving gesture and turned for the door.

"Night, Jan."

CHAPTER 19

There was a strong suggestion of fall chill in the Saturday morning air, bright blue and cloudless. Near bursting with eagerness, Calvin led Evy Walton across the parking lot of Walton's Furniture. With the determined, side to side gait of an elderly woman with bad hips, Mrs. Walton kept pace with Calvin while Ezra strolled a leisurely distance behind. Well east of Haverston on route twenty-six, Walton's was a large furniture concern started long ago by Evy and her late husband Ansel when they parted from their West Virginia kin and moved to the Midwest in '46 after the war. With Ansel gone fifteen years now, Evy still ran the business with her sons and their families every day of the week— "excepting the Sabbath." Catering to a mid and upscale clientele and widely renowned for their quality and integrity, Walton's consistently drew patrons from as far as two hundred miles.

"You're really going to like this," Calvin predicted with confidence as they approached his pickup. "I know you are."

"Well, now I told you fellas we hardly ever deal with local folk for inventory," the weathered, tight-jawed woman warned. "But I'll have a gander at what you got."

Opening the tailgate, Calvin bounded up into the pickup's bed and carefully removed the heavy furniture blankets that shrouded their work. The sharp morning light gleamed and flashed off the deep, richly mirrored surface of the cherry wood. Subtle oranges, reds, pinks, and even hints of emerald— the wood's natural colors, its fine character, and flaming grain patterns shimmered and danced in the old furniture woman's eyes. Not so often these days, but now and again, she'd come across a piece that seemed to touch someplace distant in her Appalachian memory. A place where, as a girl, she had watched her elders take the time and the effort to infuse the work of their hands with the plain love in their hearts.

"Oh," Evy Walton's face jerked up to Calvin's, then over to Ezra standing several feet distant, as if she was suddenly seeing them in a completely new light. "I didn't realize... Well, that's— that's right beautiful!"

161

Standing in his ragged jeans and tee-shirt, Calvin nearly leapt out of the pickup box with pride when he saw the furniture woman's reaction. Making mock circular motions in the air with his aching arms, he grinned widely and explained. "Elbow grease."

"I reckon so," she readily agreed. "I reckon so." She looked over again at Ezra, whom she judged to be in charge, but he appeared content to stand off and watch. Calvin gathered back her attention and proceeded to introduce each of the desk's attributes. He slid the tambour open, smooth as glass, to reveal the exquisite writing surface and the intricate details of the organizer. He pulled out one of the organizer's small drawers to show her the meticulously perfect finger joints and painted porcelain knobs. He demonstrated the beautiful dovetailed pedestal drawers gliding on ball-bearing slides. He called her attention to ornate, pull-out writing boards, to the stately raised panels, and the flawless custom moldings that wrapped the base and each of the surfaces.

"It's a fine, fine piece," Evy Walton affirmed. "How much you asking?"

Calvin was immediately stumped by the woman's query and both of them turned to Ezra who seemed to ponder the matter before speaking.

"I hear of similar pieces going for four and better over in the cities," he observed.

"True enough," the tough old woman allowed. "But we ain't in the cities and I don't pay retail." Her eyes narrowed. "I'll give you two."

The caretaker considered the offer, then nodded in Calvin's direction. "The youngster dropped a good bit of sweat on the venture. We'd like to see three."

The furniture woman scrunched her face shrewdly and considered the desk once more and then Calvin. "I'll give you fellas twenty-six, not a penny more."

Ezra smiled. "That'll do."

"Good," she said. "You can drive around back to the loading dock. I'll send my boys out to get it and I'll bring your check. Who do I make it out to?"

Ezra stared off into the morning sky. "Calvin Miller

Woodworks," he answered.

Standing behind the pickup, closing the tailgate, Calvin's stunned face spun around at the caretaker's words.

"Spelled like it sounds?" Mrs. Walton verified with Ezra.

"That's right."

"All right, then." She bustled away. "I'll see you fellas out back."

Ezra made his way to the pickup's passenger door even as Calvin remained at the tailgate in confused silence.

"You coming?"

Calvin came around to the driver's door. Finally, when he had gotten in and pulled his door shut, he hesitantly clarified, "Is that— is that twenty six hundred dollars?"

"Yes."

"To me?"

Ezra nodded.

"But, that's your... Why are you..." Calvin turned his face from the caretaker and stared down at the steering wheel. His heart was full, pushing into his throat, and his eyes grew hot. For yet another time this week, he found himself struggling to hold onto his hardened facade.

"You'll need to start a business account at the bank," Ezra noted. "Learn to keep proper records and such. Pay your taxes... so forth."

Calvin nodded slowly.

"I'll help you figure it out," Ezra added.

Calvin just nodded some more.

"You'll be paying Mrs. Peterson what you owe her."

More nodding.

"You'll have to buy more supplies this afternoon for your next project," Ezra continued. "And you'll need to keep back two sixty or better for church tomorrow."

"Church?" Calvin finally spoke.

"Church," the caretaker affirmed. Ezra gazed out the windshield at the people in the parking lot. He drew in a deep, satisfying breath, resting his folded hands atop his head. "You going to sit here all day or you going to go sell your desk?"

163

CHAPTER 20

For a consecutive Saturday, Reverend Otto Hartmann sat at his study desk talking with Ezra on his old rotary telephone. "Ya, ya, Ezra. It is good that you have been given such work to do, people to serve. You see, Ezra, how God continues to provide beyond measurement? Work hard, Ezra! With grateful heart and honest hands, work hard! Do not be slothful nor filled with arrogance."

The old man took in Ezra's respectful words and then spoke again. "Ya, good. Now, Ezra, I must tell you our Maker has used the occasion of your liberty to trouble many hearts here in Wovoka County. You must realize this, I'm sure. Some are set with fear and others with outrage. There may even be some who are seeking you. I have been told rumor that the brother of Amanda Guiness, who is a deputy sheriff, searches for you with malice in his heart. I tell you these things, Ezra, that you hear them not from another. We know you can do nothing to repair the wounds you have wrought or appease the souls you have tormented. Only, it is left for you to work, humbly and diligently, unto death. You must never forget your Creator's boundless mercy as you work and you must never give up the hope that His reconciling nature follows through the wake of your former destructions even now, restoring that which you never can. What else can you do, Ezra? You must do these things. And you must avoid trouble, Ezra!" The old German-colored voice strained with earnestness. "You are my son in Christ and I love you, Ezra, but I well know the violence that dwelt in you from your conception. And I know too well how that place of stone educated you to deal with threatening things. But you have a different Teacher at work in you now and you must never rest from heeding His good voice, from ignoring and resisting all other voices of temptation unto death. You must reason and act with the love of Christ in all things. There can be no exceptions. You have no excuse for less, Ezra. You must never forget. You must never rest from this course. We will rest together, my son, when our labors are finished and we have been borne safely across the gulf."

With gladness of heart, the old minister again received his charge's unwavering word that he would walk with Jesus to the grave, no matter what came. "Good, Ezra. Good. Now, my son, I will say goodbye, that we may both resume our work. God be with you, Ezra."

When he had hung up the phone, Reverend Hartmann permitted his mind to drift back again, to those first years he had trekked to Kalbourne. He remembered discerning the arrogance, hatred, and fear masked behind appeasing smiles and contrite, patronizing words. The old preacher remembered thinking things could not be worse, that Ezra could not be farther from his Maker, only to witness the light in his eyes, corrupt though it was, subside altogether, even as he grew so much stronger and more violent. There came a time when the minister could no longer detect anything at all in the eyes obliged to accept his visits and sit across from him. No love, no anger, no fear... no hope. Just a chilling, disconnected emptiness that esteemed nothing but its own space and silence, that, as Kalbourne infirmary reports bore witness, would shatter the bones of anyone who transgressed either.

Still, Reverend Hartmann never considered abandoning his charge. Quietly, faithfully, he and a great many of their congregation never ceased in their prayers for the son of the late Noah and Ida Watt. Not the prayers of the faint-hearted or the vainly repetitious, these were the prayers of souls suffused with the hardy confidence of Christ before their Maker. And without fail, no matter how pointless it may have seemed, the preacher made the trip to Kalbourne every three months. With simple words of righteousness imbued with fearless love, he tried to reach, to trip up, to in any way affect that apparent emptiness. Always, he reminded himself that it was God that decided who was beyond hope, not him. Whether eventually to reveal the breadth of His mercy upon the undeserved or the multiplication of His wrath upon the impenitent, God continued to preserve Ezra for His own reason. From his first youthful realizations of his own inborn corruptness, the preacher had, all his life, placed great hope in his Savior's assurance that what was impossible for men to fathom, much less overcome, was still possible for God to accomplish.

The old preacher sighed long and slow. A faint smile graced his face. Lately, he noticed the world around him growing more vague.

Sounds from quite near seemed as if coming from afar. He felt less and less a part of the scenes his eyes beheld, of the substance his hands touched, with each passing day. Though he would continue so long as he was given strength, he suspected the stepping off point wasn't so far ahead. Surely the Lord's couriers were nearing. Staring distantly beyond the study's window, the faint smile grew warm.

There came a time. There came a time! Praise God, there came a time not so many years ago— and God had privileged him to see it— when eyes so long dead, were inexplicably found alive, meeting his own full of warmth and void of pretense. A time when hands long given to destruction had clasped his own with a gentle strength, genuinely grateful for the occasion. To this day he did not know what precisely had taken place within those concealing prison walls. But he had no doubt who was responsible.

* * *

Its fixtures freshly cleaned and bulbs replaced, the downstairs hallway of the apartment house was now brightly lit. Midway down the hall, Ezra was busy patching and smoothing the scratched, gouged, and generally abused walls with drywall compound in advance of new paint. While his trowel skimmed over the wall's surface, his thoughts skimmed over his earlier phone call with Reverend Hartmann. The old man had made mention of his early days in prison, of his "education," and his thoughts drifted back to those first days in Kalbourne.

Though his mask had been as cold and threatening as he could make it, he'd entered Kalbourne very much afraid. In childhood, to fill in the spaces between his darker fantasies, he had imagined himself formidable and fearless. Reality had been decidedly less impressive, however. In plain truth, he'd bullied some smaller, mostly younger kids on occasion. But when faced with peers his own size, he'd shrunk from confrontation on more than one occasion. In the adolescent hierarchy of Jasper Mills he'd been rightly regarded as insignificant. And though his crimes had forever altered people's perceptions of him, though he'd hoped the sheer violence of his deeds would afford him some measure of respect among the inmates as he entered Kalbourne a skinny seventeen-year-old, the fact remained that his deeds were those of a miserable coward bolstered by a gun against trusting and unprepared souls. So the cowardice had remained in his heart, hidden behind layers of desperate facade, of course.

Courage is so often a fleeting thing to begin with, a thing difficult to grasp, much less hold onto. Who knows how it is that in the instant of conflict, at the moment of truth, the mind of the greater should suddenly wax confused or the heart of another, long bold, should unexpectedly fail him and still another, long lacking in courage, should inexplicably rise up with a boldness that his nature and circumstance does not predict. It is as if such currents ebbed and flowed from another's will.

Well, Ezra soon learned that Kalbourne had facades of its own. Fostered by a society trying to scare would-be criminals and by the inmates and staff themselves, trying to gain status by association with a mean place, Ezra soon observed that many of the tales told of the place were embellished, exaggerated, or downright fabricated. Oh, there was violence, sure enough, in Kalbourne. The majority of it visited by the larger upon the smaller, the sneaky upon the unaware, the group upon the singled out. In other words, Ezra found the place brimming with scores of predatory bullies like himself. Most were completely absorbed in the effort to hide a lacking heart behind cold, violent-eyed masks, behind incessant vulgar and threatening banter, behind menacing postures, fierce symbols indelibly inked or carved into the skin, strange hair, dark shades that concealed the eyes from directness— behind anything loud, shocking, confusing or distracting. Apparently, anything was preferable to facing the world simply as one was.

Now there was another sort of inmate. Not as many, mind you. A quiet sort that harbored little interest in the games of posturing and woofing. Plain looking men. Some were old-timers, tired of the rat race. Others were ordinary working folks before whatever brought them to Kalbourne. Carpenters, steel workers, farmers, and the like. These mainly preferred to spend their days working in the prison's industrial shops and maintenance facilities. Most often keeping to themselves, they rarely seemed to mingle with the others in more than an incidental way. And the others, idly lounging about the prison all day, pursuing their games of drugs, chance, and perversion, were, for all their bluster and fury, generally careful to give these simple men a cautiously wide berth.

Something began to happen to Ezra after he entered Kalbourne and not even he knew what it was. Why should he suddenly see through so much of the absurdity and pointlessness that seemed to completely enthrall many of the others? There was a time when he was thus entranced. Why not now? Words long memorized from his upbringing kept creeping into his thoughts, though he shook them off each time. Why would one new inmate be set upon and quickly devoured by the others while another would go unnoticed with the time and opportunity to grow strong? What was it that always seemed to be culling him away from the others, most often against his will, to a different course? And just what was it that could so tangle one heart in confusion and suddenly raise another up from nothingness?

Well, in time, as most did sooner or later, Ezra had found himself in a concrete alley between two buildings one day— a "blind spot" as they called the places where the guard towers could not see— facing an older, larger version of his predatory self while dozens more stood about watching the show through their narrow-eyed masks of feigned experience. As the first blows landed on his head and ribs, he had cowered behind pathetically raised arms and fell to the ground. But... something foreign happened in the midst of that blur. Something picked Ezra back up off the pavement and planted him, bloodied, scraped, and bruised, on his feet. In the space of an eerie second that seemed an hour, it had occurred to him he had nowhere to run, no one was going to come and help him, that, though he heard the echo of each blow in his skull, he didn't feel any pain, that none of it mattered anymore and that he all at once really didn't care what happened to himself— save only that he was through cowering. His fear left him, at least for that space of time, and walking through his attacker's punches without so much as a blink, he found himself in the most strange, adrenaline charged, yet oddly quiet place where each moment held long stretches of time. Perhaps by some martial skills practiced throughout an insecure youth, but really just raw animal viciousness, he'd found himself suddenly twisting side to side with stupendous violence, his hands, elbows, and knees tasting the sweet satisfaction of impact. His head butting, thumbs gouging, fingers tearing... he'd heard an odd, guttural laughter, but had not immediately recognized it as his own. His foe, reduced to his hands and knees, had garbled a scream, "Get 'im off me!" through a shattered jaw and was promptly answered by the smack of Ezra's state issued boot heel against his skull, spreading fine crimson mist across the pavement.

The trickle of his wounds still running down his face and spots of white light wafting about his periphery, Ezra had stood over his convulsing adversary that day and stared hard into the faces round about. Eyes that had been mean and haughty moments earlier darted to the ground, unnerved and unable to confront his own. He'd seen only one exception in the alley, one face that did not yield. Carrying a load of lumber over his shoulder from one building to another, old man Holbert, stolid butched gray head and detached gray eyes, glanced casually at the aftermath and squarely into Ezra's face. Without any detectable reaction, or even a glitch in stride, he had continued about his work. Ezra had left the alley without a word. The same crowd that had taunted derisively as he entered the blind spot now parted in wary silence. He'd never been certain what brought him back to his feet that day, what canceled his fears and overwhelmed his foe. It had never seemed of his own doing. Why should such a thing occur in him and not the others?

Several days later he had wandered down to the exercise yard at the far corner of the prison. There were many furiously animated inmates lifting weights there, growling, boasting, and raging with every effort. But, on concrete slabs along the back wall, he'd also seen several of the simple men lifting too. Their bearings decidedly more disciplined, their words few, they got their exercise only after a full day's work and, yet, without all the bluster, they were clearly reckoning much more weight than the screaming jackals. And when they had finished, they retired to their cells without fanfare. As Ezra had strolled by the last slab along the wall, lost in a daydream, he had heard a low voice behind him. "Did you find the void?"

He turned and met the vacant, gray-eyed stare of old man Holbert, studying him even as he chalked up a bar in the squat rack... a bar with three one hundred pound plates and some change on each end. Like every new man to Kalbourne, Ezra had heard the dire warnings, carefully whispered, concerning Holbert. They said that thirty years earlier, as a young farmer, he'd come in from the field early one afternoon and, finding his wife and neighbor together in bed, had there and then ceased to care for anything. They said that he'd beat both of them to death with such savagery that bits of bone and flesh were found throughout the house and right across the farmyard. In pleading guilty, he'd told the judge that his only regret was that they hadn't suffered more before they died. They gave him two life sentences without the possibility of parole as if one would not suffice. And Ezra had heard how Holbert had beaten other inmates over the years who made the mistake of crossing him, with merciless efficiency and no forewarning, compiling a couple more life sentences along the way and leaving some others permanent cripples. Unlike many of the other tales, Ezra had never sensed any swagger in the warnings about Holbert. Just genuine, in your bones, fear.

"What— what?" Ezra had responded tentatively, not understanding the question.

"The void," Holbert repeated in a blank tone. "The empty place. Did you find it?"

"I don't understand."

The old man had seemed slightly disappointed as he twisted the bar into position on the rack supports. "There was an old samurai a few centuries back. After he'd won about a hundred fights to the death with hot shot swordsmen, he retired undefeated and wrote a book of five rings, five states of being. He called the fifth ring the void, the place from where he fought, the place where a man believes he's already dead so nothing matters anymore. There is no pain or fear there because only what gives a damn for itself can feel either. And there aren't anymore of those little hesitations of concern for consequence. Time stretches long there, toward stillness. The void. You looked like you might have been there the other day in the alley."

Ezra had recognized something familiar in the man's words. "I don't know. Maybe."

Holbert had dipped his head under the bar without further comment and stood straight with nearly seven hundred pounds resting across his sixty-year-old back. He stepped back easily, squared his feet, and squatted down so far that his hamstrings met his calves. With astounding casualness he'd stood straight again and only after he'd repeated this motion three more times did he rack the weight.

"You come down here to gawk or train?" he asked Ezra as he removed weight from the bar.

Ezra had just shrugged.

"Pull the weight off that end," Holbert had pointed. "I'll see if I can find something you can handle. Try not to hurt yourself." The old man slid the hundred pound plates from the bar and slung them against the rack with one hand like toys. "You know, if I was a man that still gave a damn, I don't believe I'd like what they say you did to get here, boy."

Ezra had kept his mouth judiciously shut, struggling mightily with one of the plates, trying not to smash a foot.

Thus began a daily regimen for Ezra that would span the next decade. Holbert got him a job in the wood shop on industrial row. When the old man told the shop's supervisor to hire Ezra, the officer did not question. He hired Ezra.

Every weekday they worked, mostly without speaking, from early in the morning through the afternoon, reaping a few cents an hour. For a couple hours after work and twice as long on weekends, they would take to the exercise yard and "train," as the old man termed it. They would lift weights, run for miles around the graveled track, and spend grueling hours practicing skills of violence on a heavy bag or by sparring... or on the occasional poor, belligerent soul fool enough to suggest a blind spot. Through thirty years of Kalbourne clashes, the old farmer had perfected his own peculiar manner of combat. It was part boxing, part wrestling, part martial art; and it was all combined with a sacrifice all, dead man's severity. He taught Ezra to strike with the ends of his bones— fists, palms, elbows, knees, and feet— perpendicular to his opponent's long bones, snapping them with blinding ferocity. He taught Ezra not to strike at the surface of a body as other men did, but at internal targets, beyond the protection of abdominal walls, ribs, and skull. Holbert was a severe man and Ezra learned his severity. When the extremes of heat, thunderstorm, or wind-whipped blizzard drove the others from the yard, Holbert and Ezra remained, training without compromise.

But Holbert was not Ezra's friend in the manner that the word is generally understood. He was not anyone's friend. Ezra had always known that the old man would turn on him as quick as another, without sentiment or recognition, if he had ever crowded him too close. The old man instructed by example and by numbing repetition, with scarcity of words. He'd spoken more to Ezra that first day at the rack than any day thereafter for the next decade... excepting their last day.

In any case, they had worked and they had trained with no remembrance of the previous and no thought of the future and at the end of the day they went their separate ways. There was no goal to it beyond the moment, no prize to be gained. It was just a way of being. But it appealed to Ezra. He figured the old Zen teachers he read about must've had it right when they preached existence in the moment only, extinguishing all desires and forgetting all that need not carry forward, especially guilt. It seemed to work for Holbert. You didn't see him worrying about his past or whining about whatever was to come. Words learned in childhood tried to creep in and confuse Ezra, but he persistently shook them off. What they did was better than all the idle nonsense that captivated so many others in Kalbourne. And the covetous and prurient dreams that had so dominated his youthful mind finally began to dissipate along with his notion of a future. Just a way of being. A void.

Ezra was cast free of his memories by the sound of footsteps descending the apartment house stairs. Hand in hand, Bobby and Kendra Slater emerged in the foyer and turned for the front door. But, glancing back, the girl caught sight of Ezra and began tugging at her father's hand. Eagerly pointing down the hall, she whispered excitedly, "Daddy, that's E.J.!"

Bobby turned to see who Kendra was pointing at and soon calling to.

"E.J., this is my dad! We're going to the park!"

Straightening from where he worked, the caretaker focused his attention on the pair. "Very good, blue eyes."

Bobby narrowed his vision, confirming what he thought he saw. "You," he said with recognition. "You're E.J., the caretaker?"

Ezra nodded simply.

Bobby looked at him for an awkward moment, not sure what to say. "I— I guess you weren't in the parking lot by coincidence."

"Coincidence," Ezra said, stooping to continue his work. "No such thing."

Bobby wasn't sure what to make of the caretaker who now proceeded with his work as if their business was just that simply and quickly concluded. At length, Bobby bid a tentative "see you later," and he and Kendra disappeared out the front.

Ezra ran a scarred, crooked hand over the wall, checking for small blemishes. "Very good."

* * *

Saturday night, and music was blaring, loud and distorted, from an old two story house on the southern outskirts of Haverston. In states of consciousness that ranged from drunken lethargy to hallucinatory euphoria, people milled about within the house. They passed out on the floors in some rooms. They carried on raucously in others. And, in still others, they stubbornly tried to work out lusts with sweaty indiscrimination.

Soberly and somberly, Calvin walked through the house, room by ugly room, quietly watching. An acquaintance named Josh, one of several people living in the newly rented house, came up to Calvin and excitedly began to tell of a small auto shop in nearby Colton where a cousin worked. Josh had found out that the owner was gone for the weekend and he wanted Calvin to help him steal the shop's tools and equipment. "We can get three or four thousand for all that stuff. My cousin says the dude's got a safe in there, too. Man, we can stay high for weeks!"

173

Calvin stared at Josh. "We really do stuff like that, don't we? The guy needs his tools to make a living."

Nervously, Josh laughed and waited for Calvin to signal that he was joking. He knew full well that Calvin was always eager for a good score. And good at it, too.

But Calvin was not joking. "Guy probably had to work a long time to build up that shop. Probably has people depending on him. We'd be real pieces of crap to take that from him." Calvin turned away. "We really do stuff like that, don't we?" He wandered away through the raucous crowd, leaving Josh bewildered.

"Hey! Hey Calvin, man!" the gaunt couple called out from the table as he wandered through the kitchen. "Man, we ain't seen you since last Saturday night." They lowered their voices as he neared. "So what happened after we left, man? That guy was a real bummer. We figured you'd probably get your piece and teach him a lesson, man."

Calvin stood, staring at them.

"So what happened?" they persisted. "You get kicked out?"

"No."

"Well, what's up, man? Where you been all week?" they pressed.

"Working."

The gaunt couple looked at each other, then back at Calvin, waiting for the joke. "Ha ha, yeah sure, all right. Hey, man!" Their focus suddenly shifted. "You get any of Rowdy's new batch, yet? Dude, that's good crank, man!" They rolled their eyes back in their heads and flashed their teeth with pleasure. "You gotta get you some, man. He's right out back."

Calvin fumbled with the cash left in his pocket after starting a bank account, paying Mrs. Peterson, and buying more supplies earlier in the day. "Na."

"Aw, man! You gotta get some, Calvin! You'll really get off, man. It's prime stuff!"

Calvin looked at his two friends, wasted and wasting. "Yeah, it looks prime all right."

Everyone started suddenly at the sound of horrendous banging and splintering from the other end of the kitchen. People watched and then laughed and hooted as a drunken reveler kicked and smashed to pieces the old oak door that divided the kitchen from the dining room.

Then Calvin's voice shook the room. "You stupid jerk!"

The reveler spun around menacingly. "Who you calling a jerk!"

The crowd of people fell hushed against the heavy metal backdrop as Calvin made his way across the room. And when the reveler finally managed to focus his inebriated glare and realized that it was Calvin Miller he'd just challenged, he sobered with astounding haste. "Aw, man... I'm sorry, dude. I didn't know it was you. Man, come on. I'm really sorry, man."

"You know how much it took to make that door?" Calvin loomed over the reveler in the doorway. His voice bore unexpected clemency and surprised all who heard him. "Look. Look at all those mortises. They were chiseled by hand, man. Look at the raised panels, the edge work. They had to do that all by hand back when this was made. Do you know how much sweat someone had to put into that?" He pointed at the ruined door, looking into the reveler's bewildered face.

"Hey, man, come on," the reveler tried to ease. "It's just some landlord's house. It don't belong to Josh and the guys."

"Yeah, ain't we cool? We just spit on the landlord." Calvin looked around at all the puzzled expressions. And they were puzzled to be sure. For they'd all seen Calvin wreck more than all the rest of them in times not far past. But, as he turned his back on them and headed for the door, his head shook with disgust and his voice was clear and strong. "We're messed up. We don't do anything but spit and crap on people. Steal and break. Take and take and take... Ain't we just f— cool?"

175

CHAPTER 21

"Yeah, buddy." Calvin was pleased with what he saw in his closet door mirror. It felt more than a little odd to be readying himself for church on a Sunday morning. He hadn't been there in years, since his mom took him once or twice as a kid. She got on a religious kick for a while as he remembered it. Didn't last, though. He remembered the people there had seemed so... weak. Still, he knew the caretaker would be knocking at his door soon and he'd better be ready.

He'd donned his best pair of stone washed jeans and his coolest tight black tee-shirt, the one that best displayed his formidable physique and carried the same skull symbol and "death before dishonor" emblem that was tattooed high on his arm. He figured the slogan spoke to his brand of spirituality. The great mass of hair was freshly brushed and fluffed, cascading past his shoulders to the middle of his back. For good measure, he'd inserted his prized gold earring. Yeah, he estimated that the timid church types would be pretty awed by the sight of him. He would be friendly to them. He'd learned from the caretaker and he was a working man, now, with a business and everything. He'd stand tall in their midst, gracing them with his presence, and they would no doubt be impressed.

Calvin took one last look in the mirror. Yes indeed, he was quite pleased with what he saw.

When the expected knock at his door came, Calvin opened it promptly, eager to show himself ready. Dressed in his plain suit and clutching his old Bible, the caretaker studied Calvin, a flash of humor passing through his eyes. "You ready?"

A twinge of self-consciousness jabbed at Calvin, but he quickly masked it in nonchalance. "Yeah," he answered firmly, pulling the door shut behind him and swaggering ahead of Ezra down the hallway.

* * *

Edna and Janet were engaged in another Sunday morning visit

176

on the front porch and Kendra played in the yard again. This time her father played with her. They paused, both greeting and watching with curiosity as Calvin came out ahead of the caretaker and they both headed down the sidewalk. Calvin was so absorbed in his macho swagger and mask of nonchalance, that he paid little notice to the others. He turned right and headed uptown. With a good bit of amusement, the others quietly watched Calvin as he soon realized the caretaker had turned left and was strolling in the opposite direction. Quickly turning about, he darted furtive, embarrassed glances at the people in front of the house and hurried, this time without swagger, to catch up to the caretaker.

"Morning, Mr. E.J.," a man raking his yard across the street greeted as they passed. Two houses further, another couple hailed from their porch, "Morning, Mr. E.J." A little further and an elderly couple waved from their living room window. On the next block, a group of boys playing football in a yard took pause to whisper amongst themselves, then greet, "Hi, Mr. E.J." Ezra did not appear to know these people personally, yet the entire neighborhood seemed to be aware of Edna Peterson's new caretaker. As he walked at Ezra's shoulder, Calvin quietly took these things in.

In time, Calvin's attention shifted and he questioned, "How come we aren't going uptown to that New Vision place like everybody else?"

"There's a little place over here on Twelfth that'll suit us better. Serves up good portions of Bible, plain and straight."

From beneath a serious brow, Calvin considered the man's words. "You really believe all that stuff in the Bible, E.J.?"

"Yes."

"How can you? It don't make no sense to me."

"Calvin, it seems to me the old fellows that said the Creator moved them to write this," Ezra gave the book in his hand a shake, "were plain, straightforward sorts that spent their lives working and struggling in great fear and awe of God, of His purity, His justice, His truth. I don't see them being fool enough to turn around and let a lie fall from their pens. There's something different here than all the other stories and myths that have been written throughout

177

throughout history for the personal glory of the writers and the pride of their people. These guys told about their failures and sinfulness, about the shameful wickedness of their own people. Sounds more like the truth of things, doesn't it? They didn't write good things about themselves, only about our Creator and His Messiah.

"And the men who wrote the last books of the Bible and their fellow witnesses gave up everything just to get a message to you and me, to tell us that they really did meet this Messiah that had been promised, that they heard Him speak and witnessed His deeds and saw Him killed and buried... and alive again. They didn't have anything in this world to gain by it. They lost everything. Their friends, their families, their livings, and their lives. Yet they eagerly spread out in every direction and happily laid down their lives to tell the whole world what they had witnessed. I don't know many folks who will give up their lives for the truth and no one at all who'll do it for something they know to be a hoax. These people weren't crafty sorts. They were plain working people. They saw with their own eyes. They would've known if it was a hoax. They wouldn't have sacrificed all for it. Just about every one of them died violently for His testimony. Calvin, we put folks on death row nowadays with far less solid witnesses than you have here. I don't know about you, partner, but I think if so many people spilled their blood just to get this message to me, I'd better listen. And when you see that the message is exactly the same from the first book through thousands of years to the last book, it's not really so hard to see the same Writer moving all the pens."

* * *

In the front foyer area of Grace Reformed, Reverend Travis and Rose greeted the people of the congregation as they arrived on Sunday morning. Everyone much enjoyed these informal moments preceding the service. With a quick wit colored by his characteristic intensity, Reverend Travis dispersed his attention throughout the foyer. And many more, from young to old, gathered around Rose, basking in her gracious, ebony-eyed warmth, the young girls soaking in her many encouragements, the young boys mostly blushing behind their mothers' skirts.

The people were all pleased to receive the man they knew as E.J. for a consecutive Sunday. And their faces shone curious at the sight of the large, wild-looking young man that accompanied him.

Ezra introduced Calvin to the preacher and several others standing near. The preacher was not what Calvin had anticipated. He grasped hold of Calvin's hand with great strength and hands much hardened by labor. "Good to meet you, Calvin, and that's a fine reformation name, by the way." The preacher and the others standing near smiled brightly, though the reference to John Calvin was lost on Calvin. Looking up into the minister's eyes, he realized the man was not many years older than himself. Yet, in understanding and in stature, he seemed lifetimes beyond. They had walked different roads, to be sure.

Calvin carefully surveyed the foyer, but could not find the timid and weak that he had supposed would populate this place, that he had been prepared to awe. It was he who felt a twinge of timidness. He found himself wishing that he had worn a coat or something. He felt... naked. From the sturdy young minister to the old widow McVillian who came and grasped the caretaker's arm, leading him away in conversation as a mother to son, Calvin found himself in the midst of happy, friendly, and decidedly strong people. The whole foyer seemed filled with the same clear and unflinching eyes that the caretaker possessed. Calvin felt most out of place. He saw a young woman that he guessed to be about his age. She wore a sky blue dress with a white lace collar. She had soft auburn hair, porcelain perfect skin, and riveting green eyes. There was something about those eyes. Something vaguely familiar. Calvin looked away. An urge to flee took hold of him. He didn't even know why.

"Hey there young man." A large-boned, middle-aged man clasped hold of Calvin's hand and shoulder with sturdy vigor. "Name's Connor. Dane Connor. Most folks just call me Doc, though. I have a family practice uptown. This is my wife, Ivy," he indicated the demurely smiling woman at his side. "And that's our daughter, Sarah." He nodded toward the girl in the sky blue with the green eyes. "She's a sophomore over at Lakeland College—."

Doc Connor quieted as Calvin's troubled countenance raised up from the floor. "Nice to meet you, sir," he nearly whispered.

He was relieved to hear the minister's voice come across the foyer, gently cutting through the conversations and prompting people to file toward the sanctuary. "Let's get started." And Calvin was eased, as well, to be seated in the rear, next to the caretaker and the widow, out of everyone's sight. They were all kind. And they greeted him warmly. And he could not shake a spreading, thickening feeling of doom or something near to it. All the kindness and goodness he'd been shown this past week despite what he was... Something was terribly amiss.

When Reverend Travis had led them in a prayer and Rose in a hymn on the organ, the younger children followed after her to a side room for Sunday School. The preacher held class for the rest. As he read and expounded on the Bible, the caretaker's notions about people having laid down their lives to deliver these words stuck in Calvin's mind. He found himself sitting up and listening closely. To his quiet amazement, he did not hear dry irrelevance, but real, piercing words that seemed to know him as if the Writer could see his inner thoughts.

In a while, the children returned to their parents and Sunday School was concluded. And when the main service had begun and more hymns happily sung and more prayer earnestly offered and more Scripture and catechism carefully read, the congregation settled and Calvin found himself leaning forward with anticipation as Reverend Travis stood before them and began to preach.

"My dear brothers and sisters, by the witness of our Creator, his creation, and our own consciences, we plainly established, last Sunday, that there is sin in all humanity, that this sin infects and affects all of creation, and that there is a just balance inescapably attached to this sin, to be borne by the one infected or by the Acceptable Substitute. That this Substitute is Jesus Christ, droves of eyewitnesses died to make known. That we are connected to him by faith— by what we believe in our hearts to be real and true— has been shown insomuch as we have understood that there is nothing else but faith to connect us to anything in this world,

180

tangible or otherwise.

"So, what then is this process of faith by which we are united with the Messiah? How is such a thing accomplished? What does it mean to be born again? My dear friends, more than anything, I have longed to tell you what it is to be born again— that those of you who are might be edified and, if there be any among you who are not, that perhaps by grace you might be disturbed from fitful, dreamy sleeps.

"Jesus teaches us along with Nicodemus that if we are to enter the kingdom of God, to be with Him, we must be born again. Now the beginning of this rebirth is hatred and death, and the end thereof is godly love and new life.

"Yes, I did say hatred and death, but not the sort that men work. God, Himself, works this most unique manner of hatred and death in people to their great benefit. Listen to what he says through Ezekiel concerning what happens to people when they are awakened by Him. 'Then shall you remember your own evil ways, and your doings that were not good, and shall loathe yourselves in your own sight for your iniquities and for your abominations... be ashamed and confounded for your own ways...' Self-loathing. God works in the heart of the one being reborn a hatred of the sinful self. This is distinct from the sort of impetuous, self-centeredness that hates others including the Creator, and loves its wicked self. Rather, this is an earnest despising of the falseness, the wicked notions, and the conflicted heart found within. A hatred of untruth born out of the Spirit of truth.

"Remember how we said that hatred is murderous, how it seeks to separate what God has joined. And it is not good to seek the division of anything that our Creator has joined. But it is not God that joins us to sin. Our own dark hearts do this. And it is good to hate, that is, to seek separation from and yearn for the death of these natural born desires.

"The apostle Paul writes of this death. In Romans he explains that we are to reckon ourselves dead to sin. And he told the Galatians that those who are Christ's have crucified the flesh with its passions and desires. Now we know that these natural born desires assume different shapes in different people. Various lusts

181

and unwarranted mistrust. Diverse forms of hatred and dishonesty. Yet, all the shapes have a common root that passionately desires the self to be at the center of all creation. They despise the true Center in all their ways from blatant to subtle. They seek to be free from Him, deluded that they can stand alone. They strive to be specially exempted from accountability to Him. Irrespective of the particular face sin takes in each person, the inner dialogue is remarkably similar. 'I can't help it. This is the way I was born. This is the way nature made me. I can't change who I am. I've not the strength nor even the genuine desire to turn from these natural inclinations of my heart. And why should I?' Some even speak these things aloud, seeking to openly display and practice the disgraces of their hearts. But even as the inner voice fails to justify itself before the bar of conscience, so the public voices ever fail to acquit themselves before their Creator or even the eyes of upright neighbors. In our heart of hearts, we know that we are born in sin and that we cannot— will not— turn from it until and unless God works His unique brand of self-loathing, sin-hating in our hearts.

"Then this divinely worked self-loathing results in what seems remarkably like self-annihilation— like suicide. Not the manner of suicide that the world chases after, mind you, where the impetuous and ungrateful indulge while onlookers glorify. Not the murderous destruction of what God has wrought. Rather, this is the dying to, the separating from, the natural born desires that, until this very point in time, had remained the center and purpose of our life, the concealed motivation of every word and action. Take heed, this is no temporary abstinence as may have been tried of one's own purpose on previous occasions, only to be abandoned. This is an unswayable resolve to leave the sinful desires behind, no matter what the cost, to remain true to the Creator's good and simple precepts, written in His word and on our hearts, to the very end, no matter what the perceived sacrifice. Not until this self-canceling resolve to absorb any cost is brought to life in us will we finally and completely turn our back on the natural born desires. Short of this, a person only plays with God, sort of experimenting to see if acting and speaking rightly for a season will bring desired reward, only to be invariably disappointed and to find the old lusts rising up strong as ever. We like to test rather than trust our Maker. We try to manipulate that which can never be manipulated. But always in the back of our minds— and not really so far back— we know when we're hedging, when we're playing games and not being real. Our Maker exists beyond His creation of time, knowing all things simultaneously. He knows the ends of our promises before they were ever made. He knows the true motivations of our words and deeds. Just who is it that we think we're going to play a game on?"

Reverend Travis paused, gathering the congregation in eyes that gently smiled beyond their twenty-seven years. "It surely does feel like dying, too, doesn't it? Hebrews 2:15 teaches us that fear of death keeps us in bondage to sin, after all. Sin seizes one with mortal terror when the notion of cutting it off springs to life. When it recognizes its impending demise and not just another cycle of hedging, sin frantically counsels against abandonment, insisting all manner of pain and hopelessness will beset you. Arrogance, hatred, and violence assure that you will be contemptible and weak without them. Every manner of substance, from the luxuriously indulgent to the gluttonously devoured to the warmly intoxicating, desperately plead that there will be intolerable emptiness and hunger apart from their cradling comfort. But these are proven liars when left behind to wither. Our very darkest, most intractably wicked longings scream of death, swift and certain, without their purpose to order our existence. But they are proven liars, as well. They are all proven liars as they fall away, having promised a fulfillment they never delivered while delivering precisely the misery they had promised to abate. Sin, after all, never had anything of genuine substance to offer. As all truth, reality, and substance are the possessions of the One who created them, wickedness has ever only been left with untruth, unreality, and illusion with which to lure and enslave its devoted. Jesus calls Satan the father of lies. And you know that lies contain no substance.

"But the soul being reborn is made to trust its Sustainer and not the lying desires. The word 'repentance' means 'to turn away from.' So, sin is turned away from and allowed to wither and die, making no more hedges or contingencies for its harbor. Then, finally and for the first time, the will finds itself really and truly

183

free. No regret seizes hold. No wish for the selfish desires to return. No pain, hopelessness, or insatiable hunger suddenly possesses. To the contrary, an inexplicable kind of liberty and happiness springs to life. Genuine freedom for the first time from dark desires and motivations. A great joy and gratitude derives from such freedom. A simple, irrepressible knowledge, not adequately expressed in words, that everything is finally and immutably all right because, as Romans 11:29 assures, this calling and gift of God is irrevocable.

"The soul thus reborn really does desire to do good. Not for fear of punishment nor hope of reward, but honestly and simply for the sake of good. The reason Paul writes that such are no longer under the law is because it is no longer the coercion of law or the bribery of reward that motivates good behavior, but the free desire of the heart. Such a one naturally strives to serve and to share. Such long for all those who struggle fruitlessly on behalf of sin, dissatisfied and unfulfilled, miserably trapped and deceived by self-pivoting dreams, to be awakened, to perceive the true freedom and happiness in simply ceasing these vain struggles and heeding Christ's call to abandon life lived for the self, to take Him at His word, and to remand the remaining moments of one's life to a manner of gratitude-filled service, ordered by His good Word and contentedly resolved to continue in this course, no matter the cost.

"Maybe we don't always finds the words to adequately express such things, but it is our Maker who does the speaking of such things to hearts, anyway. Maybe we often don't even feel worthy to speak. But we can fix our purpose and set our shoulders to the work we find in front of us, whatever it may be. And, while we can't force others to perceive these things, we can employ our newfound liberty to maintain an example of integrity and diligence, that our Redeemer might use the course of our lives and labors to the furtherance of His good purpose in other lives. Above all, we pray and trust continually within the heart that the God who did these things, even for such as us, will most assuredly continue to use His Spirit, His Word, His regenerated servants, and the balance of His creation, to work the same miracle in other hearts.

"Make no mistake, it is a miracle. As in Jesus' day, many look to and fro today, seeking after the abnormal as if the norm of existing as living, perceiving beings amid so vast a creation were not a miraculous thing. But if it is the unnatural that you seek, you need look no further than a regenerated human heart. For in seeing a person turn from their natural inclinations, you are witnessing for yourself the most stupendous of miracles ever to be seen in this world. A genuinely supernatural event. The overruling of nature as it occurs in the sinful heart by the only One who transcends nature and is, thus capable of setting it aside. Remember, Jesus said that it is easier for a camel to pass through the eye of a needle— certainly not a naturally possible thing— than for a rich man, which the disciples clearly took to mean anyone, to enter heaven, to become right-hearted before God. Here, we see that the disciples take it to mean anyone in that they ask with astonishment, 'Who then can be saved?' and Jesus' reply is that it is impossible for men to overcome sin, to enter heaven, but with God all things, including this, are possible.

"And I will say it again, people, it is God who accomplishes these things. Never permit arrogance to charm you into believing that people possess the power to overcome what only our Creator can. If this were so, Jesus would not have been necessary and His work in vain. The German philosopher Friedrich Nietzsche was contemptuous of the notion that mankind needed his Creator to rescue him from the tangles of ignorance and evil desires. He placed all of his faith and hope in the power of the human intellect to overcome. He awaited the evolution of the 'overman,' as he termed it, a human being superior by his own self-possessed power. Is it mere coincidence that Nietzsche was betrayed by the very intellect in which he placed his hope, spending the final years of his life insane?

"People make a lot of noise about man's free will, extolling this supposed power to choose one's own course, to freely choose right or wrong from a neutral stance. To be sure, the majority choose to present a face of goodness, concealing and restraining certain of their desires for fear of consequence— and thank God for the grace of restraining consequences— but in truly overcoming the underlying inclination of the heart, free will is shown to be a fraud.

185

The fifth century theologian Augustine, in expounding the Bible's take on human will power, points out that while the first people were indeed created with a freedom of will, they used this liberty to mistrust and rebel against their very Maker, submitting their wills to the tyranny of wicked desire in the process. Thereafter, the natural born will of that first, God-given breath of life has passed on to every human being hence, so utterly entangled and enslaved to its own desires, as to be rendered quite incapable of freely choosing genuine, selfless righteousness... unless and until God intervenes and overrules this enslaved will.

"Literally, God saves human souls against their own wills. Listen to what he says through Ezekiel's pen in the thirty-sixth chapter. 'A new heart also will I give you, and a new spirit will I put within you: and I will take away the stony heart out of your flesh, and I will give you an heart of flesh. And I will put my spirit within you, and cause you to walk in my statues and ye shall keep my judgments, and do them.' Brothers and sisters, these are not the words of One passively awaiting our free will choice to repent. If He did, He would watch every last one of us eagerly chase after our selfish desires right down into the grave. But what our God says is that He Himself will take away the sinful heart. He will give a new heart. He will put his spirit within and He 'will cause' us to walk in His ways. These are not the words of a passive Creator, but of One sovereign in all things, taking action on behalf of His willfully corrupted creatures. As Paul says, speaking of Christian liberty, only when one is regenerated by God and finds their very will free from the tyranny of sinful passions, can one credibly claim anything like unto a freedom of will. Jesus reminds in John fifteen, 'You did not choose me, but I chose you...' We do not choose, but are chosen. And apart from this Divine choosing no one finds salvation.

"So, what then? Are these yet held by sin's grip to trudge about feeling sorry for themselves, helpless and hopeless against their own desires and begrudging God His sovereign choices? No. Absolutely no. We are told to repent, to turn away our hearts from selfishness and to think, speak, and live rightly. Paul told the Philippians to get busy, to 'work out their own salvation with fear and trembling.'

But, in the very next verse he notes that 'it is God who works in you both to will and to do for His good pleasure.' So we are responsible to get to it, to amend our hearts and our lives. But, when it's all said and done, those who actually do so will look behind them and perceive the hand of their Savior from the very beginning of the process right through to the end, working the hatred and death of the sinful nature, the desire to change, the will to do so, and the gumption and courage to follow through. The reborn look not with pride at what they have accomplished, but with humility and gratitude upon what their Creator has wrought within them— working all things together, both pleasant and painful, to the ultimate good of His chosen. May you discover within yourself, if you have not already, the desire to be chosen and to be changed... and then get to it!

"Next week, if God is willing, we will attempt a glimpse at His unfathomable grace in all of these things. Until then, let us pray together with David from the fifty first Psalm. 'Create in me a clean heart, O God, and renew a steadfast spirit... Deliver me from the guilt of bloodshed, O God, the God of my salvation.'"

* * *

When the service was over, the congregation remained, mingling in the sanctuary and foyer, the adults in lively conversation, the children in play, all reluctant to part.

At the far end of the foyer, feeling uncomfortably hot and wanting to leave, Calvin stood apart from everyone. He waited for the caretaker to finish his visit with the widow McVillian and others. The preacher's words were taunting him. A heaviness pulled at his insides and labored his heart. He didn't know what was happening to him and he was quietly growing petrified as he stood there. Sky blue entered his periphery and he looked up from the floor.

"Hi," Sarah Connor greeted.

"Hi." His stomach seized tight.

"Do you remember me?" she asked. "We used to go to the same school. We were even in the same home room in eighth

187

grade. Mr. Allen's room, remember?"

"Yeah, I guess so." Truth was, his memories of junior high were blunted by drinking and doping and mostly consisted of a more delinquent crowd.

"I never saw much of you in high school. Did you move away?" she queried.

"No. Just stopped going."

"Oh." She paused, studying Calvin as if debating something further. "Do you remember the time in junior high when you threw glue in my hair and hit me in the face?"

Calvin froze, caught in her sharp green eyes. Now he knew why those eyes were familiar. He remembered them filled with anguish and hurt. He remembered the sounds of his own scornful laughter. Many of the long blunted memories of that time rose out of obscurity with bewildering speed and dread gripped him strongly. "No— I don't remember that," he assured.

"Well, you did. I'll never forget that. It took my mom two days to get all the glue out of my hair." Her eyes followed his dodging face. "I never told on you."

"I'm sorry," he said, his breath shallow, his face haunted.

"Hey," she saw his upset. "It's okay. I mean, I wasn't happy about it then, but it's a long time ago. Sort of funny, looking back on it, I guess."

Calvin affected a half-hearted, watery-eyed smile. She didn't seem to want to expose him as he had feared. He stood up a little taller and his eyes ventured over the lines of her graceful figure. Then his eyes caught a glimpse of something behind her. A reflection in one of the foyer windows. His own phony, moronically smiling mask was mocking him. His leering eyes accused and taunted. His whole self-inflated, idiotic appearance laughed at him in the window. He was such a... His stomach turned at the sight of himself and he swayed. His ears rang, vision blurred. He felt as though he would fall on his face. Odd wheezing sounds came out of him when he tried to draw air through a grief swollen throat. Tears flooded onto his face before he could restrain them.

The people in the foyer grew hushed, their faces all turning as Calvin stood there blubbering, ashamed and embarrassed and quite unable to stop. He made his way quickly around Sarah and fled the church. Alternately, his hands hung resignedly at his sides, then covered his own head in disgrace as he made his way along the walkway toward Oak Street... bitterly weeping.

In the church, Ezra met the faces of concern with a calming silence. He gave a parting squeeze to Mae McVillian's arm, a wave to the others, and a reassuring smile to Sarah's apologetic green eyes on his way out the door.

Content to keep Calvin within eyesight, Ezra made no attempt to catch up, strolling a fair distance behind his distraught charge. He knew the feeling. That sickening, empty moment when a man is brought face to face with the vast gulf between what he dreamed he was and what he actually is. Even as Ezra maintained a dutiful eye on Calvin, his mind went back to Kalbourne.

After following in Holbert's pattern for more than ten years, he had caught just a glimpse of the old man subtly wince a time or two during workouts. But Holbert never let on that he was ailing. Only in the very last weeks, as legendary strength dissipated into frailty and he ceased eating, did anyone realize something was wrong. By the time the guards finally came and all but forced him to the infirmary, the cancer had already entangled most of his insides. They gave him a month or two. He lasted four days.

And on the last one, Ezra had gained entry into the infirmary, set on seeing the old warrior one more time. He'd supposed that he would find an unmoved mentor of the void drifting stoically toward final nothingness. But what he found had disturbed him greatly. Those old gray eyes had been wide, not just with pain, but with... fear. Panic. The shame of a fraud had turned Holbert's face away from Ezra's surprised expression.

Ezra had spoken to him with a deliberate derision. "You look scared, old man."

"Ezra, I— I should have forgave her," the old man had wheezed and rattled with singular desperation. "I should have forgiven them all." He sat forward, wincing and moaning with each subtle movement. "She cried and cried. Begged me for forgiveness. Begged God. Pleaded. I should have... held her. I should have... O Lord—." He began heaving sobs for a time before struggling back to some semblance of composure. "They're all crying out loud. So damn loud..."

"Who?"

"All of them!" he panted. "Everyone I hurt. Everyone was... They're telling on me!"

"Telling who?" Ezra had tried to question, but the old man just started heaving again.

"We had a son," he winced. "Named Harry— like the president, you know? Truman was president then. Harry wasn't even a year old when I... His grandfolks put him up for adoption so he wouldn't have to grow up with the— the... Look what I did, Ezra! Look what I did! I destroyed his mother! Now, where is he?! He's crying out, too!" He coughed dryly, panting with each agonizing exertion. "Oh, I'm on fire, Ezra. I'm in trouble. It's bad. This is real bad. It's got to be set right. Got to be. It hasn't ever gone away and it isn't ever going away! I can't take it! What am I going to do?!" His wide gray eyes had begun leaking again.

Ezra had just stood there dumbfounded in that room for a long time, staring at a sight he would never have believed from the mouth of another. The only things that kept coming into his mind were words the old preacher kept saying to him in the visiting room. It had surprised him greatly to hear some of those words fall clumsily from his own mouth.

"The— the preacher, he keeps telling me that a man's got hope as long as he's still breathing, that his Maker can make things right for him and have Jes— Jesus take the weight for him. You know, that's what the preacher says, anyway." Ezra had turned his face from Holbert's surprised expression, feeling the words must sound incredibly useless, yet still more fell out of him. "If— if you give up a bad heart for good, you know? If you aren't just playing. You got to really believe he's going to take your weight, really believe in— in— in Jesus. That's what the preacher says."

"You believe?" Holbert had asked him.

The room remained quiet a long time, but for the buzz of a clock on the wall and Holbert's uneven wheezing. Ezra had looked into the old man's waiting eyes and then to the relentless hands of the clock. He never answered the question.

Holbert recalled, "They say He set things right with one of the criminals that was executed with Him, didn't He?"

"That's what they say."

"Even though he never had a chance to live right and try to repay?"

"Yeah."

The old man had actually chuckled, then winced. "Ain't that something? Just odd enough to be true. It makes more sense than what we've been doing, when I think about it now. I don't guess a void ever set anything right. Emptiness isn't much to hold onto."

Holbert was quiet a long time, deliberating, then finally speaking. "You know, if I give my word to Him, I'll mean it."

"I know."

Long and slow, the old man exhaled, his face relaxing and the worry fading from his eyes. He eased his head back onto the pillow. "That's it, then. It's done." He stared at Ezra for a long time after that and then his face warmed into the most unexpected smile. The only time Ezra could ever remember seeing the man smile. The only time he ever felt like they were friends."

Then, abruptly, Holbert had insisted, "Go away. You're keeping me from my business."

And when Ezra had turned to leave, the old farmer had spoken to him for the last time. "Ezra."

"Yes."

"No more, Ezra. Don't hurt anybody. No more."

Ezra had left without answering. Not five minutes thereafter, while he was still crossing the yard for the woodshop, he'd heard the radio on a guard's hip crackle to life. "Code blue in the infirmary. Code blue in the... Negative on that. Do not resuscitate."

For weeks thereafter, Ezra had trudged about Kalbourne in a perfunctory daze. He had long thought he had things figured out. But all that time, his example Holbert had been pretending. Pretending he didn't care. Pretending he felt nothing, desired nothing, feared nothing. Was he pretending, too? Had he as much wasted the past ten years as the first seventeen? Were the old lusts and longings really gone or had they merely recast themselves in

191

subtler shapes? And were the accusing voices that could so fearfully grip really dead or only slumbering as they had been in the old man? Ezra had much dreaded the answers.

And with unrelenting regularity, the old preacher continued to afflict him. Always searching him with those perpetually hope-filled eyes. Always expending himself without want of gain. As far back as Ezra could remember, no one had disturbed him as constantly, as deeply, as that little old preacher. For all his immense strength and danger, Holbert had never possessed such power. Lord knows why, but Reverend Hartmann still gave a damn and never pretended otherwise. Indeed, there had never been any hint of pretending in him. Was this the strong man, after all, truly unafraid of death, truly unburdened by guilt? When all of his machinations were said and done, would the strength Ezra had so long and desperately craved be found in the very ones he had despised as weak? Not the awed masters of bone crushing combat, but the simply honest, the humbly productive. The ones able to admit the truth of themselves, both the obvious and the hidden, and place their trust in their Sustainer for their strength and justification and everything else.

These things would not leave him alone. All the ugliness and conflict that he'd counted dead, rose up within him anew until one evening he had found himself before one of the sink mirrors in the cellhouse shower area, trying to shave, but unable to abide his own reflection. The sight of the worthless, fraudulent piece of crap looking back at him had turned his stomach over violently and sent his vision into blackness. He'd emerged from the other end of that blackness with bloodied, wrecked hands, the stainless steel mirror and its frame replaced by a crater in the concrete wall, the other inmates in the shower area frozen in silent trepidation. That was the night he couldn't stop heaving and retching like some miserable, pathetic fool every time he considered anew what manner of man he had become. That was the night he determined to end himself, but was continually distracted from his course at every turn by tortuous thoughts. That was the night he first said a prayer without a manipulative heart and from that prayer had drifted into some uncomfortable slumber only to be violently seized out of his sleep by a most dreadful presence. A paralyzing surge of incomprehensible energy had rushed through his very core, roaring and crackling in his ears, and holding him fast, unable to move nor even to breathe while a shadow with three dimensions walked in front of his cell out on the galley and turned to face him. It was, most definitely, not a dream and it was, bar none, the most terrifying moment of Ezra's life. And when he knew that he could not last another moment without breath, the specter departed and he was released from its grip. And as he had sat there in his cell, deep in the night, gasping for air and verifying with himself, over and over, that he was awake and not asleep, he was left with two indelible thoughts. The first, that there was something— very real and terrifying— lurking just behind what the senses normally perceive. The second whispered to him like a voice passing through his mind, "As you don't want your life anymore, why don't you give it over to those who have need of it rather than destroying what you've no right to destroy?"

Ezra's attention drifted back to the present. Calvin was still walking a good ways ahead. His young charge's heaving would subside for a while. He would walk a ways, catching his breath, wiping his face... only to begin mumbling to himself again. Something about being such a piece of—. His weeping would begin anew. Ezra followed in quiet vigil. He knew the feeling.

* * *

The well-heeled man sat on his usual Zwingli Park bench. A section of the Sunday paper camouflaged eyes that quietly stalked the budding, giggling landscape even as his heart held shaded counsel and grew drunk once more on covetous dreams. Was not the heart the private domain of its inhabitant? Who was harmed by a little fantasy, a little unreality? It was harmless enough.

Some of the others in the park and the rich man, as well, took curious note of the visibly upset young man passing by on the Oak Street sidewalk. His reddened, tear-stained eyes and disheveled head were clearly visible as he passed near the bench. The guy looked a real mess and even now appeared to be mumbling something beneath his breath and breaking up again. Something certainly seemed to be upsetting him. Perhaps he had lost someone close to him.

Something else, yet distant, caught the man's glance. Then his eyes seized on the figure coming up the sidewalk. It was him! The one from the previous Sunday. The one that had ruined his tranquility with those accusing eyes. Blindly, he suddenly reacted without thinking, snatching up the rest of his paper in a crumpled heap and making his way hastily toward the far side of the park.

Carefully, he looked over his shoulder to watch the Bible-carrying stranger strolling along Oak Street. As if prompted, the stranger's head turned when he had drawn nigh to the empty bench and he looked all the way across the park... right into the rich man's face. The stranger nodded polite acknowledgment, but the rich man turned his face away, pretending not to see. For an awkwardly long time, he feigned interest in the grass at his feet. Then, ever-so-cautiously, he ventured another peek across the park. Oak Street was empty, the stranger gone, and the rich man in the park was swept with relief.

What was this world coming to when decent, law-abiding folks couldn't even relax and enjoy a Sunday in the park without being dogged by some self-righteous accuser?!

Chapter 22

His breath hanging and slowly dissipating in the crisp air, Ezra moved quietly through the early morning darkness, returning to the apartment house from uptown. In his hand he carried a small convenience store sack with breakfast for his charge. *

As he had the previous week, he entered the apartment house still a ways before five, then went to Calvin's door and softly knocked. He waited several minutes, but this Monday morning there was no response. He knocked again with more insistence. No response. Again, he tried. Not even the suggestion of a stir. His head down, Ezra stood at the door a long time. He recalled Calvin's state of mind. Then a twinge of fear as he recalled Calvin's slothfulness the previous Monday morning. A twinge of ire. For an impetuous moment, he considered walking through the closed door and retrieving his charge by force. But the destructive impulse passed and, with quiet disappointment, he turned and went out the back of the house.

Crossing the back yard, Ezra saw light coming from the shed and heard a faint rustling inside. The double doors had been opened and as he rounded them and peered inside, he saw a large silhouette, not at once familiar, back near the planer. Ezra stepped inside the doorway and narrowed his eyes, adjusting them to the light. It was Calvin, sure enough, but his hair was gone. His head was butched even closer than the caretaker's. He glanced at Ezra as he continued buffing the bed of the planer without saying a word. Ezra began to notice the shop. The jointer and table saw were freshly buffed. The floor was swept. And the entire pile of new walnut had been sorted and moved to the planer, ready for machining.

Ezra went to the far workbench and put up the breakfast sack. He took off his coat and began working. Both men continued in silence for some time. Eventually, the caretaker spoke. "Sorry I'm late."

Calvin's solemn face gave way to the suggestion of a smile. "No problem."

"So what are you going to build now?" Ezra inquired.

Calvin considered the question with some surprise. "I don't know. Whatever you say."

"It's your show now, partner," Ezra reminded. "Your decision to make."

Calvin thought carefully as he finished his buffing and put away his wax and rags. "I guess Mrs. Walton would probably buy another rolltop."

"I reckon so," Ezra agreed. "You build. I'll help."

"I'll try," Calvin said, his face filling with uncertainty. "You — you're going to make sure I do it right... right?"

"We'll get it figured out," the caretaker eased. He went over and closed the double doors to muffle the sounds of their early morning work. "You going to pay me?"

Calvin looked up from the walnut pile ominously. "What do you want?"

"The scrap."

"The scrap?" Calvin questioned. "You mean the little scraps I can't use? You don't want any money?"

"No," the caretaker assured. "The scrap is what I want."

* * *

"We're getting so old anymore, Dan. Why don't you come out and take over the farm, son? It's a good life."

Gerald and Sandy Guiness sat across the antique kitchen table from their uniformed son. "You know this farm has been in your family now for a hundred and thirty years. It'd be a shame for that to end, Dan." Gerald reasoned with his boy. "Your mom and I would be real pleased to move into town, and let you and Susan and the kids have the place."

"Yes, Daniel," his mother gently concurred. "We most certainly would."

"And I'd still come out and help with the chores as much as you like," his father assured.

"You loved this place so, when you were a boy," Mrs. Guiness reminded. "Do you remember, Daniel, how you used to run through the fields and the grove? How you used to have such fun

196

until..."

"Is that why you called me out here?" Dan's patience finally gave way. He sat in the same chair that he'd sat in all the days of his growing up. The one right next to his big sister's chair. To this day, he would not touch that chair. "You acted like it was something urgent. I thought you called me out here for something that couldn't wait. We've already had this conversation about the farm before. I told you I'm not going to be a farmer. It's too bad if the place can't stay in the family, but it's got to end sometime." He placed his hands on the table as if to get up.

"Ah, just wait a minute, Dan," Gerald Guiness urged his son. "We — your mom and I — we're worried about you, son. About how this Watt thing is affecting you."

"Sue's been talking to you, hasn't she?" Dan accused. "She should keep her mouth shut! She doesn't know anything about this. You guys know. You remember."

"Dan," his parents tried to calm. "She's just very, very worried about you and doesn't know where to turn. She says that you're not eating or sleeping, that you're out all night. She says you're ignoring your family and spending all of your savings with another child on the way, Dan. Just what do you think you're doing, son?"

Dan's voice filled with a mix of anger and anxiety in the face of his parents' questions. "She's got no business...! She doesn't understand! She doesn't know like we do. You remember! You know what he did! You know!"

"Yes, we know, Dan. We know." Sandy Guiness shook her head with a slow, introspective pain. "I so often realize that Ezra hurt us more than Amanda. Especially you, Daniel. We raised you children to hope in Jesus. Do you remember, Daniel? Amanda had that hope. We may still have pain, but hers is long past. She's alright."

"Dan," Gerald looked his son sternly in the face. "We did not abandon you to follow our anger when Amanda was killed and you cannot abandon your family now."

Dan grew increasingly exasperated. "But he's out there, Dad! Just — just walking around doing God knows what!"

"Yes, Daniel. God does know what, "his mother insisted. "It's in His hands."

"Oh, Mom, you're so naive." He looked away from her eyes, then changed the subject. "Anyway, if the guy I hired can just get a location on him, this will all be over. Things can be normal again."

"What guy? Who did you hire?" His mother's face filled with worry.

"Just what is it you're going to do if you find him, son?" His father questioned.

The wordless malice flooding their son's eyes answered the question unmistakably.

"Oh, Dan! Dan, you can't! You can't throw everything away over this! We've already lost one child to Ezra Watt. You're all that we have left in this world. If something happened to you..."

The kitchen was unnaturally silent, everyone painfully searching for words.

"You just let God handle Ezra," Dan's father finally admonished. "No one gets away with anything. It's just a grace period. The good Lord must have His reasons. It'll be set right, Dan. You just have to trust in that, son. He won't fail us."

"Really?" Dan's voice soured with scorn. "What did Mandy do to deserve what she got? Was God setting her right? Was that His justice?"

"Daniel James, you know better than to talk like that. We raised you better. You know very well none of us has a complaint for the things we receive in life, including death. We know He works it all to the good of those who love Him. All of it. Not just the easy things. Son, the community together has every right to punish, but you can't do it on your own. You know that. None of us are that righteous. You have to stop trying to make everything turn around your pain and anger. You have to think about those kids, about Susan — about something besides yourself. Let the Lord work things out where Ezra is concerned."

"Yeah, well, maybe God's just going to use me to work it out." Dan got up from his place at the table. "Know what I mean?"

"Dan, don't," his mother pleaded. "Please don't."

Their son lumbered out of the farmhouse, unwilling to abide

any more words.

Gerald saw the pain in his wife's eyes. "Dear Lord," he whispered, "Please keep our boy."

* * *

JoAnne Bundy sat uncomfortably in a low, overstuffed leather couch in a plush waiting room, fidgeting nervously with the strap of her purse and biting her lower lip. Her eyes anxiously darted about from the glossy magazines on the table before her to the exotic plants near the windows to the many impressively displayed academic degrees and professional awards on the wall to the butch-headed woman in the pin striped men's suit at the reception desk.

"Don't worry," the raspy voiced receptionist reassured across the empty waiting room. "Dr. Blackwell is quite good with children. She's one of the leading experts in the Midwest with families and children. You've come to the right place."

In the next room Michael Bundy waited uneasily in a corner of the office of psychotherapist Adrianne Boothe Blackwell. The twelve-year old felt small sitting in the large, high-backed leather arm chair and his heart beat fast with uncertainty. Perhaps, he worried, he should have kept his thoughts to himself. Maybe he should try to back out now and deny everything.

The doctor sat down in an identical chair just catty-cornered from Michael's. She was unexpectedly beautiful, dark-haired and lithe. She smelled wonderful. The boy's attention soon shifted. He watched the doctor's nylon-clad legs cross while she made preliminary notes on a pad of paper. His eyes traveled over the smartly tailored gray skirt and business suit, up to the arresting high cheekboned face and deep brown eyes peering down at her writing from behind dainty glasses. Comfortably familiar daydreams began to fill his head and soothe his troubled heart. His gaze fell back down to the doctor's supple ankles. He could imagine them bound...

"Michael, your mother seems quite concerned about you." The doctor's voice startled him from his dreams. She spoke gently, sweetly. "She indicated that you had been upset by some things a stranger said to you at your grandmother's, that you were concerned there might be something wrong with you, that you might be bad or something. Would you like to talk about any of that?"

Michael looked at the floor and shrugged without comment.

"Well, Michael, you know, it's not unusual for people to have thoughts that are different. Everyone does. It's nothing to feel bad about. Just part of the mind's natural development. Part of your own unique creative process. You understand, Michael? It's a natural thing. Nothing to feel ashamed about. Some people try to make us feel bad for the things that go on inside us, huh? But it's okay to think and feel whatever you do, Michael. Trust me."

Michael appraised Doctor Blackwell's words. "But my grandmother's caretaker, he knew what my thoughts were. He told me about a boy who had the same kind of thoughts I do and did real bad things to people and got in real bad trouble."

"Well now, Michael, we need to be careful about believing what some people tell us. Some people will try to scare us, to make us feel bad just for being who we are. You understand that, Michael? Now, Michael, I'm a doctor with a lot of experience in these sorts of things. I've been helping people like you for a long time. I think I might know a little more about these things than your grandmother's caretaker, don't you?"

Donning a sympathetic mask, the boy looked up into the woman's face and nodded agreement.

"Now, Michael, do you know what the words 'self-esteem' mean?"

The boy shook his head uncertainly, playing the role of patient.

"It means how you think of yourself, Michael. How you value yourself. Whether you think highly enough of yourself or not," she explained. "It may be that you're suffering from a lowered self-esteem. We may want to work on ways that you can learn to think more highly of yourself. And we'll want to help you get rid of any feelings of being bad or guilty and to learn to accept yourself just as you are, Michael."

"Just the way I am?" The boy's voice edged skeptical.

"That's right, Michael. We need to be able to give ourselves permission to feel good— to feel good about ourselves."

Michael seriously considered the doctor's words. "I guess I thought I was already thinking too highly of myself when I think about doing whatever I want."

"Not at all, Michael," Doctor Blackwell assured. "You are free to think and to dream anything you wish. And Michael, if you can dream it, you can achieve it!"

Michael wanted to laugh out loud. And then again, he wanted to just keep quiet and leave things at that, but something possessed him to blurt out, "Even if what I dream about is bad?"

"Oh, Michael, how do you know it's bad?" Doctor Blackwell countered soothingly. "You know, as human beings continue to evolve, we're discovering that most of the things we used to think of as bad or wrong are really just natural differences in people that we can learn to accept and accommodate. Wonderfully valid alternatives we each need to learn to develop our own special sense of good and bad, Michael, rather than allowing ourselves to be limited by someone else's sense of it. Our morality, our truth, you see, comes from inside each of us, Michael. You understand?"

"From inside of me?"

"Absolutely, Michael," the woman affirmed with conviction. "Deep down we all just want to do the right thing. We all have a spark of goodness within us, Michael. Your mother indicated that you had become interested in God. You know, we each need to look deep within and find the god inside each of us. That god just wants to love and do good. We have to create him— or her— from within ourselves."

"We create God?" Michael tried to fathom. "That doesn't sound like what I read in our Bible at home."

"Well, Michael, religious stories and myths can be very hard for children and those not properly educated to understand. They're certainly not meant to be taken literally by advanced peoples. They're very complex, Michael. Everyone can find their own meanings in them."

Michael tried to understand. "So everything— good, bad, truth, God— all comes from inside of people? Not from a Creator?"

"We're all part of the creative process," the therapist

explained. "Each of us is a creator. Isn't that exciting, Michael?"

"I guess so," the boy frowned. "It just doesn't seem like I made any of this though. Seems like someone else made it... Maybe you."

"Ha ha ha," Doctor Blackwell laughed sweetly. "Goodness, not all of it, I hope. But maybe just a little bit," she winked.

Michael really did want to leave things on such a nice, pleasant note. His juvenile eyes slipped back over the therapist's pleasing form. Her subtle perfume teased his palate. Chances are, she'll be living around here for a while, he mused to himself. In two or maybe three years he'd be big enough, strong enough to... that damned impulse to blurt things out got away from him again. "Are you sure you know what I think about, what I dream about? Didn't my mom tell you?"

"Well, Michael, she just said that you felt some of your thoughts were bad. But as we've already discus—"

Michael barged over the doctor's words, speaking very quickly as to get it out before there was time to reconsider. "I think about hurting people all the time. I— I daydream and fantasize about capturing them, hurting them, cutting, burning, rape— raping," his voice lowered with halting embarrassment to near whisper, "And killing. Ever since— ever since— for as long as I can remember that's just about the only kind of thing I think about. And I can't make it stop!"

The levity in Doctor Blackwell's eyes disintegrated into Michael's gushing confession. She paused and faltered, trying to regroup her thoughts.

It was Michael who broke the silence, once more, after several moments. "Are you sure you want me to achieve my dreams?"

"Ah— ahm, well, Michael, of course you're just a child. You don't really want to do these things. It's just— it must simply be your mind's unique way of dealing with stressful situations. You know, when you feel threatened or pressured. They're just harmless thoughts, I'm sure. You don't really want to do such things."

Michael was thoughtful, his eyes continuing to study the therapist. Her waist, her ankles, her wrists... her throat. "No, I really do want to do such things," he said matter-of-factly, his fear

202

of confession even seeming to calm some. "I play it over and over in my head, planning and getting myself ready. I don't waste my time thinking about things I don't really want to do. Do you?"

Doctor Blackwell was astounded by the boy's words. To her, it seemed that he was now speaking well beyond the level expected of a twelve-year-old and she was quite frankly uncertain how to proceed. But she was an expert in this field, of course, and she knew that if the patient was to maintain faith in her ability to deliver him from his trouble, she must continue to present herself as knowledgeable and authoritative.

"Ahm, okay— well, Michael, if you really do want to cause others pain, then it must come from some deep-seated pain within yourself. Something terribly traumatic must have happened to you. Perhaps someone has done something very horrible to you in order to make you want to lash out in such a manner. Perhaps, Michael, someone is still hurting you. Is there anything you want to tell me about?"

"No. No one's done anything bad to me," the boy answered quite plainly. "Everyone's always been real good to me."

"Well, Michael, I've had a lot of experience with these things. I think it's pretty clear from what you've told me that someone has traumatized you very badly. You may not want to talk about it yet. Or you may not even realize it's been happening to you, Michael. It may be repressed in your memory. It may take us a while to discover the exact nature of the problem and solve it."

The boy's eyes studied the therapist. "You mean I'll have to come back here a lot?"

"Mmhm," she smiled sweetly and nodded. "Would that be okay with you?"

"Sure," Michael agreed, taking in her pleasing countenance.

"Good," she smiled, then turned serious again. "Now, Michael, we still have a few minutes. I notice your father didn't come with you today. Tell me about your father, Michael..."

Out in the waiting room, JoAnne Bundy stood up from the couch and anxiously searched the eyes of her son and his therapist when they emerged from their session. Doctor Blackwell had Michael wait while she took his mother into her office for some

203

private words. Mrs. Bundy took her seat before the impressive, ornate desk, her face filled with ill-at-ease while she waited for the doctor to make her way around to the other side.

"How is Michael? Is he okay?"

"Well, frankly, Mrs. Bundy, Michael has some very serious issues." Blackwell eased into her oversized armchair. "He's clearly been very deeply traumatized by something or someone."

"Traumatized?!" Mrs. Bundy was shocked. "By what?! How?! What's happened to him?!"

"Well, I'm not sure yet, but it very probably is related to the dynamics of your family."

"What are you saying?" Michael's mother edged toward tears.

"And it may be that he's not the only one being affected. I've had a lot of experience in these matters," the doctor assured. "I'd like to schedule some sessions with you and your other child as well."

"Why? What are you getting at?" JoAnne pressed. "What's wrong?"

"Well," Blackwell's voice swelled with soothing authority. "It's been my experience in these types of situations that the man in the household is often the root cause. A very destructive influence on the family dynamic. Very abusive."

"What are you talking about?" Mrs. Bundy's eyes were washed with teary confusion. "My husband is a little gruff sometimes. But he's never abused them! He's never hit any of us. Ever!"

"Well, JoAnne. May I call you JoAnne? There are other ways in which a victimizer abuses his family. Ways that are just as devastating. Perhaps even more so because the victims may not even realize that it's happening to them. Now I know that something terribly traumatic has taken place in this case because we know that children are born basically good and innocent. And so if they have developed destructive urges, it has to be in response to something painful that has happened to them. You understand? I mean, there's no other logical explanation, is there, JoAnne?"

JoAnne nodded blindly, her mind a blur. "What do we need to do? How do we make things better?"

"As I said, JoAnne, I'd like to spend some time with you and the children, exploring the issues each of you have. Then we'll better be able to help you decide what's in your best interest."

"You mean fix our family?" JoAnne tried to clarify.

"Perhaps, JoAnne. Perhaps." Doctor Blackwell eyed Mrs. Bundy with the reassuring air of long experience. "But families can't always be fixed, now can they? I've seen this sort of thing a lot. We often find that it's more appropriate to dissolve these types of severely dysfunctional families for the good of everyone involved. Sometimes we risk more harm than good in trying to salvage such things. I'm not saying that's definitely the case here yet. But it's something we'll need to explore. Such separations can often be quite therapeutic."

"How can that be?" JoAnne argued. "You're talking about breaking up our family because Michael is having some difficulties? I don't understand. I don't understand how that can be good."

"Well, as I said, that's just something we may want to explore depending on what we find. Perhaps it may not be right for you, either. I do notice, though, that you tend to speak in terms of your family rather than yourself, JoAnne. A lot of people, especially women, tend to become so concerned with the needs of others, so dependent on a partner or children for their identity that they lose their own. We need to learn to think more in terms of self, JoAnne. You need to learn to not always focus on others, to take care of yourself first, to give yourself permission to feel and to expect of others for a change. After all," Adrianne Blackwell smiled benignly, "If we don't take care of ourselves and put ourselves first, who will?"

When they had finished scheduling more sessions, JoAnne Bundy and Doctor Blackwell emerged from the office once more and Michael and his mother departed. In thinking it over, Michael had decided he was glad he would be returning here again. He liked Doctor Blackwell. She was... stimulating.

He guessed maybe he had learned some things today. Perhaps the good doctor was right. Maybe he could create his own good and bad, right and wrong. She did seem to know about these things, after all. And maybe it was silly to always carry around these guilty feelings for just being who he was. Maybe she really could help him figure out how to stop feeling bad inside, to just be himself and feel good about it. Heck, if she was right, maybe somehow he created himself anyway. He had to admit, it was an appealing thought. The notion of not having to answer to anyone but himself made him feel warm and giddy inside.

One thing he knew for sure he had learned today. One-forty-six North Emory Drive. The address printed on the label of one of the medical journals in the therapist's office, different from all her other periodicals that bore the office address. Her home address on the north edge of the city. He had been thinking of venturing farther from home on his little after-dark excursions anyway.

CHAPTER 23

Ezra worked a soft cloth back and forth atop an exquisite cherry mantle clock made from the scraps of the previous week's desk, bringing the finish out to a steady shimmer. The Friday afternoon sunlight poured into the shed, dancing little refractive jigs on the many surfaces of Calvin's walnut rolltop desk in the middle of the shop floor. The caretaker took in the sight of his charge vigorously buffing the finish of his week's work.

Calvin had scarcely uttered a dozen sentences all week. Mostly to thank the people who continued to bring food. Mrs. Christians had taken a particular devotion to Calvin, checking on him daily, making sure he was fed enough, his clothes were warm enough... It was a source of considerable amusement for Ezra, watching his charge meekly receive the nurture and fuss of the very ones he'd terrorized.

But something had clearly turned in the younger man. It was more than merely cutting off his hair. It was more than the subdued demeanor. Every morning this week he'd been in the shed working before Ezra. And it seemed more a genuine, new-found desire to be productive than any quest to please the caretaker. Without being asked, he'd taken to helping with the refurbishment and maintenance of Mrs. Peterson's property as well.

Calvin might have seemed a little broken at first glance. More rightly, though, it was probably the strangeness of seeing him stripped of his masks. He was looking Ezra plainly in the face, now, without pretense. A little haunted, maybe, but without pretense. Real. Ezra could still remember learning to discern the difference between a real man and one still hiding behind pretenses, like that of a dead conscience. He'd watched old man Holbert's allegedly nonexistent conscience rise up and crack that rock-hard face into quivering, desperate pieces. And, by contrast, he had begun to finally see the old preacher in the visiting room— really see him— for the first time. No arrogance or coldness. No pretenses of not caring or of any other sort, for that matter. The old man had never been afraid to care openly, to expend himself for another without reserve. Even Ezra. The preacher didn't seem to esteem himself above anyone. Even Ezra. He truly saw himself as no better, no more worthy in the presence of the Creator, but ever thankful, rather, for everything great and small. So Ezra began to learn what true fearlessness was from this little old man. It wasn't a self-destructive, blind disregard for others and for self. It was not a heart settled on violent response to encroachments. Nor was it a dead eye. True courage was not to be found in any of these things. It was Reverend Hartmann's simple, indestructible, childlike trust in the providence and guardianship of his Maker. A trust that allowed him to proceed in any course, to face any obstacle or danger, without worry or fear, knowing beyond doubt that the end of it all would find him safely in the presence of his Lord.

Ezra's attention turned again to the mantle clock. He halted his buffing and examined the work. It was finished. He slid it into position on the large workbench— into just about the only space left. You see, the entire workbench was now covered with all sorts of clocks and jewelry boxes, exquisite music boxes and pen sets, puzzles and plaques and knick-knacks of every sort. Practically no scrap, whatsoever, from either the previous week's cherry of this week's walnut had gone unused.

For a satisfied moment, Ezra pondered his work. That old German-colored voice in his head seemed to approve. "Do not be wasteful, Ezra. Use what God has given prudently and thankfully." A faint smile came to the caretaker's face and he began to relax in the moment. But as soon as he did, the same earnest voice entreated anew, "Work hard, Ezra! Do not be slothful!" His smile widened and he was soon headed out of the shed.

"Where you going?" Calvin asked, still polishing his work.

"Going to finish painting the upstairs foyer," Ezra answered over his shoulder.

"Be up to help soon as I finish here."

* * *

Eyes of long experience peered out from the weathered, expressionless face of Sheriff Skoda. He carefully studied the uncomfortably rigid, hulking figure on the far side of his desk.

208

"Dan, I have some real concerns about what's going on with you, son. I've been getting a lot of calls."

"Who!?" Dan Guiness interrupted. "My parents?! Sue?!"

"It doesn't even matter who, Dan. But I'm talking about more than your family. I've been getting calls from people in the community. You haven't been responding to your routine calls. I've got complaints about you being real short and hostile with folks. You've been late for work. You haven't been reporting in on your radio checks like you're supposed to. All in all, your job performance is really flagging, son. Now you and I both know this has to do with Watt's release. You got the people that care about you scared to death that you're fixing to do something highly regrettable."

Dan remained silently rigid, staring down into the sheriff's desktop. His temples and tightly clenched jaw throbbed and flexed with agitation.

"Damn it, Dan. You told me you could handle this business all right, that there wasn't going to be a problem. I should have known better. You've been carrying around this mess ever since you were a boy, haven't you? That's what all this training is about, isn't it? The military, this job— that's what it's all about."

Guiness gave no response. Not even an effort to look up.

"Okay, well here's the way it is, Dan. I've always liked you. Long had a soft place in my heart for you, because of your family, because of everything you went through. But I'm telling you right now, if I find out you're abusing your position for personal reasons, to indulge your hatred of Ezra Watt, anything, I'll fire you on the spot, son. Clear?"

His eyes lacking any hint of contrition, Dan looked straight into the sheriff's face.

Skoda reacted to his deputy's defiant expression, gritting his teeth and lowering his voice. "You hear me, right now. I catch wind of you fixing to do anything amiss of the law— killing, going armed with intent, jaywalking, anything— I'll be the one leading the crew that comes to shut you down and I'll lock your cell door myself. You hear me, boy?"

Both men's eyes remained locked in an uncompromising stare

until Deputy Guiness finally yielded a sharp-edged, "Yup." With that, he got up and left.

When his deputy was gone, Skoda let out a long, slow breath of pent-up tension. He was not confident that his words had made any impression. He much dreaded the thought of having to take down one of his own. Especially Dan. It would hurt his heart desperately to see such an upright young man ruin his life and family, to see his folks have to go through still more grief. Besides that, the sheriff reckoned that his deputy was a one-man wrecking crew just itching to cut loose. If it came to it, he might not go down so easy.

"Dear Jesus," the old lawman whispered, not half conscious of his own words, "Don't let it come to that."

* * *

The back end filled with a fresh load of oak wood and supplies, Calvin's pickup glided along Oak Street toward the apartment house. Calvin glanced to the passenger seat, then returned his eyes to the street. He wondered more all the time about the caretaker. There were many questions he had of this E.J., but knew not how to ask. For, while the caretaker held back nothing in teaching him how to work wood or do carpentry and home repairs, he was at the same time downright unwilling to speak about himself. And there were other oddities that stuck in Calvin's mind. That he had never seen a CD before. The way he worked so ceaselessly and then just gave away whatever he made. The things he had said to that kid... He was an odd man, to be sure. Calvin glanced over again. The caretaker just sat there so quietly, watching the scenery go by the window. It wasn't so much a smile as a stillness on his face. Calvin wondered what the man thought about.

His eyes back on the street, Calvin shook his head, almost imperceptibly in wry disbelief as he considered anew this morning's events. He had sold his rolltop to the Waltons for the same twenty-six hundred as last week. And the Waltons had given him a list of other furniture items that they would be willing to buy from him well into the future, provided they were of the same quality. But

210

what left Calvin incredulous was watching the caretaker sell his clocks and boxes and things, made with nothing but the scrap, for more money than the rolltop. Hundreds more. He was a curious man.

CHAPTER 24

What a difference a week could make. A week ago Calvin had looked in the same closet door mirror, bearing his mask of arrogance and all his symbols of fierceness, imagining how he might impress others and all the while, in his heart of hearts, dreading. Just seven days hence and the face that stared back from the mirror was somehow different. A distinctly different manner of person looked back at him. The prideful adornments had been abandoned for a simple brown suit purchased the previous day. From his nightstand he retrieved the Bible he'd purchased as well. The one he'd begun reading last evening with such profound interest. It seemed to him that, no matter where he turned, the words were waiting for him.

Calvin felt a warm surge of excitement like a kid on Christmas Eve. He couldn't really explain it. He just knew he couldn't wait to go back— had to get back and be with the people in that little church. The ones he'd wanted to hide from only a week ago. The ones he'd fled from. And he couldn't even understand why, much less explain it. He just knew he had to be with them. What a difference a week could make.

Upstairs, in his apartment, Ezra opened the lid of an old cigar box on the small writing table in the living room and retrieved some money for the offering. Having converted the proceeds of his labor to cash, the old box he'd found in the shed had become the repository of his life's savings. He was straightening his tie in the entrance mirror when a knock came at his door. He opened up and saw Calvin in his new suit, carrying his new Bible.

"You about ready?" the young man pressed, only marginally able to conceal his impatience.

Ezra passed his eyes over his charge and then, staring into his face, warmed to the sort of gentle smile a father might reserve for a son.

"I'm ready."

The two descended the steps and proceeded out onto the porch. There they met Edna and Janet engaged in their Sunday morning conversation. But this time each woman wore a dress beneath an autumn coat and each bore a purse in hand. They turned expectantly to Ezra and Edna explained, "We were thinking we should stop making excuses. Would it be all right if we went to church with you?"

"Sure." Ezra answered.

Janet called past them to the yard. "Come on, you guys. It's time to go... before you get grass stains on your good clothes."

"We're being careful, Mom." Kendra came running around the corner of the porch. Her blond hair, pulled back and barretted, bounced in the dangling hood of the oversized brown jacket that covered all but the bottom bit of a white, patterned dress.

"Yeah, Mom, we're being careful," Bobby mimicked, lumbering close behind. The two stopped at the base of the porch steps and looked up at the others with identical grins.

Kendra poked a hand out of her oversized sleeve to give a friendly wave. "Hi, E.J."

"Yeah, hi E.J." Bobby agreed and grinned at his daughter's giggling.

Ezra took them in from that distant, sometimes disconcerting stare of his, then greeted them as one. "Hey there, blue eyes."

Unable to abide any further delays, Calvin descended the porch steps. "Let's go."

Ezra walked with him and the others fell in behind, engaged in happy chitchat. From out in the yards and from within the homes, Calvin could feel the eyes of the neighborhood watching their little Sunday morning procession. Some greeted as they had the previous week. Some even greeted Calvin. Calvin glanced at the caretaker, the one responsible for this little parade and so many other things in such a short amount of time, the one who seemed intent on giving things away as fast as they were accomplished. Calvin wondered about E.J. Who was he? What had brought him here, of all places, to help people he didn't even know?

Behind them, Calvin could hear Edna and Janet talking and the happy banter between Kendra and her dad. They walked a long time before he leaned close to Ezra and spoke with guarded tone so the others would not hear. "My dad left when I was little. I don't remember him."

213

"I'm sorry," Ezra said quietly.

"Yeah, me too." The men fell quiet again, walking for another block and listening to the others. "My mom lives over in Alton, with a new guy. She's had— she's had a bunch of different ones since I was a kid." They walked on some more. "She thinks I'm no good. Headed for prison and all, you know. She doesn't want me around anymore." They walked another block. "Guess I could go see her. You know, see if she needs anything... if I can do anything."

As they neared the church Ezra finally spoke up. "She could change her mind about you. Others have."

"Yeah... maybe."

"Anyway," the caretaker concluded, "it is good to do for your folks, regardless."

"Yeah." Calvin understood, then turned his focus on the caretaker. "You got parents somewhere?"

"With the Lord."

"Sorry," Calvin said. "Not that they're with the Lord, I mean. That they're gone— you know."

They came up to the church doors. "I know."

* * *

"We must not lose heart. We have to keep on diligently and faithfully. We can't give up. Sooner or later— sooner or later— God will surely meet our work with increase..." These were the sorts of encouragements that Reverend Travis and Rose had often given one another these past two years whenever they had been tempted to despair about the seeming lack of progress in their work at Grace Reformed. And these were the manner of thoughts that now quietly flooded both of their hearts as they, with the rest of the congregation, watched the man they knew as E.J., four new people, and a radically different version of Calvin come through the front doors of the church. For a moment, Reverend Travis and Rose looked past the others in the crowded foyer to meet one another's encouraging eyes.

Then the entire foyer surged with new vigor. The arrivals were

214

soon engulfed in attention. Calvin watched closely as the people gathered to Edna and the Slaters, greeting warmly, making themselves known and doting on Kendra. The widow McVillian came and took the caretaker by the arm. "Ya, there's my boy," she chuckled brightly, patting his hand. "You come with me," she said, leading him away. "I want to talk with you..."

"We almost didn't recognize you, Calvin," a cheerfully boisterous voice gave Calvin a mild start from immediately behind. He turned to find himself in the midst of the Connor family— Doc, Ivy, and Sarah.

"Yeah, guess I look a little different," Calvin answered.

"Hmm, yes you do," Doc Connor agreed, carefully taking in Calvin's face.

Mrs. Connor leaned in close speaking discreetly. "Calvin, when you left last week, we were concerned for you. You seemed most upset. We wanted to come and see you, but—"

"We didn't know where to find you," Doc explained.

"So we prayed for you," Ivy added. "That God would grant you peace of heart."

Calvin looked into the steadfast Connor eyes. "You guys prayed for me?"

"Of course."

"Wow." Calvin was without words for a time. "Well, I'm— I'm okay. I mean, I'm sorry about making a scene. I just— I guess I just had to face up to some things."

"We've all had to do that at some time or another," Doc Connor assured.

"You guys?" Calvin questioned. He found it hard to conceive that such good people could bear any resemblance to himself.

"Of course, Calvin," Doc Connor said. "Anybody who doesn't think they'll have to face themselves, sooner or later, is deluded."

They all stood quietly for a time, seeming content in one another's company. Then Mrs. Connor leaned in again. "Calvin, that's some haircut you got."

"Yeah." Calvin smiled faintly, placing a lanky hand atop his head. "I think I had a lot of foolishness caught up in there." He glanced at Sarah's attentive face. "Kind of like glue or something.

Anyway, it was time for it to go."

"Oh, you know it's funny you should say that," Mrs. Connor beamed. "Once, when Sarah was younger— I think it was in the eighth grade— she came home with a bruise on her face and glue all over her hair. Do you remember that, Sarah? I can't remember how it happened. Did you ever say? Anyway, we thought we might have to cut off her hair..."

Sarah and Calvin caught one another's eyes for an extended moment, each bearing a subtle shared humor and an unexpected warmth, before looking back to the floor as they all listened to Mrs. Connor's recitation of a long list of household products that had been tried in a determined, two-day effort to rid her daughter's hair of glue.

She was still recounting her list when the preacher's familiar voice filled the foyer, calling the gathered to worship. And when, in the course of the morning, the Sunday school was completed and the service had progressed to the appropriate place, Reverend Travis stood up and began to preach once more.

"Beloved brothers and sisters. We have considered sin and its origin in the hearts of people turning from their Creator to themselves. We've seen how this phenomenon of the spirit has infected all creation with corruption and death. And we examined the process of regeneration by which our Redeemer brings us out of sin and satisfies its just penalty with the Acceptable Substitute. Now I would like us to understand the setting within which these things take place. An environment of grace. God given grace.

"We have said often that separation is death. When we see that sin has fostered a dying world, we are seeing the Creator, who sustains this world through each moment of time, withdrawing His sustaining thought and separating from the world, unable in His purity to abide things impure. We see this dying in scientific observations and in societies trending toward moral decay.

"But that we are here bears witness that this death was not instantaneous at the moment of Adam's sin. From our perspective, this entropy has crept gradually, creating a space of time. A space during which history has continued to be worked out so that many branches of God's given breath might be raised up and renewed as

216

he foreordained from beyond time. We learn this in places like Romans 8:29-30 and the first verses of Romans 11. We exist— the entire history of the world exists— in a period of suspense between the passing of a sentence and its conclusion. A place where there is hope of deliverance from complete separation. A period of grace. God gave Noah a period of time to prepare so that he might be delivered through a portal from ancient corruption appointed for destruction into a renewed world. Likewise, God has given us the opportunity to exist in a state of grace so that we might be prepared and delivered through the portal from corruption into a completely renewed creation.

"All reality proceeds under the grace of the One to whom it belongs. This is plainly evident. Jesus says that God 'causes His sun to rise on the evil and the good and sends rain on the just and the unjust.' All live under grace.

"That this infected creation persists, that we ourselves yet breathe despite willful corruption, bespeaks our Maker's unfathomable mercy in sustaining this grace period rather than instantly severing us as our darkness justifies, allowing our substance to dissipate from memory, our souls to rage in perpetual isolation. If we possessed something so thoroughly corrupted, would we expend so much to preserve it from its insistent course? Would we lay ourselves down as a sacrifice to salvage it?

"But to say that evil continues now without balance isn't quite accurate, aside from the fact that evil is invariably its own punishment. Being perfectly holy, God cannot abide evil, even for a little while. That this is plainly true while a world of evil clearly continues for a season, gives evidence that the fearsome price of this grace period was paid in advance. From the recesses of his timeless counsel, knowing the end of all before its beginning, our Creator arranged the satisfaction of His incorruptible justice, balancing it upon the blood of His only begotten Son Jesus before He ever created anything. Our Bible says that He knew us before the foundation of the world.

"This age of grace, then, is enjoyed by all, though many despise it ungratefully, but it is maintained for the sake of the redeemed and not the reprobate. Jesus taught that His people are the salt— that is, the preservative— of the earth. It is truly for their sake that history continues until all those whom He foreknew have been born into existence and redeemed out of their corruption.

"What will we do in the face of such overwhelming grace? How will we react? Will we perceive and confess it? Will we find genuine gratitude in our hearts? Will we cease the pursuit of self obsession and lay ourselves down, a reciprocal sacrifice of love and devotion? Or will we, like the criminal who persists in despising his probation, continue in our own way until there is no more indulgence to be found at the bar and we are cast into prison without remedy. Jesus warned that one does not get out of such a prison until he has paid the last penny. And you know brothers and sisters, that we have nothing in ourselves with which to pay the first, let alone the last.

"Perhaps we are tempted to question our Creator's sovereign choices in salvation. Some people don't want to accept that grace is truly the purveyance of God, that the Maker of their souls and not they themselves shall decide who will be regenerated and redeemed... and who will not. I just spoke of prison. Let's consider God's sovereign grace in such terms for a moment. Consider a prison where every inmate is guilty as charged and fully deserves his sentence. If the governor of that prison should see fit to pardon some of the prisoners and set them free, how shall the ones who remain have any just complaint? They are guilty of their crimes, willingly committed, and rightly deserve their punishment. And of the ones pardoned, how shall they puff themselves up with any claim of merit in the matter? They were equally guilty of crimes just as eagerly committed and rightly deserved the punishment from which they have been spared. How can they do anything, but yield their faces in humbled gratitude.

"We do well in remembering it's not that some people are good in the eyes of their Maker while others have gone astray and need a little help. The prophets testify that there are none good, no not one, that all have gone astray. Far from needing a little help, we are all utterly dependent upon the mercy of our Governor. We have each sold our birthright of standing guilt-free before our Maker, a worthy citizen. With the sole exception of our brother Jesus, in deeds of the hand, of the mouth, and most certainly of the heart, all of us who gain the age of moral understanding— an age younger than we would like to admit— make ourselves deliberate criminals towards our Creator, our own consciences bearing witness against us. We, then, justly enter our prisons of gathering misery and private terrors on our way to a dreadfully permanent solitary confinement of our own insistence. But if the Governor of all things should see fit to pardon some of those thus imprisoned, extracting them from this self-made gloom, how will those who remain make any complaint? Does the world not belong to its Maker and can He not forget those who do not wish to be His? And of the ones redeemed, how will they proffer any claim of merit? They were guilty of the same treacheries, just as eagerly committed, and they just as thoroughly deserved the sentence that their good brother has served for them. How can they— how can we— but fall upon our faces in His presence, bound unalterably to His good service?

"Now we know that our Creator is completely good and always just. So, if anyone were truly innocent and came before Him with a genuinely pure heart, that person would not and could not ever be abandoned to separation. But you and I can make no such petition. The only one of us who ever did remain pure of heart and secure the right to stand blameless before our Father, laid down His pure life, making it ugly and despised in the sight of His Father with the sins of His siblings, absorbing a misery, terror, and death that did not belong to Him so that his brothers and sisters would not have to.

"We so often hear people question if God is really good or gracious at all. 'If God is so good,' they protest, 'how can he allow such terrible things to happen?' Just as often, though, these questions and accusations are found in disingenuous hearts. Sometimes hurting or grieving. But disingenuous nonetheless. For in our heart of hearts, we know very well that the miseries and catastrophes of this present world have their genesis in the evil and corruption born by the hearts of humankind. If anyone would feign doubt at this, let him examine himself and every other person and group of persons that has ever set foot on this planet. Let him see in this examination that every culture and tribe from the ancient to

219

the contemporary, no matter how remote, no matter how far removed from the knowledge of the Bible, nevertheless seeks to offer some sacrifice, some manner of appeasement for their own misdoings whenever something terrible happens or is feared to happen. To their Maker or to their imagined gods and spirits or to anyone or thing that they hope might listen and grant clemency, do they offer these meager appeasements. By this desire to appease in times of trouble, we confirm that we have indelibly written on our consciences from conception, the sure knowledge that the evil of this world is directly linked to the evil in our hearts. Passed to us from our ancestors, along with the spiritual and physical infection of sin, is the guilt of it, the desperation to somehow appease for it when its inevitable results begin to rain down. The charge for terrible things happening, then, is properly laid upon mankind, not God.

"The depth of God's grace is such that He will work all these things, including the miserable results of our evil, to His righteous purpose, to the benefit and redemption of His people. As Paul wrote to Rome, 'we know that all things work together for good to those who love God, to those who are the called according to His purpose.' God is able to turn the greatest curses of misery that this world reserves for some, into the greatest of blessings. What did Joseph say to his brothers? 'You meant it for evil, but God meant it for good.' As many as have been ruined by riches and pleasure with the oft accompanying pride and ingratitude, how many more have been broken from foolishness and turned to their Redeemer by the sufferings of this world? You know, few people die instantaneously. Most see it coming from a few minutes, a few hours, or a few days off. Many suffer from pain and from the fears and humiliations of death. Is this without purpose, without reason? Nay, we know well that the closeness of such stark realities can change a person as perhaps nothing else can. There are people such as Doctor Kevorkian and his followers who would have us believe that such things have no meaning. They would lay charge against our Governor, that He is arbitrary and cruel. They would claim that we somehow own what we have no hand in creating or sustaining, and that we may destroy it, if it so suits us, rather than face those

220

hard things that our Maker might employ to turn our hearts. The
Bible has a clear voice, however. 'Do not despise the chastening of
the Lord, nor be discouraged.'

"And what of this alleged capriciousness of God? How is it that
He chooses some for redemption while allowing others to continue
on their merry way to hell if it is not of merit? In the ninth chapter
of Romans we are told, concerning Jacob and Esau, that God
elected one for restoration and determined that the other would be
abandoned to his own way before they had been born or done
anything good or evil, 'that His purpose might stand, not of deeds,
but of Him who calls.' Paul goes on to echo what God told Moses
in Exodus, 'I will have mercy on whomever I will have mercy, and
I will have compassion on whomever I will have compassion.'
Which guilty criminal will level a charge against a righteous Judge
for exercising compassion as He pleases?

"It's not really for me to say, brothers and sisters, but I just
believe that we will be very surprised one day at just who and how
many were finally genuinely broken and turned about in the last
hard moments of their lives, even as the criminal crucified with
Jesus was. Jesus teaches in parable that the owner of the vineyard
will give to those who served one hour, the same as those who
served the entire day. Yet let no one test God's patience lest he be
cut off suddenly and without remedy. Whatever the final outcome
will be, beloved, we know that it will be good, because we know
that the God who controls the outcome is good. We will be in
never-ending awe of His grace.

"So it is, that absolutely everything in creation is proven to be
a blessing toward the ultimate good of God's people. Not always to
the immediate good of their bodies, but to their persons. For we
well know that we are not merely these fleeting and infected
vessels, but living souls bound for a more sure existence. He
weaves together the hardships with the pleasant things, the evil
conducted by His creatures with the goodness ministered by His
host, into the intricate fabric of history, from beginning to end, so
that His sovereignty, goodness and grace might be plainly
manifested in the sight of all. We see that both the pleasant, easy
things and the hard, miserable things serve to humble and turn the

redeemed to their Redeemer, all of it inducing humility and gratitude, contentment and compassion... love. And, at the very same time, the very same things received as good by the redeemed are received as curses by the reprobate, I mean, those that will be left to their own devices. Wealth and pleasure only serve to inflate, pervert, dissatisfy, and numb with ingratitude while pain and hardship only produce melodramatic self-pity, cursing, bitter raging... hatred.

"As we conclude this morning, let me ask of you— which is our Creator's woven fabric of history producing in you? See to it that it is gratitude and love. You've no excuse for less. You get to it. You work it out 'with fear and trembling,' the Bible says. And when you raise your eyes from your work and pause to reflect, you will have no trouble seeing Who it is that has produced these things within you and all around you. Amen."

* * *

The group from the apartment house made their way along Oak Street after church. Ezra trailed behind, his mind still set on the young preacher's sermon. As time advanced, he could indeed see how all things, even one's own willfulness, were conducted in perfect concert to influence the course of one's life, to entice, lead, or seize hold and force one to his appointed path. He supposed that if the Creator had determined from before time to retrieve a soul, He would orchestrate all means to block that soul from its own desire, to frustrate it at every turn, and shake it from its delusions. If gentle and pleasant things would not do it, then miserable and painful things would. And if even these were not sufficient, then perhaps plain old terror would be. Whatever it took, the Lord's foreordained history would provide it. Ezra often recalled the shadow that had laid hold of him in his cell that night so many years ago and paralyzed him with such overwhelming terror. He had never told anyone of this thing, though it followed him still. When it had happened, he'd thought it the most dreadful of demons, or some such suffocating evil. But, as he considered it with each advancing year, he realized that evil had never sought to scare him.

It had always come to him sweetly, full of rousing promise. No, he came to believe that this thing that had scared the hell out of him, shaking him from so much delusion and numbness, chasing him toward his Maker like a frightened child to its parent, was more likely angel than demon, more likely grace than curse. And though he did not speak of this with others, considering it a personal message meant for him alone, he often wondered how many others quietly carried with them similar encounters with that which resides just behind the appearance of things.

* * *

Once again, the well-heeled man sat on his Zwingli Park bench. The autumn weather was still pleasant enough to draw the young objects of his lust. And he tried stubbornly to pursue his normal Sunday morning routine. But he was not able just now to slip comfortably into his dreams. He was filled with nervousness and discomfort. His eyes incessantly darted from the park's voluptuous scenery to the threatening distance of the sidewalk. He feared those watching eyes. Others were content to leave him alone with his heart. But this one... Why did he plague him so?

He returned his fitful attention to the park for only a few moments when his dreamy periphery was jolted by movement on the sidewalk's distance. His attention wielded and he eyed the approaching figures while they were yet a long way off. A couple of women, a couple of men, a child— he did not recognize his accuser among them. He waited. He squinted, watching intently. There was another figure behind them, only visible now and again through the bustling figures. Adrenaline surged into his veins. The Zwingli Park air grew thick and inadequate. It was him!

Hurriedly snatching up the sections of his paper in a disheveled heap, the rich man started for the far side of the park in near-panic. He looked back again and again, watching them— watching him— coming nearer and nearer. Remembering how the stranger had seen him from across the park the previous Sunday, he suddenly changed his course. Now he hastened for the cement block restroom facilities in the center of Zwingli. He pressed into the men's room and hurried to the far corner, next to the last stall. He waited. He listened. He could hear the faint sounds of traffic from the streets. He could hear the muffled sounds of people out in the park, talking, laughing, and playing. But mostly what he heard, echoing off the bare walls of this dim place, was the crumple and crinkle of the clump of newspaper in his arms and his own constricted breathing.

He waited a long time. And many fears crept around him. What if the man with the accusing eyes followed him in here? He would be trapped. What if his tormentor was at the door... waiting? Though the men's room was cool this autumn day, sweat beaded on his forehead. His breath continued unevenly, interrupted often by uncomfortable swallowing. It must have been twenty minutes or even more before, ever-so-cautiously, he emerged from the restroom. Carefully, he surveyed the park, the sidewalk, the neighborhood. There was no sign of the stranger or his group.

But, as he looked about, he began to notice others watching him. Oh, they were pretending to be involved in their own affairs, talking and laughing. But he could see the elusive, indirect glances... the accusations. He could see. Did they all know? Well-manicured hands hastily deposited the crumpled paper in the nearest trash receptacle and worldly eyes darted all about as he fled Zwingli Park for the refuge of a well-secured home. The others in the park pretended not to notice him, but he knew what they all thought of him. He could see.

CHAPTER 25

A tall, lean man with blond hair and wearing a Levi jacket treaded carefully on the rain-softened ground near the east barn of Grey's Stables. It was mid-November. Nearly two and a half months had passed since Ezra Watt's release and, rumor had it, Lynn Younger was not well. But every spring around Memorial Day and every fall near Thanksgiving time, Jess Anders would make this trip to see Lynn, to ask if she would like to spend some time together, to search her deep, doleful eyes for any glimmer of the happy, slightly mischievous soul he'd known and quietly loved since their youthful school days.

Back then, he hadn't had the sense or the courage to rightly express such a thing. Anyway, he'd always seemed too busy working construction for his cousin after school and on weekends. After graduation, Lynn had gone off to college and he'd struck out on his own, working fourteen and sixteen hour days, determined to build a solid little contracting business. When Lynn had been attacked it had hurt so many people. It had privately crushed Jess. He hadn't known what to say or do, but had wanted so very much to somehow bear her pain for her. He still didn't know quite what he could do, but he kept going to see her with the seasons, always hopeful that she might be ready to venture from her shell. Some meager show of commitment, he supposed. Each time she would gently decline his offers and send him away. Still, it did seem to him that in recent years she was taking more time to consider. In any event, by now he imagined that she might be a little disappointed if he didn't show up and try.

When Jess rounded the corner and peered down the aisle of the east barn, he was dismayed by the sight that greeted him. Startled by his presence, Lynn jerked around and stared hard at him from frighteningly haunted eyes. She was frail and thin. Her face sunken and pale gray from lack of sleep and sanity. Jess's heart waxed exceedingly heavy and he bounded down the aisle for her. But Lynn's whole countenance began to quiver with panic and she quickly turned her face away from him, dropping a bucket of feed and bolting in the opposite direction.

"Get out of here!" she yelled hoarsely.

"Lynn, it's all right. It's me— it's Jess."

Bender's massive head protruded over his gate, into the aisle and Lynn took refuge behind it, hiding her face from Jess as her strained voice grew more panicked and insistent. "Get out of here! I don't want to see you! Leave me alone!"

"Lynn, I'm so sorry." Jess's steady eyes filled with tears. "Let me help you."

"Leave me alone!" she cried. "Go!"

The heavy steel gate creaked and groaned, bowing outward under the strain of Bender's great shoulders. The horse's eyes locked menacingly on Jess, his ears laid back on his head and nostrils flaring.

Jess was flooded with heartbreak. He relented and turned around. "I'm so sorry, Lynn. I'm so sorry."

When he had gone, Lynn wept long and bitter, pounding Bender's gate in anguished frustration, the horse standing quiet vigil.

* * *

There was a happy banter at the evening supper table in the Slater apartment. Janet, Kendra, and Bobby were finishing their meals and soaking in one another's company with genuine affection. It had become their steady routine during the past two and a half months since Bobby had left Jillians behind. Mrs. Peterson now eagerly took Kendra in after school, helping with homework and indulging the girl with snacks. Bobby and Janet would come to pick her up after their work and they would make supper and spend the evening together. When Bobby had seen Kendra off to bed, he would quietly return to his house on the edge of town. On the weekends he would come early and they would all spend the days together. And they had continued at Grace Reformed each Sunday since their first walk there with the caretaker.

Kendra was thoroughly pleased by these events, by her father's attention and her family's togetherness. But there was still a separateness to her parents. An unnatural space between them. She would say her regimented prayers for them each night as they put her to bed. But when the lights were out, her parents gone, she would whisper the true earnestness of her heart. "I know You can hear me. I know You can make them love each other..."

As for Janet, she kept waiting for Bobby to falter, to abandon them for his old ways. But he showed no sign of it, no interest in the things that had always drawn him away before. It was very hard for her to accept that he could just so abruptly change. And yet, there it was. She still didn't know just what had happened to him. He was taking care of their expenses now, still sending child support to the agency besides. For a while, Janet had suspicioned that he was just trying to get back with her for a "good time." But he had yet to even attempt anything intimate with her. A perfect gentleman. As her trust and her heart grew warmer, Janet now found herself wishing that he might be just a little less of a "gentleman."

This November evening, their supper finished, Kendra scurried off to retrieve a package from her room. She laid the flat, rectangular parcel with colorful wrapped paper and bow on the table in front of her mother. The girl's eyes were filled with anticipation. "I didn't forget your birthday, Mom."

"What's this?" Janet's face warmed with surprise. She looked to Bobby, but he only shrugged his lack of involvement in the deed. "Did you do this by yourself?" Janet inquired of Kendra.

"E.J. and Calvin helped me!" the girl eagerly explained. "And Mrs. Peterson helped me wrap it. Come on, Mom! Open it!"

"Okay, okay." Janet's face beamed as she busied herself with the wrapping until it was removed and a truly outstanding colored pencil drawing set behind glass in a beautiful walnut frame was revealed. The drawing of a man, woman and girl, standing in a yard next to a house, was well beyond anything Kendra had ever drawn before. It must have taken weeks to complete, Janet estimated. The woman's eyes swelled full. "Kendy, this is so awesome. You worked a long, long time on this, didn't you?"

The girl beamed proudly. "At Mrs. Peterson's, after school. E.J. and Calvin made the frame. I helped."

"It's so beautiful, Kendy."

"It's our— it's our family, Mom."

"Yeah, I see that," Janet agreed. She looked across the table at Bobby, but his head was lowered, his eyes on the floor.

Kendra drew in a great, hope-filled breath and turned toward her father. "Dad, did you remember it was Mom's birthday?"

He answered quietly, raising his eyes from the floor, "I remembered." He reached into the pocket of his coat, draped over the back of his chair, and produced a small cubicle box wrapped in elegant white tissue paper and bound with red ribbon. He held it out to his daughter, who in turn, bore it with utmost care and import to her mother's hand.

Janet received the box with caution. Her soft eyes grew intense, searching Bobby's face. Her voice held a subtle waver. "Robert, what is this?"

"It's a birthday present, Jan."

Kendra could scarcely contain herself. "Open it, Mom! Open it!"

She eyed Bobby with much uncertainty as she removed the wrapping and then opened the little box. Inside, resting on a tuft of cotton, was a single bright, shiny—

Janet stared in the box, perplexed. "A key," she finally said. "What is this for, Robert?"

"The house," Bobby answered.

"The house," Janet repeated flatly. Then a sudden realization flashed in her eyes. "You mean your house, the one you built?"

"Yes."

Janet's eyes lifted from the key. "Robert, why?" she near pleaded for an explanation. "You built that for yourself. You haven't even paid it off, have you? How can you..."

"I want you and Kendy to have a nice place," he shrugged. "It's too much for me. Anyway, I took back some of the electronics and stuff. Made some accelerated payments. It's pretty much paid for."

Listening to him, Janet suddenly had another flash of realization. "Where's your hotrod, Robert? I haven't seen it for a month. Is that— is that what you used to pay off the house?"

Though he didn't say anything, the look in Bobby's eyes gave

"Robert." Janet's voice strained with emotion, her eyes welling. She watched her daughter's face for a long time, as if pondering a decision. "We won't live there unless you are with us."

Now, Bobby was quiet, also gazing into his daughter's earnest face. "I guess we should be married for something like that."

Janet wiped her eyes with the heels of her hands. "Are you asking?"

Bobby got up from his chair and went to her. "You want me to?"

Janet stood and, laughing softly through her tears, melted into his arms, her head nodding against her neck. "Yes."

Scarcely noticed, Kendra had begun to softly weep and to repeat over and over, "I knew You heard me! I knew You heard me..."

"Oh, Kendy, what are you saying?" Janet soothed. She and Bobby turned to their girl. "Come here, sweetheart. Come on." Mother and father knelt, taking her into their midst.

* * *

A midnight blue Lebaron crawled through the dark along route forty-three toward Jasper Mills. It moved at little more than thirty miles an hour. Inside, steady, silent tears streamed down Lynn Younger's face. Fear, regret, rage, shame— her constant companions and they all rode with her now. She could feel them. She could hear them. She could even see them. Acrid, unnatural shadows— she could see their reflections, or lack of them, surrounding her own in the windshield. Living beings, they were. Demons.

She was so tired. She was so very, very tired. The car slowed and turned off onto a gravel road. It was a road that terminated at the Hoyt's old hayfield. Her body was just too spent to sustain the terror anymore. A heart that had pounded and raced for weeks and weeks without mercy, simply could not sustain the effort any longer and it, just that abruptly, quieted. She drew in the most wonderfully satisfying breath and her foot relaxed downward on the accelerator. The car lurched ahead, propelled at a climbing velocity.

229

A mind so wearied from racing discord, stilled. In the distance, the light of her headlamps reached the reflective yellow T-intersection sign and the hayfield's embankment that backed it. The end was in sight. She could see her companions in the windshield. They still accompanied her, but they were no longer tormenting her. They seemed... satisfied. The tears that rolled down now were those of relief. Her mind was blissfully numb. The foot on the accelerator pressed down heavily to the floor. Beyond the reflections of her companions, the sign raced up quickly, bright yellow, until it filled the whole windshield.

CHAPTER 26

Dan Guiness sat nervously in Gilbert Harms' Northfield office, impatiently waiting for the investigator to get to the point of why he had finally called him in after more than ten weeks.

"I haven't been able to find anything on Watt's name or Social Security number. Must be avoiding any official use of his identity. And I tried following his trail along the bus route for a while, which proved time consuming and fruitless." The investigator shifted forward in his chair. "So I started trying to make some cautious contact with a couple of fellows who work inside of Kalbourne. Now one guy in particular— and, of course, he's not keen on having his name come up— agreed to help us. And, after some time, he was able to get us this." Harms pulled a thick manilla envelope from a drawer and plopped it in the middle of the desk.

Dan eyed the envelope with much anticipation.

"Copies of a whole bunch of Watt's prison records," Harms explained. "I wanted a chance to go through them first, but you got here so fast after I called that I haven't had a chance yet."

Dan's eyes were fixed intently on the envelope, then on Harms. He leaned forward and reached for the envelope. Right there, on the detective's desk, he emptied out the contents and began rifling through them. The first thing he found and culled from the pile was an up-to-date list of vital statistics and an official photograph taken of Ezra right before his release. Now he knew what his target looked like. Dan continued in strange silence to rummage through the papers, pushing them all over the desktop.

Watching the deputy's behavior, Gilbert Harms suddenly had an uneasy feeling about the whole business, but kept his concerns to himself for the moment. "Don't know if there's actually anything in there that will help us or not. You Wovoka County guys are pretty single-minded about your work, huh?"

Dan made no attempt to respond, his eyes hurriedly scanning document after document. There were work evaluations, cellhouse reports, dental records, and behavioral notes. There were investigation reports that suspected Ezra in bone-breaking altercations. No talkative witnesses, though, and no charges. And there were subsequent dated evaluations and notes that suggested pronounced changes in Ezra's demeanor and behavior. No identified reasons given. Dan combed the files, looking for something— anything— that he could use. Then, at last, near the bottom of the mess, a single photocopied sheet of handwritten log entries. Names, dates, times. The same name, actually, recorded over and over, every few months. The log of Ezra's visits. Paydirt!

Dan was on his feet in an instant, grabbing up the visiting log along with the picture and vital stats, stuffing them all in the pocket of his department coat.

"You find something there?" Harms probed. "Something we can use?"

Dan glanced hollowly at the old investigator, fumbling inside his shirt pocket. "Your services are no longer required." He tossed the last of his family's savings atop the mess of files.

In another moment, Dan was gone and Gilbert Harms was left alone in his office with a distinctly bad feeling creeping over him.

* * *

It was mid-morning at Wovoka Christian and Reverend Hartmann was tending to chores, mopping the old tile floor of the modest Sunday school and reception wing. He glanced out the windows to the front lot. On the one side sat the parsonage, a simple one-story ranch. On the other a well-kept cemetery that bore the discarded shells of a century and a half of departed parishoners. The sky was growing gray. Rain, maybe even snow, on the way.

The eighty-seven-year-old man maneuvered the mop with measured, efficient strokes, working his way to the far end of the wing, then taking another swath back again. He drowned the mop in his bucket of water and squeezed off the excess, readying for another pass. Things continued to grow distant and out of focus. Not so long now and his bones would rest out there. Next to his beloved's. He glanced outside again and his brow crinkled. There was a sheriff's car parked in front of the parsonage.

Reverend Hartmann was curious. Rarely did law officers stray from the paved roads without a definite purpose. He leaned the mop against the wall and retrieved his old black coat from the office. He made his way out the door and across the gravel lot with careful, steady strides. As he neared the house, a large young deputy emerged from his front door and stood on the porch, glaring down at him with cold, metal eyes.

"Good morning, officer," the preacher greeted. "Is there a problem?"

The deputy descended the porch steps and walked past the preacher. There was much hostility and agitation in the deputy's manner, though his voice attempted to disguise with pleasantness when he finally spoke, his back yet turned to the preacher. "Just came by to see you. Your door was unlocked, so I checked to make sure everything was okay." He continued toward his car.

"Ya, all right. Thank you for the concern, officer," Reverend Hartmann responded. "What was it you wanted to see me about, then?"

The deputy stopped for a long, silent moment, his back still to the preacher before finally turning around. "Kids. Have you seen any kids vandalizing out this way?"

The preacher's eyes came to rest squarely on the officer's face. "No, I have seen neither kids nor vandalizing, Officer Guiness."

Dan's eyes flickered at the little old man's unexpected recognition. He quickly donned a mask of friendly ease, a mask that carried no chance of deceiving the old shepherd of hearts. So Dan turned away and made haste for his patrol car. There was no need to remain a moment longer, anyway.

With gravity, Reverend Hartmann watched the car back around in the drive and speed out of sight down the country road. The preacher remained for several minutes, staring blankly at a gray horizon that was all but featureless to him by now. With reluctance, he pushed out of his thoughts and looked at the parsonage's open door, knowing that he would have to go and see what he did not want to see. He made his way up the porch and into the house. He passed by the drawers that were askew in the kitchen and the papers strewn over the countertops and onto the floor. He passed through the living room where the bureau had been ransacked. These things mattered little to him. He headed straight for his study and looked immediately to his desk. There, he saw what he had not wanted to see. With a resigned sigh, he dropped his head. Atop the rifled desk, next to the old rotary phone, his well-worn address book lay open to the "w"s.

CHAPTER 27

Ezra sat at the small table in his apartment, quietly listening to the heartfelt voice in his telephone's earpiece.

"Ezra, I'm sorry that I must tell you these things, my son. I know that you have grown to love your new home, your work and your friends. But, it would seem, our Maker has other intentions for you. The desire in this deputy's heart is betrayed in his eyes. I have heard it said that he has abandoned his pregnant wife and family and spent all in his search for you. I confess I know not what to do, Ezra. Perhaps I should call the young man's sheriff."

Ezra's head was cast down, his eyes on distant things. "No, Reverend. Don't call the sheriff. There's no need to get him in trouble."

"What will you do, Ezra?"

"I feel like standing still. Let him have his way. It would be more than fair…"

"You must not, Ezra." The preacher responded. "You're not a child in our faith any longer and you must not entertain childish things. Your life is at our Father's disposition, not your own. You've no more sanction to destroy yourself than another, Ezra. And destroy yourself you surely would if you stood before this man without defense. As surely as standing in front of a train. You must not, my son. You do him no goodness in such a thing. To allow him such evil is to harm him." Reverend Hartmann paused, listening to the silence. "Do you hear me, Ezra?"

"I hear you, Reverend. It's all right. I know what to do."

"What is it that you will do, Ezra?"

There was another space of quiet before he answered. "I just know now what must be done, Reverend. Don't worry. It'll be all right."

"Ya, very well, Ezra. Very well. I will leave it with you, then. God is good." The old preacher and his charge sat in one another's silent company across the phone until Reverend Hartmann spoke again. "Ezra, I must also tell you now that the young woman Lynette Younger is in the hospital. She drove straight off the road at Hoyt's place at a very fast speed. There weren't any skid marks found. Had the rain not greatly softened the embankment, they say she most surely would have died..."

When their conversation had ended, Ezra replaced the receiver and sat in silence a long time. Finally, he raised his eyes and focused them on the old cigar box at the back of the table. He pulled the box to himself and opened it. Inside was more than twenty thousand dollars in cash, the fruit of his labor since arriving in Haverston ten weeks ago. He slid open the table's small drawer and retrieved a pen, a couple of manila envelopes, a roll of stamps, and tax forms. He filled out the forms. He listed his name and his government issued numbers. He gave his occupation, "caretaker," and his address, "among the living." He listed all the money he'd received from his efforts in Haverston, took no deductions, and signed his name. Counting out stacks of bills, he placed them in the envelopes with the forms, addressed them to their respective federal and state destinations, and affixed a generous row of stamps to each.

Ezra considered the money that remained on the table, the season of freedom, friendships, and labors it represented. A wistful smile came into his eyes and he got up from the table. The fifteen thousand or so that remained went back into the cigar box. He even found a few more dollars in his pocket and tossed them in as well. There were a couple strips of postage stamps remaining and Ezra made use of them to seal the cigar box shut. Walking easily about the apartment, he gathered his things and placed them in his old gray duffel. Last of all, he put in the envelopes with his taxes. He'd render them to Caesar the next mailbox he passed.

* * *

Out in the upstairs foyer, Ezra set his duffel on the floor while he locked up the apartment.

An enthusiastic little voice hailed, "E.J."

Ezra turned to see Kendra rising from the floor near the window that overlooked Oak Street. She left paper and colored pencils behind and approached the caretaker with exuberance.

"Hey there, blue eyes."

"E.J., we're moving to the house my dad built!" she reported. "My mom and dad are going to get married all over again!"

Ezra absorbed her words, then smiled. "That's good news, Kendra. About time those two figured things out."

"Mmhmm," Kendy agreed. Her eyes widened and her voice fell to an astonished whisper. "Jesus heard inside me, just like you said."

Ezra knelt, his broad, rugged skull nearing the delicate, little blond head. His dark, vivid eyes gazed far into the trusting blue. "That's a good thing to know, my friend."

"Hmm, yeah," the girl concurred and both pairs of eyes grew bright with satisfaction.

Ezra straightened again, shouldering the strap of his duffel.

"Where are you going?" The child's brow creased with questions.

"It's time for me to leave, Kendra."

"Where are you going?" She grew concerned. "Why do you have to go?"

Ezra gave the inquiry genuine consideration before answering. "Well, I guess I'm done here. And there is another place that I have to go now." His smile grew warm. "Jesus is always with us, though. And I will ask Him often to bring good wishes from my heart to yours. Okay?"

"Okay," the girl agreed. "Me too."

"So you will be good and work hard after I'm gone, yes?"

The girl nodded her accord.

"And you'll not be slothful or forget to eat your vegetables, no?"

"Hehee, no," she giggled.

"All right then. Very good," the caretaker said, descending the stairs and slipping from sight. "Very good."

* * *

All the photocopied prison records were sifted into well-organized stacks on Gilbert Harms' desk, now. An ill-at-ease feeling tugging at him, the investigator had begun carefully reading

237

through the papers after Deputy Guiness left his office earlier in the day. Now Harms sat with the phone receiver to his ear, his heart stricken with disquiet, as he waited for his call to be transferred through to the Wovoka County sheriff. What he had eventually come upon amid the records, what sat on the desk in front of him now, was a document labeled "Summary Crime Report." It amounted to a detailed report of Watt's case, including evidence, witnesses, victims, and families... and the name "Guiness."

The voice came on the other end. "Hello, Sheriff Skoda speaking. Mr. Harms, is it?"

"Yes."

"My girl says you're an investigator over in Northfield?"

"Yes, Sheriff, that's right."

"How is it I can help you, Mr. Harms," Skoda offered.

"Well, Sheriff," Harms hesitated, "I guess I need to try to confirm a couple of things. First of all, do you have a deputy by the name of Guiness working for you?"

There was a stark pause at Skoda's end. "Yes," he finally answered, a rising unease in his voice.

"Sheriff, did you authorize Deputy Guiness to retain my services for the purpose of locating Ezra Jacob Watt?"

There was another space of silence and then a long sigh. "No, I didn't."

"Sheriff," Harms voice turned grave, "I think we have a problem."

CHAPTER 28

The rich aromas of baking spilled out of Edna Peterson's apartment when she opened the door to Ezra's knock.

"Well, hello, E.J.," she greeted. "Please come in. Come in the kitchen. I'm just in the middle of taking some bread from the oven. I'm going with some of the ladies from Grace Reformed to visit the nursing home tomorrow. We're taking some food with us."

Her table and countertops were scarcely visible beneath the blanket of fresh breads, cakes, and pies.

"You've made enough for the entire western hemisphere," Ezra proclaimed.

"Oh, no," Edna chuckled. "I don't think quite that much."

"You've been visiting the folks at the nursing home quite a bit," Ezra observed.

The landlady chuckled some more, removing another loaf from the oven. "Well, it beats moping around the house feeling sorry for myself, now, doesn't it?" She looked back and focused in on Ezra, the duffel in tow. Her face grew curious.

But, before she could ask the question forming in her mind, Ezra laid his apartment key on the corner of the table, saying simply, "Time for me to go."

Mrs. Peterson was taken aback. "So suddenly?"

"I'm afraid so."

"Is everything all right? Are you okay?"

"Everything will be all right," he answered with direct eyes. "I wish I could stay longer. But I have to go now."

Edna gave the appearance of confusion at his words.

But her caretaker reassured her with a smile. "I expect you'll hear more about it soon enough." His eyes declared small hints of weariness. An unwanted loneliness, perhaps. "I believe we're square through the end of this month, yes?"

"Oh, goodness," she said. "We're more than square. You've done so much and— and asked so little I won't know what to— how to... You know, the Slaters are moving out, too."

"That's what I hear," Ezra watched her face. "You have a fine place here, Mrs. Peterson, and reasonable rent. You'll find some

239

good tenants. And you have Calvin here to look after you."

"Yes," Edna acknowledged, smiling through full eyes. "I suppose he will. That's funny, isn't it?" she chuckled. "Who would've ever believed it?"

"God is good." Ezra repeated the words he'd first said to her ten weeks ago.

"He is," she agreed with conviction.

Ezra made his way to the door. He opened it up and turned once more to the trailing landlady. "It stands for Ezra Jacob," he said.

"Oh," she smiled. "Well, that's a fine name."

"Thank you."

"Thank you, Ezra Jacob."

* * *

Hanging up the phone, Sheriff Skoda felt heavy and sick. What Gilbert Harms had just told him led him to believe that Dan must've found something on Ezra Watt's location and that he'd taken that clue with him. But the Northfield investigator was not able to discover anything else in the files that would shed light on what Dan had found, much less where he might be headed. The worried sheriff reached for the radio microphone on the credenza adjacent to his desk.

"Four, this is one. Come in." He waited several moments, then keyed the mike again. "Four, this is one. Respond four... Damn it, Dan. Report it right now." No answer. "Anyone seen Dan?"

"One, this is six. Haven't seen him since roll call."

"One, this is three. Haven't heard from him all morning, Sheriff."

"All right, try to find him and get his butt in here," Skoda ordered. He considered his words a moment and then keyed the mike once more. "Boys, you better use some caution here."

Skoda put down the mike and was immediately at the telephone again, quickly punching in a local number.

"Hello?" came the wavering voice of a woman trying hard to conceal her anguish.

240

"Susan, this is Al Skoda. I need for you to tell me where Dan is at, if you know."

There was an awkward, telling silence.

"Ahm, no," she sniffed, "I don't know where he's at. What's—what's going on?"

"Why are you crying, Susan?"

"Crying?" she attempted to steady her voice. "I'm not—"

"Susan," the sheriff interrupted. "This is no time for games. Neither one of us wants Dan to do something we'll all regret. If you know where he is, it's important that you tell me right now."

Susan's voice broke into sobbing. "I don't know where he is. He came home and left his patrol car and uniform. He took our car. He said he was taking some personal time. I don't know where he went."

"Susan, did he take a weapon with him?"

The pregnant woman tried to get hold of her emotions. "Ahm, I'm sorry, Sheriff. I have to go now."

* * *

"You bothering that guy again?"

"I was helping," Sarah Connor flashed mischievous green eyes at Ezra and then scolded as she passed him on her way from the workshop to her car. "You better be nice to me. I know the boss."

"Yes, ma'am," Ezra smiled.

Inside the shop Ezra found Calvin stooped over a router, preparing to edge a walnut dining table. To one side, there was a finished set of oak bookcases. To the other, a half dozen other projects in various stages of completion. Strewn about the workbenches were woodworking books and magazines, pages of notes, and piles of project plans, most of which had been hand drawn by Ezra. These things now demanded the majority of Calvin's waking attention.

"Looks like you're gonna need to hire some help one of these days," Ezra noted.

"Yeah." Calvin looked up with a smile. But when he saw the

duffel on Ezra's shoulder and the look on his face, his smile faded. The young man's eyes flickered and he stooped again, resuming his work on the router, pretending not to see. "I'll need your help cutting some plywood a little later."

"You'll have to find someone else," Ezra answered.

"Why? Where you going?" Calvin attempted nonchalance. He dreaded the answer he already saw in the older man's eyes.

"It's time for me to go."

"What do you mean? You coming back?" Calvin tampered blindly with the collect on the router.

"No."

Calvin straightened, dropping his collet wrench to the table. "Where do you have to go so suddenly that you're leaving like this?!"

Ezra ignored the question and Calvin's emotion. Coming near, he offered his hand. Calvin stood, blinking and feeling helpless. He awkwardly and reluctantly raised his own dusty, callused hand and grasped the caretaker's.

Ezra saw the fullness of heart swelling in Calvin's eyes. He felt the same pressing at himself. With his free hand, he gently cuffed the young man on the arm. "All right. This is not where I belong, see. This is where you belong, my friend. I have to go. And you have to stay. You're the caretaker here, now. You must see to Mrs. Peterson. You understand this, right?"

Though Calvin said nothing, his sober nod and straight-eyed stare was a promise, sure as any. Eventually, his eyes passed over all the clocks and boxes and such that Ezra had built, but not yet sold. "What about your projects?"

"Sell them."

"Where should I sent the money? There's probably a couple grand there."

With a slow shuffle through the sawdust, Ezra started toward the door. "You know, I read an interesting article in the Haverston Gazette the other day. It seems some people around here, who had been stolen from, are being paid back anonymously. Some getting back their property. Others money. One guy even got his gun back in the mail." Ezra paused near the double doors. "I guess someone must've had a change of heart."

Calvin looked into Ezra's face. "Not really worth mentioning. Shouldn't be so much attention on a person for just doing what he should. Anyway, he probably didn't even have a choice in the matter. They should write about the One that changed his mind."

"Ya," Ezra agreed. "You're going to be all right there." He gave a nod toward the unsold projects. "You send the money wherever you figure it'll do some good."

He opened one of the double doors enough to pass through and, just before he disappeared, added some final words over his shoulder. "I might see you again someday, Calvin. And if I find out that you've been harassing the neighbors again..."

The door closed and Ezra was gone, his sentence still hanging. His heart full, Calvin began to laugh. He swiped his eyes with a sleeve and returned to work with the diligence of one that had no more patience for idleness.

CHAPTER 29

The Guiness family car, a two-year-old green Saturn, sped south on the highway to Haverston, pushing past the speed limit just as much as Dan calculated he could get away with. It was finally happening. No more dreaming and visualizing. No more preparation and planning. It was really happening. This is what he wanted... He knew how it was supposed to feel. After all, how many times since boyhood had he imagined how this trip would be? If there were certain unanticipated deliberations now roiling within him, it would not dissuade him from his course.

Random thoughts here and there. What would now happen to his parents? Where would Susan and the children go? Would Sheriff Skoda's stare cast him down as a common criminal? In truth, all these years, he'd never actually thought about what would come after his time with Ezra Watt was finished. It had never seemed to matter.

That's what he had to keep straight in his head now. All those people and things that had gotten him to this point were behind him now. They had served their purpose, but they were expendable bridges that could be left to burn away at this point. The sweet sight of his little daughter, the inquisitive voice of his son, the softness of his wife— these things flittered in and out of his consciousness.

He gave his head a hard, quick shake. He would keep to his purpose. There was a well-rehearsed program to follow and so he would. No allowances for deviation. Voices and faces fleeting and fading. His mother, his father, his wife and children, Sheriff Skoda...

He shook his head still harder and edged the accelerator down a little more. Focus had to be maintained. There would be no turning back.

* * *

Knitted mittens and winter hats of many colors and sizes filled two large wicker baskets beside a very well-worn rocking chair. Each year as winter approached, the baskets would be delivered, overflowing, to the Haverston Pantry, a place that provided food, clothing, and other forms of help to area families in need. Gently rocking in the chair with purposeful rhythm, as she nimbly fashioned yet another pair of mittens, the old widow Mae McVillian presided over the view beyond the window of her Pleasant View apartment. The modest, one-level retirement home rested in a small grassy field next to U.S. Highway seventy-five on the north edge of Haverston.

From this vantage, ninety-year-old eyes could gaze across the field and watch vehicles as they entered and departed Haverston on seventy-five. The late afternoon grew increasingly gray and wind-chilled. What started as spats of November rain on the window soon turned to bits of sleet tapping out a grainy rhythm. Out on the road, Mae saw a man walking the shoulder, headed out of town. Her hands stilled momentarily from their labor and she focused intently. Sure enough, she recognized the sturdy form and the blue denim. He'd walked out to visit her several times this fall. Mae's weathered face found its familiar smile and, though she sat alone in the spartan apartment, she spoke aloud. "Ahh, there's my boy," she chuckled brightly.

But, as her sinuous hands resumed knitting, she saw that he did not turn up the Pleasant View drive as expected. Rather, he continued north. And when he'd come up to a point along the road that was directly across from her window, he stopped for a moment and turned toward Pleasant View, more clearly revealing the duffel slung at his side. His eyes searched until he found her in the window and he gave a large, salutary wave.

"Oh," she spoke aloud again. "I suppose that's that, then. Go finish your work, then, my son. We'll see you, soon enough."

Ezra turned north again, and continued up the road. The wind picked up, driving the sleet into the window with increasing velocity.

"Burrr," the old woman shrugged. "It's getting right chilly out there. Would You please give that boy a ride?"

Before Ezra had even passed from her sight, a tan Buick heading out of town slowed and then stopped. It took Ezra in and drove on, disappearing over the prairie horizon. "Thank you Jesus,"

245

the old woman chuckled pleasantly amid the austere sounds of rocking and knitting.

* * *

Carefully ascending the porch steps of the Oak Street apartment house, Dan remembered to measure his respirations and maintain his focus, just the way he'd always trained. He pushed through the front door and was immediately startled by a group of people gathered in the foyer, apparently engaged in discussion. Adrenaline surged and his eyes locked on the people. Deftly, he slipped a hand into his coat's lower side pocket. He scanned the faces, carefully and quickly. A pair of women, one older, one younger. A child. Two men, but neither fit Watt's parameters. His eyes gravitated to the child a second moment. A little blond girl, not much larger than his own. The adrenaline flickered and his hand came out of the pocket, empty.

Calvin had already been at Mrs. Peterson's door, discussing Ezra's sudden departure, when Janet and then Bobby had arrived home from work to pick up Kendra. Now they all paused from their discourse, turning their focus to the large, tense stranger standing just inside the door.

"Hello," Edna greeted. "May I help you?"

Dan blinked and refocused. Abruptly he affected a pleasant smiling mask. "Yes, I wonder if you folks might be able to help me? I'm looking for a man named Ezra Watt."

"Oh, yes," Edna flashed recognition. "We know him as E.J."

Dan's smile flickered ever-so-slightly. "E.J.," he repeated. "Yes, ol' E.J. That's who I'm looking for. Does he live here?"

"Oh, I'm sorry," Edna answered. "You just missed him. He left very suddenly earlier today. Just said he had to go. That's what we're talking about now."

"Left?" Dan repeated, not wanting to comprehend.

"Yes. Packed his things, turned in his key, and said goodbye."

"Where was he headed?" Dan pressed.

"He didn't say," Calvin answered, privately nurturing a growing suspicion of the man.

"Well, do you know what kind of vehicle he's driving?"

"He doesn't have one." They answered. "He walks everywhere."

"Do you at least know which way he went?" Dan's pleasant mask began to show small rifts. "Anyone who might know where he went... where I can find him?"

"No." They all looked to one another, shaking their heads. Then Janet, trying to help, offered that he might try Reverend Travis. And when Guiness frowned, Bobby clarified, offering directions to Grace Reformed.

"We're sure going to miss him," Dan heard the older woman say as he was turning back for the door. "He did so much for all of us in the short time he was here. Always working. Always taking care of things.... but I guess you would already know that about him. Where did you say you knew him from?"

Dan turned back around, the mask of pleasantness evaporated, a disturbing malevolence in its place. He quickly produced a folded document from within his coat and, when it was unfolded, brought it uncomfortably close to their faces.

"Is this him? Is this your E.J.?!" He searched their faces with unnerving intensity, his eyes quivering in wrath.

They all stood quiet, thrown into shock and confusion by the penitentiary mug shot. Gradually, reluctantly, they began to nod in the affirmative.

"Yeah, huh?!" No longer could Guiness conceal a contempt that extended even to these people he did not know. "He's a real good guy, all right. He's a killer and a rapist! He murdered my sister! How's that for a good guy?!" Dan pivoted and opened the door. "He belongs in hell!"

Kendra's eyes, full of bewilderment and hurt, gazed up at the adults, hunting for answers, but they appeared to have none. They stood in the foyer in a stunned hush, trying to absorb what they'd just been told even as the sound of Dan's footfalls receded from the house.

CHAPTER 30

The decade-old tan Buick that had picked up Ezra on the fringe of Haverston was driven by a man of fifty or so, immediately friendly and talkative. Ezra had lofted his duffel over the seat into the back, atop stacks of sample cases of the sort lugged about the country by salespeople. A rather sturdy-looking gray-haired man with just a slight paunch beneath a wrinkled dress shirt and tie, the driver reached out and turned down the volume of a bluegrass harmony on the radio.

"They always warn about picking up strangers," he said. "But I've never paid that much mind. In sales, you know. Always on the road. And I haven't ever had a bad experience with anyone I've given a ride to. Anyway, I was adopted as a baby. So I guess I've always kind of figured I got picked up from the side of the road, myself." He smiled and offered his hand. "Name's Harry. Harry S.... like the President."

Ezra's eyes narrowed. He studied the man's face closely and tried to grasp what he'd just said. The eyes were indeed gray and familiar. Ezra's head perked subtly with private incredulousness and the smile came into his eyes.

"You all right there, Mister?" Harry asked.

"Sure." Ezra took his hand. "Name's Ezra. Ezra J. And I'm pleased to meet you, Harry S."

"I'm headed up and over to the Twin Cities," Harry offered. "How far you in for?"

"About half of that," Ezra answered.

So they drove on into the sleet. The afternoon gray turned into nighttime black. Harry spoke happily of many things. He seemed grateful for the company. He spoke of baseball and his intractable Cubs, of football and his beloved Vikings. To hear Harry tell it, that blasted dome was the "worst thing that ever happened to them." He shared his love of bluegrass music. He liked the songs that were long, high and lonesome. With great tenderness in his voice, Harry told of his adoptive parents, both now passed on, and of his wife and son waiting for him at home. With the spray of passing vehicles floating in the yellow of the headlights, Harry's heart eventually turned to the parents he had never known as if something of them yet lingered at the edge of his consciousness, mired in that haze of infancy, just out of grasp. Ezra was sure that it was a place Harry visited often. He wondered how many lonely nights on these highways had this salesman spent puzzling over his beginnings, how many strangers had listened to his earnest speculations.

"Don't guess I'll ever meet them or know anything about them at this point," Harry conceded. "But I've always held good hopes for them. You know... prayed for them and such. Guess they might not even be alive anymore. Still," he glanced wistfully at Ezra. "It would be such peace to know. What I wouldn't give..."

Ezra quietly considered Harry's words for a long time. He marveled inwardly at this amazing intersection of lives. No such thing as coincidence. Of this, he was convinced anew. But what could he say to Harry? Could he tell him of a mother's murder and a father's life in prison?

Ezra listened to the soft, doleful strains of the bluegrass a while longer and then, finally, the glint of his eye shining through the darkened car, he spoke. "I expect things are kept from us for a reason, Harry. Until it's time for us to know. But I believe there's a peace in knowing that our Maker is in control of it all. He is always good. I expect that in His good time, here or hereafter, He'll show us things that will leave us in awe. Things that happened all around us, Harry. Things we were too small to see. Anyway, you've hoped and prayed for your folks and I bet your heart was sincere. I don't guess our Maker would ignore that..."

The conversation passed the hours and the road quickly by. Before Harry knew it, Ezra was grabbing up his duffel from behind the seat and climbing out of the car at a desolate-looking rural intersection. Harry was very reluctant to leave Ezra in such a lonely, wind-chilled place. Repeatedly, he offered to take him to a town or a filling station. He offered to buy him a meal or a room at a motel, but Ezra just smiled and held out his hand. "I'm glad the Lord crossed our paths, Harry S. You're a good fellow. Your folks would be proud."

The last time Harry S. saw Ezra J., it was a couple hours shy of midnight. He was pulling a worn black stocking hat down over his skull and lifting his collar against the driving sleet as he walked off into the night down an empty highway.

* * *

Dan Guiness sat in a pew near the front of the Grace Reformed sanctuary, not far from where he'd first found Reverend Travis and Rose passing the evening, diligently polishing and scrubbing. He'd made friendly pretense again, trying to gain a lead on Ezra. But, when it became clear that the young couple didn't even know that Ezra had left town, much less where he was headed, and when they commenced to cheerfully extol his many virtues just as the people in the apartment house had, Dan could stand it no more. His mask disintegrated into furious, violent eyes. All that Ezra had done— what he'd defiled, what he'd destroyed— came gushing out in a raging tirade of words and frustrated tears.

The Travis' were plainly dumbfounded by the things he said. Yet they remained Ezra's friends. They stood calm amid Dan's storming rage, unshaken by his menacing and fury. But neither were they cold and unmindful of him for their friend's sake. Rose and the Reverend saw the long years of anguish that colored his anger and they had compassion for him, sitting him down in the pew and speaking to him with kindness and ease, meeting his fury with undaunted gentleness. Though younger and physically lesser, Reverend Travis bore an irrefutable air of authority. At once kind and firmly purposed, he spoke straightly with Dan and the angry Guiness found himself obliged to still himself and behave calmly. He'd not even noted that Rose had gone until she reappeared, bearing a glass of water and a towel.

So they sat him down in the empty church and the three of them talked well into the night. They listened quietly as he told them with much bitterness and detail of the deeds and heart of a man named Ezra Watt. And they, in measured turn, told him of the deeds and apparent heart of the man they had known as E.J. Each described a man bearing the same face and identity. Each spoke truly. Yet, the former and the latter were so far removed from one

250

another as to be different men, opposites in nearly every way that a man can be measured.

Dan could not help but like this young preacher and his wife. They were genuine and engaging. It was near impossible not to be civil in their presence. But Dan was still determined that his will would not be swayed from its course nor his heart turned aside from its malice. "I know you are good people," he conceded. "And I know you believe that Ezra is good. But you have made a terrible mistake. He has fooled you. He's fooled everyone here. There's just no other explanation." Dan's face bore hints of bewilderment. "It's just not possible for someone like that to change. I will never believe it. And— and, even if it were, why should he be allowed to? He shouldn't even be given the chance. Some things are unforgivable and no amount of doing good can change it."

"Well, that's the heart of it right there, isn't it?" Reverend Travis responded. "We all make inquiry— don't we? — in that secret place that no one but our Maker knows. We ask whether our treacheries, done openly and done in the shadows of our heart, can ever be undone or overcome by any amount of penitent effort, by any change of heart. The answer that greets us is demoralizing and terrifying. And, Mr. Guiness, if we find this to be true in ourselves, we needn't doubt that, deep down, everyone knows the same thing about themselves. Ezra doesn't need you to tell him that he can never do enough good. He already knows it. But you and I are not the authors of justice. We draw our breath by mercy, same as the next guy. I suppose that's why we need a government to carry out the things that we're not righteous enough to carry out by ourselves.

"You're right, Mr. Guiness, that those who murder should themselves be separated from the communion of this life. Even as all of us who have ever birthed hatred in our heart for our Creator and his creatures deserve to be forever separated from the communion of all things by our ultimate Government."

The earnest preacher searched Dan's angry eyes. "It seems our government, for whatever reason, has failed to carry out the sentence that Ezra deserves. If Ezra did the things you say, he deserved to die. And I say this as his friend. But you are not the one ordained to set things right. Do not despair that justice has failed. All of these things are in the hands of an unfailing Judge. All will be balanced. It will be made right. In fact, my friend it has already been done, if you can fathom, sealed from before time.

"If Ezra's heart is fraudulent, will it not be added to his terror when Justice finally falls on him? But, if Ezra's heart is real, then who is it that you struggle against, Mr. Guiness, but the One who changes hearts? It may very well be that the man you seek is already dead, destroyed by the indwelling of Christ. If so, you now stalk after nothing more than a ghost of your own tormented making... one that will always escape you."

Dan's head shook subtly as he stared at the floor, his jaw clenched tightly. Though his ears received the preacher's words, his heart fought them. And Reverend Travis continued to reason with him.

"A long time ago, Mr. Guiness, a man named Augustine wrote about an evil man named Victorinius. Victorinius lived in Rome and enjoyed a high position and great wealth. He loved all the pagan sacrifices and the murderous entertainments of the amphitheater. Throughout all of the city, Victorinius was known for his love of these revelries. But one day he heard the Word of God preached and, just like that, had a change of heart. To the city's astonishment, Victorinius suddenly regretted his evil and left behind all that he had been and that he had possessed to become a lowly student of the Christian way. Augustine said that it was precisely in people so plainly and publicly held by evil, that God sometimes displayed his most remarkable presence, causing change where there appeared no reason or hope for it. The apostle Paul was a man who started out as the most zealous tormenter and murderer of Christ's people. Then in plain sight of everyone, he was turned against his own will, ending up the most devoted and fearless defender of Christ unto death. What is this, Mr. Guiness, but God breathing directly in the face of all whom he causes to witness such things, daring them to deny His changing presence? What is this thing in Ezra, but God's breath in your face, Mr. Guiness?"

"No. No!" Dan shook his head. "No more words. No more talking. I can't hear any more of this. I won't—"

"Mr. Guiness, let's try—"

"No!" Dan interrupted. He stood and turned his back on the couple. "I won't listen to anymore."

Reverend Travis and Rose stood as well, their faces filled with concern. The preacher called after Dan, "Mr. Guiness, please go home. Leave justice to its Author."

Dan turned back once more before leaving the sanctuary, his face again marred by bitter anguish. "I can't!" he gritted. "I can't go back now. It's too late. It's who I am."

CHAPTER 31

A clock on the wall of the darkened hospital room labored past midnight. The second hand marked each moment with agonizing slowness for Lynn. It already seemed just shy of an eternity since her parents had departed at the end of visiting hours. They'd been much reluctant to leave her alone, though she continued to maintain that it was just an accident. She just hadn't seen the end of the road, she told them. The skepticism in Sheriff Skoda's face and the pain in her parents' eyes said they were less than convinced, though they nodded politely and said that they believed her.

She had a concussion, cracked ribs, and internal bruising. They had given her a pleasing dose of opiate and her first night here had been one of wonderfully oblivious sleep. But now the clutching apparitions had managed to press their way through the drugs and sleep was beyond her, again. Fear beyond reason, beyond restraint. Black spiraling despair. They were here with her, tangible beings more intensely discernable than ever. They seized, mugged, and tortured her from without and suffocated her with unbearable agony from within. She knew they would not relent until she yielded once more to their desire.

She pushed her head back into the pillow and stared at the darkened ceiling. Tomorrow they would discharge her from the hospital. This time she would need to find a method more calculated, more certain. And without arousing suspicion. She felt the monsters shifting around her. In her periphery, something else moved. She adjusted her head on the pillow and watched the door to her room easing inward. When it had opened a quarter of the way, the figure of a man slipped quietly through and closed the door again. Illumination from the room's nightlight and from the streetlights outside the window outlined the man's form, though not the details of his face. Slowly, he moved near her bed. The monsters seemed to adjust their grip on her, jealous for their quarry.

"Who are you?" Lynn raised from her pillow. "Are you a doctor?"

"No," the man answered softly.

254

"It's— it's not visiting hours," she pointed out with burgeoning apprehension.

"I know," he acknowledged. "I won't stay long. I knew you probably wouldn't be asleep, though."

Lynn sat up straighter and scooted back against the headboard. "How would you know if I'm sleeping?"

The man was quiet for a time and she caught the shine of his eyes passing over her face. "They would never let me sleep, either," he finally said. "They had hold of me for a long, long time. Couldn't find a moment's peace. They came from within, of course, but they sure seemed to have a mind of their own. Always luring and pushing, gripping and tearing. They never leave you alone, do they? I guess there was a while there when I thought they might have gone away. But they had just relaxed their grip a little, waiting. The day came when they grabbed back ahold of me so damn tight I couldn't breath right, couldn't sleep, couldn't even think straight. They just would not let go. Some of mine were different than yours. Some, about the same. Hate, anger, desires— burning desires for terrible things. And fear. Lots of fear. But I reckon, whatever their names are, they all have the same aim... to take us down to the grave. They won't be satisfied with less."

"You can see them?" Lynn questioned. "I thought I was the only one who saw them. I figured I was losing my mind."

The man lowered his voice. "You know our Creator really can send them away. He can send far greater to displace these dark ones and stand watch over us."

Tighter, still, the specters cinched their possessive clutch on Lynn and she half-gasped beneath the pressure. "Did He do that for you?"

"Yes!" was the man's emphatic whisper. He stood vigil over her for a time, both of them listening to her respirations, weak and unsteady.

"Lynn, there came a time when I despised myself so completely and didn't know how to break the hold of this darkness. It smothered me. I decided in my heart to end the struggle, to kill myself, and this pleased these spirits that torment. You know what I mean? But that very night there came another. A different spirit.

It terrified me more than all the others, more than anything I've ever met. It shook me awake as nothing else ever had, from self-concern, from struggles and torments, from my own darkness, Lynn. Since that time, I haven't had any excuse left for not knowing that there is more to this world than we see with our eyes. It's right here with us, just behind what our senses discern. And it's all good, Lynn, because its Creator is good. He truly is alive and aware and in control of it all. He is our Father and He knows us, you and me, and He has never forgotten us.

"That same night, it was taught to me that since I didn't want my life anymore, anyway, I should give it over to our Father's use, rather than selfishly throwing away what was never mine to throw away. And anyway, how could I be afraid anymore? I didn't care about living."

"That's what you did?" Lynn asked. "Gave up your life to God?"

"Yes."

"Just like that?"

"Just like that," he affirmed. "A different way of dying. The right way. Dying to the fear, the self-concern, and the dark desires. It changed everything, Lynn. Nothing was the same. Stillness. I didn't have to hang onto anything, anymore. Didn't have to hide. I let go of everything and I was free. I 'let' our Maker have control of things... as if it had ever been any other way. Now I'm where I should be, along for the ride and happy to see where our Father will take us. There is no more doubt that He is good, that He should be trusted. No reason not to. I let go of everything and instead of losing, I gained. It's just like Jesus says— if we try to hang onto our lives, we lose them. If we let them go to Him, we find our lives returned to us, better than we imagined possible.

"I read that the opposite of fear is faith. I think if we ever find out in our heart that God is with us, that He is working everything out to our ultimate, everlasting good, fear can never find a comfortable place to dwell in us again. And so goes bitterness and hatred and any other ugly inclination that is unable to trust God."

Lynn sighed and winced. "I wish," she said. "I wish I could have relief like that."

"Some believe that it is God himself who sparks that wish in you, that He's working out every detail of your life to grow that desire for Him within you. And when it dawns on us that if He begins such a work in us, He will never fail to finish it, we have great assurance and happiness in discovering this simple, genuine wish growing within us. Some never do have that desire, you know. They just go on and drown in their darkness without ever looking up out of it."

Lynn shook her head in the dark. "It's hard to see how God's working things out for me. If you knew all the things I've been through... everything that's happened to me. I mean... why?"

A long silence trailed her question. "Lynn, I don't know why you've had to go through so much. Who knows our Father's mind? But He knows you and He knows why. And even though the evil has no excuse for itself and will die, I believe He will use even this to accomplish what He desires in you. How can it be any other way in the mind of a Creator who has colored His entire creation with the awareness of goodness and mercy?"

The man grew more earnest. "Lynn, He wasn't ready for you or you weren't ready for Him. Maybe both. Who knows His thoughts? But He caused a bullet to bounce off you. He brought you back to consciousness and gave you strength to survive. I can't know what went through your mind in that field. I have so often tried. But I don't believe you were fighting to hold onto a life of fear and misery. I have to believe you were clinging to the good things of life, to family and friends, to happiness, kindness, humor, and love, that you were not willing to let darkness take these from you. And now look. Even when you try to give them up, He won't let you. He continues to hold on to you. Still not your time. You have life left to live, people to see, work to do..."

Lynn slowly, cautiously scooted back further and sat up straighter against the headboard. "How do you know so much about me?" she pressed. "Who are you? Did you work at the hospital back then?"

There was another space of silence, the man answering her questions neither immediately nor directly. "It has become my most persistent hope and prayer in life that the One who has seen fit to deliver me from evil and bring me such relief, will not fail to do the same for those who have suffered because of me. You are chief among those, Lynn. With all my heart, I believe this prayer will be answered."

Lynn gasped weakly. "You?" Then, with gathering breath and recognition her voice grew strong. "You!"

"Yes."

Lynn braced for the expected terror to jump on her and rip her to shreds. But, strangely, it didn't. This was the moment she had always dreaded, but there wasn't anything in the room to be afraid of. She knew this, now. She wasn't sure how, but she knew it.

"There just aren't any words, Lynn. Nothing I can do now to fix what I broke in you." He turned toward the door. "But, Lynn... think about it. If our Father has had this kind of mercy on me, what is there for you to any longer fear or doubt? If He remembers even me, how could He possibly forget you? It is not possible."

Ezra slipped from her room in the same manner he had come. And, though he made no effort to conceal himself as he walked past the nurses' station, things just seemed to work out, both in his coming and in his going, so that he was unnoticed.

CHAPTER 32

Night's black shroud gradually lifted. The cold, northerly wind subsided and the sky cleared. A layer of sleet and slush covered the ground outside, waiting for the sun to wax strong in the sky and melt it away.

It'd been a long time since Reverend Hartmann had remained in bed past the dawn's first glimmers. When his Rachel was still with him they would, now and again, take an extra hour... A smile warmed his face with the memory. Then he winced just a little. The dull fullness in his chest had, by degrees, grown sharper through the night. It had now spread down his left arm and into his jaw. He had not slept, but rested peaceably straight through until now. Even as many things continued to fade into an echoing distance, others were now coming into focus. Two long figures, one at either corner of the bedroom, had stood vigil all night and even now continued at their posts. Merely strange shadows in the beginning, lacking a backdrop and standing freely, they'd become ever more delineated as the dawn neared. "Thy rod and Thy staff," the old preacher had said right out loud with the wonderment of a child. He felt certain why they had come, yet they waited. Why? What prevented them from taking him? What was left undone?

While he lay pondering these things in the muted company of his escorts, he gradually grew aware of the swooshing and scraping noises outside the parsonage. Reluctantly and with great effort, he rose up out of his bed. He pulled an old burgundy robe over his flannel pajamas, slid his feet into ancient slippers, and shuffled to his door. When he opened it and stepped onto the porch, he was able, clouded vision notwithstanding, to make out the figure of Ezra, scooping the sleet from his walkway.

"Morning, Reverend," his charge greeted.

Ezra seemed so far away to the preacher. Nearly untouchable. His words had a distant, garbled quality as passing through water more than air.

There was unexpected sternness from Reverend Hartmann. Impatience, even. "What are you doing here?"

"Just passing through, Reverend." Ezra was puzzled by the

preacher's manner. "Wanted to see you again before I go do what I have to do."

"You don't belong here, Ezra. You will only trouble hearts here."

"I know," Ezra acknowledged. He put the shovel down and eyed his old mentor closely. "I'll be on my way shortly. I just... I miss our visits, Reverend. Thought we might have another." Smiling, he pointed to the shovel. "Figured I'd make myself useful while I was here."

The old man's eyes returned from the shovel to Ezra's face with finality. "No reason to shovel the walk. I won't be needing it. And we'll not be having a visit just now."

The smile faded from Ezra's eyes, replaced with growing realization. "You all right, Reverend?"

"I've never been better. But I have company waiting and they've come a great distance to receive me. My business is with them now so you will kindly leave us to get on with it."

An unforeseen loneliness sank into Ezra's heart. Logically, he'd always known this day would come, but it didn't help him feel any less a helpless child left at the side of a treacherous trail, unable to follow after his quickly vanishing father. Ezra knew such things must be. Nevertheless, for Ezra, the world would become a more desolate place without the Reverend Otto Hartmann in it. Though as a younger man he'd shed no tears, even at the loss of family, he now silently shed them in the presence of his much beloved overseer.

The old preacher considered the heart of his fading charge. The earnest, German-tinged voice softened with compassion. "Ya. Ya. That's fine, Ezra. You will be just fine now, my son. You know this, of course. Jesus is with you. And I am near enough now to see the others that walk with you. Can you see them, Ezra?"

Ezra shook his head.

"Ya, well, that's all right. They are there, sure enough. Each as formidable as the two that have come to bear me away. They go before you, Ezra, and they follow behind. They hedge both your left and your right that you turn not aside from your appointed course. So go now and willingly walk the path that our Father has set before you. Work hard, Ezra! Do not be slothful, lest your heart should have pause to wander near darkness."

While Ezra watched, Reverend Hartmann turned and disappeared into the parsonage, his voice lingering behind. "If such a thing is permitted, I will be watching. And others must, as well, I'm sure. Do not forget that we will see you again, Ezra..."

* * *

Dan Guiness sat in a dim motel room on the outskirts of the state's capitol city. It was midmorning. He had been here since very early this morning. He'd not known where else to go. He was weary and disheveled and had not slept at all. So fiercely did his mind rage through the night, that he had not the slightest occasion for rest. And, curiously, it was not even Ezra Watt, so much, that his mind seemed to rage with as it was with its own self. He was mired in thick, smothering turmoil. If Ezra had just been in Haverston when he arrived, it would have been so simple. It would be over now, just as he'd always seen it happening. No time to think about it. He'd gotten so damn close. Damn it! He'd been close!

But now the starkness of what he was really trying to do— kill a human being— was beginning to catch up with him, prick at him... mock him. But this was not a human being. This was Ezra Watt, a soulless evil creature that merited not even the status of an animal. There should be no conflict in it. There should be no turmoil. Words from that intense young preacher, words from his parents, words from far down in the haze of his youth— they all twisted and squirmed in his heart, torturing him without relent. Back and forth, back and forth— his mind could no longer stay settled on its purpose. A heart so singular in its purpose, so driven for so long, now seemed to crumble into paralysis, divided against itself and unable to move.

There was a knock at Dan's motel room door and he tried to shake off the chaos and put on a mask of composure. Whatever his struggle, he thought bitterly, there was still one thing he could do without a conflicted heart. He opened up to the senior staff reporter

261

for the statewide newspaper, the one that put out the Sunday edition everyone would see.

"Mr. Guiness?" the narrow-eyed man of fifty inquired. "Jack Whitmeier... We spoke on the phone?"

"Yeah," Dan acknowledged darkly. He turned and walked back into the room, leaving the door wide open and the reporter still standing outside, puzzled and hesitant.

Minding the apparent graveness of the deputy, Whitmeier finally entered the room cautiously, taking a seat at the small round table near the door. "When my editor heard that you have recent information on Ezra Watt, he was nearly bursting to hear details. I called up to Wovoka County. You know, to verify that you were a deputy and everything. They wanted to know where you were. I guess I didn't know if I should say. Got the impression they weren't happy with you. Anyway, I didn't tell. But I guess you should know they're looking for you."

"Okay," was all Dan said.

"So you got a story for me?"

"Yeah, I got a story for you. And a current picture to go with it." Dan returned to the table with his little dossier.

"That's good," the reporter said. "I don't guess someone like that should be walking around anonymous."

* * *

Jeremy and Amanda Guiness sat at the breakfast table, their eyes following their mother around the kitchen with concern. Though she tried desperately to conceal it from them, they clearly saw the fear and anguish in her eyes when they asked for their father. From their beds, they had listened to their mother's weeping through the night. Now her face was drawn and drained, her eyes puffy and filled with tears on the constant verge of falling. Yet she continued to meet their mounting worries with gentle, reassuring words.

Susan subtly flinched and paused from her cooking momentarily, holding her abdomen. As if sensing her turbulence, the baby had been squirming and thrashing within her throughout the night. It seemed likely to her that their child would come at any time now. Where Dan was at, what he was doing, if he was all right— she had no idea. She had no idea, either, how she could take care of everything and make it through without him. She closed her eyes, her mind quietly squeezing out yet another string of frantic pleas to God even as her eyes squeezed out fresh tears.

"Mom," Jeremy's voice broke through her prayers, "I need a new lunch ticket for school."

Susan kept her back to the table as she wiped her face. "Ahm, I'll fix you a sack lunch, sweetie."

"No, Mom, I don't want a sack lunch. I want to eat lunch like everybody else."

"Mom doesn't have money to buy you a ticket, Jeremy!" Susan snapped. She took a deep breath and turned toward the table. "I'm sorry, Jeremy," her voice softened. "I know you don't want one, but you'll probably have to have a sack lunch for a while. I'll make you a good one, sweetheart... okay?"

The children continued their breakfast while Susan went out to the back entry and prepared the weeks' garbage for the curb. And when she had hefted the large plastic bag with one hand, she opened the back door with the other. But, before she could push open the storm door, something caught her attention and caused her to stop. She frowned and set the bag of garbage back down. Just inside the storm door, resting on the threshold at her feet, was a cigar box, sealed shut with postage stamps. With the effort of one so pregnant, she knelt and retrieved the box and when, at length, she had severed the seals, she gasped so loudly that the children scurried from the kitchen to her side.

263

CHAPTER 33

Avery Loomis cursed vehemently beneath his breath staring up the long, foreboding flight of stairs to the second floor of the courthouse. Advancing age and three packs of cigarettes a day made these steps an ever more daunting affair for the Wovoka County prosecutor. And, as his own office was on the first floor, he was able to avoid them for the most part. But now Alvin Skoda suddenly insisted that he come up to the sheriff's office at once, though he refused to say why. What was so damned important that it could not be said on the phone nor brought down to his office, he knew not. Skoda simply demanded that he come up immediately.

Loomis gripped hold of the railing with icy tenacity and began his labored ascent, wheezing and muttering every step of the way. No one who passed him gave more than a furtive glance to the frail man in the rumpled suit. And no one dared speak to him. He was, of course, well known to most. Which is why most, be they county employee or general public, had learned to stay well clear of the bitter old prosecutor.

Not that folks didn't have a certain kind of respect for the man. Most don't really care for the snake in their barn, but it does keep the vermin at bay. Thus, the voters of Wovoka County repeatedly assented to Loomis as their prosecutor each election time, regarding his effectiveness and utter refusal to lose in the courtroom, even while scrupulously avoiding personal contact with him. Among the other lawyers, his reputation for thorough, painstaking preparation and unrelenting attack was legendary. Most of them would've preferred to tangle with a rabid wolverine in the woods than face Avery Loomis in the courtroom. And those poor souls foolish enough to transgress the law in Wovoka County, in even the most minor way, soon learned to fear him. "Don't breathe wrong in Wovoka County," they said. "Or lynching Loomis will bury you." He never plea-bargained nor did he ever willingly agree to probation or reduced sentences. The guilty must pay the full price, Loomis believed, and even when the sentence was completed, it would never truly cleanse their guilt in his eyes.

But those who could remember, insisted that Avery Loomis had not always been such a man. They told of a man who was engaging and pleasant, a man interested and active in the community, a man devoted to his wife and two children. And those who could remember, agreed that these things had all changed abruptly the day old Judge Skoda had pronounced Ezra Watt "not guilty" of murdering Brian Helms and Amanda Guiness. The embittered heart, the icy, animus stare that followed Ezra from the courtroom as he left with an inadequate sentence, had never faded from Loomis. Nay, rather, it was turned back with a vengeance upon every subsequent defendant and defense attorney to cross his path. Community involvement, social niceties, wife and children— all were forsaken for eighteen and twenty hour workdays, seven days a week, insuring that he would never— never— be vanquished in a courtroom again.

As he leaned on the baluster atop the steps and gulped air, he looked out wretchedly from beneath his lowered brow at all the people in the upper hallway stealing glances at him. He was quite certain what they were all thinking. Even all this time since the Watt case, he still saw it in every pair of eyes that so much as glanced at him. The accusation. The reproach. He had failed them. And the looks were only more ghastly now that Watt walked free. It was his fault and no matter how thorough and invincible he had been ever since, no matter how hard he worked to atone, the guilt would not lessen its grip on his heart. Just as he found any amount of penance on the part of the people he prosecuted to be worthless, so also did he ever labor under the looming specter that no amount of diligence and unfailing service would ever mitigate the weight of this one unforgivable failure.

Loomis made his way down the hallway and through the door to the sheriff's offices. The sheriff's receptionist received not the slightest concession to her existence when she politely greeted the passing man. He pushed open the door to Skoda's office and saw a man sitting with his back to him and the sheriff across the desk with some strange, grave grin on his face.

"Damn it, Alvin!" Loomis wheezed. "What the hell did you make me come up here for?! What's so damned important you can't say it on the phone?!" He neared Skoda's desk, but struggled to refrain from leaning on it, not willing that the extent of his frailty be known. The profile in his periphery was vaguely disturbing and familiar at close range.

"Avery," Skoda said calmly, "In case you don't recognize him, this is Ezra Watt." Skoda paused from his speaking to take in Loomis' cadaverous appall as he heard the name and spun around to take full measure of his nemesis. "He's come here to turn himself in, Avery."

"What— what did you..." Looking hard into Ezra's face, Loomis stopped his sentence and then spun his glare back to Skoda. "Oh, Lord, what's he done now? And why isn't he in cuffs?!"

"Avery," Skoda eased. "Mr. Watt, here, wants to confess to the attacks on Brian Helms and Amanda Guiness."

Loomis now had to catch the corner of Sheriff Skoda's desk to prevent his collapse. He began to think on what he'd just been told and his expression grew angry. "You know damn well you were acquitted for those murders, Ezra." He spoke the name with hideous contempt. "I'm not about to listen to you gloat, now that you know we can't retry you! I'll be damned..."

"You charged me with their murders," Ezra softly agreed. "And I was acquitted, sure enough. But you never charged me with their kidnappings or any of the other sufferings that were done to them."

Loomis' eyes danced back and forth quickly as he tried to comprehend. "There's— there's no evidence. It was all thrown out. No witnesses."

"There is one witness." Ezra paused, taking in the frail prosecutor's bewildered countenance. "I am your witness, Mr. Loomis." Ezra fell quiet again, he and the sheriff waiting for Loomis to register understanding. "Look, I know this is unusual, Mr. Loomis, but it's not complicated. The sheriff assures me there is no statute of limitations on any of these crimes. Plain and simple, I will confess to everything that I did to them. You then bring charges. Not murder, of course, but every other charge, however remotely applicable, and I will plead guilty to them all. No trial. No hassles. Then, if you have been thorough and if you convince the court to boxcar each sentence on each charge, you should be

266

able to pile up enough years to bury me in Kalbourne for good."

Loomis' eyes grew frigid as the proposition sunk in. His jaw began to quiver and he stammered, gathering his strength. "Oh, don't think I wouldn't be thorough, Ezra! I don't know what kind of sick game you're trying to play now. I don't even care. But, where your imprisonment is concerned, I'll be most happy to oblige. A confession will buy you no sympathy with me! None!... If I'm thorough, huh? Oh yes, Ezra," he gritted. "I'll be very thorough!"

Ezra smiled, faint and tired, and he answered the angry man. "I believe you will. Everyone is counting on you."

CHAPTER 34

The foyer of Grace Reformed was full on Sunday morning. As full as it had ever been. Calvin was there. And the Slater family. And Edna. And so were four other new families and several individuals, all of whom had added their number to the Grace Reformed fellowship during the ten weeks of Ezra's presence in Haverston. Some had been drawn by the rumors concerning the Oak Street caretaker, of the things done at the Peterson apartment house. Others had grown so curious of those happy Sunday morning processions passing through their neighborhood that they had decided to join in.

But despite all of its increase, the foyer was subdued, the mood of its inhabitants somber and unsettled. The impetus of their surging population was gone and they had all seen his prison mug shot on the front page of the morning's paper and read of his horrible past. They spoke in hushed tones, their eyes searching one another with confusion and sadness. Such a vile past. Had he been a pretender among them... a fraud? They'd invited him into their homes and near their children. Had they been wrong to so readily trust someone they'd known so little about? Yet how do you ever know anyone, but by their actions and their words? There was much uncertainty and heartache.

Standing amongst them, the Reverend and Rose watched the faces full of concern, listened to the voices of quiet dismay, and even shared in these things. But Reverend Travis' voice began, bit by bit, to rise up out of the immediate group with which he visited until, at last, he was being listened to by the entire congregation right there in the foyer.

"For many of us here in Haverston this fall, a lot has happened. A lot of changes. A lot of good changes." His gaze passed over Edna. "From sorrow and pain we've seen relief." His eyes took in Calvin standing next to the Connors. "We have watched peace and order grow out of anger and chaos." His face settled finally on the Slaters. "We've witnessed love and unity rise from the tombs of separation."

"Many blessings, my friends. Many great blessings and all of them from God. And even if it were shown that the one He used to bring forth so many of these things was purely evil, it would cast no darkness on these good things. Lest we ever forget that our Father works all things, including the ugly, to His good purpose.

"But I don't believe that the E.J. we knew was a false soul. Often we have read in the Word and often you have heard me say that precisely in the heart most darkly fixed does our Redeemer sometimes see fit to shine forth and make Himself most plainly visible to all. The apostle Paul, Nebuchadnezzar, the people from whom Jesus drove dark spirits..."

"Barrabas," the widow McVillian interrupted with a crackled forcefulness. The preacher and the others turned their attention to her. "Barabbas," she repeated insistently. "For all of my life, since I heard of him as a little girl, I have always ached to know what happened to Barabbas. The good Book says that he was a murderer waiting to be executed, but he was released in Jesus' stead. It never says what happened to him. Did he go on hating and murdering, blind to God's pardon, or did he come to realize just who it was that died in his place?" The widow looked at all of them, a slight quiver in her jaw, a glossy fullness behind her spectacles. "He knows... He knows who died for him. His heart is true. He's a good boy. I know it."

A comforting arm fell around Mae. Then another. They all knew it was of the caretaker as much as Barabbas that she spoke.

"Indeed," Reverend Travis agreed. "And sure as we claim to have faith, something will be sent to try that faith, to see if it is only professed or if it is real. We say we believe that God can change a heart from darkest evil to righteousness and, sure enough, a block has been set in our path to try us and see if we will stumble or hold fast to His Word. So let us be tried, then. And let us be found true." He smiled in all of their faces. "We believe. We believe and are not shaken. We believe in miracles of the heart."

* * *

The well-heeled man sat at a table of prominence on the upper lounge deck of the Haverston Community Center. From this

269

vantage he was able to take in all of the indoor swimming facilities below. He sipped a cafe au lait, feeling most relaxed and self-satisfied. Better than he had in weeks. In front of him on the table was the front page story and accompanying picture of Ezra, how he'd lived anonymously in Haverston since his release from prison two and a half months ago, how a deputy sheriff from up north— the brother of one of his victims— had uncovered him and chased him out.

"We always know where to find you on a Sunday when the weather's cold," Sam Parker said, a friendly smile on his face as he approached the rich man's table. Sam was the Community Center's director and he always stopped in after church to make sure things were running smoothly. "Of course," Parker added, squeezing the man's shoulder, "If I had donated most of the money for this place and even insisted on paying for indoor pool facilities, I suppose I'd want to get some use out of the place, too."

"I just want to give something back to the community, Sam." His eyes left their much loved place on the backs of Haverston's frolicsome poolside daughters to gaze up at Parker. "If we can just make a difference in one of these children's lives, it will have all been worth it."

"Yes, yes," Parker piously agreed, his attention then drawn to the newspaper on the table. "That's sure something about that serial killer living right here in town. All that time and nobody knew who he was. Damn creepy to think someone like that could walk around here without anyone knowing it. Makes you wonder why he didn't kill anyone around here. I guess he either doesn't have the heart for it anymore or else we just got lucky."

"We got lucky is all." The rich man's eyes narrowed with the veneer of sage experience. "You know, I actually saw him on several occasions, lurking around Zwingli Park... watching. I didn't know who he was at the time, but I could sense that he was no good. You develop a feeling about people like that. You can just sense something's not right. Yup," he returned his gaze to the pool, "it's a good thing he got run out of here when he did. It was only a matter of time before he would've struck. God only knows what he had in mind."

When he looked up again, Parker was staring at him. "What?" he demanded.

"Nothing." Parker's brow wrinkled, perplexed. "I was just listening to you."

"Oh."

Parker remained slightly perplexed, but he smiled and bid the rich man a good day, then continued on his way.

Cautiously, the well-heeled man watched the center's director until he was gone. Then, drawing a satisfactory breath, he relaxed once more, returning his yes and his heart to their secret hiding places.

CHAPTER 35

Thanksgiving came and went. Some were thankful. Some were not. The December snows took flight and laid their flattering blanket of white over the upper midwest. And the days pushed their way to the brink of Christmas.

In Haverston a young heart roiled amidst conflict and paralysis. Michael Bundy sat staring out the window of his bedroom. On his lap was the workbook that Dr. Blackwell had assigned to help improve his self-esteem. From out in the hallway, his little brother Jonathan kept a quiet vigil. With great curiosity he watched his big brother, wondering what it was that troubled Michael so greatly that he had forgotten to visit any form of abuse or torment upon him for many weeks now.

Much had happened in the past couple of months. Since they'd met Dr. Blackwell, that is. She'd finally talked their mom into kicking their father out of the house. It hadn't been pretty. A lot of yelling and crying, pain and anger, confusion and fear. But, though he still didn't really understand, their father had finally given in and left. I don't guess any of them really understood... except Dr. Blackwell, of course.

Their dad didn't seem the same now. Whenever they would see him now, he was very quiet and sad. Their mom felt bad, too. She cried a lot. She wanted to take him back, but Dr. Blackwell was very insistent. She warned that he was only trying to manipulate them. She said that people like him— abusers and such— never truly change. She is an expert on these things.

Michael gazed down at the words in the workbook, yet again. "You must give yourself permission to feel what you feel and to want what you want. You must learn to feel good about yourself just as you are. You deserve the things that you desire. You are worthy to have them. You have the power within yourself to achieve your desires and your happiness. You must learn to put yourself first and to never allow yourself to be burdened and abused by the needs, demands, and intolerances of others."

These things agreed well with many of the other things he heard all around him. "We are nothing more than natural organisms, evolved from animals, evolved from little organisms, evolved from... nothing," many said or implied. Ultimately, it seemed there was nothing to us of lasting significance and we would soon enough escape back into oblivion. Michael's natural born heart wanted desperately for these things to be true and it warred within him to prevail, to be set free by such doctrine and pursue its own prurient, violent course without fear of lasting consequence.

But there was another voice in this war. One that seemed emboldened by the words of the caretaker. One that seemed equal to the battle and left him paralyzed in indecision and inaction. The doggedly persistent suspicion that Dr. Blackwell and the like-minded were woefully amiss, that their incessant prattling about following one's own nature obstinately ignored a plainly perceivable tug to transcend this ignoble nature and be held to a higher standard. Did they not feel it? Did they not perceive it?

He did. It was not people that gave him pause. Not a society or a philosophy that troubled his heart. It was a Presence. A Presence just behind everything that his senses could perceive, awake, organizing, animating.... watching.

He looked down again at the printed words. "You must learn to fulfill yourself. You must learn to put yourself first."

Michael slid the workbook aside and stared at the words in the book that he held beneath. "Let him who would follow Me deny himself and take up his cross..."

They say that the word Israel translates something like "struggles with God." So it is that another struggle is joined in Haverston. Blessed is the one thus engaged, whose natural inclinations are thus paralyzed and frustrated from their goal until they are, at last, brought to nothing.

* * *

While up in Wovoka County, in the pediatric ward of the hospital, a very sick little boy rested quietly between the waves of pain and nausea brought on by his chemotherapy. He was enveloped in warm, gentle arms. Long months of cancer and chemo had left the child bald and frail, but with an iron spirit forged by the furnace of suffering and an understanding that exceeded his five years.

His mother had no husband and she was overwhelmed by the medical bills and by the two other young children she had to take care of. So she worked both days and evenings, leaving little time to see the children she had at home, much less visit her son in the hospital for more than the painfully fleeting moments squeezed in here and there. The boy understood. Nevertheless, much of his time on the ward had been very lonely.

About a month ago, though, one night very late, a quiet woman, herself a patient, had wandered into the ward and seen him suffering in his bed. Without any words, but oh, such gentleness, she had picked him up and held him straight through until morning. The pain and illness somehow seemed more bearable within such warmth. She had finally spoken a few quiet words in the morning, saying that she was to leave the hospital that day, but that she would return in the evening, after her work, and sit with him.

That day, the boy had endured his treatments with unusual ease, watching the door to the ward, filled by the hope that the quiet woman with the gentle hands would not forget him. He had learned already in life that sometimes people make promises, whether in pity or for the benefit of others present, that they soon forgot or never really meant to keep, like his dad saying that he would come to see him and take him to wonderful places. But, before the sun had faded, the woman had appeared on the ward in her sweet smelling clothes, her pretty dark-eyed face passing by the others and fixing on him. She held him with rare and abiding patience, speaking softly now and again, listening carefully to the five-year-old concerns and interests that bubbled out here and there during the troughs of relief. Sometime in the night he had found wondrous sound sleep and when he awoke it was bright morning, the nice woman gone.

In the evening his eyes watched the entrance to the ward again with steadfast anticipation. And she did not disappoint. Nor had she missed an evening since she said her name was Lynn and that she worked with horses by day. She promised, if his mother would allow, to take him to see the horses and to ride her friend Bender

274

as soon as he was well enough. He believed Lynn's promise and held it in his heart.

This night, Lynn asked if it would be alright for her to bring a friend along tomorrow night. She said his name was Jess and that he was a good man. She said they would go to dinner after they visited him. Maybe a movie.

The boy sensed subtle anticipation in his comforter's words and he twisted his head to gaze up into her face. "Is he your boyfriend?" the child inquired.

A reticent smile flickered in the woman's face. "We used to go to school together a long time ago." Then she beamed brightly, lowering her head to his. "You're my boyfriend," she mock-scolded the bashfully giggling boy.

"So do you think that would be okay?" she asked again after some time.

The child nodded.

"We'll stay to tuck you in, okay?"

He nodded again, sleepily.

Another long stretch of quiet and Lynn thought that her charge had fallen asleep when, from beneath closed eyes, he softly sought to verify, "You won't forget to come?"

"I won't forget."

* * *

The orange-red glow of a radiant heater forestalled the December cold from the shed. With Sarah's help, Calvin worked harder than ever to get as many orders as possible out in the two days remaining until Christmas. And there was a mountain of orders besides these holiday ones. There were many from Mrs. Walton, of course, and many more from a multitude of people throughout the neighborhood. Enough, already, to keep him working steady through June. And there were other responsibilities now, such as Mrs. Peterson and the apartment house. Calvin knew he would need help if he was to keep up.

He gazed at Sarah, sanding away with steadfast care. She was excellent. A quick study and she liked working with him, as did he, her. But she had school to attend and other responsibilities, besides. He needed full time help. Calvin decided that he would look for someone next week, after Christmas.

The apartment house was running smoothly. He'd been keeping up with the maintenance, learning as he went. The Slaters had moved out, but they still visited often and he always saw them at church. They were friends now, everyone that had been living here when Ezra arrived. The Slater apartment had not been vacant long at all. Mrs. Peterson's son-in-law Karl lived there now. Mrs. Peterson's daughter had made him leave their home. They didn't see too much of him. When they did, he mostly seemed untalkative. Sometimes, early in the morning, Calvin would see him leaving for work, his eyes red with tears.

Calvin's eyes wandered to the shelf he'd built above the large workbench. There was a row of covered breads and meats and cheeses. More, he fretted, than he would ever be able to eat. He could not help but smile. In his apartment there was still more. Casseroles and baking, jams and jellies, cookies and brittles... It just kept coming from everywhere. From Mrs. Christians, from Mrs. Peterson, from Sarah and Sarah's mom, the Slaters, people all over the neighborhood— it just kept coming. Every time someone brought him more, it was as if the caretaker were still here, laughing at his doubt again and again. It was to the point that he couldn't eat a meal anymore without a warm gratitude welling up in his heart along with the memory of Ezra's teasing confidence that if they worked hard and didn't fret about it, God would remember them.

"What are you smiling about?" Sarah drew him from his thoughts. "You're always smiling. What gives?" she kidded. "You shouldn't be so happy."

The two looked into one another's faces with warmth and he finally shrugged. "Guess I like the way things have worked out." He reached out a dusty hand and mussed Sarah's hair.

"Calvin John, you be nice," she scolded. There was a certain formal diction in the way she spoke his name that never failed to send his heart dancing. Her parents had heard it, too. They had invited him to spend Christmas with them.

He looked forward to doing so. He would be visiting his mother, as well. He had gone to see her several times recently. She seemed troubled by him, as if, though his face was the same, she was not entirely certain that he was the same son that she had born into the world.

Sarah and Calvin had continued their work for a time when the gaunt couple timidly peeked their faces into the shed from the double doors. Calvin had not seen them in a couple of months. They looked very ragged, cold, and tired. They eased their way further into the shop at Calvin's invite. The gaunt woman was showing the unmistakable signs of pregnancy. They'd been "booted" from their apartment for not paying rent and wanted to know if they could "crash" at Calvin's for a while. Also, the gaunt man asked Calvin in a hushed voice, eyeing Sarah with suspicion, if he had any "stuff" they could get. They were out, he explained, and they "really needed some bad."

Calvin took in the sight of his old friends for an uncomfortably long time. They stood there, awkward and hopeful, in his studious gaze. Finally, he spoke to Sarah even as he regarded the gaunt woman. "Sarah, take her to Mrs. Peterson and say that I want them to have the empty upstairs apartment. Tell her that I will take responsibility for them. And then if you would, Sarah, please help her move in." Calvin turned his stare hard on the gaunt man. "He won't have time to help. He's going to work... right now."

When Sarah had taken the gaunt woman from the shed, Calvin moved in real close and loomed over the gaunt man. "Might as well take off your coat. You're going to be here a while."

"Wha— what's up with all that, man?" The gaunt man weakly protested.

"Don't even start," Calvin warned. "You don't even have a choice anymore. You're going to work right now... We messed up too much, man. I remember when she was still a straight girl in high school. You brought her around and got her all messed up, man! Now she's carrying your child. Your child!" Calvin emphasized. "No more, man. No more. You're going to take care of your family." Calvin put his face right in his gaunt friend's face. "You got a problem with anything I just said?"

277

The young gaunt man swallowed hard and shook his head timidly.

"Good," Calvin said, turning toward his work. "Let's get on with it."

* * *

The scent of fresh spruce mingled with that of cooking and filled the Guiness farmhouse. In the kitchen, Susan helped her mother-in-law prepare dinner, both of them with a vigilant eye on the family's newest addition, now nearly a month old. At the other end of the home, in the long, country-styled living room, Gerald Guiness sat on the floor with his arm around his grandson, Jeremy. The two talked of many things, not the least of which were their speculations on the contents of the many presents beneath the tree. At the far end of the room, little Amanda stared out the window, watching the farm's two Labrador puppies frolicking in the snowy farmyard. And behind them all, on the couch, Dan Guiness sat with the resignate posture of a defeated man.

When he'd finally made his way back home, out of options and frustrated by Ezra's presence here in jail, he'd very nearly lost his mind with despair. Sheriff Skoda had fired him on the spot and banned him from all county property, especially the jail and courthouse, until such time as Ezra was moved on. Then the old lawman had literally taken him by the arm and forced him to Susan's side as she delivered their child.

And so now here he sat, unable to realize his one goal in life. They said that Ezra would never get out again. Most had a strange amazement on their faces pondering the notion that a man would willingly bring down such a fate upon himself. Not that Dan hadn't quietly considered committing a crime of sufficiently heinous nature to get himself sent away to prison and, thus, continue his pursuit. But alas, he knew they would never send him to the same place as Ezra. His plans had been frustrated at every turn and there was no reason to think this would change. Dan was beginning to suspect an organized conspiracy against his designs, but he was most reluctant to confront the notion of just who the organizer might be.

278

He quietly watched his father with his son. Now that he'd lost his job and Ezra Watt was history, his folks were pushing hard for him to take over the family's farm. They were bending over backwards to offer him every financial advantage they could. And he and Susan suddenly had a good little nest egg of their own. Gilbert Harms had come over from Northfield and personally returned all of the money Dan had given him. And there was that mysterious cigar box... Neighbors? Relatives? Nobody would claim any knowledge of it. Susan just kept saying that they were left with God to thank... which is probably what he intended.

Amanda had shifted her interest from the puppies in the yard to her father. For a long time she quietly considered the brooding man, then came across the room to his side. With big brown eyes and an engaging warmth vaguely reminiscent of her namesake, she gained her father's attention. "Don't worry, Daddy," she comforted. "It will be okay."

"It will, huh?"

"Mmhm," she nodded with confidence.

"How do you know it will be okay?" he quizzed.

The girl frowned, giving her father's question serious thought. Then her face abruptly relaxed. Her shoulders scrunched and she opened her hands to the sky. "I just know it."

CHAPTER 36

There is a room at Kalbourne, just inside the first two electrically operated, sliding steel entrance gates and off to one side. It's called "Receiving and Discharge" — "R and D" for short. It's where both incoming and outgoing prisoners are processed. For the incoming it is where their transport chains are removed and they are stripped of clothes, property, and of any lingering illusions about where they are at. They are given their standard issue— clothes and boots, rule book and drinking cup, toothbrush and soap— then expelled through the final two gates onto the yard with the general population.

It is from the heavily barred window of this R and D room that the new inmates gain their first glimpse out onto the yard, their first indication of this isolated, alien world hidden away behind massive walls. It never looks the way they had imagined, what they'd seen in a movie or on a television show. Reality is so seldom acquainted with things of the imagination, but it's generally more disquieting.

So it was for young Kyle Johnson as he mutely gazed out this window at all the raging, ravenous souls milling about the snow-covered Kalbourne yard the day after Christmas. Though he didn't want to be called Kyle Johnson as he had loudly explained to the transport guards when they loaded him, chained and shackled, into the back of a Kalbourne prison van at the Orde City jail. "Stony" was the name he preferred to go by. It was short for "Stone Cold Killer," which is what he proclaimed himself to be. They sat him next to an older man, also in chains, that they'd brought from up north.

His head bowed, Ezra appeared resting when they sat the boisterous kid with the odd haircut next to him. He didn't really know why, but he was reminded of his bus ride to Haverston a few months back, of little blue eyes. Stony had brown eyes that were willfully narrowed, desperately clinging to a mask of cold hostility so that everyone who looked upon him would realize how scary and dangerous he was. At least that seemed to be the plan. As they'd proceeded on to Kalbourne, Stony had explained to the transport guards up front, with particular vulgarity, just what a couple of "punks" they both were. They remained silent, giving no indication that they'd even heard him .The transport guards were often older, experienced officers who'd done their stints inside the walls and now served out their time to pension ferrying convicts to and fro all over the state.

Unable to provoke any response from his transporters, the nineteen-year-old turned his attention to the man in the long, loose denim that sat next to him. The kid sneered with disdain. "Damn, man! Guess you ain't been down before. You look like a punk your damn self. Some kind of stupid geek or something, heh heh heh."

The van was starkly quiet, but for the young man's cackling. The two guards had both worked inside the walls for years and knew Ezra well. At one time or another, they had both helped carry the results of his brutality to the prison's infirmary and they now shook their heads subtly and winced with something akin to sympathy for the imprudent young man. In their estimation, he might as well have been nipping at the ears of a sleeping grizzly. Then again, Ezra had mellowed over the years, but... why tempt fate?

The nearer they drew to Kalbourne, the more the woofing and cackling ebbed. By the time the walls came into view the most notable sound within the transport had been the rapid, shallow respirations of the stone cold killer.

"Damn, this is the real deal, here," the kid finally said through awkward swallows. "You ain't getting scared are you, pops?"

For the first time, Ezra turned his face fully to the rattled young man and spoke very softly. "What's to fear? I have you to protect me."

Kyle plainly saw in the older man's face something quite other than he had supposed and he was rendered silent and shaken for the remainder of their ride and their awkward, shackled shuffle into the front of the prison.

And now, here they stood in the R and D room, searched and dressed. Ezra, it seemed, had merely traded old state issue for new. They clutched their meager possessions and a cellhouse assignment slip. It was time to take the walk through the last gates and face the yard. Kyle noted that the older man did not seem terribly concerned. He'd watched one of the R and D officers speaking to Ezra with familiarity— "Couldn't make it out there, ay Watt?" "No... you free people are crazy," had been the old convict's response. And the kid did not fail to observe what general deference both the guards and the inmates working in the room afforded his transport companion.

Kyle lingered at the window. Not only did he see a general crush of souls in the yard, but he noticed that many were gathered into groups... and that several of these groups were already watching him. They would turn and confer among themselves, then look back up at the window again. They looked, for all the world, like voracious wolves, intent upon the fresh carcass about to be dropped into their midst.

"Come on, son," the head receiving officer coaxed. "It's time to go."

Stony looked hopefully at the two transport officers busily gathering their chains and shackles into a metal carrying box. "Are you guys going to take us to our cellhouse?"

"I put my time in there," the one said, chuckling. "You couldn't get me back inside that hellhole for nothing on earth, kid."

"Besides," the other added, "You don't need a couple of punks like us slowing you down."

The young man looked around the stark room at all the faces watching him. He looked at Ezra who was quietly waiting by the door and he began to bitterly regret his brash words in the transport.

For Ezra's part, he studied the young man frozen by the window. He reminded himself that he did not believe in coincidental circumstances. He sighed, then spoke. "You have the same cellhouse assignment as me, Stony. You could probably get a cell near mine and hang around with me for a while. I doubt anyone would bother you much."

The kid looked around the room at the others, searching for a hint. A couple of the officers and one of the older inmates gave him barely perceptible nods. He looked back at Ezra. "Yeah, okay... Cool." He hesitated awkwardly, then added, "I'm sorry about what I said on the way."

282

"Yup," Ezra agreed, then added, "If you're going to run with me, you'll have to work. We can probably get jobs in the wood shop."

"All day?" Stony balked.

"That's right," Ezra confirmed. "And you won't be playing stupid prison games around me, either." He was thoughtful again, then added still further, "And you'll come to hear the Word preached by the chaplain on Sundays."

Stony faltered, uncertain of his decision. "I don't know, man. You're trying to run my whole life."

Ezra shrugged. "Suit yourself." he turned and passed through the door, heading down the corridor for the final gates.

Stony took another look out the window at all the expectant eyes.

"Let's go, Johnson." The receiving officer was more insistent.

Abruptly, Stony broke free of his spot by the window and hurried out the door. The men in the R and D room all heard him speaking quite quickly out in the corridor. "Hey, wait up, man. Wait up. That stuff, what you said. That's cool, man. I'll hang out with you... okay?"

"Okay," Ezra agreed as the last gate closed behind them with a heavy iron clank. "You go down there by the yard door. I'll be along in a minute."

And so, while Stony continued on to the end of the hall, Ezra turned back again. He stared through the bars of the gate, up the long, empty corridor one last time... and he spoke.

"Well, what did you expect? It just wasn't ever gonna square, me walking around out there. What does divine clemency have to do with corporeal debt? Our bones still fall apart. So here it is. My name is Ezra Watt and I am home. My mind rests easy, my heart warms, as a man returning to his native ground from a long and arduous journey to an alien land. Does this seem strange to you? Does it seem askew? Yet what place is home to you, but the place where you were born and raised, the place where your forbears rest? So is this place to me. For it is here that my predecessor was slain. And it is here that I was born. I love this place. She is my mother. She receives me back, now, and hides me within her protective stone embrace and you shall not see me again while we yet walk among these shadows. And if you are my friend, I say that I am humbled by our Father's lenience in such a thing and that I am, as well, your friend. And if you are my enemy, I say that it doth make the plainest sense if all the universe should seek to spit me from its taste and yet, for the sake of Another, it is otherwise and I am your friend so much the more.

"Do not imagine that I walk about this place in gloom or that I begrudge the walls their strictures. We all have our boundaries. But I will stand out in the middle of this yard with a soaring spirit, burdened neither by possession nor by worry... free as any that have ever tread this sphere of travail. And because you are truly my friend, do I ever hope that you, too, are thus unburdened. That though we walk opposite sides of these walls, our journeys may be parallel, following in the wondrous wake of our good Brother unto the land of our Father... where we shall never know separation again."

With that, Ezra turned his back and departed for the yard. The frigid masses parted as he moved out among them... a frightened stone cold killer following very close in his wake.

THE END

"...and I have reason to believe that we both shall be received at Graceland..."

Paul Simon

284